June 21, 2001

Dear Debra,

Thank you so much for inviting me to your lovely organization. See you soon at your blessed event.

Love
Phyllis-Lori Gold

SAVING GRACE
A SPIRITUAL LOVE STORY

Phyllis-Terri Gold

ISBN 0-7414-0381-1

Cover design by Cathi A. Wong

Published by:

Infinity Publishing.com
519 West Lancaster Avenue
Haverford, PA 19041-1413
Info@buybooksontheweb.com
www.buybooksontheweb.com
Toll-free (877) BUY BOOK
Local Phone (610) 520-2500
Fax (610) 519-0261

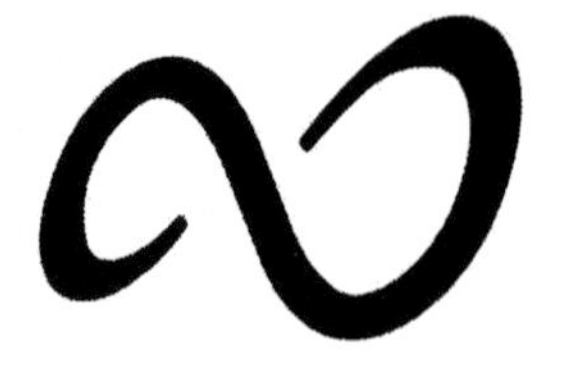

Printed in the United States of America

Printed on Recycled Paper

Published January 2001

ABOUT SAVING GRACE
A SPIRITUAL LOVE STORY

It is rare to find a work of fiction with a page-turner story and engaging characters within the context of simply presented spiritual teachings, yet that does describe *Saving Grace: A Spiritual Love Story*. It allows the readers to experience that spirituality can be fun. *Saving Grace: A Spiritual Love Story* is inspirational fiction about true love, real magic and ordinary miracles set in this, the Age of Anxiety. It is a story about a group of "romantically impared" individuals (much like you and I are, or were), searching for love and happiness without knowing what they really are or where to find them.

Through a "chance" meeting with a very wise Eastern teacher, the protagonist, Valentine, along with the readers, goes to his Life School, where he presents eleven authentic spiritual lessons about love and happiness – truths from Yoga, the ancient Eastern Indian philosophy applicable to us all regardless of religion and belief. Yoga teaches, "When you choose your actions, you choose your results." The classes are interspersed throughout this engaging romantic novel that touches upon just about every important life area, as the main characters struggle through a modern life which is as harried as *is* life in this new century. By the end of the book they've learned better ways toward discovering happiness and love.

Experience the difficulties and joys of Valentines' relationships and growth as a person. Enjoy and suffer with her in her love relationships...welcome the explanations about how our world is changing...see the advantage of incorporating these concepts into our lives. Appreciate the pragmatics revealed about love, relationships, parenthood, the differences between men and women, atypical individuals, and why science and spirituality, which are often at odds, need not be.

This, a didactic spiritual novel, may well represent a welcome new genre for the new age in which we live.

ABOUT THE AUTHOR

Dr. Phyllis-Terri Gold, Ph.D, NCC, is a Board Certified Clinical Mental Health Counselor and Psychologist who specializes in integrating conventional and alternative therapies. Formerly adjunct professor of Hofstra University and Long Island University, C.W. Post College, she served a doctoral residency as a research associate at State University of New York, Stony Brook. Dr. Gold is founding director of Mindworks Center for the Self. She is in private practice in Fort Salonga, Long Island, New York, and also gives lectures and workshops for corporations as well as the general public.

Since the early 70's Phyllis-Terri has been a student/teacher of meditation and spirituality. A student of two Eastern Indian masters – one of whom is still her teacher – she was director of one of their meditation centers for ten years.

Phyllis-Terri is an Intuitive and a Reiki Healing Master. She, her patients and students have experienced many miracles. She is also an ordained interfaith Reverend.

In *Saving Grace: A Spiritual Love Story* Phyllis-Terri writes not as a doctor, but as a woman, humanist and friend.

Grateful acknowledgement is made for

Quotation from the following songs

I Remember You by Johnny Mercer and Shertzinger
Our Love is Here To Stay by George and Ira Gershwin
Joy To The World by Hoyt Axton
All I Wanna Do by Sheryl Crow, Wyn Cooper, Bill Botrell, David Baerwald, and Kevin Gilbert
American Beauty Rose by Hal David, Redd Evens, and Arthur Altman
When You Wish Upon A Star by Ned Washington and Leigh Harline

Also To:

Toni Wolfe for her identification of the four archtypes of woman as specified in her paper, *Structural Forms of the Feminine Psyche*.
Mary Renault, for her retelling of the amazon tale from *The Bull of the Sea.*
Pantanjali's *Yoga Sutras.*

Cathi Wong, *for her cover art*
(The cover conceptualization by Phyllis-Terri Gold)
Lizbeth K. Lindley for photograph of author: March 2000.

Acknowledgements

The journey from first writing through publication of a book, especially in today's publishing world and most especially when it's a first novel and a unique type of spiritual novel at that, could be a very lonely, arduous and discouraging process if not for the help of others. I was most fortunate along the way to have had the help, support and encouragement of many wonderfully giving people; it's my delight to thank them here from my heart.

First and foremost as always, I thank my Siddha teachers... for everything.

A very special tribute to atypical persons everywhere as well as to all those who courageously support them. May we soon see the day when diversity is honored and respected.

Thank you, Valerie Arena, Gloria Freeda, Fran Frumkin, Leslie Funda, Kathy Palermo, and Denise Rohlfs for typing earlier drafts of the manuscript before I bought my computer and learned to use it. Thank you, my terrific assistant Andrea Macellaro for helping me to edit the final draft, and for in so many ways assisting me with my other work thus freeing me more to write. Thank you to the following people for supporting me by reading and critiquing parts of the manuscript, for inadvertently supplying funny lines or suggesting apropos situations and for offering technical assistance, inspiration, and/or encouragement to continue pursuing rewrites and finally publication: Marla and Bill Abraham, Myrtle Banis, Vegatirado ("Bessie") Basilisa, Yomaira ("Jo") Blanco, Dr. Doug Biklen (and all the fine people at the Syracuse University Facilitated Communication Institute), Dr. Harman Bro, R.D. Chin, Pat Conlan, Lorraine Courounis, Frank Darmstadt, Robert Faulkner, Janet Garr, Steve Geraci, Mitchell Goldberg, Joyce St. Germain Hopkins, Diane Jacobs, the dedicated devoted staff at Jamesport A.D.D, Barbara Lieber, Lizbeth Goldberg Lindley and Jeff Lindley, Sharon Jennings, John McDonald, Peggy McDonald, Sue McManus, Florence Meyer, Margaret Norton, Muriel and Harry Oksner, Wilma Pordin, Rev. Anne Puryear, Dr. Hae Su Pyun, Rajnish Rametra, Lisa Reisner, Kathy and Walter Rhind, Richard Savage ("Dick's Discs"), Judy

Schneider, Mary Ann Scribner, Judy Steel, Lois and Kenneth Stern, Chris Terry, Eileen Vein, my parents Blanche and Jim Weissman. Special thank-yous to free lance editor Elmer Luke for your editorial ideas, to Executive Editor of Warner Books Rick Wolff for your invaluable suggestions and for your encouragement of, "Don't give up the dream!" to Norma Fox, then Vice- President of Plenum Publishing for supporting and encouraging me in the writing and publication of my first book, and to John F. Harnish of Infinity Publishing who, from our first contact onward, so generously gave of your advise, support, and optimism in the publication of *Saving Grace: A Spiritual Love Story.* I also want to thank everyone at Infinity who worked on my book. You have heart. Thank you Cathi ("Cat") Wong for beautifully capturing the essence of *Saving Grace: A Spiritual Love Story* in your art for my book cover, and in giving generously in many other ways. I want to offer an extra special thank-you and a warm embrace to each of my patients, clients, students, workshop attendees and newsletter subscribers from whom I've learned multitudes and who kept me going when the going got tough by exclaiming, after reading excerpts of *Saving Grace: A Spiritual Love Story*, things like, "I loved it! I can't wait until it gets published so that I can read the entire book! *When* did you say that will be?"

To all the special people in my world - past, present and future-

"When my life is through,
and the angels ask me to recall
the thrill of it all,
then I shall tell them that
I remember you."

To Paul, my husband

"...the Rockies may crumble,
Gibraltar may tumble
...but, our love is here to stay."

AUTHOR'S INTRODUCTION

I began writing this book over seventeen years ago; within that time period I have completely rewritten it at least three times. So, when it does well - I somehow know that it will- it won't exactly be "an overnight success"! I simply had other priorities: my children, working for my masters and doctoral degrees - the doctorate requiring that I write my first "big book," my dissertation - years of advocating for the rights of my son with autism and his peers, and attending to my profession as a psychologist which includes a demanding stimulating schedule of lecturing, teaching, the media, and a busy private psychotherapy practice combining alternative and traditional methods. I should not fail to mention the time-consuming two years of thirty-something submissions of the manuscript followed by letters of rejection from editors and literary agents; *Saving Grace: A Spiritual Love Story* was "too much" this…"not enough" that. No matter; each time my book was rejected I worked on it further, hopefully improving it.

I believe, though, that the above were just worldly ways of serving the primary reason that this book took so long to get out there – that until now it wasn't the time. First I had to work many, many years on myself spiritually, until I could write this with enough high energy behind it to really affect readers in a positive, elevating way.

I wrote this version differently than before. I had a certain intent about its key ideas, but other than that I was totally committed to allowing it to come through me, from my Higher Self, keeping my logical self out of the way. Thus I was continuously surprised at what unfolded. Currently one hears the phrase "channeled" material. This book was not that if by that is meant listening to words dictated to one from some other being or collective other beings with me being the scribe. No; what I was intended to do at this stage was to go to my Truth deep within, to make my decisions and to write from there with my Self as my own highest authority, from that place of faith, self-trust and honesty.

For that is what my teachers have been preparing me to do all these years. It is for that reason that they made me face myself, forced me to go deeper and deeper to where I didn't always want to go, to places where I sometimes with all my might resisted going. But they would have none of that. I had to do it. To face my own fears, to peel away my layers of self-dislike and insecurities (even when others probably believed that I had none, and I'd fooled myself into believing the same), and to rid myself of them. To discover certain attitudes and behaviors of mine which didn't work and to find new ones which did. To get in touch with my own heart. In this, I had to do what everyone must eventually.

I've taken this journey and since it is by no means over, I sense that this book is also going to be a powerful teaching for me, one which will bring me - and hopefully others - higher and deeper, to echoes of the heart which we all have in common.

Good fiction for me has three important ingredients: an appealing protagonist with vivid characters around him or her, a credible landscape in which they interact, and a teaching of something important and unique which in a practical attractive way help readers to solve their problems of living. I believe that *Saving Grace: A Spiritual Love Story* satisfies each of those criteria.

Yet for me there must be more. One great precept underlying all successful literary work is, "Look into your own heart and write. Do not primarily seek approval. Be true. Be fearless. And be loyal to the promptings of your own soul." An author can write no more than he or she is. In order to write more she or he first must be more. Any decent writer can write nice-sounding phrases, and initially, at least, impress people. But if the author writes with strong purpose, deep feeling and open to the highest inspiration, then the energy of that author gets into those pages rendering what's between the lines even more powerful than what's written in the lines. Making the book breathe forth such a vital, living power that the reader is inspired and uplifted by some indefinable something in that book. It is this indefinable something that takes a book out of the medium or good category and makes it exceptional and truly successful. It is this type book which is recommended by one reader to the next and causes readers to buy numbers of copies to pass on to others. The writer who writes not with the thought of having what he writes sell, but with the thought of reaching people's hearts, giving them something of vital value that will broaden, sweeten, enrich and beautiful their lives, writes a book that sells itself. I do not mean to sound immodest, but I believe this describes me and *Saving Grace: A Spiritual Love Story*. The reactions from those who have read excerpts or the entire manuscript seem to confirm that. I feel comfortable saying that because I give the credit to God. If in reading this book, you experience good feelings surging through you, that will be your proof. You won't have to take my word for it.

Saving Grace: A Spiritual Love Story is inspirational fiction using my own life challenges merely as a springboard. Only the spiritual precepts within are totally true. It presents Yogic doctrine, ancient Eastern Indian teachings handed down from prehistoric times. Yoga, translated into English to mean "yoke", consists of ancient methods - one of many kinds - by which individuals of all religions and beliefs may become united with God or Reality.

My recommendation is to do the practices suggested in the Discourses for a year, then re-evaluate yourself and your life. However, please take from this book whatever you find useful and applicable at this time. Not least of all, as you read *Saving Grace: A Spiritual Love Story*, please enjoy your adventure. If you feel inspired to get in touch with me, I'll be delighted to hear from you. You can see how to do that in "Epilogue"

"I write fiction and I'm told it's autobiography. I write autobiography and I'm told it's fiction. So, since I'm so dim and they're so smart, let them decide."

--Philip Roth

BOOK I

THE PRELIMINARIES

CHAPTER ONE: LA DOLCE VALENTINE

Seeker: "Baba, how can you say that maya (illusion) doesn't exist?"
Baba Muktananda: "Show me maya and I will believe in it."
Seeker: "How can you expect me to show you maya?"
Baba Muktananda: "Then how can you expect me to believe in it?"
--Swami Muktananda and a Seeker

"No matter what is happening in our lives, it isn't really happening. It appears to be real, but it's real only in the sense that a dream is real. It is just maya as they call it in the East, not ultimate reality.

So, in reading this story, probably your mind will want to know, 'is this Valentine's story, or Phyllis-Terri's story?' Dear Ones, why does that matter? Whether it's Valentine's maya, or Phyllis-Terri's maya, it's still all just maya.

Yet it's fine to get very involved with it. And, don't forget to have some fun."

-- Dr. Cheng Ho

I'm Valentine Jordan. I want to tell you my story because I suppose in many ways I'm like you. I began to learn what real love is only after a point in my life when I felt painfully deprived of love. It was only then that anything truly important happened to me. But in order to understand, you'll need to know something about what came first.

When I think back upon that time of my life I do so with reverence, because life is precious – however it plays. If I have any regrets, it's but one. That it took me so long to have none.

Late March, 1975

The wind smacked the windows and pummeled the roof, partially awakening me. Spring, but on Long Island it was still winter. The next thing I sensed was a man's arm around me lightly brushing my breast. My second awareness vastly upset me. Try as I did in my half asleep state, I could not tell which of the two men I was with.

"Sweetheart, beautiful Valen," the man was whispering, "You awake?"

"No o o o," I murmured. Only one person called me Valen; the man who was holding me was my husband; I was at home in my own bed; our bed; I was also soaked with perspiration.

Outside a chilling sleet/rain fell. By contrast, our sophisticatedly sleek silver, red and black bedroom was a cozy cocoon. It was the kind of Monday morning when sleeping-in would have been a world class thrill.

Especially with Richard beside me. My good looking husband of nine years, a minor-league Paul Newman look-alike, now gazing at me with his half-closed waterfall blue eyes, touching me in a place I need not name. I rubbed the hairs on his arm. Then as my hand moved to between his legs too, I saw the clock on my night table.

"Goodness me! It's 5:00!" In one movement I threw off the covers and jumped out of bed, in the process unintentionally pushing Richard onto his side.

"Shit! The day's almost over." Richard's sarcasm sandwiched in between his struggle to regain his balance, sent me into a fit of laughter. But as I moved to get out of bed my husband's expression turned serious. "Did you know you were in a sweat when you woke up?" he asked. "Have you a fever?"

"No," I told him, "It's due to the dream. I had it again."

"What dream? And what does that have to do with sweating?"

"How many times have I told you about this?" I was becoming annoyed. "Alright, once more. As always, there's the close-up of that big clock on the wall with the small hand on the eight and the big hand – somewhere, I forget. Then the brief cases are falling and flying. Ambulances are screeching. Thre's a tight-two shot of two medics carrying a stretcher. I try to help but I cannot move. I awaken in a sweat. That's it."

"You dream close-ups and camera angles?" Richard chortled. "Talk about bringing one's work home." Sensing me not amused, he added, "It's only a dream, honey. Why make so much of it?"

There were two reasons. The first one I kept to myself; it seemed too real to be just a dream. The second reason I shared with Richard; "Because what I can't understand frightens me."

But, my weekday mornings left no time for real conversation, especially mornings like this one when I'd overslept in the first place. I looked down at Richard, still reclining, and asked impatiently, "Are you getting out of bed soon?"

"Why?"

"I want to make the bed."

"Don't let me stop you. Make it with me still in it," Richard grumbled, pulling himself to his feet. "Valen, I brought paper work home last night. I didn't get to sleep until 1:30. Would it be a sign of sloth if I lounged around in bed until 5:15 A.M? More to the point, will the world end if you don't make the bed one morning?"

I half closed my eyes, pursed my lips, struck a seductive pose and said, "Five minutes ago you didn't exactly look like sleep was what you were craving."

"That's a whole other thing," Richard moaned, climbing out of bed. " This career of yours does nothing for our sex life. Except that one couldn't find a better method of birth control."

"Effective, yes. Better, I could think of," I answered as I hurriedly smoothed the sheets and comforter on my side, then plumped the pillow. "You don't like my having to catch a 6:10 train every morning?" I darted to Richard's side of the bed and rapidly smoothed the bed covers as Richard watched in apparent fascination. Why could he not lift a hand to place a pillow; his arm was broken? "Funny, *I* love leaving so early, especially when it's sleeting and storming out like today." I hurried into my walk-in closet – about which my best friend Casse had remarked, "If you'd put a bathroom in there you could rent it out" - calling to Richard, "When there's a *snow*storm things become even better out there." I pulled my new skirt off of its hanger and grabbed a sweater from the shelf which I hoped matched. I rushed out of the closet, hurried to my bureau and pulled a few undergarments from a drawer. "As I think about it all," I continued, "I can hardly *wait* to get out there today and get *drenched*!" My arms loaded with clothes, I dashed into my bathroom and shoved the door shut with my foot.

By 5:25 I was showered and dressed except for jewelry. From my top bureau drawer I selected a pair of earrings, squares of mahogany red jasper swirled with dramatic black inclusions and poised beautifully above delicate teardrops of carnelian, handcrafted with sterling silver frames. I'd had them for awhile; I loved their burnished elegance which was all that I needed with my skirt and sweater. I scribbled a long list of directions for Mrs. Becket, the sitter, who'd arrive soon to help Richard get the children ready and off to school. Mrs. Becket was filling in until our live-in housekeeper, Esmerelda, returned from a month's vacation.

When I re-entered our bedroom Richard was seated on our bed in his robe. "Hadn't you better take your shower now before the children are up?" I reminded him.

"I presume you mean a COLD shower."

"Really funny, Richard."

"We're becoming like two ships in the night."

"Two ships in the night *meet* in the night. Could be worse," I offered. I wondered if Richard actually believed it was a lark for me commuting to New York City five days a week, rarely getting home before eight at night, while striving to be a good enough wife and mother to two children? Make that ten children; Brenna counted as one, Willie as nine!

Richard came out of the bathroom wrapped in a towel as the radio announced, "probably all day rainstorms." I was glad I'd decided to wear my old but still presentable Treetorn boots. My job as representative to advertising photographers required a split personality wardrobe depending on what I'd be doing each day. It was a fashion-your-own-dress-code job description; some reps wore clothes that were funky or sexy to the extreme. I watched out. With conservative clients I let my clothes fade into the background, making the work the important thing. It was when showing to younger clients that I could wear my leather pants outfits and other clothes with panache. I needed a versatile wardrobe, which fortunately also suited my personality if not my current finances.

I was pulling on my boots when a naked Richard crossed the room, faced his closet, then holding a shirt in one hand, a tie in the other and without looking around asked me, "These go together?"

"Uh uh. You need something brighter. Try one with red in it."

Richard pulled out another tie. "Better?"

"Much. Perfect, actually."

Turning then to face me, Richard's eyes widened as he whistled. I looked at him and asked, "What?"

"Talk about perfect!" he exclaimed. "The men in New York will go nuts when they see you! You look BEAUTIFUL!"

Instead of that accolade making me feel great as it probably should have, it made me instantly uncomfortable. All such compliments did that these days. Furthermore, the beautiful thing puzzled me. Women and men said I was, men reacted to me as if I was, yet I wasn't relating to it. I tried to remember whether I'd felt pretty before Willie.

Richard, following me down the stairs, interrupted my musing by asking anxiously, "When's Esmerelda coming back?"

"Next Monday. She'll be a week late. She missed her plane."

"Did you ever notice how maids never miss their planes going on vacation, only returning?"

"Cynic!"

"Realist!"

"And, I say 'pataato', you say 'Patayto', so let's call the whole thing off?"

"Now that you've brought it up, why *don't* you ever call? Richard complained.

To be fair, he had a point. Lately I'd been so busy from the moment I arrived at the studio until I got on the train for home that I'd not found a minute to phone Richard. Whenever he called me I was in a shoot or otherwise tied up. When I returned his call he was with a client or had left for the day. Even our phone communications were missing the mark.

"What time will you be home tonight?" Richard asked.

"I can't say yet. I'll phone you from the studio once I know, is that alright?"

"That sounds like a plan."

I pulled my raincoat from the hall closet, kissed Richard hurriedly, then standing in the doorway - how could I have almost forgotten? - I asked, "Oh, honey will you let Jonah and Sammy out? And take the cover off of Si's cage, then give him his seed? Tabitha gets fed at night; I'll do it. Pisces is just fine."

"Wonderful! Now that I know the fish is fine, all day I'll be at peace. I needed this menagerie?!" Richard grumbled. "If I hadn't stopped you you'd have brought home a moose!"

I picked up my purse, slung the strap over my shoulder, and opened the front door. "If I don't leave this second I'll miss my train," I said, pulling my keys from the bag as I stepped out the front door and closed it after me.

I slid behind the steering wheel of my '72 Porsche Speedster, with one hand shook a Parliament cigarette out of the pack and slipped it between my lips, shoved in the car lighter with the other. What a downpour; in the dash from the house to the car alone I'd become soaked! I turned on the ignition, windshield wipers and heater. When the cigarette lighter popped out I pressed it against the cigarette tip, took a drag, replaced the lighter as I pushed the car clutch, shifted into reverse, and backed down the driveway. As I strained to see through the downpour I felt the crumbling blacktop under the wheels. Again I dragged in deeply on the Parliament. In less than a minute our 100 foot long brick ranch, the wood trim with the peeling paint, would be a dot. By the time I got on the train at the Coldport station, the people who lived in the house with me would cease to exist. I would have entered another world. I exhaled smoke. Was that also a sigh of relief?

I arrived at the station just as the train was pulling in. The Long Island Railroad! Nobody would have believed it; the dirt on the outside was so thick, it looked like one of the cattle cars to Dachau! Judging from the grime on the windows, I'd guess they had last been washed in 1920 – maybe. The interior of the train matched the exterior. I boarded the abomination, with it all feeling fortunate to get a seat.

I felt a hand on my shoulder. "Are you asleep?" he whispered softly.

"*Now* who?" I thought, unnerved. As I partially opened my eyes, with my peripheral vision I saw the side of a white Styrofoam coffee container waving slightly as the train jostled us. Slowly, I reoriented myself. I was sitting beside Max. Max Witkin, fellow commuter and friend. Intelligent, kind, caring Max. At the same time I felt something cold and wet fall into my eye. I looked toward the ceiling and saw some water dripping from my raincoat which I'd shoved onto the luggage rack above my seat. Maybe it had been sleet that had just melted. "Jeez!" I said, wiping my face with a Kleenex. And the day hadn't really even begun yet.

I clearly remembered the morning about three months earlier when I'd met Max for the first time, at least the first time I could remember. Often Richard had told people, "Men and V...like moths to a flame."

That morning, like this one, I had been traveling to my job. The seat on the train next to mine had been vacant. Then Max had come along, taken that seat, stretched his long legs out as much as space allowed and asked redundantly, "Mind if I sit here?"

"That's fine," I'd lied. This man looked like he wanted to talk, whereas I'd needed to meditate, maybe catch up on sleep a little as well. Due to a combination of my late work hours, Willie's erratic nocturnal habits, and my eerie recurring dream, my sleep deprivation was starting to tell. I'd gladly have settled for just meditation. Not that meditating on trains was for a novice; I was a little more than that. That morning too Max was holding his Styrofoam coffee container straight out so that his coffee wouldn't spill on me. But it did, on my skirt.

"Oh, Lord, this was so foolhardy of me! I'm so sorry." Max pulled out a handkerchief and began to dab at the spot. Then, perhaps thinking that might be inappropriate, along with realizing that it wasn't working, he became even more flustered and embarrassed.

"Wonderful!" I thought. With good money riding on me in my work, I was expected to dress well and to look just right. I had nothing to change into.

"Don't worry. It will come out in the cleaners," I assured Max, standing up. "Will you excuse me for a few minutes, please?"

Max stood up to allow me to pass, uttering further apologies as I did so. I answered with a few more, "It's all right's," and dashed to the rest room where I scrubbed the spot with soap and water, to no avail. When I returned to my seat with an obviously still stained skirt, in fact made worse by my ministrations, Max looked distressed. I mustered up a broad smile and in my most nonchalant voice offered, "Goodness me, must be strong coffee." It was after this whole scene that Max introduced himself and told me we'd actually met once before.

"Some time ago, on the return trip during the rush hour, seats were finally available. We obtained adjacent seats, like today," he said, in his unique way of speaking. "I remember how pleasant the trip was because of such a lovely interesting companion."

Considering that oration, I was now feeling guilty that I hadn't remembered that meeting. Max's appearance was rather unremarkable. He had honest brown eyes, straight brown hair, and wore a brown suit. He was of average height, stocky but not heavy. He reminded me of a friendly chocolate lab. But his speech was memorably formal, like from another era.

"Well, I'll surely not forget you *this* time," I tried for the light approach. I'd paid more than I could afford for the new skirt, especially retrospectively considering the outcome.

"Yes, I'm sure I left my mark," Max answered. "I intend to pay for your beautiful skirt that I ruined. I know that doesn't compensate for the inconvenience, but at least hopefully you can replace it." I was about to answer, "Thank you, but that won't be necessary," when Max added, " I must say you look fetching in that skirt. I do hope the replacement will fit you… as well."

"Here it comes! Why are you surprised?" I silenly asked myself.

I must have given Max a cold look without even realizing it, because he quickly explained, "Please, that wasn't an overture, I promise you. I'm sorry if it sounded like one. Kindly tell me about your work and how you got into that field?"

So I gave Max a brief synopsis, then asked "And what do you do?"

"I'm chief of the Neuropsychiatric Institute at New York Chelsea Hospital."

"Really! You're a psychiatrist? A Medical Doctor?"

"I am. When I was younger my heritage emerged from somewhere within my cells. The idea I was raised with was that a Doctor was what God would have been if his parents had *really* been Jewish. So, I did what my parents felt was required to surpass God; graduated from medical school. I teach at the hospital also."

"That's admirable, Max. Do you like your work?"

"Much of the time I do. I feel that I perform a useful service. So does the man who fixes my car. It's that simple for me now."

"I'm impressed. How do you remain so...unassuming?"

"I guess life has a way of bringing us down a peg," Max answered, then looking me directly in the eye, asked, "Are you married?"

"Yes."

"Your husband is very fortunate. Children?"

"I have two. My son Willie is six and my daughter Brenna is seven and a half. And, you?"

"Technically -- yes, I'm married. If it could ever have been called a marriage. Separated six months, in the middle of a divorce. My wife is seeing to it that it will be as hellish a one for me as possible. She's making a career out of it. Weak moment; I don't usually bad-mouth her. She was a good woman in a bad union. I do have two wondrous sons, though, so good came out of it."

I did not care to go there. All I really needed to know about Max I had figured out. He was an exceptionally nice man whom I'd love to have as a friend.

Now, months later, on the same train line at approximately the same hour, listening to Max I felt our relationship threatening to take a turn that I didn't welcome.

"I'm asking you to lunch Valentine, nothing more. Why the major stand-off?"

"I'd love to, but things have been very busy lately." At least that last part was true.

"What about those tedious advertising industry two hour lunches during which nobody works?" Max persisted.

"A myth, at least for me lately. I've been eating lunch at my desk. It's when I try to get caught up."

Actually I was telling the truth about eating at my desk. I simply left out that what I was primarily catching up on was stuff with Willie; the housekeepers who came and left, necessitating constant training, retraining, getting their feedback and making changes in the plans. That for five years straight, until Willie had entered school, the majority of each day I'd done mostly everything for him myself. I didn't speak to many people about autism then. My attempts at telling people, "I have a son who's autistic," had been strangely received; either the listener looked at me blankly because they had no idea what autism was, or looked at me like I was a leper's mother because they *thought* they knew what autism was. Or there was that classic response when they'd look at me brightly and say something like, "Artistic! Aren't you lucky. Does he paint?"

Nor was I prepared to tell straight-arrow Doctor Witkin that lately, whenever I could leave the studio at lunch time – when we weren't in the middle of a shoot, when I didn't have to entertain a client at lunch, and when all the domestic holes were temporarily filled - or on evenings when I could leave early, I'd been rushing over to the Mid-Town Zen Meditation Center. If it was true, as my friend Cassandra said, that I was growing painfully thinner, I was also growing happily calmer. Before I'd started meditating I'd been having such anxiety attacks due to Willie that I'd thought I'd have a heart attack before I turned 33. Meditation had stopped them. Anything that accomplished that I gave precedence to over lunch. I apologized again to Max for having fallen asleep.

"I've had some late nights," I told him.

"Why don't you catch a few winks," Max kindly suggested. "I'll read the paper and awaken you when we get to Penn Station." He was the epitome of empathy and compassion, and *he* lived fifteen minutes from my home. Go figure.

Let's backtrack a bit. As I said, I'm Valentine Jordan. People call me a variety of other names some of which I answer to. A few conservatives call me Valentine. Richard calls me Valen, or V. At work they call me V.J. People I've known since college, like Casse, call me Val. Presently at least I'm wife of Richard T. Jordan, Mother of Willie and Brenna, and until three years ago was a stay- at- home mom, except if the term had existed then it would have been a redundancy; then it was assumed that a mother of young children stayed at home with her kids.

Richard's in the field of finance and had success in it. But when another Richard, last name Nixon, had become president a few years earlier and the Republican economy had crashed, a substantial portion of Richard Jordan's income had flown out the window. In its place soon had flown the realization that what we'd been spending on tutors and therapy for Willie had been more than most people live on per year. It was indeed more than we had to spend.

And so I, with a Bachelor's Degree in psychology and a minor in English literature (in other words, trained to do absolutely nothing) went out job hunting. Which brought me to an exact realization of what my BA degree was worth in the job market; considerably less than a high school diploma in the hands of anyone who could type 60 words per minute. It was what my Zen teachers would have called an enlightening experience; I called it a lousy one.

It must have been because I didn't try to hide my discouragement from close friends that Casse's present husband Albert -her fourth, but who's counting?- suggested that I try my luck at modeling in Manhattan. "There could be good money in it for you," he said.

My reaction was immediate. "Of *course* I can model! Unless I decide to be a rocket scientist instead! Come onnnnn, Albert..."

"I can give you a list of modeling agencies and names; that's about it. I believe you've got a chance. Have some balls," Albert suggested succinctly.

I liked and respected Albert, a nice no-nonsense guy. Because of that and because he was a knowledgeable art director, I decided to go for it. I put together a portfolio, got an agency willing to represent me, and not long after, my first go-see, or interview for a modeling job. It will be forever etched in my memory.

Heart fluttering and palms sweating, I tentatively stepped into the ground floor studio of photographer Calvin Lichenstein. He had just begun to gain recognition in the business. Recently I'd seen his photographs in magazines along with articles about him. He was very handsome, like a model himself.

A receptionist took my name and directed me to an alcove reception area where two other models were seated with one empty chair between them. After I timidly took that middle chair I glanced to my companion model on my right, a blonde. Then I stared. I couldn't help it. I hadn't remembered ever seeing anyone as stunning. She wore a tight jump suit with a V-neck revealing impossibly perfect breasts that shouted, "Implants!" I wondered why she was showing *those* at a go-see for a stocking ad. Who would notice she even had legs?! She was so engrossed in a magazine I don't think she noticed me looking at her. Then I looked over at the model seated to my left, a more flashy but equally striking red head, whose perfect nose screamed, "Rhinoplasty!" and whose thigh length skirt revealed long legs which I assumed were her own. Although it's not been an adjective used to describe me, I was feeling plain. In the background the hit single of the day, 'My Eyes Adored You' sung by Frankie Valli wafted softly from an invisible stereo speaker. I ached to smoke but there were no ashtrays around.

A door leading into the alcove opened and a man walked out gracefully. "I'm James, Mr. Lichenstein's representative," he told us, gesturing toward the door. "Mr. Lichenstein is ready for go-sees now. He'll see each of you separately."

The blonde stood up, put her magazine down on the chair, and with a nod from James they disappeared together into the office. Shortly, James came out alone, semi-smiled at each of us and then disappcared into another part of the studio.

I heard a scratching sound to my right. I turned in my seat to look in that direction and found myself staring directly into the redhead's mascared eyes. She had dragged her chair a bit to the left to make eye contact with me. She silently looked at me without blinking.

"Hello, I'm Valentine," I offered.

"I'm Jacy, how ya doin'?" she answered, in one of the most glass- shattering Bronx accented voices I'd ever heard, punctuated by a crack of her bubble gum. For me, there went gorgeous. Jacy then casually lifted the blonde's magazine from the latter's chair and proceeded to thumb through it. I gathered our conversation had ended. Her seeming repose in this situation made my nervousness all the more obvious. I had to hold my hands on my knees to keep them from knocking together.

Before long the blonde came out of the office. "Next girl, go right in," she told us in a practiced voice.

I instantly indicated, by not moving one body part out of my chair, that Jacy was the next girl. She gave a shrug, stood up and walked into Calvin's office, hips swaying, gum cracking. In a second I heard voices. I looked at Calvin's office door and saw that Jacy had left it slightly ajar, enough for me to hear her's and Calvin's conversation. Feeling like a captive eavesdropper, I thought to get up and close the door, then decided that might appear presumptuous.

I heard Calvin tell Jacy, "I'll just unzip your portfolio and take a look."

"Be my guest," Jacy answered.

I heard the sound of a zipper as Calvin asked, "Bathing suit shots in back? I need to see all of your legs."

"I can do better than that," Jacy said.

Silence from Calvin.

"You see, I need this job." Jacy went on. I leaned forward in my chair to hear better. I couldn't help it.

Calvin was calmness and reasonableness personified. "I'm sure the other girls need the job too. *My* job is to pick the best model for it."

"Perhaps I should be clearer," Jacy said. "For you, *I* am the best girl for this job; I'm willing to pay for it."

There was the sound of another zipper, followed by the sound of Calvin's drawing in his breath. Out in the alcove I did the same.

"What do you mean?" Calvin asked her.

Was he real? *I* knew what Jacy meant and I wasn't even in the room with her.

After a long pause, Calvin told Jacy, "You can stop there. I see that you have good legs. I'd like you to leave your head sheet, and if you're chosen we'll contact your agency. Thank you very much for coming here today. On your way out, will you please send in the next model?"

Jacy walked out, her jump suit unzipped from the waist. As I stared at this half unclad female walking directly in front of me, she gave me a 'what's a girl to do?!' shrug. She followed that with a nod of her head in the direction of the office and screeched, in the process possibly breaking several windows somewhere in the building, "YOU CAN GO IN." With that, she carefully zipped her jumpsuit up to but not covering one bit of her cleavage. As she swayed down the hallway, I heard her gum crack.

When I walked into Calvin Lichenstein's office I could not have been more nervous. Calvin, standing there in his tight jeans - what was his waist measurement, for heaven's sake, all of 30 inches? - and close fitting shirt tucked casually into them, with his olive skin, emerald eyes and wavy black hair, was even more attractive in person than in his photographs. That seemed to make things worse. I was aware of my legs shaking and hoped he hadn't noticed.

"Hard act to follow," I said with a nervous laugh, nodding to the door where the model had just exited.

Cal didn't answer. He was concentrating on the data on me that my agency had forwarded him. "Valentine Jordan," he read aloud. "Your own name, or professional?"

"My given name is something else, but my father began calling me Valentine when I was three. He said it suited me because I was very feminine and romantic. It stuck."

"Your father was right. What's your real name?" Calvin asked.

"I never tell that."

"Fine," Calvin answered. "Valentine suits you. I like it."

"I sort of do too. With a name like Valentine at least people remember you."

"People would remember *you* if your name were Sue." Cal gave me a quick smile. "I just thought of a good name for you if you don't mind the suggestion. How about V.J?"

I thought for a moment, then told Calvin, "I like it for work. It's very…corporate."

"Good, then when you return to the agency today, remember to tell them that from now on your billing is V.J. So, that's settled. Now let's see." Cal turned his attention back to my bio. "Age 25," he read aloud.

"That's a lie," I blurted out.

Calvin looked up in surprise, but he couldn't have been more surprised by my outburst of truth than I.

"I'm 29," I told him.

"You could have fooled ME," Calvin said, scrutinizing me.

"Yes -- well – I'd been advised to lie because otherwise the client or photographer might think I'm too old so not even want to see me."

"You're probably right. In fact, from now on say you're 20." Calvin returned to my vital statistics. "Weight 115. Looks more like about 112."

"I've lost weight since that was recorded. You're good."

"You get to tell," he answered matter of factly.

Before Calvin could say more, I astonished myself a second time.

"You'd better take – Jacy for this job," I told him. Calvin peered at me the way one would any curiosity. "I've never heard *that* before. Why?"

"Because she'll pay for it. I won't."

"God, you heard all that?" Calvin became busy for a few minutes wiping his forehead, blushed, then laughed. "Well, right now let's focus on you. You're not only beautiful, you make me laugh. How could I not suggest you for the job! You even have a good voice. Many models don't."

"I noticed." I tried to sound cool. He wanted me for the job! My first go-see!

"It seems like you have it all," Cal added.

"You have no idea -- all I have," I said, sighing.

"What?"

"Oh…. nothing."

Calvin looked at me inquiringly for a second, then shrugged and turned his attention back to my portfolio. While he looked through it I glanced over at a table beside us and saw on top of it the photos which the other two models had left. Both photographed exquisitely.

Calvin handed my book back to me, saying, "These are alright, but you can look better." My face fell. "Don't worry about it," he reassured me, adding "Please understand, V.J, I don't have final choice of model, the client does." I felt my hopes nosedive. "But" he added brightly, "My regular clients trust me so they usually go with my choices. This client has used me many times." Calvin winked.

"What will be will be," I managed. Cool. If I was going to do this work, I'd better start now with an attitude. "Thank you so much, Mr. Lichenstein. I'm glad to have had this chance to meet you."

"I believe we'll see each other again—soon," he answered, "but only if you promise never again to call me Mr. Lichenstein."

"All right, then. Calvin"

"If you call me Calvin you *definitely* will never see me again. Nobody calls me that but my mother. One mother is enough."

"But, the magazine article I read…said you like to be called Calvin."

"There's always somebody who has to change everything, good or otherwise," he shrugged. "Everybody who knows me calls me Cal."

"Well, then, thank you, Cal."

The following day my agency notified me that I had the job!

After that first job Cal took a complete new set of pictures of me that didn't cost me anything. It was called testing. A photographer would experiment with lighting and technique to perfect his art, the model would get the pictures. From the first time Cal and I worked together we were as easy with each other as two fish swimming side by side upstream. Cal said that as a model I was a natural, and I must say there was truth in that. Although I had never done anything like it before, from the start in front of the lights I came alive. True, at first I'd been shy, but with Cal's continuing ego boosts I soon responded. And so as current hits like 'Love Will Keep Us Together' by Captain and Tenille played in the background, Cal, with his Nikon pointed at me, would purr to me, insinuate, call me "beautiful," and say, "My camera is loving you right now!" And so due to Cal I gained confidence, becoming bolder, saucier, more impudent, sexier.

I learned there had to be a special chemistry going between photographer and model. Mine and Cal's making of a picture together was something like making love. Despite that, there was only friendship and professionalism between us. As for Cal's photographs of me, they were so fantastic that the first time I looked at them I had to wonder who that beautiful woman was. It was only because I'd posed for the pictures that I knew it really was me –in a sense.

Then one day Cal, after staring at me for quite awhile, said, "V.J, I'd like to do some nudes of you." My head shot up. Cal added quickly, "Of course not for publication. Just testing. Working with lights and shadows. How about it, Valentine? Your body's beautiful clothed. It's got to be lovely naked."

After gaining back my equilibrium I answered mischievously, "No Cal. My naked body is for just a select few." I told him I'd decided that I wouldn't take my clothes off in front of a camera for anybody or anything, ever. I must have been convincing. He never asked again.

I did all right in modeling, certainly better than I'd ever expected. I even made the cover of several magazines. However, the whole thing was a catch twenty-two. I would have done far better if, like Jacy, I'd been "willing to pay for it," and I damned well had been made aware of that. I often thought that if I had $100 for every proposition I received with the promise of a job in exchange, I could have retired at thirty-two and lived well for the rest of my life. It was a, "if you won't fish, cut bait" situation, especially since I met many models who openly admitted "doing it." I won't say I was never tempted, but I never did. My thought was, "I guess either you're cut out that way or you're not." In retrospect I'm not sure that's true either. At that point I wasn't quite financially desperate. Although we were short of money my children were eating and clothed and we all had what we needed. I would never judge any of those who "did."

Looking back after the fact, I realize that strange as it sounds in some ways being a model had been good for my spirituality. Discipline was a requisite. Whatever was going on in your personal life, however you were feeling, in front of the camera you turned on when and how it was called for. No waiting for the muse to smile down on you. I also learned discipline in eating, exercising, and yes, in moving quickly how and when necessary, and that carried over. As an example, I would bet that any woman who has modeled can get herself dressed and out in her personal life faster than any man in her life can get dressed and out. Not many women - or the men who are with them - can make *that* happy statement!

One afternoon, after Cal and I had finished a shoot together, he made a career suggestion. "V.J, why don't you consider becoming a photographer's representative?" he asked. My ears perked up. "You're rare," he continued. "You're as much interested in what goes on behind the camera as in front of it, and understand much of it. You've got the brains for it, and lets face it, beauty helps. I'd want you as a rep myself if I didn't have James. Even though I'd hate to lose you as a model because you're a star, if I were you I'd consider it. Why continue being propositioned every two minutes, not that that will totally disappear whatever you do. Just, repping could be better for you all around."

The more I thought about Cal's suggestion the more it made sense. I had no aspirations toward becoming a movie star, so what was I doing in this silly business anyway? At first modeling had been a fascinating novelty to me, and as I've said it did give me growth experiences, but I had to admit to myself that it was becoming destructive to me too. At times I was beginning to be recognized in public. Teen aged girls would ask me how I did my hair and how I kept so slim, obviously idealizing me, wanting to be models too, or at least to look like one, whereas I wanted to tell them how secondary and meaningless it all was. I wanted to shout, "Can't you see! This isn't brain surgery, it's just a female impersonator having her picture taken! The inner Self is what really matters." Yet I felt like a hypocrite because I was not making the inner Self my priority. In fact, with all that concentration on appearance, being praised and rejected by turns because of it and objectified through it all, I was a living antithesis of concentration on inner beauty. Cal's suggestion made me become honest with myself. There was only one thing keeping me in modeling; the money. That alone had stopped being worth getting up for in the mornings. I might like repping better, and perhaps I could do as well financially with it. I decided to call Albert to discuss it.

Albert once again was helpful. He told me that there was a photographer whom he used occasionally who might be interested in hiring me for the job. "His name is Ernie. Ernie Ernest," he said. I started to giggle. "Ernest Ernest?" I repeated. "Goodness me! Did his mother name him in a tunnel?"

"That's quite funny," Albert said dryly. Albert never laughed. Smiling would be a stretch. " If you think his *name's* funny, wait until you meet *him,*" he offered. "A funny looking thin little guy from "New Joisey," so rough around the edges that I can hardly see him and you together, Val. (Albert called me Val because Casse, whom I'd known forever, did.) On the other hand, the man is street-smart. Few photographers I've met have such a good business sense. Some people in the business like to work with him because they find him amusing. His charm eludes *me,* but immaterial. Since his rep quit the business a few years ago he's successfully been his own rep. He's not a great artist, but he's good enough to be able to shoot whatever they put in front of the no seam, enough to pull in about one hundred fifty thousand a year." I was impressed. One hundred and fifty thousand in the seventies was a lot of money. "You could learn, and make good money with him. I'll introduce you," Albert concluded. Two days later he kept his word.

As Albert and I stood together in front of Ernie Ernest, I realized what a good eye Albert had. His description of Ernie couldn't have been more accurate. Ernie was indeed so skinny that he could lurk behind a needle and not be seen. He darted around the studio like a launched rocket looking for a landing pad. His hair bounced over his forehead, galloping like a horse's mane, his voice was high like a seal's, and I felt he was as slippery as an eel. When Ernie left the room for a moment, I told Albert about the horse, seal and eel. "This man of yours is all animal," I commented, giggling hysterically.

Albert answered, without cracking a facial muscle, "He's also smart as a fox. So don't be an ass. You could do worse."

In a minute Ernie, now a hawk, flew back into the room, stating, "I make one hundred fifty thou a year by myself, so what do I need a rep for?"

I really thought he meant it as a question. "I don't know. What *do* you need one for?" I asked in return.

"I NEED A REP FOR NOTHING, THAT'S WHAT FOR!" Ernie bellowed at me.

I took a step backward and looked at Albert, who almost smiled.

"But," Ernie added, "call me tomorra."

Going down in the elevator, feeling dejected, I asked Albert, "If Ernie isn't interested, why does he want me to call him?"

"Oh, he's interested."

"Albert, he said, 'What do I need a rep for?' That's being interested? Explain this to me."

"That means he wants you."

"That means he *wants* me?!"

"Call him," Albert said. "You'll see."

"Albert, is everybody in this business crazy?"

"Definitely. It's a prerequisite."

When I called Ernie the following day I discovered how right Albert had been. Ernie, wasting no time, asked me to become his rep. "I'm good, ya' look good and I can train ya; ya've got the brains. I think we can make a lot of money togetha. Interested?" he shrieked.

"When do we start?"

I've been with Ernie five months now. To say that it's been interesting does not do the experience justice!

My thoughts were interrupted by the screeching of brakes as the train came to a halt at Penn station. When we stood up Max said, "Here, Valentine," as he pressed his still folded New York Times into my hand, "I haven't even read it. Maybe you'll find time to, later." I was about to decline when Max added, "Please, Valentine, take it. I... want to... give you something." I took the paper. As we allowed ourselves to be pushed toward the doorway by eager commuters, Max asked, "Did you have a good sleep?"

"I didn't really sleep, I just rested."

"I wish you had slept," Max said.

"Why?"

"Because I slept. Then, we could have slept together." I gave Max a look indicating that I was both surprised and displeased by his adolescent joke. A train friendship with Max seemed fine. I could even see it expanding into a broader friendship. But complicating my life with any further involvement, with anybody, was the last thing that I needed.

"Sorry," Max apologized. "I didn't mean to step over the line." I gave him a quick nod to indicate, 'It's alright.'

Once in the waiting room I pointed to the "up" escalator.

"I have to go now," I said.

"Yes-- uh, well, I go the other way," Max told me unnecessarily, then asked, "What train will you be taking home tonight?"

"I honestly don't know yet."

"Well, see you same time tomorrow on the train, I guess?"

"I guess. Bye, Max."

One third of the way up on the escalator I looked down. Max was standing where I'd left him, looking up at me. I gave a small wave, then quickly turned around and faced front. When I got to the top I furtively glanced down again. Max was gone.

I stepped off the escalator realizing that I was still clutching Max's Times in my right fist. It felt oddly comforting. There was a trashcan near the door. With one swift motion I plunged the Times into the can, where it stood on end. Then I took one deep breath, exhaled, and pushing open the door, stepped outside into the cacophony that is New York City.

CHAPTER 2: THE SOUND AND THE ERNEST

"Don't abandon the world, Beloved People. Stay with your business, crafts, skills and talents. The truth is, life in the world can be a magnificent way to happiness, but only if God is in it completely. Otherwise life is crippled, has no savor, no delight."

-- Swami Muktananda

"I've come a long way--maybe."

--Lena Horne

Sights and sounds assaulted my senses; the head splitting rapid fire burst of a pneumatic drill digging up the northeast corner of Seventh Avenue; the rattling of big yellow busses creeping in traffic like huge futuristic animals; the magazine man on the corner shouting out the headlines; people of every dress, race and distinction, hurrying, running, rushing by. It was loud, insane, ridiculous, exciting. New York! There's no way you could be here and mistake it for any place else. The adrenaline started to rise. I was awake.

People asked, about my commuting daily to Manhattan, "How can you stand the stress?" Stress? New York *was* challenging, but stress? I *knew* what stress was; this wasn't it.

Remembering that we were low on polaroid film at the studio – we went through cases per month – I dashed through the rain to a photography supply store not far from the station and picked up the film. Now, lugging the box, I signaled for a taxi – any taxi.

I'd waved my hand in the air for less than a minute when a taxi pulled over. A taxi, this fast, during morning rush hour, in the rain? Who said there are no miracles?

I folded my umbrella and climbed into the back of the cab while telling the driver, "296 Park Avenue South, please." I sat down, felt something sticky under my leg, reached there and found a wad of gum stuck to the seat. My disgust diminished as I reminded myself that this was still better than standing outside in the downpour. I shrugged, loosened the gum as much as possible, put what came off in the ashtray, then slid to the other side of the seat. "It's near 23rd street," I added.

"Lady," the driver barked, turning his head around so he was looking directly at me. "Ya gotta tell me where 296 Park is?" This was when taxi drivers in New York still spoke English… so-called. "Ya know how long I bin drivin' a hack here? Ya shud liff so long, lady!"

"Sorry," I answered meekly, wondering why I was apologizing.

"Hey, ya tawk diffrent. What country ya from, lady?"

"Long Island. I'm a native," I suppressed a laugh. What *country* indeed! Here you were a foreigner if you didn't say "cawfee" and "dawg."

"Nah," the cabby insisted, "I drive lotsa people from Lon-giland. Dey don't sound like you. Ya talk too funny fer a Lon-gilanda, lady."

I wasn't going to bother arguing with him that my speech *was* native Long Island, that many "Lon-gilandas" today had come from Brooklyn or the Bronx so had carried those accents with them. Something more crucial was happening here. The driver thought I *talk* funny? He *drove* funny, although labeling this cabby's driving "funny" was like calling a terrorist's behavior "hilarious." Aloud I asked, "Would you mind facing front please and watching the road?" (Before we rear-end another cab or, worse yet, a pedestrian). "I never watch da road. The traffic makes me noivous," he answered, adding, "Ya tellin ME how ta drive?"

"Naturally not," I answered under my breath. "*You're* the driver. If you collide with a truck, what business is that of *mine*?"

With that he rammed down the accelerator, came within one inch of the gasoline truck in front of us, slammed on his breaks, then veered in front of the truck nearly hitting a bus. At that moment I decided if the driver wasn't going to watch the road, why should I? I closed my eyes and meditated, poorly.

The traffic was especially heavy as was always true when foul weather merged with the rush hour. Even with all the cabby's darts and dashes it took us one half hour to arrive at the studio. I could have walked it in twenty minutes. I kept peering at my watch. Now I was not only nervous from the ride, but from knowing I'd be late for work as well.

Finally we arrived at 296 Park South. Once inside the building I pressed the elevator "up" button. As usual it took forever to descend. When it finally did, I got in, pressed the tenth floor button, and again nervously looked at my watch. It was already 8:30 AM. Ernie would be exploding at that very minute.

The door opened at the tenth floor letting me out inside the studio. The noise level here almost made Penn Station seem like a monastery. The stereo was blaring "Jer-i-miah was a bull frog - was a good friend - of my-an..." while several male voices were inharmoniously whistling and singing to it. Ernie and Stu, the photographer Ernie shared studio space with, were obviously having their early morning spat. Ernie's screams of, "What the fuck do you want from me?!" rebounded off the walls from around the corner. In the seventies few people used four letter words in public, not even actors in movies. That didn't stop Ernie. "never understood a word he said" the song continued blaring from the stereo, "but he let me drink his wine. Joy…to the world…"

As usual I first made a pit stop at the ladies' room, ran a brush through my hair, checked out my make-up, then walked out of the rest room and toward the sets where some of the technicians were setting up. I stopped for a brief "hello," then started to move on when I heard from behind me a low whistle. I turned. Jayson was approaching me, calling "Hell—oo, GOR..geous!" When close, he kissed me on both cheeks and exclaimed, "Let me LOOK at you." With a practiced eye he did so carefully, then raptured, "Fab…ulous, dear. If Scarlett had looked like this, Rhett would have stayed. Even Ashley might have had a change of mind. The outfit is to die for! Have you a magician at home? The look of your outfit has me spellbound. Soft and dressy, yet casual enough for the simplest parlor trick." Quickly I placed my hand over the coffee stain as I cooed, "Thank you for pulling that compliment out of your hat." Jayson continued, "I'd ditch the boots, but I know why you wore them in this drench. Heavens, *I* only had to travel fifteen minutes uptown and I thought *I* was swimming the English Channel! "

Multi-faceted Jayson was a free lance make-up artist, stylist and set designer, good at the latter two however at make-up he excelled. I'd never seen anyone do a face like he could. He wasn't famous yet but I felt he would be. We'd been terrific friends since the day I'd started with Ernie. Ernie and I used Jayson almost exclusively for our shoots.

Now Jayson was cupping my face with his hands. "What a face! WHAT A FACE! he extolled. "Do you mind if I do a little something here?" He touched the area near my right eye.

"Please, go ahead."

Jayson dashed to his make-up case, grabbed a few tools of his trade, ran back to me and gently caressed the area over my eyes on the bone under the eyebrows. "Subtle here, darling. BLEND! Always remember to BLEND." He placed a mirror before my face. "See the difference?"

What he'd done in two minutes was amazing. "Jayson, you're incredible," I told him, then added, "Can I ask you something?

Jayson, totally attentive, replied, "Of course, my loveliness, what?"

"Jayson, give me an honest answer? Objective now, please? What is this beauty-wow wow- thing about me? My mouth is too big… you can walk down any shopping mall and find ten girls prettier."

"You stop that!" Jayson said firmly. "None of it is true. Models would get collagen injections for your sensuous mouth! And your eyes, my God! Your beauty appeal *is* your lack of perfection. You're…lush…exquisite. You have a high L.Q also."

"L.Q?"

"Likeability quotient, darling. Men and women like you." Now Jayson shook his finger at me. "So, don't let me hear you knock my favorite face and figure ever again!"

With that morale boost I entered the office adjacent to the elevator that Ernie and I shared, and had just unburdened myself of raincoat and umbrella when Zarela Mendez, the studio manager/receptionist, dashed in, breathless, with a sheet of paper in her outstretched hand.

"Glad you finally got here, V.J. Fifteen more minutes, Ernie would have had a stroke. "Your messages," she said, handing me a memo pad.

"Thanks, Zarela." I took the pad. "It sounds like I'm not Ernie's main source of aggravation this morning. What's wrong between him and Stu this time?"

"Leave them alone," Zarela replied cryptically, "They're having a relationship. I'm going out to get coffee. Want anything?"

"Well, decaf would be good, black please." I reached into my wallet and handed her a dollar bill. "How was your weekend?"

"Oh, the usual relationship problems at home. Then I have to come to my relationship problem here."

"You mean Stu."

"None other than."

"I know you don't like one another."

"It's not so simplistic. We can't stand one another. See you in a bit."

After Zarela left I thought about Stu. I was beginning to understand how she felt. I was getting the impression that Stu couldn't stand me either. Worse, the feeling was becoming mutual. Not an ideal climate with somebody you had to see every day.

Zarela stuck her head back into the office "I don't believe it. I just don't," she said. "Stu has a new complaint. Guess what now?"

"Surprise me. Although since I've been working here that would be difficult."

"He asked me to tell you to stop twisting the cord when you talk on the telephone."

"WHAT??!!"

"You heard right."

"You did it after all. Surprised me."

"I asked him, 'Why don't you tell her yourself?' Do you know what he answered?"

"Surprise me again."

"He said, 'That's a woman's job.' Or something equally idiotic. But don't worry, I know why he won't tell you."

"Why?"

"Because he's afraid of you."

"Stu, afraid of ME?!"

"Yes, because you're so very intelligent."

"Zarela," I asked, "what is this "very intelligent" nonsense? My nickname Val doesn't stand for valedictorian, I promise you. I'm no different than anyone else here."

"Not true. You're very smart," Zarela insisted, "and Stu's very afraid of very smart women. Me, he can talk to. One decaf medium, right?"

"Black"

"Of course, black. My mind this morning…forget it! See you soon. Oh, don't forget your messages." Zarela left.

I studied the dust on my desktop. I wondered if I really did twist the phone cord. I took some Kleenex out of my pocketbook and started to dust the desk while I read Zarela's scrawl. The first message said, "Art Director Alfredo Schneck called 'at 8' this morning." She was mistaken. He had called at exactly 8:05. Schneck always called at exactly 8:05. The man was a fanatic!

At that moment Ernie hurled himself through the doorway much like a tornado wondering what to hit first.

"Why the hell can't ya get in on time?!" he squeaked, then collapsed into his chair which faced mine. He reminded me now of a coiled-up snake.

I was learning how to handle Ernie. "And, that's hello?" I asked.

Ernie's tone softened. "I like the way ya' look today, V.J." Again I smiled coyly as once again my hand covered the coffee stain. Ernie continued, "Bob Mauer will like it too. He'll be here later. I saw how he was takin' ya in last time. Is your skirt shorta than usual?"

"Maybe slightly." I continued to hold my hand over the stain.

"Hike it up some more."

"I'd tell you to feel ashamed of yourself," I said, "but there's as much chance of that happening as there is of me teaching my bird to meow."

"Your bird *doesn't* meow?"

Ernie was indeed a unique character, I'd never known anyone like him. What he lacked in class he compensated for in humor and street smarts. That last quality especially made it possible for me to overlook all his shortcomings. Call it a flaw in me, I'd forgive anyone anything if they were intelligent.

"Schneck called," I said making a face. It wasn't just that Schneck was a nut; we had many of those; he was also repulsive.

"I talked wid Schneck," Ernie said. "He wants ta discuss some work he may have for us over dinna -- wid you. He don't really want dinna. He wants you." Ernie smirked.

"Excuse me while I retch."

"Listen kid, ya knew this was part a the job when ya took it."

"Are you crazy! THAT never was discussed as part ..." I got so emotional I couldn't even finish my sentence.

"Don't be a jerk. I don't mean THAT's part of da job. I just mean lunch or dinna with clients is."

"Oh." I breathed a sigh in relief. "Well, with Schneck that's more than enough."

"Don't be so dramatic. Just entertain'im."

"When did *you* last eat with a client who had ten pair of hands, every one of them very busy trying to entertain *you*?"

"Not lately," Ernie said, "Because I'm a guy, not a beautiful woman. Unless the guy's a fagala, I'm safe."

"Unless he's a what?" I asked.

"Sorry, I forgot you ain't Jewish. In Yiddish fagala means gay."

"But I am Jewish."

"Yeah, yeah, sure. Ya grew up on Lon-giland – where I come from that ain't Jewish. Anyway, suggest lunch with Schneck instead of dinna; with dinna comes dessert; that'd be you. Find out what work he has in mind, be charmin', make the whole deal one and a half-hours door to door. Gotta lot to do ta day. We still gotta work on the BR & D ad this afternoon."

"You mean the Spanish wine ad?" I asked. "But, that's all set. I finished taking care of that Friday."

"Like hell it's all set!" Ernie screeched, hitting his forehead with his wrist, knocking the cowlick over his eye; he brushed it away with the back of his hand. "It was all set. Then Dresdo, the client, phones this morning. He sez we can cancel our model cause he's bringin' his own."

"But why?"

"BABY, welcome to the real world! This can only mean he's got a girlfriend who wants to model, so he's puttin' her in his ad. Indicating the ad will stink, cause if she was any damned good what would she need an old goat like him for?"

"I thought they only did that in movies," I said, surprised.

Ernie hit his forehead again. "Oy, I don't believe ya' sometimes! Everythin' they do in the movies, they do here. Simple reason. This *is* the movies!"

"Goodness me. What do we do now?"

"Goodness me," Ernie parroted me. "I never hoid anybody use language like you."

"Likewise. But tell me, what do we do now?"

"YOU," Ernie said emphatically, "call Dresdo and try ta talk him out a it. If that don't work, tactfully suggest he pay for the model we hired as well as bring his model. We'll shoot twice. That way, ya' tell him, he can choose the shots dat work best."

I was genuinely impressed. "Ernie, that's clever!"

"Maybe yeah, maybe no," Ernie answered. "It will depend on whether, when the results are in and Dresdo sees that there's no contest between our model and his, he'll swear by us or at us from then on. A lot will ride on whether or not he's by then grown tired of that babe of his as a piece of ass. Oy. When will the schmucks learn, you don't play where you eat!"

I'd surmised that Ernie was very smart about more than just his work. He had a wife and son in the Jersey suburbs, and no one had ever heard of him being involved with anyone he worked with. In fact, I'd have been surprised if he fooled around at all. That gave me a certain feeling of trust with him. Ironically. I really didn't believe in infidelity, nor did I trust people who engaged in it.

Zarela came back into the office, placed a paper bag with my decaf on my desk as she announced, "The models are here on the go-see." It was for an ad we were shooting the following week for a medical brochure, specifically for a preparation for - of all things - a medication for the skin disease ringworm. When Ernie had first been told, he had asked, "Sure we'll do it. *What* kind of worm did you say that is?" As Albert had told me, "For a buck Ernie will shoot anything!"

Ernie had described the simple layout to me, a nude girl reclining. As the art director had explained it, this was to show that ringworm could afflict any area of the body. Ernie had a different explanation: "The fuck it is," he'd told me, "It's to get the attention of all them horny doctors! But - that's their problem. It pays us $3,000 plus expenses for the model and incidentals. A nice piece of change for two hours of color shooting."

As I'd thought about it, though, I'd realized that the layout the art director had drawn - a ring of fire around the nude girl, to show how ringworm burns - would be technically implausible. Where were we going to find a model willing to pose inside a ring of fire, even if the client were willing to up the standard $200.00 per hour for nude work? But, even if somehow we did find such a model, we'd all be foolish, liability wise, to even try to execute that. I felt the art director's idea was astonishingly impractical.

I'd pondered the situation and finally suggested to him that instead of trying to photograph a fire ring, we shoot the model as if the ring were there and later have an artist draw it around her.

"It would be exactly as you want, and most cost effective." I told him.

The art director went for my idea, whereupon Ernie told me, "Baby, you're learnin'!" I felt delighted. From Ernic that was high praise.

I removed my container of decaf from the paper bag and lifted the lid. It wasn't black. It wasn't even medium. It was light. Damn, milk and my stomach had been in disagreement lately. But, I craved something hot. I took a sip. Which, maybe fortunately, was all I had time for, as at that moment Ernie was leading a young model into the office, shrieking, "This is Valentine; Valentine, this is Bunny Howe from Marlana Agency. Bunny, show Valentine your book." Bunny handed me her portfolio which I unzipped from both ends meanwhile studying the young model. Her white angora sweater and pink ribbon in her hair made me think she'd aptly named herself. Bunny. The gimmicks! She had green eyes and long dark hair. She looked very familiar. I asked, "have you been up here before? Maybe on a job with the other photographer in the studio?"

"No, never," she answered in a tiny voice.

"Strange, I thought I'd met you before. Well, no matter. Let's look at these." I turned the black pages which held 8½ x 11" glossy shots. There weren't many photographs in there, but those that were, were good. They were the standards; the bathing suit shot, the evening gown shot, the outdoor shot.

"Bunny," I said, "I'd like to see a nude picture of you if you have one, although from these pictures your face and figure seem perfect for the job. Don't you think so, Ernie?"

I put my hand into the back pocket of the portfolio. Some of the girls carried their nude photographs in there to show just for nude work. There was nothing there. So I pointed to the bathing suit shot and asked, "Bunny, have you any scars on the parts of your body that this bathing suit is covering? Like appendectomy?"

"Oh, no... but, why?" Bunny was staring wide-eyed.

I wondered… could it be? I asked Bunny, "Did your agency tell you this was nude work?"

Bunny looked stunned. "Oh, no…I…I didn't know," the scared little bunny exclaimed. This was no gimmick.

"How would you feel about posing nude?"

"I…don't know. I might but I …hadn't thought about it." Bunny stammered, fidgeting.

Through the entire exchange Ernie had remained atypically quiet, although shifting nervously from foot to foot. Now he reverted to form. "Listen, Honey Bunny or whatever ya name is," he shrieked, "Could ya think about it fast? The rate for nude work is $200.00 an hour. That's $400.00 fer two hours work. What do ya say?"

At the mention of the fee Bunny's eyes widened further. "I don't k-k- k-k-know if I could," she stuttered. "I'd like to but.. I don't k-k-know…"

Ernie's patience - if you could call it that - expired. "Look baby," he shrieked. "If I were yer shrink maybe I could tell ya if ya could. As it is, I got five other girls picked out dyin' ta make an easy 400 bucks."

I looked at Ernie in surprise. We didn't even have one other girl selected. Ernie continued, "Ya come in here not even known' what the job is. That ain't professional. It's stupid! I need a dame who won't freeze on me and I can't wait all day. So, what d'ya say?"

Bunny was at this point fighting back tears. Seeing this, Ernie asked me, "What the fuck did I do now?" then told me, "You handle it," and blew out of the room.

As calmly as I could, I asked, "Bunny, how old are you?"

"Fifteen," she answered.

I wanted to shoot the agency who'd taken her on and sent her for this gig, and not with a camera.

"How long have you been a model?"

"About a week. This is my first…interview. Maybe if I knew what it would be like, to pose nude, I mean. I'm sorry, but..." She was wiping tears from her cheeks as she spoke.

I touched Bunny's arm. "Oh, but don't apologize, that's a very reasonable question," I assured her. I knew physically she'd be perfect for it and the client would be pleased. I could convince her, so why not do so? After all, she'd been hired by her agency to be a model and I hadn't been hired by Ernie to be a social worker. These days I needed every good break I could get. I told Bunny, "This is an ad for a reputable drug company. It's very tasteful, not girlie caliber. You're just right for it, and where can you make that kind of money so fast?" Even as I said it, I asked myself, "Valentine, what *are* you doing?" and a feeling of guilt flooded my being. The next thing I knew I was telling her, "On the other hand, it's important that you feel comfortable with it, Bunny. Some girls feel fine about doing it, others don't."

"What is it like? Who would be there?" Bunny asked.

"The photographer of course, probably one assistant on a job like this, the art director, the client and myself," I continued, soft-pedaling nothing.

Bunny gasped and exclaimed, "Oh, that's like posing nude in Grand Central Station!"

I pushed the door closed, then whispered quickly, "Bunny, I'd hire you. But I don't think you should take this job." I smiled at Bunny, who smiling back weakly and said, "Thank you...very much... for saying that. I really didn't want to." I told her, "Then leave me your head sheet. We'll use you for something else, I promise." Bunny put her composite page of photographs on my desk, gave me a relieved look, opened the door and left.

I thought of myself at fifteen. At seventeen. Seventeen? God, I thought of myself now! Never would I be able to bring myself to pose nude. Yet when I began this work I would have been terribly embarrassed to have even been in the same room with four men, watching a naked member of my own sex being looked at and photographed. Amazing how that had so rapidly become routine to me.

I found Ernie on the set. "That Bunny's somethin'," Ernie whistled. "So, is it all set?"

"Not exactly. She turned it down" I told him. When Ernie gave me a look of dismay, I said, honestly enough in a way, "I tried everything to make this right, I promise you." I felt relieved in the sense of someone who had just shot herself in the foot in lieu of getting hit in the head.

Fortunately other models did come in on the go-see. The next to last one really did look familiar. Red haired, beautiful in a more blatant way than Bunny, great body. I looked at the name on her headsheet. "Jacy Marks." I'd be damned. Jacy, the model from Cal's studio that day, the "I'm willing to pay for it" girl! She didn't seem to remember me, and I left it at that. She would be as cool in this shoot as if she were dressed in a raincoat. And this one, at least, was out of kindergarten. The other models qualified too, but I felt strongly compelled to take Jacy. Maybe it was karma. I, not she, had gotten that job with Cal. Perhaps I owed this to her.

Somewhere in between all that activity I called Schneck and made a date for lunch at 1:00.

At 12:30, I put on my raincoat, zipped up and left a note for Zarela—who'd gone out for lunch—that I'd be back at 2:30 the latest in case anybody phoned. I pushed the main floor elevator button and waited the inevitable wait.

Finaly I entered the elevator, as Zarela stepped out with a bag of lunch from the deli. Before the door closed she called to me. "Hey, V.J – did you realize how much that model Bunny looks like you - take away ten years?"

I answered truthfully, "No, I didn't. Try seventeen years. I have shoes that are older." So, *that* was it.

I stepped into the elevator as "Philadelphia Freedom" by Elton John blared forth from the stereo.

Lunch with Schneck wasn't as bad as I'd thought it would be. It was worse. Since I'd last seen him he seemed to have shrunk two feet and grown two more hands.

Each time he looked at me his eyes appeared to spin in his head. "I'm having lunch with the pinball wizard," I thought. I wondered when his forehead would light up with the word, 'TILT'. I felt it a major accomplishment that I survived that lunch without choking on my hot roast beef sandwich. However, I managed to fend off all Schneck's advances but not to offend, to avoid choking on my meat, to nail down the job and to do it all in 1 1/2 hours door to door.

It HAD been a feat.

"Are you proud of me?" I asked Ernie.

"A' course. Ya can't tell?"

"How?"

"Did you hea me complain?"

"I see. I assume that means you've noticed I'm getting shrewder?"

"Um."

"And more efficient?"

"Sure, but..."

"And of course you're aware you've got one of the best reps in New York -- and pretty too?"

"What the hell's this all about?"

"Thank you Ernie, you say the nicest things."

I phoned Jacy's agency and committed with them for the shoot. There were other calls to return, among them to Casse who wanted to know if I was going to leave soon and if so, if we could take the same train home? She was the only person I'd told about some of my spiritual activities. After all, she was my "oldest" friend. Her reaction was always the same; I was crazy to mess with such nonsense and should drop it from my life as soon as possible. For that very reason I didn't often talk to Casse about it. This evening was a perfect example. I told Casse I'd be taking a later train. I didn't lie, but neither did I explain. Apparently she assumed I'd be working overtime, because she said, "Don't overdo it, Val. I told you, you're getting too thin. Ha -- it should happen to ME!" I exhaled. "Getting too thin," from Casse, was better than, "getting too crazy."

I also called Richard to tell him that I'd be taking a later train. "When will you be home, Valen?" he asked. "You're never home."

It was 6 PM. I ran to the elevator and pushed the button. If I hurried I could make the early evening session.

I waited a full five minutes before the elevator came to our floor. But naturally.

CHAPTER THREE: A PLACE IN THE HEART

"The senses of the yogi (one who practices Eastern Indian spiritual practices) are introverted and thus behold the drama of the inmost Self who delights in exhibiting the world of drama."

--Siva Sutras

"Rather than withdrawing from the world, meditation can help you enjoy it more fully, more effectively, and more peacefully."

--Dean Ornish, M.D.

The Mid-Town Zen Meditation Center was cross-town, not far from the studio.

Inside it seemed even more peaceful than usual tonight. A leader announced the start of the session with a gong. Each hall had its own system to begin and end the session. Some used two claps of a clapper, some a bell, and there were variations.

I hanged up my coat, removed my shoes, walked into the long narrow meditation room and took a place. I kneeled on the special round cushion used to perform Zen meditation, usually round as was this one, filled with panya, a special kind of cotton from a plant; it worked well for support during long sessions.

I, along with the other meditators, assumed the lotus posture, or kekka -- left foot resting on right thigh and right foot on the left. I made the trunk of my body perpendicular to the floor and held my head so my spinal column was straight and the tip of my nose directly over my navel. At first this posture had been very difficult for me to perform, so I'd begun with the Hanka, or half lotus, with only one foot resting on opposite thigh. My eyes, slightly opened, were focused on a point of the opposite wall approximately a yard away from me. I adapted the Zen position of the hands which was called Join -- palms up, one hand on the other thumb, tips barely touching.

If the postures were difficult for me the concentration required was harder still. Each sitting began for me with my own mantra: "I don't want to do this!" "I don't want to do this!" Yet, some force stronger than my resistance kept drawing me back. I began Tokiho, a Zazen breathing method, rounding my lips, exhaling the stale air, and concurrently bringing my torso forward. Now I put my lips tightly together as I inhaled through my nose and raised my torso to an erect posture. Concentrating fiercely, I then exhaled through my mouth, letting my torso once more go forward but this time not as far. Finally I began to breathe through my nose only, tongue against my palette, my eyes still half closed. Accumulation of saliva had become a problem; one had either to hold it, which was uncomfortable, or swallow it, which was noisily distracting to the other meditators. The answer was to avoid saliva formation altogether by keeping the teeth and lips only lightly together and pressing the tip of the tongue against the roof of the mouth. Harder done than said. Most important was that the entire body remain relaxed. "Sure!" I thought, persevering.

After I had exhaled three times through my mouth to rid my body of no longer useful things, trying to take two or three times longer to exhale than inhale, I began to count my breaths from one to ten, breathing in on the odd numbers, exhaling on the even ones. There were varied choices for counting a breath...thank you very much. As a beginner I'd settled on counting it as it reached an imaginary point ten inches from my nose; this had been after I'd tried the method of following the breath once it had moved into my nose; that had made my nose itch. Sometimes I breathed by focusing on my navel. They said that breathing in and out of one's navel, or centering on one's chest, reminded one of the peace within.

I shifted my body on the cushion. I didn't feel ready yet to do without it. I wasn't certain I felt ready to be in this strange setting in the first place.

How had I arrived here? I did what I wasn't supposed to be doing at this moment. I let my thoughts wander backward.

***

1969. It had been an interesting year for the world, and certainly for me as well. That year Nixon had been inaugurated as president, Vietnam having been the dominant factor in Johnson's decision not to seek re-election. That year over 100 persons had claimed to be aboard strange craft from other worlds, while from 1947 until 1969, according to the Gallup poll, another five million Americans reported to have seen flying saucers. Also, a twenty year project headed by Major Hector Quintinilla-Wright of Patterson Base in Ohio, costing seventy-two thousand dollars, had come up with scientific answers for all but eight percent of them; a voluntary civilian organization, the National Investigation Committee on Aerial Phenomena, headed by retired Major Don Keyhoe, conducted an investigation costing fifty thousand dollars, and was among the groups that charged the Air Force with an "intolerable degree of secrecy."

And, that year began my conscious exploration of my inner being. At the time I was not seeking anything as esoteric as self-realization. I was simply trying not to go crazy, if indeed I had not already crossed that line. I had a child who was from Mars, who at the time either screamed for hours on end or sat staring at his hands as if I weren't there. For a long while Richard and I had to sleep in shifts: Willie had taken to getting up in the middle of the night, breaking things and smearing food, or worse, all over the house. When we became too exhausted to continue that vigil, we put a chain and lock around the refrigerator before turning in and let it go at that. The ghastly messes we still found in the morning were the price we paid to get some sleep. Except I didn't, not really. Part of me was always listening.

For Richard and me, getting out together was a near impossibility; baby sitters called us an hour after we'd left the house asking us to come home; Willie was out of control. Once sitters sat for Willie they usually were unwilling to return. So I was up nights, then spending almost all day, every day, trying to get through to Willie, trying to help him. I was rung out to dry. Additionally, since I didn't know anyone else who had a child like Willie, my sense of isolation was formidable; I was losing weight and also developing a nervous stomach.

I tried psychotherapy first. My experience was, to put it mildly, a disaster.

Dr. Raddler, the psychiatrist, asked me, "Why did you come here?" I told him about Willie, and explained, "One of the worst things about it is the loneliness."

Dr. Raddler's reply was less than sensitive. "How could someone who looks like you feel lonely?" Something felt wrong here. I'd come to this doctor in trust and respect for his credentials and knowledge, but I couldn't understand how what I looked like had to do with how I felt. I glanced at the good doctor again. Was it my imagination or was he leering? I was not imagining anything. Dr. Raddler didn't want to do my analysis, he wanted to do my seduction. I might have been lonely but not that lonely. I stood up and announced, "I'm leaving." Dr. Raddler answered, "But, we aren't finished yet." I told him, "You might not be, but I am." I got up and walked out; that was that for psychotherapy and me.

Next I searched for answers by going to various synagogues and churches. I remember visiting a Jewish temple service on a Saturday. I sat down and immediately realized I was the only woman sitting on that side of the room. I had unknowingly walked into an Orthodox synagogue and had sat down on the men's side. After the seventy minute service –conducted by a rabbi who was unfortunately boring-- ended, I left the synagogue with the same feelings I'd had at Sunday School as a little girl: "What does any of this have to do with God?"

My next step was to bring Willie to Saint Patrick's Cathedral, a large well-known Catholic Church in New York. The moment I walked through the door the entire scenario was familiar to me. I'd grown up primarily with Catholic children and visited their churches often. But this déjà vu feeling seemed deeper than that. Willie was occasionally verbal, usually at the wrong times. This was to be one such time. After we'd sat there in the stillness two minutes, he shouted out, "WHEN DOES THE MOVIE START?" After that he was relatively well behaved in the church. I even managed to be able to speak to a priest there that day without Willie's behaviors interrupting too much. Still, I felt there were no answers here to whatever I was seeking.

I then heard of Paradigm, a large human potential center on the West Coast, the only one of its kind then in the country. It was a self-awareness education laboratory, a sort of counter-culture university. I grew excited, feeling that might be closer to what I needed then. I asked my mother if she would come stay with Willie and the English maid we then had (we had started importing housekeepers from foreign countries. My reasoning was, since everything in America would be weird and difficult for them, Willie might seem no more weird than anything else.) I told my mother and Richard that I wanted to take some college courses to keep my mind alert. It was falsehood of self-preservation. I knew that if I told them the truth they'd never cooperate with something so "wacky." They bought my story and agreed to help out. I went to Paradigm for two weeks.

Paradigm was certainly different from organized religion or from anything else I was used to. As I arrived, I saw a blindfolded person being led across the grounds. I was told that was to build trust. People in groups were rolling over and over each other on the lawn; I had seen kids do that but never adults. If the churches and synagogue had been away from the point and boring, this seemed stratospherically beyond the point. I wondered if I told them that I wanted to go home immediately, they'd refund my money.

Yet another part of me wanted to stay.

The sheer physical beauty was in itself seemingly illusionary; the ocean with rocks jutting forth, the garden with statuary. There were no newspapers or televisions, just one remotely located telephone. It was a sensual peaceful place. Primarily due to that, and since I'd gone through a great deal to get there, I decided to embrace it completely, peculiar though it was, at least for the duration of my stay. Maybe the peace would come later.

That was easier said than done. The first workshop I attended was one to encourage freedom. The facilitator spoke to us of being free, and then told the thirty or so of us assembled, "Now take off your clothes." As the others disrobed I stood there helplessly, still fully clothed and feeling very conspicuous. I saw that a man across the room was having the same predicament.

"But, how do I do it?" I wailed to the facilitator. He answered, simply, "You just do it despite your fear. You remember that your goal is more important than your fear, so move through your fear toward your goal."

Even the man across the room had disrobed. I was the only one in the room with clothes on. It was embarrassing! But I was sorry, I wasn't going to undress. However, the facilitator had given me an important teaching; do things despite my fear, not necessarily instead of it.

I walked out of that workshop and found myself by the communal baths under the stars. That looked inviting - until I saw that the bathers, too, were naked. I passed that one up also.

The wealth and variety of programs offered amazed me. Methods I and the majority had never yet heard of. Gestalt theory and practice. The process of group dynamics. And Shiatsu, meaning finger pressure in Japanese, a form of pressure using needles as in acupuncture to stimulate points along lines of energy flow, (which they call "Ki") believed to be situated throughout the body thus stimulating the blood circulation, bringing more oxygen into the system thereby removing waste products from muscles.

There were courses in expanding to move with the flow, that is, without effort. Classes in sensory awareness, in exercises to cut out excessive verbiage to get to authentic feelings; we had to "converse" with our eyes and our vocal expressions only. And courses for awakening the intuitive powers to enable us to then move through life with greater ease.

I took workshops on self-love and energy, on Hinduism, Buddhism and Zen, and even read material on dolphin research as applied to humans. (At that time nobody I knew had heard of dolphin research; maybe not even of dolphins.)

There were therapists who put one correctly in line with gravity. They claimed that insults and injuries, emotional and otherwise, had settled themselves in our body parts. These therapists, then, manipulated the fasciae, the tissues that surround and support the muscles, using their fingers, elbows, and fists. It was called Rolfing. I signed up the minute I learned that for this one I was permitted to at least keep my underwear on.

I lied down on the table wondering if I was crazy for doing so. Two minutes into the treatment the Rolfer removed all doubt when he gave a painful thrust of his elbow into my right armpit.

"OUCH!" I screeched. The Rolfer silently continued.

"OW!" I shouted at the next thrust. "That hurts!"

"I'd like you to stop resisting me. Relax."

"How, with your fist in my chest?" I asked reasonably enough.

Finally it was over. The Rolfer smiled and helped me off of the table, "See" he asked, "don't you feel better already?" I actually did, a trifle; but I always felt better after the dentist stopped drilling, too.

Toward the latter part of my time at Paradigm I joined a dance seminar. It turned out to be the most consciousness-changing experience of my stay. I had always had a natural love and affinity for music and dancing, but I had never danced like this before. It was with drumbeats, primitive, atavistic, at a level beyond words. As I got more and more into it, suddenly I was without any form of self-consciousness. I was completely into the dance and more totally free than I'd ever remembered feeling before.

The entire atmosphere at Paradigm was so different than how I, or most people then, had been raised. As much as possible it was the way I wanted to raise my children. It was know yourself and be yourself so long as you don't hurt anyone else.

Some of the staff had a profound impact upon me. There was more than just an unusual beauty about them. They had amazing eyes, as if the irises contained all the sparkle yet peace and harmony of the stars and sky above. There was a grace, strength and beauty within them which drew me to them. I wanted it for myself, and felt it could be very accessible to me. Yet, I sensed it had to be earned after much effort.

Although not all the modalities at Paradigm were for me, it was the start of a new direction. By the time I left the place my stomach pains had abated, and I had some degree of inner peace to replace the bundle of nerves with which I had arrived.

Back on Long Island I began looking for ways to continue my new direction, but rapidly learned, to my great disappointment, that there was nothing. I did find a Hatha Yoga class which I took and found very helpful. But I craved more.

One day, soon after I'd begun working in New York, I was walking on the street when an oddly dressed man approached me. I opened my purse to reach for my wallet, thinking he was one of the city's many homeless about to ask me for a handout. The last time Richard and I had walked together in New York he had complained, "We've been walking only four minutes and already you've given money to five beggars." He had then pointed up to an imaginary structure and suggested, "There's a bridge up there. Why don't you climb up and cross it. Surely on the other side there's a bum you overlooked! For God's sake, Valentine, let them get a job!" But this odd character didn't want money. He wanted to hand me a flyer, which I took. It was about The Mid-Town Zen Center. When I decided to investigate it, I also decided to keep that, too, a secret 'lest I be considered "gone 'round the bend."

I was realizing that I felt attracted to Eastern philosophies in a most positive way, different from my ambivalent attraction to Catholicism and my then indifference to Judaism. I was learning that Zen was something one couldn't understand except by direct experience, through methods such as meditation; that enlightenment meant the clarification of one's mind, the ceasing to attach oneself to externals, rather grasping one's inner core of being; that Zen isn't interested in the "Young" -- the outer active mental and emotional facets of the mind, which hate, reason, judge, or "Love"; it concerns itself only with the "hissing" layer -- the one of pure feeling and knowing. I was taught that one who discovers this layer of being interacts fully in life yet a part of this one is always established in a peaceful, joyful state; that an enlightened person doesn't need to ponder; answers are all just there. Well, it *sounded* wonderful anyway.

My retrospection was rudely interrupted. The Sensei, or Zen priest, was whacking me on the shoulder with his keisaku, or flat stick about three feet long. Although I knew my body posture and facial expression had been beyond reproach, the Sensei had known my mind had wandered. Talk about the intuition of a clarified mind! He had used his stick to bring me back. With the feel of it, I promptly went into a deep meditation.

I remained in that deep state until the gong announced the end of the session. At that signal I narrowed my mouth into an oval, exhaled deeply but quietly several times and began to move my body. As I'd been taught, I rubbed my numb legs. I then began to move my body. Then I got up.

I felt relaxed and together. The Sensei had said Eastern philosophy realizes that meditation is not only in a hall, but also with us always. I would try to carry that feeling with me.

Apropos of nothing I've just told you, I should relate an incident that happened exactly one week after that day Max spilled the coffee on my skirt. Since the cleaner hadn't been able to remove the stain either, I'd stuffed the skirt into one of the Salvation Army drops and thought that was that. Now a week later, it was lunchtime. Most everyone was out of the studio. As usual I was on the phone with "Willie's people," when a rather large package addressed to me was delivered. Inside was a beautiful skirt, startlingly close in design and color to the original. I looked at the label. It was my size and carried the name of a very prestigious designer. The skirt was a much more expensive skirt than my original. Accompanying the skirt was a note: "Dear Valentine. To compliment your beauty and apologize for my clumsiness. No need to tell *you* to 'wear it well.' Yours with love, Max."

CHAPTER FOUR: MYSTERIES OF THE MIND

"My friend mind,
What is the use of so much idle talk?
My friend mind,
all this is a matter of conjecture.
I have told you what is the quintessence:
You are indeed the Reality."
--Avadhuta Gita

"Rabbit's clever," said Pooh thoughtfully.
"Yes," said Piglet, "Rabbit's clever and he has a brain."
There was a long silence.
"I suppose," said Pooh, "That's why he never understands anything."
--A.A. Milne, The House at Pooh Corner

It was the dream again, but intensified. Now the hands on the eerie clock on the wall were turning to fire, then back to normal, then the fire again. The cycle repeated three times. Next, there were people on stretchers, others screaming.

I heard Richard's voice, concerned. "Honey, you were moaning." The images vanished.

I sat up, soaked once again. "I'm getting bored with that damned dream."

"Well, that's better than scared, honey."

"I'm that too."

"Here, sit up." Richard helped me to a seated position. "Forget it now."

Obviously I didn't forget it since on the train that morning I mentioned it to Max. "It's definitely metaphorical," he explained assuredly. "It's your subconscious whispering in your ear, trying to get through to you that you're overtired; that if you don't take a rest you might get sick and have to go to the hospital. That's what the stretchers and the like are about. My prescription: take a few days off."

I felt relaxed after Max's explanation. I even liked his prescription. But I didn't fill it.

My only concession was to go in to work slightly later with Casse the next day. For several weeks she and I had no contact at all. Finally we'd connected by phone. She'd been eager to tell me something - I knew that from her tone. We agreed to take the train in together. She'd be calling for me in an hour.

Richard grumbled as we were getting dressed that morning. "Cassandra is ordinarily hard enough to take, but first thing in the morning? Impossible! Her and that damned pew organization."

"P.H.W." I corrected. "People for the Help of Women"

"You see it your way, I mine," Richard answered.

"It's to help women in all ways."

"Yeah? Well Cassandra's a woman who needs help!"

"Come on Rick, Casses's not bad. Why can't you be nice to her?" I ventured.

"Maybe I just resent her because she's more masculine than I am."

I couldn't argue that. Casse certainly dressed mannish, with short straight hair, slacks, vests, flat chunky shoes (not yet in style for women). She was very into the still young feminist movement. Richard asked, "If Casse's a lesbian, why does she keep marrying men?"

"Because she ISN'T a lesbian, DARLING."

"She could have fooled me."

"Not all lesbians dress masculine, Richard. Some are very feminine looking. We use some female models who are lesbian yet if you saw them, *you'd* be turned on."

"With my current luck, probably."

Casse and I had been friends since our freshman year in college. She'd gone on to law school and after graduation had become a very successful attorney. So, I'd been most surprised when she'd told me that she was leaving law to become a representative for the advertising photographer Desmond Blake. Casse had explained, "Law and advertising are male dominated. I've already made it in law. Advertising's a challenge."

I told Richard, "You have to admit Casse's done well."

"You call three divorces doing *well*?"

"I mean professionally. Besides, I think she's finally got a good marriage, with Albert."

"The man deserves a medal! Don't think I don't know Casse's been trying to get you knee-deep into her PEW organization," Richard said, looking terrified at the thought.

Richard was very threatened by PHW. Due to Casse I think he equated it with women getting divorced at least once, and by that reasoning, Richard being my first husband, he was up at bat. His thinking here was not totally off-base. Having realized several years ago that our relationship needed help, I'd more than once suggested marriage counseling. Richard wouldn't hear of it.

As I gave Brenna her breakfast, she asked, "Mommy, will you be home when I get back from school today?"

"No, Bree, but Mrs. Becket will be here and I'll call you from work, close to the time that you get home."

"No you won't, Mommy."

"Why would you say that, Bree?"

"Because you didn't call me yesterday."

I gasped. She was right. I'd started out tired due to having that damned dream the night before, on top of having to get up numerous times during the night with Willie, then work had been so hectic from start to end that I'd forgotten. Feeling like a worse mother than Medea, I apologized profusely to Brenna, promising it would never happen again.

"Could you come home early?" Brenna pleaded. "Betsy's Mommy is always home in the afternoon."

"Well, that's different, honey. Mrs. Syms is a school teacher." My daughter was killing me.

"Why couldn't you have been a school teacher?" she implored. It began to dawn on me that consciously or otherwise Brenna might be laying a guilt trip on me. She had to know the truth, that next to her father, nobody was more important to me than her and Willie.

"Because I wasn't smart enough," I retorted. "Now please finish your breakfast so you won't be late for school."

"Oh, yes you are. Mrs. Syms thinks you are very smart."

"Mrs. Syms? What makes you say that?"

"Once at Betsy's house I heard her on the phone telling somebody that she wondered why a smart woman like you was traipsing all over New York every day leaving her children alone while you did God-knows-what."

"You aren't left ALONE," I answered, "And I'm not traipsing! I'm working!" I shook my head! This is what it had come to? Me arguing with an absent gossip and a 7 year old?

"When is Essie coming back? Daddy keeps burning my toast," Brenna complained.

The doorbell chimed.

I searched in my pocketbook for my keys while Brenna asked, "Is that Aunt Casse?" then ran to the door. "She's like you, gregarious," Richard often said.

"Brenna!" I called to her, "Do we open the door before we ask who's there?"

At that Brenna called, "Who's there?" as she opened the door before anyone had answered. I shook my head and whispered to myself, "Keep trying. That's all you can do, keep trying." I was searching through my bag for my keys as Casse breezed in. "Hell-oo, my little dar...ling," she cooed in a high uncharacteristic voice. "Aunt Casse hasn't seen Brenna in so long. Does Bree have a kiss for me?"

My head jerked upward at the sound of Casse's new voice. Then I stared at her in amazement. "Uh, oh," I said, before I could censor myself. Little wonder that Casse had been so eager to see me. Something was up and I believed I knew what. All the telltale signs were in place.

Instead of her usual pants and vest, Casse was wearing a flowered dress with a lace collar. In place of her black flats were high-heeled red shoes. But it was her hair that really got my attention. It was bleached blonde from its former light brown, and in tight ringlets all over her head. I know the description *sound*s attractive so I'm at a loss to explain just how hideous the entire effect was. Cassandra in Shirley Temple curls simply did not make it.

Brenna, of course, noticed. "Aunt Casse, what did you do to your hair?" she asked.

"It's a perm," Casse answered, twirling around so we could view the abomination from all angles. "Do you like it?"

I thought, "Uh-oh!," but Brenna surprised me.

"It's very nice," she said. I swelled with pride at Brenna's newly developed…thank God… social graces. With her next remark I deflated.

"Aunt Casse?"

"Yes, darling?"

"Are you going to look like that for the rest of your life?"

"Bree, don't you have to get your homework together?" I hurriedly interjected.

"No..."

"Yes, you DO!" I insisted. "Anyway, it's also time for Aunt Casse and me to go to the train station."

After hugs and good-byes Casse and I walked out the door. As we were heading toward the car Casse asked me, "Do *you* like my hair, Val?"

I thought fast. "I think... once you brush the curls out a bit... it will be very... uh... lovely."

"One doesn't brush THIS perm," Casse informed me. "One molds the curls gently with one's fingers." And she proceeded to do so, coyly and gingerly.

"Oh, Lord!" I thought.

"Put your keys away, I'll drive," Casse commanded.

I obeyed, realizing why Richard took offense to Casse. You just had to understand her. She didn't *intend* her statements to sound like orders from the Third Reich.

At the Coldport station Casse became impatient. "Look at this!" she exclaimed, pointing to the big clock on the wall. "8:05, and no sign of the train yet! At this rate we'll get to work in time for dinner."

I couldn't answer. Casse turned to look at me. "Val, what's up?"

"I want to leave here," I blurted out. Oh, God! Max had been right. I had not taken his advice. I had pushed the envelope too far so now I was having a nervous collapse.

Misconstruing, Casse assured me, "Don't worry. We won't have too much of a wait. In fact, look down there, the train's coming now. Come on. Let's walk down the platform a way so we can get on near the middle."

"I CAN'T," I said too loudly. Internally I told myself, "Get a grip!"

At least I had gotten Casse's attention. Although impatiently shifting her feet, she had stopped walking and was standing, staring at me.

"I can't get on," I repeated.

Casse now looked at me sympathetically. "You don't look well, honey. Are you getting the flu?"

"No, nothing like that…"

"Val honey, I know what it is, then. All that…mysticism stuff you've been messing with. It's making you paranoid. You just drop that from your life, get on the train with me, and everything will be all right again…"

"I don't like this train," I explained inadequately

"You don't like this train?" Casse was not a nurse. Her patience had expired before her patient did. "That's very interesting, Val. Nor do I. I don't particularly love any one of them, however, they do get me to work where I make all that lovely money, so I live with it. NOW LET'S GO BEFORE THEY CLOSE THE DOORS AND WE'RE SCREWED!" She took my arm and jerked me toward the train.

"NO!!" This time I shouted while pushing Casse's hand off of me. This *wasn't* just imagination. I was now also sensing internally what the dream had been warning me about. "We're not getting on! Something is going to happen to this train."

"What about work?"

"We can drive to Crystal Bay. They have a train to New York every hour."

"CRYSTAL BAY! It will take us half an hour to arrive there!"

"At least we'll arrive."

"I will NOT let the inmates run the asylum!" Casse spat out at me. "I'm not going to Crystal Bay and neither are you giving in to this insanity, because I'm driving -- and that's final!"

The train whistle announced that the 8:35 was pulling out of the station. And so it did.

"Shit!" Casse exclaimed. "Come on. Let's go to Crystal Bay."

She sounded and looked like a drill sergeant as she marched toward her car, snapping her fingers, with me following meekly like a private first class. Casse drove to Crystal Bay so aggressively, hands gripping the wheel, at intervals lifting one hand off to give a slow driver - one going only 65 MPH - the finger and a curse, that I wondered if we wouldn't have been safer on the 8:35! At one point I asked her, "How is it, Casse, that anyone going slower than you is 'an idiot' and anyone driving faster is 'a maniac?'" In all that, this was the old Casse again, incongruously decked out in tight blond curls and flowers with lace.

As we pulled into Crystal Bay we heard a train whistle. "I hope that isn't what I think it is," Casse said. It was. A turn into the parking lot revealed a westbound train pulling out of the station, which meant the next train wasn't for an hour. "Fuck!" Casse exclaimed, smacking her thigh over the flowered dress.

We decided we might as well wait at the next-door diner and have breakfast. Before our coffee arrived Casse told me what she'd been wanting to all week.

"Val?"

"Casse?"

"Must you pick this time to be cute?"

"I'm sorry. I've been very tense this morning."

"You *have*?!" Casse asked sarcastically.

The waiter appeared at our table. "Are you ready to order?" he asked pleasantly.

"I'll have a toasted bran muffin and decaf, black," I told him. Then he and I looked at Casse.

"Bring me a toasted English muffin, two scrambled eggs, potatoes, bacon and regular coffee," she said. The waiter nodded, smiled and left, whereupon I raised an eyebrow.

"Potatoes AND bacon?" I repeated. "I thought you wanted to get in shape?"

"I am in shape," Casse shot back. "Round's a shape." Then she lowered her voice. "Look, I don't want to add to your stress, Val, and I know you aren't going to approve. I met somebody."

"What else is new?" I asked. I'd been through three prior Casse meeting- somebody's, new- image, divorce, new- marriage scenarios. By the third marriage Richard had complained, "I'm getting tired of buying that woman wedding presents."

Casse spoke rapidly. "I know how you feel about affairs, Of course you and Richard are the PERFECT couple; the word "affair" isn't in your vocabulary..."

"There's no such thing as perfect," I interrupted uncomfortably.

"Well, then as perfect as it gets. Everybody who knows you two knows that, honey. Besides, I realize this goes against your moral grain, so try not to judge me too much?"

"I'm not judging you at all," I answered. "What's *this one's* name?"

"I surely can hear you not judging."

"I didn't mean it how it sounded."

"All right, then, let me go back a bit. About a month ago I started to think maybe Albert's screwing around."

"Albert?! Goodness me!"

"I know what you're thinking. Dear straight-arrow Albert, right? But under it all, a man is a man."

"What makes you think he's cheating?"

"He started acting strange."

"How?"

I heard a rustle, looked up and saw our waiter standing beside our table. "Will that be all, girls?" he asked, smiling broadly.

Casse's head snapped up like a bull spotting a red flag, she fixed her eyes in a fierce expression, stared at the waiter and snarled, "Mister, this is the seventies?! We are not *girls*!"

The smile left the waiter's face.

"That's right, this *is* the seventies all right," I interjected. "We are not *girls*. We are *men*."

As Casse then turned her threatening look upon me, the castrated waiter took this opportunity to slap our check onto the table and to split.

Casse put her head closer to mine and resumed about Albert. "He's developed strange sexual tastes. He wants me to wear... costumes... garter belts... sexy nighties... that sort of thing. I was shocked. I told him, 'Albert Sann! You of all people. Into women's rights, supporting me in PHW, yet you'd demean me in this way!'"

"But will you wear them?" I asked.

"ARE YOU CRAZY?!" Casse asked loudly. Several fellow diners turned to stare whereupon Casse again lowered her voice. "Of course not!" Then with second thought she asked, "You mean you think I should have?"

"I think you could at least try."

"HOW CAN YOU SAY THAT?! What the hell *for*?!"

"What do you mean, what *for*? Because he likes it. You might too, if you'd try."

"Like it?! But I forgot. You aren't at all interested in the cause I and so many other women - your sisters, Val - are fighting for. Equality, for us all."

"Casse, I've told you before, I'm not that far from you. I support equal opportunity for both men and women, equal pay and a chance for advancement for the same job. I believe in community supported day care centers. I just don't believe that social roles should necessarily be transferred into a private relationship, nor do I feel that a man and woman together should strive to be consistent privately and politically. I think the fairly recent incredible big changes in human values have confused many women as to which social template they should follow -- and I think this is YOUR confusion, Casse."

Realizing that I was lecturing, I stopped there. But Casse seemed interested in what I had said. "You're telling me I'm confused?" she answered. "Go on."

"It's just that I think you and probably many of your other P.H.W. members sometimes confuse economic and political issues with personal ones. What two people do in the bedroom should be pleasurable for both and have nothing to do with economics, unless one of them is a prostitute."

Was Casse now looking at me with admiration in her eyes?

"Val, Val," she said, "You're incredibly intelligent. A bit nuts lately... I mean, witness what happened this morning at the train station. But you sure are smart. P.H.W. could use you. Come with me to the next meeting?"

"Thanks, Casse. But with Willie, Brenna, Richard, my work, the autism society, my hands are full now."

"I know, I know. I don't know how you do it," Casse conceded. "But about Albert. You don't think he's fooling around?"

"For whatever it's worth, no, I don't. I feel Albert's an honest reliable man, trying to be very honest with you. I think you should be glad he wants that with YOU; take it as a compliment."

"You've done... those things... with Richard?"

Casse's question took me so off guard that I answered, before thinking, "Not with him, no."

Fortunately Casse was so wrapped up in her own life drama that she didn't take note of my slip.

"I haven't... been unfaithful to Albert -- yet." She went on. "Maybe I should just forget the other man and concentrate on Albert?"

I nodded affirmatively, "You don't talk with your men, Casse," I offered. "You just emulate them. You assume Albert's having an affair so based on that you find another man. It's what you've always done. Are three divorces enough for you? Then talk with Albert. Tune in. Men are people too."

I was surprised, for never before had I been so honest to a fault. Certainly I'd worried about Casse ever since she'd rejected everything frilly and decorative, and worried about her even more each time she embraced those very things, because at such times only her garb was feminine. Her actions never veered from what was considered classic male acting-out behavior. None of it seemed…healthy.

The bigger surprise was how receptive Casse was to my candor. "Spike heels... garter belts... hmm…interesting," Casse mused. "Want to hit Bloomingdales at lunch?"

"Sorry," I declined, "By the time we get in today the words lunch hour won't be in my vocabulary." My answer brought Casse back to reality. "You're right, same for me."

I added, "Besides, maybe you can ask Albert to take this shopping trip with you one evening."

Casse looked at me as if I'd just revealed to her the eighth wonder of the world. "MY friend," she said, patting my arm from across the table, "You may just have saved a marriage." It was an ironic conversation, all considered.

The train ride in was actually fun. Casse and I laughed as we shared stories about working in New York.

"So, I'm taking this client out for lunch," she related. "Hallers. You've been there; fine restaurant, right? I tell the waiter, 'We'll have two roast beefs, one well-done, the other medium rare.' And completely sincerely the waiter answers, 'Fine Madame. And how would you like the roast beefs done?' It wasn't that he had a language difficulty; he was American."

"He had the New York language difficulty," I offered, "Can talk, won't listen."

As we swapped New York City work stories and giggled like old times, now, with those ominous feelings I'd had at the railroad station completely gone, I knew that I'd behaved totally irrationally. Max had been right. The strange uncomfortable feeling and the dream had been tension, nothing more. I'd stupidly become a slave to my feelings instead of just taking them for what they *were* a sign of; stress. I'd meditate more and take a few days off just for myself. Now comfortably back on familiar ground, I mentally began to plan my days off.

I arrived at the studio at 11:30. "Ernie's going to explode!" I thought steeling myself on the way up in the elevator.

When I entered the studio Zarela spotted me first. She ran over and threw her arms around me.

"Oh, V.J, Thank God, thank God!" Then she called out, "ERNIE, EVERYONE, V.J is here, she's all right!"

Ernie, assistants Duke, Dave, Tony, Hank, Jayson, and Dawn the stylist, all ascended on me at once, uttering similar "Thank Gods!"

"Will somebody please tell me what this is all about?" I asked, unnecessarily. I knew; felt it in my gut; the ominous feelings were back. My dream had happened. It *had* been a warning afterall. Now I was *really* terrified.

"I don't think she's heard," Zarela told everybody, and then turned to me and said, "The 8:35 train from Coldport crashed this morning. First time in history. Many people were badly injured, some critically. Five were killed."

"Oh, my God, I knew it was going to happen!" I blurted out, beginning to perspire. Damn! I hadn't meant to say that. Cautiously I looked around at everybody. They were staring at me with utmost curiosity. "I took an alternate train. That's why I'm late," I added, trying to bring in the mundane, hopefully to draw attention away from my first outburst.

The phone rang from my office. "Zarela, please tell Charlie Anderson I'll call him back this afternoon," I managed. "He wants an appointment to see Ernie's work." Again they all stared. Inwardly I asked "What the hell's happening to me? Maybe it's just another form of insanity?"

Zarela disappeared, soon to return. "It *was* Charlie Anderson," she announced. Everybody stared at me again.

"All right, all right, the party's over, everybody," Ernie shrieked. "I'm not payin' you all ta stand around doin' nothin'."

Hank mumbled to me, "No, he's just paying us next to nothing, period. The cheapskate." He then walked toward the set with Duke, Dave, Tony and the others.

The phone rang again. "Tell Richard I'm all right and I'll take his call in a minute," I mumbled to nobody in particular.

This time Ernie disappeared into my office. In a moment he came out again, looking pale. "It *is* Richard," he said, and with a shake of his head walked out into the studio.

I went into the office, took the phone and reassured Richard that I was uninjured. Then I simply sat quietly at my desk. In a few minutes Ernie returned and sat down beside me.

"I don't get it, V.J," he said. "How did ya know that train was gonna crash?! And how did ya know who was callin' on the phone, twice?!"

The phone rang again. I moved to answer it but Ernie cradled his hand over the receiver, preventing that. "Who is it this time?" he asked.

"Hal Lindley about the new ad?" I asked weakly.

Ernie picked up the receiver. "Studio," he said. Then he put his hand over the earpiece. "It's Casse," he said.

"Tell her I'll call her back."

Ernie hanged up. "Well, ya missed this time. But, ya still got two out of three. And ya knew about the train. How do ya do it?"

"It's hard to explain," I answered. That was certainly true, considering that I didn't understand it myself. I was now soaked with perspiration and shaking. Ernie was reacting quite differently. A glint had entered his eye. "Hey, could we make money with -- this thing ya do? Like with the lottery"

"No!! I mean…I don't know." "Well, let me be the second ta know, once *you* do," Ernie said with a wink, then quickly left the office.

I took a Kleenex off of the table and wiped my brow, then took a deep breath before returning Casse's call. "My God!" she raved, "Like I told you, I don't go for this supernatural stuff, Val, but a serious injury or my death I don't go for right now either. I don't understand any of it but if what's just happened is a result, then do- do- your- voodoo, and thank you!"

Finally alone, I turned on the radio in my office. I listened to reports of the accident and remarks from on-lookers: "I could see one dead body. Some passengers were pulling him out and then covered his face. I'd never seen anything like it in my life."

I felt greatly upset and guilty. I wondered if I should have done something beforehand to alert the other people before they took that train. "Sure" I told myself, "why didn't you make an announcement over the loud speaker system, 'Everybody, this is Valentine Jordan warning you to get off this train; it's going to crash.' And then get hauled off to the nearest mental institution, idiot!"

Zarela walked into the office and turned off the radio. "V.J, you should just rest quietly for a while here," she offered.

I don't know what made me decide to choose Zarela to confide in, except that she was always solicitous, kind and right then she was there. "I dreamed about the crash for weeks before," I whispered, "Sometimes I know who's on the phone before I take the call. I'm… scared."

Zarela answered, "What's there to be scared of? You are just very psychic. In my country, Peru, unlike here, we simply accept such things as a natural part of life."

"I never was...psychic…until now. Does it just come, like that?"

"You probably always were. You just never realized it before."

"But I have nobody to talk to about it. I mean, I can talk to you, but…"

After a moment's thought Zarela offered, "There's a man. A professor of Eastern philosophy. He lives on Long Island, in fact. Although he shuns publicity, he was featured in the National Inquirer several years ago."

"There's a reliable source," I muttered.

Zarela, either not having heard that or choosing to ignore it, was writing on my pad. She pulled the sheet of paper off the pad and handed it to me.

"I suggest you call him," she said. "Now, just sit quietly awhile." She left the room.

I looked at the paper that Zarela had given me, with the name, "Dr. Cheng Ho" and a phone number written beside it. Zarela had always amazed me with her remarkable ability to remember a phone number after hearing or reading it once. I stuck the paper in my pocket book wedged between my note pad and wallet.

From the set I heard Ernie, above the stereo music, shouting at Stu, "What the fuck do you want from me?" He was partially drowned out by the screech of the stereo. It was again like a normal work day. I tried to pull myself together and to pretend that it really was.

CHAPTER FIVE: LIPS LIKE HERS

"There is no happiness in the world that can be gained without tapasya (austerities)."

-- Shiva Purana

"Life is difficult."

--M. Scott Peck, M.D.

When Esmerelda returned, Richard didn't want to let on how thrilled he was to be relieved of his morning duties with the children. To me he boasted, "I was getting to make a mean toast!" However when he came home at night and saw Essie there, he couldn't quite hide his elation. He nearly jumped in the air and then kissed her on the rebound.

Once Richard was out of earshot, Esmerelda, looking frightened, asked me, "Senora, Mr. Jordan, he es fine?"

"Yes, Essie," I answered, "Just excited to see you. I think taking care of the children in the morning was difficult for him." Essie smiled extremely broadly and said nothing, my clue that she hadn't understood. "Si, Essie," I translated, thankful for my college Spanish. "Muy emocion al verte. Yo creolque el cuidar de los ninos en la manana era mucho tension papa el."

"Si, Senora," Essie responded, this time breaking out into a genuine grin.

"Essie, let Mr. Jordan help with things now and then," I said, speaking more slowly. "He is very macho about his kitchen. Deja que el ayude con las cosas de vez en cuando."

"Si, Senora," Essie nodded, laughing.

That morning nothing facilitated my getting to work. First, as I was about to walk out the door the washing machine overflowed, not a rarity these days; it was getting tired and needed a replacement. Once I'd mopped up the suds I myself was soaking wet, so I went upstairs and changed my entire well thought-out outfit into something that I just threw on. After several more such domestic crises I was convinced that my life consisted of only all the worst that life had to offer to both the housewife and to the working mother. I was beginning to feel that I was being guided to stay home that day, but told myself, "Stop it, Valentine!" and took the train in regardless.

Of course on top of everything I missed my regular train, so arrived at the studio later than expected.

"Hi, Ernie" I said with forced cheerfulness.

"Ya couldn't get in earlia?"

I was in no mood for it. "Have you forgotten all the mornings I've been here before the crow cawed?" I asked him. "Let's start over. Hello, Ernie."

"Hello," he managed.

"It's nice out," I offered pleasantly.

"Then I'll take it out," Ernie rejoined.

"To the manor born!" I replied. "Have I told you lately that you're disgusting?!"

"Wow," Ernie switched the subject, "You look gorgeous today; what happened?" Conversationally the man had the attention span of a gnat.

"Nothing yet – but, wait a second…" I gave him a fake swat.

An hour later we were going over some proofs together when Zarela walked over to tell me that I had a phone call. I picked up the extension beside us and heard an agitated Esmerelda on the line. "Senora Jordan," she said, sounding upset, "The school of Willie, she call. She say he not feel well. She say you to take heem home today."

"Willie, not feel well?"

"Si,"

"He looked fine this morning before I left."

"Si"

"Don't worry Essie," I reassured her, "I'll take care of it." I hanged up the phone, excused myself, went into the office and called the school director.

"Hello, this is Mrs. Jordan," I said. "I received a call from my housekeeper. I'm here in New York working. You have my work number, you can always call me here. Is Willie all right?"

"Well, no, not exactly, Mrs. Jordan," the director answered. "William is very agitated today. He even engaged in S.I.Bs this morning."

"He engaged in what?"

"S.I.Bs, Mrs. Jordan. Self-injurious behaviors" By her tone she might as well have been saying, "Idiot who works and doesn't take care of her child, knows nothing!"

"What kind of…S.I.Bs*?*" I used the unfamiliar term.

"He hit his head a few times. He obviously isn't feeling well. We believe he should be home until he feels better."

"Does he have a fever?"

"I don't know. These children don't like their temperature taken."

How dare she put Willie in a box that way! I felt myself getting hot from anger.

"Well, you can feel his head, can't you?" I was trying hard to hide my agitation.

"Mrs. Jordan," the director said in a tone of voice that one would use with a petulant child. "The teacher doesn't feel she can handle William as he is today, so we ask that he be taken home until he feels better. However, if *you* are too busy to come get him, could your husband pick him up, or, your maid?"

Now I knew why I'd felt that I shouldn't go into work today. Silently I cursed myself for this time ignoring my inner voice or whatever the hell it was. I phoned Richard.

"Rick," I said, "They're having trouble with Willie today. Can you pick him up and bring him home?"

"Again! What's wrong with those people?"

"I agree Rick, but they insist."

"Valen, how often can we do this?"

"I know."

"I'm about to go into a crucial meeting. If I left now it could cost me a bundle of money. They'll just have to keep Willie there for the day. We can only do what we can do." I sighed. "I'll take care of it, then."

I called the school again and told them, "I'll catch the first train home and pick Willie up as soon as I can."

I called Esmerelda and told her my plans, and then went in to tell Ernie that I had to leave on some personal business. I had never mentioned Willie's condition at work and wanted to keep it that way. To my relief Ernie neither asked any questions nor raised any objections.

But, on the train ride home I was like a pressure cooker with the lid on tight and nobody in sight to remove it. I was indeed steamed! I had a gut feeling Willie wasn't ill, just the victim of some teacher who didn't want to bother. By the time the train arrived on Long Island, I couldn't decide who I was angry with; the school people, Richard who couldn't leave his damn work to travel one-half hour to get Willie so that I had to travel two, or with Willie himself for being who he was.

At the school I hugged Willie, who didn't seem sick to me, rather his usual self. I felt his forehead. It was cool. The director said, with a sigh, "Willie isn't easy, you know." "Yes, I know" I answered, managing only a modicum of politeness. "that's why he's here." I felt like adding, "If you wanted to work with 'normal children,' why didn't you go teach at P.S. # 25? Pay enough to get a teacher who knows how to handle Willie." But as usual I didn't indulge myself with that risk. They could take it out on Willie.

I helped Willie on with his coat, then put him and his little belongings into the car. "Come on," I said, my love for him overtaking all the anger and other emotions I'd felt earlier. "Mommy and Willie will have fun today. Are you hungry? Should we go to a restaurant?"

Willie got excited. "Re-re-re," he repeated, his way of saying restaurant. He loved to eat.

"Willie, listen to mommy. Restaurant. I'll say it slowly, you say it after me. Rest au rant." Willie turned away. "I'll take you in when you say it, Willie. You can say it. Listen." I took his beautiful perfect-featured face in mine and turned it toward me so that he was looking at me. "Listen, now. Rest au rant." Willie said, "Rest ran" "Willie, good enough. Good!" I hugged him. "You said restaurant, so we can go to one."

Underlying everything every day, I had a constant thought: What would happen to Willie if I had an untimely death tomorrow? Who would understand his speech? I was the only one who always had to explain him to everybody. I felt I had two choices: to outlive Willie, or to help him become normal, now, while I could. I'd made up my mind to do all that I could in both areas; so for one full year after his diagnosis, I'd spent nearly every minute with Willie, often to the point of exhaustion - mine, not his; he had more energy than an entire Olympic team! I would talk to him, enter his world, and love him. Now - and every opportunity I had – I'd do the same. I'd hired and trained the tutors, speech therapists, teenagers, sitters, maids, and taught them all the things to do based on what I'd figured out worked best. As a result Willie had gone from totally withdrawn and non-verbal to more outward and verbal; he now had some meaningful speech. This was a definite improvement. The thing was, for all the time, energy and money spent, it seemed not enough.

So often I felt I'd failed; that for putting so much into this child I must be the biggest fool in town. I'd fluctuated from wanting to shout at professionals like the director of the school, "Has it ever crossed your mind that you might possibly be the stupidest person on this planet!" to thoughts of, "What's wrong with me that my effort with Willie isn't going anywhere?"

I took Willie to a diner for a late lunch.

In public Willie and I rarely went unnoticed, because he looked so extraordinarily beautiful yet (by ordinary standards) often behaved so extraordinarily badly.

Today in the restaurant we attracted attention as usual.

Once seated, in the most remote empty booth I could find, I asked, "Well, Willie, what do you want to eat today?"

"HAMBURGAIRE," Willie shouted. "YOU WANT HAMBURGAIRE!" In case you think I exaggerate, we had ten people's attention immediately.

"Shhh, not so loud," I cautioned, but Willie either didn't know how to modulate his voice or saw no reason to. "Willie should say, '*I* want hamburger,'" I added, correcting his autistic tendency to refer to himself in the third person. At least he assured us prompt service! Almost instantly a waitress was at our table, pad and pencil poised.

"I'll have a chef salad and decaf, and my son would like..."

"HAMBURGAIRE! WANT HAMBURGAIRE!" Willie again shouted.

"What a cute accent," the waitress said. "Is he from France?"

"From much further," I answered. I hardly heeded the waitress's confused expression. I was tired from the paranormal events of the past few days, from this day of commuting to New York only to be called home almost immediately, and to be truthful, I had started to think I must be "out to lunch" to have brought Willie here in the first place! Judging by what next came from my mouth, I was by then so wired that I no longer cared what I said.

"No, my son does not have a French accent," I told the waitress, "It's an Orkian accent."

"Orkian, ma'am?"

"Yes, Orkian. My son is Mork from the planet Ork."

"I see, Ma'am. I'll go put your order in." The waitress didn't walk away, she sprinted.

Willie did not sit idly waiting for his food. Willie rarely sat still. His movements were astoundingly rapid. Before I could take his hand or a "NO!" could escape my lips, Willie had grabbed and opened the salt shaker and probably thinking the content was sugar, dumped it all in his mouth. Finding it was not sugar, he made a pained face and spit the salt out on the tablecloth. He then drank his entire glass of water, took mine and did the same. Two women at the next table dropped open their mouths in unison, then stared disapprovingly.

"No, not good, Willie," I told him, doing my best to wipe up the recycled salt. The women, like two cows chewing their cud, continued to simultaneously chew and stare. "This too will pass," I consoled myself.

The meal over, I sighed with relief as I left two bills and four quarters for the waitress. Willie, a delighted expression spreading across his face, grabbed the four quarters and began to spin them all at once on the table. Now we had the astonished attention of about ten more patrons.

Perhaps I should have previously explained that Willie, like many children with autism, liked to spin - himself (at times he'd sit down on the ground, or the floor, depending upon where we were, and spin himself like a top) and any round thing that he could get a hold of. I must say that he was extraordinarily good at it. Once he took a handful of coins off of Richard's dresser and got them spinning all at once, giving each a twist at the correct interval to keep them going; Richard said we should book Willie on a TV talent show.

Willie then began to carry at least ten dimes in his pant pocket to spin in public whenever he chose to. I can't say if he cared or not, but he was definitely the focus of attention and admiration of many neighborhood kids who tried to emulate that feat but failed.

Once we'd been at an out door restaurant and suddenly Willie was on the ground spinning something. We looked more closely at the object. It was what must have been at least a three-carat diamond ring. A few minutes later we saw a woman frantically searching the ground. When we had to take the ring away from Willie and give it back to the woman, she looked greatly relieved, whereas Willie screamed for an hour. As she began to walk away I whispered under my breath, "No reward? Ten dimes would be more than sufficient."

Now the table adjacent to ours, where a family sat lunching on salads and sandwiches, was becoming the focus of Willie's attention. His eyes zeroed in on their food, then, like a dart, as I watched helplessly, Willie was beside their table lifting a slice of tomato from the stunned mother's salad plate, and standing it on end, ready for the spin. I jumped up to retrieve Willie with the thought forefront in mind, "If he can spin that tomato, lets reconsider what we HAVE here.......!" However, the tomato hung limp in Willie's fingers, causing him to shriek in frustration. By the time I apologized to the family, who sat frozen in incredulity, and had maneuvered Willie back to our table, I needn't tell you that there wasn't one person anywhere in the restaurant not looking at us, some in fascination as if watching a circus act, others very disapprovingly. Willie seemed oblivious or unperturbed about the cold or stunned looks. "God," I thought, "I could use a little more of that trait!"

Willie and I walked toward the cashier, as did the two staring women. As we four stood on line waiting our turn to pay, they continued to stare at Willie and me as if we were worms.

I'd been taught by my mother to be a lady, to be polite, to be pleasant. But at this moment I'd had it. My years of being polite at other's disapproval and criticism of Willie, and me as a mother, all came together. I stared back at the two deliberately, and then icily asked, "Why didn't you take out binoculars? You could have seen him better."

"Your child is very spoiled," one of the two answered.

"If a child can't behave he doesn't belong here ruining other people's meals," the other added, pointedly moving away from Willie as if avoiding something unclean.

"That's right," said the first. "He should have been removed the moment he began acting up. He made us very nervous."

In essence I agreed, however there was no way to explain that Willie wasn't spoiled, he was different, and that his behavior was so unpredictable that I could not have known in advance how he'd behave in the restaurant. So I certainly wasn't going to deprive him of a possible good learning experience to please people who didn't care in the first place.

Their moving away from Willie was the last straw.

"Don't worry," I spat out, "he won't tarnish your aura."

They looked absolutely repulsed. That did it!

"He *made* you nervous?!" I continued, "You *start out* nervous. I doubt either one of you can finish a thought on your own. If we ever have the bad fortune to end up again in a restaurant with you, I suggest YOU get up and go twitch someplace else."

Clutching Willie's hand, I told him, "Come on, honey, let's get away from these bad women. Let's go home."

"Bad." Willie parroted. "Go home. Bad."

Brenna was home from school when we returned. I wanted to spend some time alone with her, so I asked Essie to take Willie and his bicycle outside and to let him ride it on the sidewalk in front of the house for awhile. Willie loved his bicycle. The two went out, but five minutes later, when the doorbell rang and I went to the door, it was Essie, pointing to the sidewalk. I looked. A few boys around Willie's age were standing near Willie as he sat on his bike. Children could be thoughtless, but Bobby The Bully as I referred to him, was more than that. He was a mean kid.

I saw Bobby put his hands on Willie's bike. "I think I'll ride this bike," I heard him say. The worst was, there were several women sitting outside the house across the street. One of them was Bobby's mother. I watched, waiting for her to intervene. She did nothing but look away and continue to talk to the other women. When Bobby pushed Willie off the bike, I quickly moved out the front door and forward. Hurrying toward my child, I knew that maybe I was wrong. It was a tough world; maybe I should have stood back and let Willie handle it the best he could, so he could learn. And maybe after that I should have gone over to Bobby and empathized with him, told him I understood, that I forgave him and trusted him to do better the next time. Maybe.

But that wasn't what I did. Instead, I rushed over to Willie, hugged him as Bobby and the others stood aside, and asked him, "Are you alright honey?" Willie just stood mute, looking frightened. "This is *your* bike, honey," I told him. "You can get back on it if you want to." Willie pulled away from his bike, then just stood and hung his head. At that I walked over to Bobby, took his arm, pulled him over to me so he faced me, and crouched down to his eye level. Next I made the most menacing face he'd probably ever seen outside of a horror movie, and told him, "Listen. You see this boy over here? I'm his mommy. I don't like mean boys who try to push my son off his bike. If you ever try anything like that again, I'll be right in your face so fast, you'll find out then what that's like." I hadn't any idea what that meant but it felt right and I hoped it impressed the kid, and perhaps also his mother who now sat watching us from across the street.

As days with Willie went, this had been a pretty good day.

"Is this ironic?" I said to Richard later that evening over the phone, just after he had told me that he had to attend a meeting that night. "You're always home early, but the one night I'm home, you're out."

"I know, honey. I wish I didn't have to go. But it's important."

"I understand that; it's all right." Actually, I meant it. After the day that I'd just finished, I'd welcome the time alone.

Once the children were asleep, early, I thanked God, I took my pocketbook and went into the bedroom. I'd rearrange my purse's contents, then go to bed. As I began to remove everything, the slip of paper Zarela had given to me fell out. I looked at the name Dr. Cheng Ho with his phone number beneath it. I'd almost forgotten about him. I got up and shut the bedroom door. I reached for the phone, then hesitated. "What are you getting into here?" I asked myself. "The National Inquirer isn't exactly the New England Journal of Medicine." "Fool!" I answered myself, "Does an inmate at Riker's Island ask for the wine list? You're thirsty for information and this Cheng whatever is all that you've got!" I carried the number to the chaise, upholstered in white fake fur and positioned near our telephone. I sat down, kicked off my shoes and swung my legs up, rubbing my feet into the soft material. I dialed the number.

The phone rang several times before I heard the sound of the receiver being lifted at the other end.

"Hello, Cheng Ho here. And, you are?" The man spoke with a lilting accent, yes, but that didn't begin to describe his voice. I found it most pleasant and compelling. It just gave me a very powerful, joyful and safe feeling.

"Dr. Cheng," I began, "my name is Valentine Jordan, and..."

"Not Dr. Cheng. Dr. Ho," he corrected. "Please. You will call me Cheng."

"All right, Cheng." I said. "I...uh...needed to talk to somebody. So although we don't know each other..."

"Ah, but we do. I can see you now, Val-teen. Long dark brown hair. Olive skin, large green eyes. Unusual combination... Very beautiful. Straight nose. VERY full lips. Slim body but not skinny. Curvy."

I was speechless! He had in essence described my coloration and features as accurately as if he were standing in front of me. And "Val-teen" yet.

"How..did..you do that?"

"Was I accurate?"

"Not bad. Although you didn't say that my lips are too big," I told him.

"Not big, luscious. Ah, yes. You are -- something -- Val-teen!"

"But I asked how you did that."

"Psychicness. Intuition. The same thing in yourself that unnerves you lately. Is that not why you call me?"

Again he had startled me. "Yes, Cheng. It's so sudden. I don't know what to do with it."

"Let it come, what else? You have no choice anyway. One can't go back."

Cheng's answer failed to reassure me! "It scares me, Cheng," I told him. "I never asked for or wanted any of it."

"You worry because you have started to function as you're intended?" Cheng asked rhetorically. "Not a rare reaction. You should read Herman Hess's *Damian.* In it he wrote, 'Nothing in the world is so distasteful to a man than to take the path that leads to himself.' Meditation is a way to yourself, Val-teen. It leads to a pure heart and clear head. Those lead to great power for good. Accept the psychic gifts which come to you along the way without dwelling upon them. Primarily, allow yourself to feel the increasing love in your heart. The purer your mind gets the more love you will feel. That love will increasingly echo to other hearts, until one day you and love will be one."

I was digesting Cheng's words so I didn't reply right away. Cheng filled the conversational gap by remarkably reverting to a Chinese accent as he told me, "I give course Thursday evenings at Chelsea University." "Self-awareness. If you want, you come. Would help."

"What's the subject?"

"It is Life School. Awareness of God. Self-Realization, in other words"

When I didn't respond, Cheng asked, "What's wrong?"

"Just…if there *is* a God, s/he has a lot to answer for."

"That's profound," Cheng said, punctuating that with the most infectious giggles. "Now you *really* can come to my class."

I sighed. "Why not? It has to be better than that orthodox service I went to. Listening to that Rabbi for seventy minutes was the closest thing I've ever had to a near-death experience."

Cheng again giggled gleefully. "You are amusing- at times," he offered. "Of course not every Rabbi is so long-winded. Some give very good talks indeed. So, you want to come Thursday?"

"Very much." As I said it I realized how *much* I wanted to. Not that I wasn't apprehensive about what I might be getting into. Mostly, at the moment I was just wondering about how I could fit yet another commitment into my schedule. Again, seemingly reading my mind, Cheng said, "When it is right, there will be enough time. This one will come to trust Dr. Cheng Ho."

Cheng's next sentence totally stunned me! "Just one further thing. The relationship with the West Coast man needs to be re-evaluated. Before it weighs you down. That never good. In fact, at this stage of your development could be bad for you."

I gasped. I'd told nobody about Brandt. Yet this total stranger had accurately evaluated one of the most personal aspects of my life.

"We'll be talking about him soon. A lot." Cheng said.

At those words, feelings of relief flooded my being such as I can't describe.

"Oh, yes!" I exclaimed, "I need to talk about this with ... somebody - very much. I'd want to discuss that alone. Do you have private sessions?"

"No problem."

"Then, should I call to set one up as soon as I know my schedule for next week?" I asked eagerly.

"Yes. If doesn't happen on it's own before then." Cheng replied. "Blessings." And he hung up.

I placed the phone back on the receiver and rested my head on thc back of the chaise. I ran the phone cord through my hands, twirled it, stopped myself, and then twirled a lock of my hair instead, thinking of Cheng's mysterious answer. How could a first meeting between him and me happen on its own? It was a comment that stymied me, something that I was to learn Cheng did often and, I would guess, deliberately. Because the mysterious intrigues us and propels us forward in search of answers.

CHAPTER SIX: WHEN VICE IS NICE

"People use karma as an excuse to hide their own weaknesses. People indulge in adultery and say, 'God has ordained that.' This attitude is nothing but a wile of the mind. Our tricky mind is a thousand headed cobra which will try to prevent us from traversing the path of righteousness."

--Darshan Singh

"Your friends will know you better in the first minute you meet them than your acquaintances will know you in a thousand years."

--Richard Bach, Illusions

For the rest of the week everything went so smoothly at the studio and at home that I first asked myself, "What's gone wrong?!" Then it crossed my mind, "Does this have anything to do with Cheng?"

Whatever the reason, among the good things, I was able to leave the studio early each evening and to spend some really lovely, and loving, evenings with Richard. Even Willie cooperated by sleeping. If this was not the current normal way of things for us, I loved the abnormality. For Richard and me, romance was definitely in the air. Some things simply can't be rushed, and we didn't.

On the way to the Zen Center the Monday night after a delightful weekend between Richard and me, I decided that I would tell Richard that I was a meditator and other things of the like about myself. After the intimate times we'd just shared, it seemed natural to also share with him this important part of my life. Having decided that, I meditated especially well in the hall.

In the shoe room I bent down to put on my shoes, then as I straightened up my chin collided with somebody's head.

"Oh, I'm sorry," I apologized, rubbing my chin while looking into the most beautiful deep brown almond shaped eyes that I had ever seen, eyes which reminded me of those of some of my teachers at Paradigm, except this pair was one hundred times more compellingly beautiful. They drew me into them as invitingly as being pulled out of a cold winter night into a warm spring.

"It's all right," the one with the eyes assured me. "I'm Cheng Ho. How are you, Val-teen?"

"Goodness me." Totally startled, I took a moment to compose myself, then looked at the rest of Cheng. My first impression was that he was very tall, but I soon realized that could not be since at his full height he came up only to my chin. Yet it was strange, the feeling of largeness that one got from him. More importantly, his face emanated wisdom and love. There was something angelic about this man, although his behavior seemed extremely down to earth.

"No need for apology," Cheng said. "I knew we be bumping into each other sooner or later." His pun obviously amused him so that he began to giggle with such infectious intensity that I had to giggle too. It felt good to laugh with Cheng.

"Do you come here regularly, Cheng?"

"No. I just decided to drop in tonight. I didn't know why. Now I do. Shall we go to train?" Cheng invited. "We take the same line."

On the train we were fortunate in finding two adjacent vacant seats at the end of a car facing the wall instead of other passengers.

I was realizing that I felt emotionally elevated near Cheng. He giggled and chuckled often. I got the feeling that whatever was going on, he was having a very good time. There was something childlike about him, yet just as I'd be thinking that, in the next breath he would say the wisest thing. I'd never met anyone like him. Most interesting was that although I'd just met Cheng, I felt like I was in an oasis with an old dear friend. As safe and comfortable as an evening curled up at home in my old bathrobe, with a bowl of popcorn and a favorite television movie. I told Cheng so. He had a ready answer. "Old karmic friends. Our relationship here a continuation from prior lifetime."

"You really believe that?" I asked.

"I don't BELIEVE. I KNOW." Cheng answered with conviction. "I was born with unusual ability, knowledge of many of my past lives."

I drew in a breath and exhaled slowly, my way of trying to handle all the unaccustomed positive energy coming to me from my new friend, or whatever he was. I would say that he'd been born with MANY unusual abilities!

"When I meet person," Cheng continued, "I know who we were to each other, where, when and why, in past lifetimes."

"You know all that about you and me?" Goodness, I'd never met anyone as intriguing!

"Yes."

I waited for Cheng to elaborate. Finally, he said, "I can't tell you more right now. One thing we must learn; there is a time for everything. This is not the time."

"Will you tell me at another time, then?" I heard the eagerness in my voice.

"Yes," Cheng said. "unless you realize it for yourself first."

"Unless…I..realize it…myself first?" I parroted his words. "How could I do that?"

Cheng changed the subject. "Now tell me about the West Coast man." I gulped. "From your perceptions, from the beginning," he added. Could this be happening? "And don't spare the details." Again Cheng punctuated with a giggle, then continued, "It is a long ride home, and you have been waiting a long time for this moment."

"That" I admitted, "is an understatement. But are you sure, Cheng? It won't be an imposition?"

"Not at all," Cheng said smiling. "It is why we met tonight."

His brown eyes looked into my green ones, once more drawing me in, giving me the feeling that there was nothing more important in his world than what I was about to say.

And so, I went back for Cheng to that hot summer in Atlanta, Georgia of July 1972. To, as Cheng had requested, "The beginning."

The words came haltingly at first, but then I began describing everything effortlessly, as if I were there again.

CHAPTER SEVEN: BRANDT, PART I

"He who sits restraining his organs of action, while in his mind brooding over the objects of the senses with a deluded mind, is said to be a hypocrite."

--Janeshwar Gita

"It's such a waste of time, this not being a slut."

--Kim Bassinger

When I started to write this part I believed it was about Brandt. To think about him, to help me to understand what he did, and why. And to some extent it did just that. But now I realize that this wasn't about Brandt, it was about me; that the person I really needed to understand was myself.

I'm still astonished that I did what I did back then. I don't believe I could today. But things were different then. As Cheng was to teach us, there are no mistakes, only decisions; any "consequences" are learning experiences. Or as Maya Angelou would say years later, "Ya'do what ya' know. When ya' know better, ya' do better." In any case, as Cheng would teach, we are responsible for our actions.

* * *

July 21, 1972

At about one PM my plane landed in sweltering Atlanta. In slow-motion Southern time a taxi finally got me to the hotel. Once I'd checked in and the bellhop had deposited my two heavy suitcases on the floor of my room, I realized that if I unpacked just then I'd be late. (I always took too much with me). I left the suitcases just where they were and hurried to join the others at the meeting.

Gradually the national autism organization, For Our Children, Inc. (FOCI) board assembled. This, our first two-day annual national convention, was to begin the next morning. Attendees were expected from throughout the country as well as from several foreign countries.

As we reviewed final plans for our virgin conference, our collective energies were high and our nervousness palpable. Wilson, our president, a native of Georgia and father of an autistic boy, was seated at the head of the table. I, first vice-president, was to his left, then clockwise around the table sat second vice-president Mike McCue, third vice-president Eydie Larson, an RN and mother of an autistic girl; slightly older than the rest of us, she was the self-assumed den mother. Mark Sloan, an attorney from California and father of an autistic boy, was our treasurer and legal advisor. Then there was Sally Miller, our secretary from South Carolina who didn't have an autistic child, just liked to help the needy. Finally sat our board members at large, Steve, Jim, Harry and Rosalie. The latter two, college professors, were a married couple.

We finalized scheduling. I was to introduce our Saturday evening keynote speaker Dr. Bill Roll, the "vitamin psychiatrist" from New York. That seemed appropriate, since once I'd started taking Willie to him and began then referring other parents to him, within six months Dr. Roll had moved out of his cubbyhole office to a plush Park Avenue address. I smiled remembering Richard's quip at the time, "I don't know if the vitamins are doing anything for the kids, but Dr. Roll is THRIVING!"

We assigned the second primary speaking spot, 2:00 PM Saturday, to a medical doctor from the West Coast named Dr. Mancino. Although none of us had met him, we had invited him on the strength of a New York Times article I'd spotted with a long headline, "West Coast MD says the severe childhood disorder called autism is not caused by intrapsychic conflict or improper familial handling of the child, rather, by biological abnormalities. Dr. Mancino hopes his studies will uncover clues to causation."

That one article had been reason enough. After reading that I'd eagerly told the board about, "the Italian doctor" who defended mothers, and subsequently Wilson had extended the invitation. Dr. Mancino was the first expert we'd heard of, ever, to publicly refute that autism was caused by improper parental treatment, especially by the mothers. Additionally, he was engaged in research studies to uncover biochemical causation. Dr. Mancino's extensive background and current involvements had led me to conclude that he must be a rather old albeit still vital man.

The speaker scheduled to close the conference Sunday morning was a professor named Dr. Julian from Syracuse University; he had some unique ideas for educating autistic youngsters. The conference would open with a panel discussion composed of some of us board members, followed by informal discussion among attendees and us. This, a first, was a rare chance for parents of autistic children to schmooze on a grand scale.

Saturday morning the conference opened beautifully with our panel. At noon all of us board members except Wilson met for lunch at one large table reserved for us in the dining room. Wilson had left for the airport to meet Doctors Julian and Mancino's planes, with scheduled arrival times - conveniently enough - fifteen minutes apart.

We animatedly chatted about the morning's events. For most of us this was the only chance we had to share with others who were undergoing similar experiences and leading similar lives. Nowhere else could I talk about and receive empathetic recognition over Willie's spinning peccadillo's and Richard's and my difficulties in keeping baby sitters. Although at times we board members had our differences, some heated, now the pooled energy of this new exciting undertaking had made us feel very close, like family; we were high and happy.

I had put on a white suit, which I could never wear to work due to the New York dirt, but for a business event would be quite perfect. I'd begun to wear white more often ever since one day in the studio when Jayson, after seeing me in a white dress, a mistake in New York City, practically speaking, had rhapsodized, "Dahrling, you in white, with your dark coloring and green eyes, will lay to rest anyone's notion that angels must be blonde!" In deference to the heat I had French braided my hair and plaited it to the back of my head with white mother of pearl combs. It was so hot, in fact, that the air conditioner was as if non-existent. Finally I put on my white pearl necklace and earrings set, along with a gold heart on a chain which had been a gift from Richard a few years back.

Richard. Handling the necklace, I thought of him. Our marriage of late was on shaky ground. I realized that he was probably worried about business - which at best *was* a guess; he never told me what was bothering him. The only thing that I definitely knew was that for the past month he had been nervous, worried and disapproving of everything that I did, especially in regard to Willie and me. He made it seem like Willie's behavior and condition were entirely my fault. As if I'd somehow been tainted for having the child. There were enough people on the outside thinking that. I hardly needed one in my home. Not that any of that was verbalized, but by Richard's actions and remarks it was how I perceived him to feel. He either criticized or clamed up.

It all hit the fan the night before I was to go to Atlanta…

I had arrived home from work after a hard, hot, New York City day, given the children dinner with Esmerelda's help, read a story to Willie and two to Brenna (because *she* asked. With Willie you didn't even know if *he* wanted *one*). Then I sang to Willie for half an hour which finally coaxed him to sleep, thank goodness. I was in our bedroom peeling off my heels and pantyhose, literally stuck to me with perspiration, when Richard walked in with his current usual sour unhappy puss. One of the things I'd fallen in love with had been Richard's great sense of humor. Had I seen it lately? Don't make me laugh! (I only wished he would!)

Richard walked directly over to the telephone, lifted it from the receiver and holding it by the cord, allowing the cord to unravel down, exclaimed, "Damn it, Valentine, do you have to twist the cord? I have to untangle this every time I want to use the phone." I couldn't argue that I didn't, since at the studio Stu continued to accuse me of the same thing. I didn't answer Richard; I just stood silently, twisting my hair this time, while he made a business call. After the call Richard had a new complaint. "You're rarely home anymore. Why?"

"What do you mean, why?"

Richard repeated it again slowly as if talking to a mentally deficient person. "Why aren't you home anymore?"

"I'm playing Mah Jong." How had that sarcastic woman entered our bedroom? "Come on, Rick, what kind of question is that? When I'm not home I'm working, same as you."

"Cavorting all over, like to Atlanta, is working?"

"Certainly FOCI's work. Surely you know that."

"Of *course* I know. Luxury accommodations, fine food, a chance to gab your heads off away from all your responsibilities. It's hard work but somebody's got to do it, right?"

"If you think that, then you haven't been paying attention to any of the things I've been doing all year, not the least of which has been to work my head off for FOCI. The conference is just the culmination. Why is Atlanta different than any of *your* business trips?"

"My business travel's for money, Valen. How much money will you make in Atlanta?"

"For goodness sake, Richard, is money the only thing that's important to you? If a mugger accosted you saying 'Your money or your life,' would you answer, 'I'm thinking about it?'"

"Money is the most important thing - when you haven't enough of it," Richard answered, "which is definitely the position we are in right now."

"I see. Then you believe that the welfare of Willie and the others should be put on hold until we have – I quote - enough money?"

"No, but...I don't see FOCI or anything else you're doing helping Willie."

"You don't see him improving? Everybody else says…"

"Everybody else doesn't live here, Valen," Richard interrupted "Everybody else isn't paying for the tutors and the vitamin doctors and the God knows who else's who come in here ostensibly on Willie's behalf. If I'd installed a turnstile at the front door last year, from that alone we'd be millionaires. Everybody else is sleeping in their beds all night while we're up every night that Willie gets the midnight urge to jump and roam around until 5 in the morning. Please, hear me, V. I wouldn't mind the hard earned money spent and the hard work, if it showed. With it all, Valen, you still have an abnormal child."

"*I* have?" I asked, "*I* have? You're Willie's father."

"A father without a son."

I heard my voice as a whisper when I answered. "You do have a son, Richard."

"Valen, Willie doesn't *know* I'm his father. He doesn't even know whether I'm here or I'm not…"

"That's *not* true, Rick. He knows more than you think. Just because he can't express things doesn't mean he doesn't know."

"You believe what you want to believe. I'm a realist."

"So am I! The reality is, you made a commitment to this marriage."

"I committed to you. Not to this." Richard turned his back.

I felt my breath leave my body as I broke into tears.

Richard turned to face me again. In a softer voice, looking like he wanted to apologize but had forgotten how to reach out, he replied, "I just -- feel you shouldn't…be away right now."

I looked into Richard's eyes. He appeared so lost. While ordinarily I would have felt love and pity for whatever pain he was experiencing, right then I could feel nothing, except a giant abyss between us. "I'm sorry you feel that way," I told him, "but I have to go to Atlanta. My plane leaves early in the morning."

In the morning Richard left for work without kissing me goodbye or offering to drive me to the airport, so I called a taxi.

When I boarded the plane I felt miles apart from him, physically, emotionally and spiritually. Totally alone in the world with Willie.

* * *

Something was happening here at our dining room table. Rosalie was talking to Harry while Harry was coming on to me.

I didn't have to be psychic to pick up Rosalie's resentment of me just then. Her expression was enough indication. I turned to her, smiled and asked, "What were you saying?" It was far from the first time that this had happened to me. Each time, just as now, I had wondered, "Why did men do this in front of their wives?"

With a grateful look, Rosalie resumed. "Dr. You-know-who," she said, "still insists mothers cause autism? We should have invited him here - the bastard - and put him in front of a firing squad of us mothers!"

I was wholeheartedly agreeing with Rosalie when I happened to look toward the doorway just as Wilson walked through it followed by two men, one about 70 years old; Dr. Mancino, of course. The much younger man with them would be Dr. Julian.

The trio made their way to our table. Wilson, jovial as usual, boomed, "Well, here they are, our illustrious board. At least we're not notorious -- not YET!" He punctuated that with raising his arm to the air and laughing heartily. He directed his next remark to us.

"Everybody, this is Dr. Julian," he said while at the same time gesturing to the older man. "And this," he continued, putting his hand on the younger man's shoulder, "Is Dr. Mancino." Wilson then went around the table introducing each of us to the two guest speakers.

The introductions completed, Dr. Julian immediately pulled up a chair, sat down and loquaciously engaged the majority of the Board in his theories about special education. Suddenly I felt a presence standing beside me, looked up and saw that it was Dr. Mancino. I hadn't realized that he had been making his way around the table toward me during Dr. Julian's sitting oration. I was still in process of digesting my surprise at his age.

I looked Dr. Mancino over - a look up, down, up again kind of thing. I guessed he was in his late thirties to early forties, and somewhat over six feet tall. As close as I could determine his build in his business suit, he had broad shoulders tapering to a slim waist, and strong muscular arms and legs. Dr. Mancino had straight medium brown hair, professorially long in back and with sideburns. His hazel eyes, as they peered through horn-rimmed glasses, had a very alert intelligent expression. His glasses rested on a slightly down-turned nose, giving him an appealingly masculine appearance.

"Miss Jordan?" he said (only he pronounced it "Jaaa-don," without the r) in a voice that was incredibly deep, masculine and sensual, and with a Boston accent that made him sound somewhat like President John Kennedy in a lower pitch. A Boston accent with laid-back California style; that was a combination! I decided that Dr. Mancino was, while not classically handsome like Richard, a very attractive package. You knew you were with a man.

"*Mrs.* Jordan," I corrected him.

As if he hadn't heard that, he continued in a purr, "Well, hi there." (he said there like "thay-aa"). So, you're from New York?" (New "Yaak," he said)

Dr. Mancino's conversation and manner were very polite and proper. It was the way that he was looking at me. That wasn't improper either. His eyes weren't roving over my body in the overtly sexual way of some of the New York sleaze. Although the steadiness of his stare was unsettling, it was also quietly compelling. I can best describe his look as – it sounds crazy –total appreciation of and delight with me. He was enthralled with me. Men said they wanted me, women became jealous until they knew me and *then* they liked me. But it had been a long while since anyone had looked at me with such unconditional acceptance. If anyone ever had.

Meanwhile, I was having my own reactions to Dr. Mancino. I was feeling very connected to him. Like two people sharing memories of the distant strains of a fiddle - but with Dr. Mancino I sensed it would be more like the Philharmonic. It sounds fairy-tale banal, but the feelings of closeness and intimacy that I experienced with him immediately astounded me. I had never felt their like before. Despite what one might suppose, that fact did not make me feel comfortable with him; on the contrary, his presence made me nervous, somehow.

Feeling the need to disguise my unrest, I took out a pack of cigarettes, extracted one, tapped it on my wrist, put it to my lips and clicked my silver lighter three times; it wouldn't even generate a spark.

"Must need a new flint," I muttered awkwardly.

Dr. Mancino began a series of staccato pats to his jacket and pants pockets, looking so much like a huge monkey scratching itself that I'm sure I would have laughed had I not felt so tense.

"I thought I had matches in heeaa; I'm sorry," he told me.

"Don't bother. I'm sure I have some." I was feeling unsettled enough to act arrogant. Fishing around the bottom of my pocketbook and finally locating a book of matches which I held up triumphantly, I announced (rather inanely, I later thought), "See. I believe in women's lib; I'm able to light my own cigarette."

"You have the curse of the beautiful woman," Dr. Mancino said. Following that he took the book of matches from me and proceeded to light my cigarette for me. In so doing his hand lightly touched mine. I saw that he had large hands. I wanted them to stay on mine. Then, handing the matches back to me he said, "You don't need it."

Due to the intensity between us I had to look away to compose myself. When I looked back again Dr. Mancino was gone. Leaving me to wonder what it was he'd meant I didn't need; Cigarettes? Women's lib? Him?

Of all the insane things, I felt a void, a sense of loss. I missed him. I began to visually search the dining room for sight of him.

As if from miles away I heard Rosalie, at my table, saying to Dr. Julian, "Dr. What's-His-Name says that maybe a break in the mother-child bond occurs as early as at the breast."

"Breast?" I thought. I wondered how Dr. Mancino's hands would feel on my breast. "Snap out of it!" I scolded myself. "You want none of this. This- this total stranger- which is all that he is to you - could be The Boston Strangler! Even if he's a reincarnation of Albert Schweitzer, the point stands. You are married! You love Richard!" But, my heart wouldn't believe me. Love at first sight, it was.

The next time that I saw Dr. Mancino was at two that afternoon, when he gave his speech in the lecture hall. As I sat in the third row listening to and watching him, part of me began wishing that I wasn't experiencing him here this way. If I'd found him attractive before, seeing him in front of the audience intensified that. He was electric, brilliantly charismatic and so in command that when he finished, he received a standing ovation. During the question and answer period he was extremely kind and caring, empathizing with our plight, offering more than he had to. Dr.

Mancino was somewhat like the man who painted for tourists on the banks of the Seine. You knew that in part he was showing off but were charmed just the same. Suddenly questions came to me to ask him, so I raised my hand. When he called on me and I asked the first question, he walked a little closer to the edge of the stage and looked at me longer and answered more personally than he had with the others. Concerned lest the others sense the intimacy, I said, "Thank you," formally, thus cutting off the exchange. Standing up there Dr. Mancino actually shined and I mean that literally; when I looked at him, standing behind the lectern, I actually saw a shining silvery aura around him. By the time his presentation had ended I thought the board and members would hand him the entire organization on a gold platter.

The air conditioning was doing what it did in the late afternoon July Georgia heat; nothing. Sticky from perspiration on my chest and neck, I decided this was a good time to go shower and dress for dinner.

I turned the shower to cool, stayed under the near chilly water for at least five minutes, then washed, stepped out and patted myself dry with a fluffy towel. I felt my skin still hot. Had my body temperature more to do with my inner climate than the outer one? I put on a white silk dress with a romantic side to it, which still was quite perfect for a business event. It was subtly buttoned from collar to hem, yet the exquisite fabric was lush as white liqueur. It had seed pearls on the neck, and a flowing ankle length skirt. The dress material had hearts embroidered into it. I wore sheer white stockings, white silk pumps and my gold heart on a chain. I'd washed and blow dried my hair and brushed it straight and loose. I pinned three filmy white heart ornaments to the back of my hair.

I was going to a lot of trouble because of the honor I'd been given of introducing Dr. Roll that evening. Life's accolades rarely go to the understudy, and tonight I unabashedly was playing the star in an outfit that was anything but incognito, giving my own dramatic side free rein. Dr. Mancino had nothing to do with it. That's what I told myself. In fact he probably wouldn't even be there. I'd overheard Dr. Julian saying he was sorry but he had to leave directly after his talk because his work called him. Busy guests often did that. Dr. Mancino had no doubt left as well.

When I stepped out of the elevator the first person that I saw standing in front of it in the lobby was Dr. Roll. He looked at me, said, "Oh, MY!" and appeared flustered. I took that to mean I looked nice. I muttered "see you later" and hurried to the dining-room/lecture hall.

At the dais I took my place as the other board members began to take theirs. I hadn't realized how distracting the sexual tension with Dr. Mancino had been until now that he was gone. I smiled, exhaled deeply and... felt eyes upon me. I turned my head and looked two chairs away from mine to my left. Dr. Roll was seated there, staring at me. When he saw me notice, he quickly turned away. A few seconds later I felt the eyes again. I looked in Dr. Roll's direction, but this time he was engaged in conversation with Mark Sloan. I looked to my left past Dr. Roll down the long narrow table directly to the last seat at the end; Dr. Mancino was seated there, staring at me with a closed-mouth smile. I managed to smile back faintly, then again drew in my breath, quickly looked away and forced myself to pay attention as Wilson welcomed everyone to the evening session. Soon he'd be inviting me up to the microphone to introduce Dr. Roll.

Dr. Roll. It was a miracle to begin with that the board had invited him here. I well remembered the board meeting not that long ago where my admission to the others that I was trying mega-vitamins for Willie had brought warnings of, "Valentine, people already think parents of autistic children are crackers. You can't represent FOCI and go public with fringe things like vitamin therapy." If they thought vitamins were far out, what would they say if they found out about my interest in the mystical? I'd make damned certain that they didn't.

Throughout my introduction to Dr. Roll I felt Dr. Mancino's gaze upon me. I have to admit knowing that he was interested inspired me to be very good in inspiring the assemblage –with a there- is- hope kind of message. They loved it. I was also beginning to feel thankful to Dr. Roll for his silent confirmation near the elevator that I looked good that night.

During dinner Dr. Mancino openly flirted with me with his eyes and smile. Let me clarify, I think men and women flirting in work situations is natural. It went on at the studio all the time. I think as long as you know the difference between flirtation and seduction, flirting's a fine pleasurable reminder that we enjoy being attractive sexual beings. Me Tarzan, You Jane. One could then take that home and have great sex with one's partner.

However, this from Dr. Mancino, like at our first meeting in the dining room, was more potent than that. It was for this reason that I decided that *whatever* it was best be nipped in the bud.

I did not nip particularly maturely or graciously. Rather, as soon as dinner ended I stood up abruptly and rushed out without a glance in Dr. Mancino's direction, dashed to the elevator, and hurried to Wilson and his wife Olivia's suite, where a good-bye party exclusively for us board members was scheduled.

I knocked on the door. Finally Olivia opened it wearing a robe and shower cap. "Oh, I'm so sorry...I'm early...I'll come back later," I stammered, embarrassed.

"You all will do no such thing, darlin," Olivia answered. "Y'all come right in now and sit down." She showed me to a chair near an already set-up bar. It was a bedroom, not a suite, representative of FOCI's austerity budget.

"Just help yourself, honay. I'll be out in a jiffy." Olivia disappeared into the bathroom. In a few minutes she came out again, gathered up a man's pair of pants, shirt, some women's clothes, smiled at me and disappeared again into the bathroom.

"Oh my God," I thought, "because of me they're getting dressed in their bathroom. Due to Dr. Mancino, what a rude idiot I'm being."

In a while Wilson emerged, came over and hugged me warmly, then sat down on the bed and proceeded to put on his shoes. A minute after that Olivia came out of the bathroom and did the same.

"Here, honay, come sit on the bed; it's the most comfortable seat in the house," Wilson offered. I went and sat down on the bed beside them. Wilson propped a pillow on the headboard.

"Here, be comfortable" he invited. I moved over and positioned my back upon the pillow while remaining seated. It *was* comfortable. I thought, "These two give new meaning to the term Southern Hospitality!"

After awhile the others attendees began to drift in, some with their spouses, some on their own. Olivia and Wilson stood at the door greeting each one warmly.

I remained seated on the bed. Soon all the party sounds could be heard. Ice clinking in glasses, liquid being poured, bantering, jokes and chatter, congratulations to one another on a successful conference, and discussions about next year's and maybe getting a celebrity then to publicize it.

"Ah vote we get an actuh," Olivia drawled more than ever due to excitement. "How 'bout Paul Newman, an' ah be sent ta greet heem. An ah furtha vote Valentine not be permitted anywhae neah heem -- or he won't even see *me*!"

Mark and Harry had pulled chairs up beside me. I was seated yoga style with my legs folded. Harry put his hand casually on my ankle. Everybody was joking and laughing, the rest after the storm.

I was feeling strong, triumphant and relaxed. I had walked away from Dr. Mancino, who was on a plane back to L.A. by now, thank God!

I felt a stir in the room. I looked toward the doorway and saw Dr. Mancino standing there. I saw Wilson get up and walk toward him, then heard him say, "We're honored. Come IN, Doctor!"

How had Dr. Mancino known about this party? It hadn't been in the program. My heart took a leap. Indeed, I personified ambivalence at that moment. I had never in my life felt so happy to see a person I'd hoped never to see again.

I gazed at Dr. Mancino, mesmerized. He had a lion walk, this man, proud, graceful, unhurried, and in command. And there was that shiny silvery aura around him. I wasn't the only one who saw, or at least sensed it, as certainly every woman in the room had come to life at his entrance. They now began to congregate around him, even little Sally who ordinarily disliked all men.

I sat rooted on the bed, comparing Dr. Mancino's appeal with Richard's. Richard would walk into a room and just standing there attract woman with his handsomeness. With that, to his credit he was faithful to me. As much as one can be sure of anything about another person, I was of that. Dr. Mancino, on the other hand, magnetized women by his masculine charismatic take-command manner, empathy and deep-voiced brilliance, so evident through his talk; after that, they were his slaves. He was a horse of a different color all right, which sounds pretty racy and quite exciting. But had I thought at all, really, I might have realized that catching up with a race horse would be quite another thing.

Dr. Mancino lion-walked over to me. As he stood beside me, Mark and Harry got to their feet and ambled away, whereupon Dr. Mancino took Harry's chair. It was like a play with all the actors performing their parts perfectly. Incredulous, I wondered, "Is this the universe arranging for us two to be together?"

We all have conversations we'll remember forever. That which next ensued between Dr. Mancino and me was such a one.

"Hi, theeaa,"

"Hello. I thought you'd left already."

"I'd intended to. In fact, I had a plane resaavation back around five, and everyaathing."

"Oh?"

"I changed it for tomorrow. It was some trouble, but wotth it."

"I see." I didn't exactly. Where was he going with this?

"I wanted to see you again." Once more, this was said with total pleasure and appreciation, not innuendo.

"Well, look, then."

"I am."

"How did you know where to find me?"

"I asked at the desk wheaa the afta-confaance paaty for the board was being held. Conventions usually have those. When I came in heeaa and I saw that man Harry – I know him, he's from my home state – sitting heeaa with his hand on your leg, I wanted to knock it off."

My reaction was immediately indignant. "His hand was on my foot, not my leg. Besides, isn't that presumptuous of you, considering that you don't even know me?"

"That isn't true," Dr. Mancino answered.

"Dr, I *know* the difference between my foot and my leg."

"I didn't mean *that* isn't true. I mean the paat about my not *knowing* you isn't true. We've known each othaa 100 yeaas."

In retrospect I was to consider that quite a statement from a man who would later tell me, "I don't believe in past lives or any of that other crap!"

Suddenly, in that crowded room, Dr. Mancino and I were a couple.

The party continued. One by one the men stood up and told jokes. Dr. Mancino, definitely one of them although with me, told his share with relish, then each time returned to my side. Miraculously, each time he did that everyone else left us alone.

Slowly, people were saying, "Good Night" and departing. Finally, with the exception of our hosts, only Dr. Mancino and I remained.

I looked at my watch; it was midnight. I stood up and said, "Well, we'd better be going too." Flustered, I corrected myself, "I meant to say… *I'll* be going."

It was too late. Dr. Mancino was by my side as together we left the room and entered the hallway.

I began to walk down the corridor with him. Short of running as if from a rapist, what else was I to do? Finally, I turned to face him and striving for my most formal manner, said, "Dr. Mancino, I'm not certain if you know that I'm the FOCI research coordinator. I hope you'll send me your research reports. Hopefully we'll get studies like yours funded, to help your important work to continue."

"I certainly will get on top of it, soon as I get back to the hospital." Then added, "I've observed youaa very giving."

"Thank you," I answered with great dignity, extending my hand. "Our L.I. FOCI P.O. Box address is on the conference brochure. I'll look forward to receiving your report. Such a pleasure to meet you, Dr. Mancino. Oh, by the way, your talk was excellent. Good night." I took a step away, but Dr. Mancino's next words stopped me.

"Oh, you don't want me to go."

"No. I don't." Although I perceived my voice as inaudible, Dr. Mancino had obviously heard me. He put his arm around my shoulder. Then, my arm, which I'd extended to shake his hand, found its way around his waist.

Grief is something we all hear about today, and it's quite commonly understood that without doubt the most painful grief is the grief of a parent over the loss of a child. That's hard-core grief. What may come as a surprise is that I was in grief over the death of *my* child – the death of my expectations. I would not measure kinds of grief but I'd say my grief then was as painful as over a physical death; I could not imagine feeling greater pain over a child whatever the circumstances. In a way it had been even worse than the physical death of one's child. There had been no funeral, no public or private acknowledgement of my mourning, little expressed empathy for what I was enduring. I realized people feared that if they said something it would be something stupid, which is true at funerals too but there at least people say the stupid things anyway.

In my situation it was what people didn't say that spoke loudest. Take relatives who hadn't seen me in awhile. "And…how's your pretty little daughter doing?" No mention of Willie. They acted as if he were dead. When people said things like that, I had started to answer, "Fine, and my son Willie's doing well too." They'd look embarrassed, but let them learn! Still, it hurt, every time.

Despite it all, I'd had to continue being a wife, mother, employee and everything that went with each, and of course a mother, and *then* some. The only people who had real empathy were my FOCI colleagues, yet often they were too much in their own pain to support me in mine. Little wonder that in order to carry on, my feelings had become almost armor-encased. While that helped numb the pain, it was no way to live; not feeling, with nothing mattering.

The thing here was, something about Dr. Mancino was making me feel again. It was terribly frightening and extremely exhilarating all at once.

"Wheaa is your room?" he asked.

How could I walk away from feeling again, and – important question at that moment- *why* should I? Me in my crap-filled life. When had Richard last eased my way? When had *he* last been my friend? When had *he* last given me reason to feel about *him*?

"My room's at the end of the hall."

At my door, as I pulled my keys from my purse my hand was shaking so that when I tried to fit the key into the lock I actually couldn't. Helplessly, I handed the key to Dr. Mancino, who unlocked my door. I faced him then.

"Dr. Mancino. I'm married. I told you, *Mrs.* Jordan, remember? I've never done anything like this before. I'm... very nervous."

He took my hand in his. His hand was so big that inside his, my own hand felt like that of a child.

"Don't be sixteen yeas old," he said, but kindly. "I just want us to talk."

Interesting that he'd used that analogy. An awkward teenager was exactly what I felt like.

Inside, the bedside lamp lit the room dimly. I sat down upon the bed – thinking how since I'd met Dr. Mancino I was becoming expert at bed sitting - and he took a chair which was about twelve feet away from me. "*Sitting* on the bed is good," I thought.

"Do you always weaaa white?" he asked.

"No, but I wear it often." I was surprised and pleased that he'd noticed. At that point I was finding Dr. Mancino's accent and deep voice very appealing. As far as I was concerned he could keep talking all night long.

"You look like an angel in it." Again, the angel thing? Hardly, if tonight was any indication.

"Tell me something about youaaself?" he asked.

"Well – I work in Manhattan. Advertising. I'm a photographer's agent."

"I thought you weaa a model or actress."

"I was, before. Model."

"You must look wondaful on camera. Did you like modeling?"

"Not much," I smiled, "but I liked the money."

"I come from the East myself. Boston," he continued.

"Get out of heaaa! I nevaa would have guessed."

He laughed. "Do I really sound like that?"

"No. *Your* accent's heavier. Why did you leave Boston?"

"To get away from my mothaa." He said it straight-out. Then his eyes twinkled. "What's the diffaaence between a Rottweiler and a Jewish mothaa?" he asked.

I hadn't expected Jewish jokes from an Italian man. In a way I resented it. I shrugged as in, "I don't know."

"Eventually the Rottweiler lets go," Brandt said. He was so amused, and it *was* funny enough, that I had to laugh too.

"Well, how is it woaaking in New Yoaak City?" Brandt then asked.

"It's like working everyday amidst millions of people who look like they belong in a mental institution. You could set up a booth in any corner, like Lucy in that cartoon, with the sign, 'Psychotherapy, 5 Cents.'"

"So if the L.A practice fails I have options. Only I thought in NYC I could get more like 10 cents." Dr. Mancino grinned boyishly. I wished he wouldn't do that. It was too disarming. "And you love it? Wooking in Manhattan?" he asked.

"Much of the time."

"Tell me about youaa children?"

"Brenna's four and one half and Willie, the autistic one, he's three and a half."

"I'm certain it has been very haad?" he said. The sympathy in his voice reached inside me and caressed my heart.

"Yes, it has. The guilt made it worse. You know, that thing that mothers caused autism."

"No possible basis to that," Dr. Mancino said very emphatically and professionally. "Abused kids have serious problems, true, but they communicate. They relate. Nobody has evaa made a kid autistic. It's a physical problem."

"You seem sure of that."

"Definitely. No question. That Dr. You- Know -Who who said othaarwise is an asshole."

Although in my heart I'd known all along that was true about autism, that confirmation from Dr. Mancino was reassuring.

"How old aaa you?" he asked.

"Twenty-nine."

"I caan't believe it! You look twenty-five."

They said such things about age all the time in my business. It always struck me as so ludicrous and annoying that now, hearing it from Dr. Mancino too, I felt inspired to do something with it.

"Can you please help me understand how that works?" I asked, with a very serious face. "I know how they can tell the age of a *tree*. They count the rings around the trunk. But can you explain how you can tell the age of a *person* by looking?"

I picked up a pencil and pad from the night table beside the bed, got up and handed it to Dr. Mancino. I then returned to the bed and again sat down upon it. "Here, could you please draw me what a 25 year old woman and a 29 year old look like so I can see the difference?"

Dr. Mancino first looked very confused. Then, he somewhat chuckled. "I guess I see what you mean. It does sound silly."

I giggled. "You were thinking, 'maybe this woman should be my first NYC patient,' weren't you?"

"Something like that." The disarming grin again. "You do look very young, though."

"That comes from the easy life I've had. No aggravations."

Dr. Mancino's laughter then, indicating his understanding of my irony stemming from his knowledge of autism, was an additional immediate bond.

I wanted to know all about him. "Are you married?"

Dr. Mancino answered, "I'm divossed. I was married to an obstetrician."

"What went wrong?"

"Oh, she competed with me professionally, it just wasn't good."

"Do you have children?"

"Five, four gils and a boy. The fist two are teens and they live with Joan, theea mothaa, in Boston. The other two gils and a boy all under nine yeaas of age, live with their mothaa too."

"*She* must be busy."

"The youngaa three are heaaa with me. This was my week to have them and they wanted to ride on a 747, so..."

"Where are they tonight?"

"With my Uncle Jack. He has a home heeaa in Atlanta. We're staying with him during the confeaance. He's a psychiatrist."

"Like you?"

"Yes, I am a psychoanalyst like him. And child psychiatrist."

"You mean, you're also an adult psychiatrist?"

"Well, lets hope so. I am foaty yeaas old!"

"I can't believe it. You look 39."

"I guess I deserved that." He smiled.

I thought, "He did say at the door that he only wanted to talk. Was that true? When it came to me, was his research proposal the only thing he intended to get on top of? If so, I had mixed feelings about that too. I could not possibly put into words all the feelings that this man elicited in me just by his presence. My pain over Willie. My deep loneliness of late with Richard. Dr. Mancino being deeply involved with a cause dear to me. It was good to feel that close to a man again. And, let me face it, he - with his keys to the mystery of autism – was the white knight who had suddenly appeared by my side, who could save me. Me, who was ready to be saved. Everything about him - his kindness, his empathy and caring about my situation with Willie, the felt intimacy, the chemistry between us - was too much for me. It undammed something in me.

"With Willie- sometimes it's been so hard, and painful—I've wondered... if I can do this anymore? At times...I've even...wished...he would... die." I had never admitted that to myself before much less to another person. Dr. Mancino's being had elicited it from me. The floodgates opened. I felt the tears flood my eyes and overflow onto my cheeks. Appalled at myself, I fumbled in my pocketbook for a tissue. But Dr. Mancino was right beside me handing me his handkerchief, after which he returned to his chair and sat patiently, allowing me to get myself together.

I had never been an aggressor with men, so I surprised myself then by patting a place beside me on the bed, and saying, "I want you here."

He got up, said, "I was just thinking the same thing," and came and sat beside me.

I surprised myself a second time by leaning my face toward his and lightly brushing his lips with mine. I heard him draw in his breath quickly, then whisper, "You'aa so beautiful. I caan't believe this is happening."

Whatever he thought would be happening, didn't. What we mostly did was what the kids used to call, "making out." And we talked, about seemingly everything. Dr. Mancino was as open and communicative as Richard, lately, was remote and closed. I savored each word as I drank it in, not having realized how thirsty I'd been for intimate conversation with a partner.

It's strange. You tell yourself you're faithful to a primary partner because you're not having sex with anyone else, but what I was getting from Brandt was a kind of intimacy that was even more potent than sex. Due to this, in my heart I was feeling as unfaithful to Richard as if Brandt and I had had intercourse, yet I'd felt as long as we didn't I wasn't really being unfaithful. So despite the tremendous animal magnetism and sexual tension between us, I wouldn't go further nor did Dr. Mancino, in any way, push me to.

Finally, Dr. Mancino looked at his watch and said, "Do you know we've been making love for five houraas!" Interesting that he used that term rather than saying, "We've been together for five hours" or "been here." Was he feeling the intimacy as much as I was?

I looked at my watch. It was nearly five am. Then I asked an unbelievable question, all considered.

"Dr. Mancino, what's your first name?"

He answered, "Brandt. Brandt R. Mancino."

"What's the R for?"

"My middle name, Richard. Richard was supposed to be my first name but at the last minute my mother changed that to Brandt. God knows why."

"That's interesting." He had no idea *how* interesting.

Brandt asked, "And what do people call you, Valentine?"

"Everything."

"So, I have my choice. Well, I'm not too original; I'll call you Valentine." Looking at his watch, then pulling himself bolt-upright Brandt exclaimed, "Oh, my God, my plane leaves at 9:07. I've got to call my uncle and, forgive me, I'm going to tell a small lie."

He dialed a number, waited briefly, then said, "Hi, theea Jack. Yea, I'm fine. Boaaing meeting so had a little too much to drink. Yes, spent the last five houaas sleepin' it off. You get the kids dressed, all right? Be theea soon, thanks, 'bye." He put the phone back on the receiver.

"Thanks a lot," I was laughing "You surely hid your boredom well."

"I love to see you laugh. You are so gorgeous. You enjoy being a woman."

"Brandt," I thought to ask, "Did you have so many children because it's your ethnic tradition?"

"What ethnic tradition?"

"I mean because you're Italian."

"Who's Italian? I'm Jewish. My mothaa still keeps a koshaa home."

"Mancino? Jewish?" I asked. I found myself feeling pleased, while at the same time amused at that reaction of mine. Did I feel that Brandt being Jewish instead of Italian exonerated me?

"What did you change your name from?" I asked.

"I didn't. Maybe my foaa faathers subtracted and rearranged a few syllables. Maybe once it was Manichevitz or something."

"Brandt Mancino." I repeated. "Nice." I remembered once asking Richard something similar about *his* non-Jewish sounding last name, and his reply of, " Jordan's always been my name but maybe my forefathers changed it from Jampolsky, or something." The similarities were becoming, ah... interesting.

"Brandt *Richard* Mancino," Brandt said. "I'll leave now," he kissed me lightly, "And then maybe you'll catch some sleep."

"Maybe," I agreed, doubting it.

I was sitting up in bed as Brandt, shiny silvery aura and all, walked out the door. I never did get to unpack my suitcases.

That evening my plane took off in a hailstorm. In the adjoining seat was a woman named Ruth, an operating room RN from New York City whom I'd met briefly at the conference. Her first words to me out of the blue were, "God! I wonder if Dr. Mancino's married. He is really something!"

I replied, somewhat defensively and surprised by it, "He isn't that handsome, actually."

"Doesn't matter," Ruth declared. "He's so masculine!" She opened her book and became instantly elsewhere. At that we flew directly into the fringes of a hail storm out of Texas. For the rest of the flight our plane bounced around like a sliver of wood in the wind. I was convinced God was punishing me.

"Do you think we'll make it?" I blurted out anxiously at the next bout of terrible turbulence.

Ruth moved her eyes from her book and turned them patronizingly upon me. "We'll just have to see, won't we," she answered, then returned to her book. Blase! It could have been her tenth operation of the day.

I prayed silently. Oh, how I prayed. This marked the beginning of what would become my fear of flying. "God, I promise. If you will deliver us home safely, I'll never be with Brandt Mancino again – never! God…I promise…never..I promise."

I kept repeating it – until we landed safely.

* * *

As I said those last words I heard the screech of brakes and a cessation of movement. For a moment I thought it was three years ago and that I had just landed at Kennedy Airport on that plane from Atlanta. Only when Cheng spoke did I realize that the screech of brakes I'd just heard had been those of the train as it arrived at our station, Coldport. That it was 1975, not 1972, and that I was seated beside Cheng.

"That is something, Val–teen!" Cheng said. "Tomorrow night meet me at the L.I.R.R. information booth at 6:35. On the train you will tell me part two."

CHAPTER EIGHT: BRANDT, PART TWO

"The true man embodies life to the fullest and unattached leaves no trail."
--Chuang-Tsu

"God, she loved him so... she would have done anything for him except destroy her family and maybe him as well."
--Robert James Waller,
Bridges of Madison County

Miraculously – one of many recent small miracles – the following evening Cheng and I got the same train seats as we'd had the night before. Once comfortably nestled into our space, Cheng immediately brought me to the purpose of our meeting.

"So you landed safely after all," he reiterated. "Take it from there, please."

Smiling at Cheng's use of the idiom, I proceeded to indeed, "Take it from there."

"Truly, Cheng, I neither intended to talk with nor to see Brandt again. Once home, I convinced myself that I could chalk up the entire Atlanta scenario to loneliness in a strange city. That I could not possibly have felt all those emotions for a total stranger..."

"Except," Cheng interrupted, "He was NOT a total stranger."

After a puzzled moment, I understood. "That past-life stuff again, huh?"

"You got THAT right!" Cheng answered gleefully.

"I suppose you also won't tell me what Brandt and I were together, when, and why?" I told him.

"You got THAT right too." Cheng responded. "Just, it is old karmic ties. What an attraction! You both felt it."

I asked, "Brandt did, too?"

"And HOW, Blandt too!" Cheng answered with his giggle-chuckle.

I laughed at Cheng's mispronunciation of Brandt's name. Then, immediately fearing that I might have hurt his feelings, I lamely offered, "I'm sorry. I sometimes laugh when I'm nervous."

"I know that. No problem. Continue, please," Cheng urged, totally unperturbed.

"Well, then...weeks passed. Very busy ones. Made it easier for me to dismiss Brandt from my mind. I'd been out of town alone, an incident had occured, now it was over. Once home that's how I chose to think about it. I dug snuggly into my life and that was the end of it. It probably would have remained that way too, but then something happened to change everything."

"Destiny intervened," Cheng interjected, smiling.

"I believe you're right, Cheng, because I had no choice but to talk with Brandt again. It was totally outside of my control."

"Prarabdha karma" Cheng muttered.

"Excuse me?"

"No matter for now. About Blandt, tell me," Cheng encouraged. As if I needed encouragement! And so I did:

"About a month after Atlanta, Wilson, our FOCI national president called me. 'Honay,' Wilson drawled charmingly, 'Everyone has sent in his or her fundin' proposals 'cept one. Be a love an' call ta' give him a reminda, darlin'? I need not tell you whom he meant! Wilson then gave me 'Dr. Mancino's" office telephone number. I just couldn't believe I was being put in this position. Brandt's research into causation held such great promise that we needed it to be considered for funding. Coordinating such research proposals was one of my vice-presidential duties. Showing Wilson any reluctance to phone Brandt personally could lead to speculation that something beyond business had taken place between Brandt and me –especially since Wilson and Olivia had seen the two of us leave their hotel room together. Becoming the talk of the FOCI board was something that I didn't need! There was no way out of or around this.

So I devised an entire scenario. I'd call Brandt from home around 7 PM our time, which would be four PM West Coast time. Hopefully Brandt would still be at his office then, while Richard, who'd recently been having some rare shorter hours, as well as the children and animals, would likely be congregated in our den. From Brandt's end, I'd obviously come off as what indeed I was, a committed wife and mother. I'd deliver FOCI's message briefly, cordially and professionally, then get off the phone.

It sounded like a good plan, yet it took another week before I could bring myself to execute it.

When I finally did call Brandt, a secretary, not Brandt, answered. "Dr. Mancino is in a meeting," she said officiously. "He will probably be out around six." That would be nine our time. I gave her our home phone number and asked for "Dr. Mancino" to return my call when he got back to the office. Then I told Richard, in case he should answer the phone, "A doctor might be calling me here later; a FOCI thing."

Richard responded, "What else is new?" He'd resigned himself that FOCI phone calls had become a regular part of our life.

I thought, fine, I'd manage to be engaged in something else at around nine so Richard would pick up. Just hearing a husband's voice would be a strong message.

I'm sure I need not tell you that it didn't work out that way. At around 7:15 PM. Richard, who, among all people I know had long held the world record for a seemingly strong immune system, announced, "I think I'm coming down with the flu; God, everything hurts."

I thought, "Oh, fine; great timing!" Then, feeling really contrite for my self-centered thought, offered, "Oh, Rick, I'm sorry. Want some tea or cold medicine?"

"Nothing," Richard said, "I've just got to sleep it off. Honey, maybe I should sleep in the guest room tonight so I don't give whatever this is to you?" I could quarrel with his timing but not with his logic. We blew each other a goodnight kiss, and Richard went upstairs. Around eight, when I looked in on him in the bedroom down the long hallway from ours, he was sound asleep. The children went to bed and fell asleep soon afterwards, even Willie; I in fact almost prayed, "please, let tonight be one of Willie's Young Insomniac nights." But of course this night Willie fell asleep early and slept like an angel.

I read for awhile in the den, then said goodnight to Esmerelda and went upstairs, Jonah following me. He went and sniffed at the closed guest room door, came back into our bedroom and circled around the bed. Accustomed to sleeping on the floor on Richard's side, he was puzzled and uneasy. I rubbed his head, telling him everything was all right. Finally he settled down on the floor at my side of the bed and soon was asleep.

I showered, put on a nightgown, took Ernie's portfolio to the chaise and got comfortable on it. I began to thumb through Ernie's pictures, rearranging their order. When I do something I get fully involved in it, so the phone startled me when it rang slightly after nine PM.

"Well, Hi theeaa." There was no way of mistaking that Boston accented low sensual voice. Or my reaction to it. The moment I heard it I was like a candle formerly cool and decorative, which now, having been ignited by Brandt, was BURNING.

I managed a weak, "I... didn't... know.. if.. you'd.. remember me."

"NATURALLY, I do. How've you been?"

"I've been well. You?"

"I'm wondaaful... NOW," he said.

You might be thinking, as I did in retrospect, '*That's* the best he could do?' But I didn't think that, then. My reaction to Brandt then was totally visceral. So the candle began to melt. Like smoke, my plans for brief, cordial and professional blew out the window.

Brandt and I spoke for over an hour. Although our words may have been casual the undertones were anything but. It was as if no time at all had elapsed since Atlanta, and the same feelings prevailed.

Finally, feeling that I should explain how I was able to talk with him so long this way, I said, "My husband's not feeling too well. Sleeping in the guest room tonight."

"Oh. I'm sorry to heaaa that."

"His name is Richard." There was a pregnant pause. "Like your middle name. Some coincidence, don't you think?"

"Quite." Another pause.

"Well, I have to get up early tomorrow morning, so..." Truthfully, I could have stayed on the phone with Brandt all night and then some, but even my mention of Richard made me feel uneasy about this conversation.

"Well then, can I phone you next week?"

"It isn't a good idea for you to call me here at home."

"How about at the studio numbaa?"

"That isn't a good idea either."

Brandt, after another pause, said, "Well then, you've got my numbaa heeaa at the hospital, and I'll also give you my apaatment numbaa. Got a pencil?" I jotted down both numbers as he gave them to me. "I live alone," he continued. "If you want to, call me collect next week at eithaa numbaa."

"I'll... think... about it," I answered feebly.

"Yes." Brandt answered. "Only if you want to." Then he added, "Valentine?"

"Yes."

"I hope... you will... want to."

I greatly wanted to call Brandt. But for two weeks I fought with myself against it. Instead, I did everything I knew to bring Richard and myself closer together. He'd apparently only had a twenty-four hour virus, not flu; he was better the following day.

I'd think things were improving emotionally between us, then Richard would revert to being closed and uncommunicative, shutting me out. My contacts with Brandt made me realize how thirsty I was for closeness with a partner. That a very basic human need was not being fulfilled in me, had not been for quite a while. I was in an arid desert, dying of thirst.

Three weeks after Brandt's and my first phone conversation, I placed my initial collect call to him.

He sounded thrilled to hear from me. Although there was fire beneath our words, at the end of the conversation I told Brandt, "I can't be any more than a friend to you, but we'll be good friends. Is that all right?"

I don't think I even heard Brandt's answer, possibly because it was drowned out by my own inner voice sardonically screaming, "Yea, right!" So you see, inwardly I knew. I think we both knew.

It seems it should have been difficult for Brandt and me to connect every week, two people with such busy irregular schedules, and the three-hour time difference besides. Since I began working I'd even had difficulty connecting by phone with Richard, and that was without any time difference. In fact, from the start connecting with Brandt by phone wasn't all that difficult. As fate would have it, I guess you would say, Cheng, soon after my first call to Brandt I was required to work a number of late nights at the studio; since my calls to Brandt were collect, often I could phone him from work. Nine PM our time, six PM Pacific time he was still at the hospital.

At first we kept it light, verbally at least. The undercurrents were something else again. We'd share events of our week, his and mine. Brandt had eventually sent me his research proposal, so we talked about that; it excited me greatly - research into the causation of autism, the first of its genre I'd heard of. I'm the kind of woman who has to be turned on in the head first. Brandt's kind of work, intelligence and success did stimulate me tremendously. And Brandt talked about his children, and asked me about mine. I thought he must be a great father. His kind of interest in them, especially Willie, and in everything about me, was a further aphrodisiac.

Then I wrote my first letter to Brandt. It began, "What do I say to a man I've just met yet have known one hundred years?"

Well, Cheng, you should have heard him carry on about that letter! "What feeling you have! What writing talent! Why don't you do something with it!" You would have thought I was Shakespeare. Richard, who had once been supportive and encouraging, had neither supported nor encouraged me in much for quite awhile. Now here was Brandt telling me he couldn't wait for another letter. So, of course there was one.

Then, even that early on, Brandt did something odd in a negative way. I asked him to reciprocate in the letter writing mode. I wanted something tangible from him. In this I didn't worry about Richard, who was the least nosy person I knew; I could leave a paper under his nose but he'd never read it; besides, any envelope from Brandt, with hospital stationery, would look like just one more part of my voluminous FOCI correspondence.

Brandt said, "Alright, I'll send you a lettaa." But even after he said that he'd mailed it, none arrived. When I asked Brandt about it, he said, "I caan't understand that. Alright, I'll write you anothaa lettaa." That letter never arrived either. When I tried to pin Brandt down about it, I couldn't. Of course I was disappointed. But I excused him; probably Brandt, like many men, was awkward at letter writing and hadn't known how to say "no" to me. He was so nice in every other respect that I forgave him for what I considered his benign lie.

Several weeks later Brandt did something even odder. We were talking over the phone when suddenly he said, "Oh, we won't be able to speak next week. I'm going to take the week off."

"Really. Are you going away?"

"I'll be staying at my ex's house, to be with the children." While that news didn't delight me, on the other hand I remembered that he'd told me that his ex-wife still lived in the Boston area.

"Oh, you're coming east?" I asked, excited, hoping he'd suggest that before or after Boston he'd fly to New York.

Brandt answered, "No, Mary lives in Brentwood, just a stone's throw from me. It's the house we used to live in togethaa. Theaa's a pool theeaa, so I can swim with the kids and all."

Mary?! Brentwood?! I was confused. For one thing, I was certain he'd said that his ex-wife's name was Joan. But then maybe I'd heard incorrectly?' Did your ex-wife move from Boston to Brentwood?" I asked, believing that a plausible explanation.

Brandt explained, "Oh, you're thinking of my first wife Joan. No, she still lives in Boston vicinity."

I was totally nonplused. I asked, "You mean you've been divorced TWICE?"

"Nah, just once," Brandt answered nonchalantly. "I'm divossed from Joyce. Mary and I are sepaaated."

When I could find my voice I said, "I find it very strange that you didn't tell me you were married twice."

Brandt's answer floored me. "I did tell you; you must have faagotten."

Now, I don't claim that my mind is consistently like a steel trap. Concerns of Willie's care *were* sometimes overriding. So I'd forgotten to pick up shoes at the shoemaker and remembered three weeks later, been late for an appointment because I couldn't locate my car keys, and buying belated birthday cards had become routine for me. But me...novice that I was in all this...forget something like the existence of an additional former (or, *was* she?) wife of my boyfriend? I don't *think* so! Yet in retrospect it simply astounds me that at the time I even considered Brandt's explanation plausible. After all, Brandt was simply too nice and considerate for any other explanation to apply.

Still confused, I asked, "You and Mary are separated, yet you're going to stay with her for a week?"

Brandt's answer didn't thrill me. "We're friends," he said. "Actually, I'm going theaa to spend time with my kids. It's a way to be closaa to them."

I wondered if it was also a way to be closer to Mary. After all, Brandt had said that they were friends. Who does a man go to bed with, his enemies? I have to admit that I was jealous.

But I spoke logic to myself: "Look here, I'm married. Brandt obviously knows that I make love with Richard (not that it was a world record for frequency, lately). So, if he sleeps with Mary now and again, it isn't fair for me to take exception." Yet my wiser voice within said a firm, "It isn't the same thing! From moment one you told Brandt about Richard. You don't object to that there's a Mary as much as you mind having been kept in the dark for two months that there's a Mary!"

I then asked a new question of Brandt. An interesting question.

"Mary??" I asked, "is Jewish?"

Brandt answered, "She is now; she convaated."

"What about your first wife?" I asked. "Was she Jewish?"

"Joan," Brandt answered, "was Jewish, and remains so as faa as I know; there's been no contact between us foaa yeeaas."

I thought, "Well *that's* a plus at least."

I had a rather miserable week emotionally. But the following week when we spoke again Brandt sounded happier than ever to hear from me. As pleasantly as I could manage, I asked, "How was your week away?"

Brandt answered, "Well, we managed to get through it."

I remember thinking, "You sound like it was root canal. Who forced you to go in the first place, and to stay the entire week in the bargain?" I suppose what I said next was more curiosity than it was benevolence. "Brandt, since you say you and Mary are friends, and you miss your children so much, why don't you two get back together?"

Brandt answered, "It wouldn't waak. If I had any doubt about that which I actually didn't, laast weekend extinguished them."

His words made me wonder if this past week, then, had been a reconciliation attempt.

Whatever had happened or not happened that week between Brandt and his so-called "ex-wife" certainly had seemed to cause Brandt to long for me. The animal passion which had been felt since we'd reconnected by phone yet had been largely unexpressed, was now unleashed. I don't believe the term phone sex was around then. I thought Brandt and I had invented it!

Finally Brandt said, "Well, I guess I'm going to have to come to New Yooak."

I asked, "You MEAN it?"

Brandt said, "I do what I have to do. I can only spend a day away right now, but I can do that. I'll fly out in the eaaly morning, and return heeaa at night."

Among all else, I was immensely flattered that this busy very famous doctor was going to fly over about twelve hours all told in one day, just to be with me! But then my intelligent self asked him something which, as I think about it now, was curiously phrased.

"Brandt, why are you coming here? Is it to be with ME?"

Brandt, sounding annoyed with me for the first time since we'd met, answered, "Of caas I'm coming to see you. I've already seen Kennedy Aiipaat." He added, "You sound ambivalent."

I responded that since I felt such a one-day round trip was a bit unusual, I wondered why he'd do it, that was all.

Brandt answered, "Because I'm crazy."

Many times thereafter I thought of that remark. I've decided that when at the start of a relationship a man tells you something about himself, believe him! He knows himself better than you do!

But my heart and all my other parts yearned for Brandt. I wanted him here and told him so. Half-kidding, I asked him, "This has been happening over the phone only for awhile. Suppose we don't like each other in person?"

"Then it's time we found that out," Brandt answered, "Although theaa's no way that could be so."

We proceeded to make plans. It would be a day in September. When I asked him, "When?" he answered, "*You* tell *me*."

Understanding, I chose a date when I wasn't due to be... you know...menstruating.

Brandt told me that he'd make a reservation at the Inn at Kennedy. He'd get there at ten AM, register and go to the room. I'd arrive around ten also, call on the hotel phone in the lobby, he'd answer and give me the room number, and then I'd go up. When I didn't respond to that suggestion, Brandt, seeming to read me, asked, "Want me to come down and meet you in the lobby? Would that be bettaa?" Without waiting for my reply, he said, "That will be bettaa. We'll do that, then."

I admit that from the time we made that plan until Brandt's actual arrival, I drove him crazy with my "ambivalence" as he'd correctly named it. I fluctuated from passionate promises of our soon-time together, to proclamations of reminding him that I wasn't that kind of woman. I really don't know how he remained so patient with me. The day before he was to fly here, I told him,

"There's something you should know. I... don't.. do this... easily. I mean, I've... never done... this before."

Brandt replied, with disbelief in his tone, "My God, did you think you had to TELL me that!"

I had some things to attend to before Brandt's arrival. Richard's had had a vasectomy, so for awhile I personally had used no birth control. This was before the AIDS era when condoms became all too popular. At the time medical science had advanced beyond them. Still, I summoned up my courage and went into a Manhattan drug store. Ignoring the snickers of the two young men behind the counter as they looked at me every which way, I bought a one-dozen box of Trojans. When I found the chance at home, I gift wrapped them in tissue paper with a pink ribbon, and hid the package among some shoeboxes on my closet shelf.

The day of Brandt's and my meeting began with incident. I was so nervous that although I'd been to Kennedy Airport at least one thousand times before, on this morning I got lost en route, so arrived an hour late. When I finally did arrive, I parked, walked into the lobby, looked around but no sign of Brandt. Slightly panicked, I looked further and finally found him seated behind a potted palm patiently waiting for me. I walked up to him and said, "I thought by now maybe you'd have found another woman."

Smiling, while giving me a light kiss, he said, "Nah, I wouldn't have wanted one." I looked around.

"Nice hotel" I offered, then thought, "that was the stupid remark of the day, sounding like I spend a lot of time in hotels." Just then I spotted the fireplace with a deer's head on the wall. I pointed to it in disgust and said, "Yuck! That's disgraceful. Why do they do that?"

Brandt answered, "It's a tribute, they say, because it's such a beautiful animal."

"There you GO," I answered. "I think my daughter's beautiful too, but in *my* living room I have only *photographs* of *her*."

Brandt chuckled, then offered, "you're funny."

Our day and evening together was all that I'd wished for, and more. Brandt had reserved not just a room but an entire luxury suite. We sat in the living room for a long time talking. When hours passed and Brandt had made no move, I went over to him, sat down on his lap, put my face close to his and asked, "Brandt, don't you want to make love to me?"

My boldness surprised me, as did his answer. "I thought we'd just talk."

Again startling myself, I said, "Well I thought we wouldn't. So I brought a present for you." I handed him the tissue wrapped box with pink ribbon.

"I'm going into the bedroom while you open it. Then join me there... if you want to."

Once in the bedroom I waited a few minutes, during which it was so still in the livingroom that I knew Brandt had left the suite. I admonished myself, "You were too damned blatant. You offended him!"

At that thought Brandt appeared in the bedroom doorway, the shiny silvery aura around him, the opened box in his large left hand, the pink ribbon dangling from his right one. He came over and looked down at me on the bed. He said, "Yoaa present is unique. As you aah." He sat down beside me and said, "Well, I guess I'll put on one of these."

"Let me do it?" I asked.

By the time the day was over, Brandt, looking at the remaining condoms in the box, said, "I used six of them, anyway."

Lazily, I teased him, "What's wrong with the remaining six?"

Brandt answered, "My name is Simon, not Samson."

I might have argued with him there. The lovemaking was incredible! I'm not saying it isn't good, often exciting, with Richard...as my memory served me... this was... incredible in a different way. To be blunt... and I can't believe I'm telling you this... Brandt has a large penis. I'm sure you've heard all that stuff about how a man's size doesn't make any difference. I say that's a crock. With Brandt I felt, well, totally filled up. I thought of it this way: Some men excel at sports, some as singers, some as dancers. They are naturals, gifted with the right requirements. Well, Brandt is a super-star in bed. He has the skill, the motivation, and the equipment.

After one of our particularly passionate sessions that afternoon, I asked Brandt, "Does your ex-wife (I emphasized 'ex') Mary know how lucky she was?" The past tense here was deliberate also.

Brandt answered, "No, she wasn't interested in sex."

I thought about that. Since Brandt's penis hadn't done it for Mary, clearly I'd been wrong about the importance of the size of a man's penis. Obviously, all of this had to do with far beyond anatomy. Mary, who had lived with this man, wasn't interested in making love with him, whereas I'd practically have an orgasm upon hearing his voice. It also had much to do with the great mental and emotional rapport between Brandt and me, to say nothing of the tremendous chemical attraction.

Before Brandt left that early evening, I told him that although many men made offers, I hadn't been interested in being with any of them this way.

"Good." he replied "Let them all look and want you. Only I will know how satisfying you aaa."

I said, "Yes in this way we can be faithful to each other. It's extremely essential to me that it be that way between us." I don't remember Brandt answering.

Why had he wanted to "just talk" until I had to seduce him? Was it due to all the mixed messages I'd previously given him, making him feel - and not inaccurately- that being with me the first time would be like with a virgin? Maybe he believed, also accurately so, that sex with me would require a degree of commitment from him which he wasn't prepared to make? Or was it because sometimes when a man really likes a woman, he wants to delay having sex with her – the double standard thing? Or maybe this was just one of the many complexities of this very intelligent, appealing and complicated man.

Amazingly, and shockingly, since I'd never believed in cheating, (the word made me cringe!), once home I didn't feel at all guilty about what Brandt and I had done. Interestingly, with him I didn't feel I was being unfaithful. I felt we belonged there. In a sense he had become like my husband, whereas Richard was becoming the odd man out. Certainly that Brandt knew about Richard's existence but the reverse was not so, made this relationship even more close and precious to me. In a certain sense, Brandt was like a first love. Ironically, it was when Richard and I had sex that I felt unfaithful -- to Brandt!

The following week when Brandt and I spoke by phone, he sounded somewhat removed and preoccupied. Instead of telling me how wonderful it had been with me, he told me how much work had piled up for him during his day away from the hospital. I was puzzled and hurt, but I tried to humor him out of it.

"Well, we're back to practicing safe oral sex. We just talk about it." I said, then added, "Oh, Brandt, we're so far away!"

He answered, "Yes, we aah that. Well, maybe it's a protection." Then, laughing, he added, "We have a good foaam of contraception, huh?"

I was startled. For a moment once again he'd sounded just like Richard.

"I prefer condoms," I said flirtatiously. Brandt became warm and loving again.

"Give me a kiss?" he asked, before we hanged up. I'd started that just before Brandt had come to New York. At first he'd said, "Look, I've never gone in for that kind of thing." That was when I first realized that Brandt could be shy. But with me he seemed to go for it and then some.

What Brandt was doing to me now would have been greatly appreciated had we not been three thousand miles apart. You could say Brandt and I created cybersex before it was actually invented.

We expanded upon it until, I remember, I exclaimed, "DOC-Tur? Have you got the FEEL-Thy pictures to go with those words? Are you trying to give me multiple ear-gasms?" At that Brandt laughed. By the time we hanged up we were both in a light happy mood.

The next time we talked Brandt was remote again, to the point where I finally asked him if anything was wrong. At first he said no, he was just very busy. Then he floored me.

"Valentine" he said, "It would be bettaa, for awhile, if you call me only at the office, not at the apaatment."

Of course I asked, "Why?"

Then he hit me with it. "A formaaa gilfriend is moving back in with me. We'aa going to try it again for awhile."

I was so stunned I could neither speak nor be quiet. After a pause, I heard myself turning into the CIA, FBI and Gestapo combined, a hateful creature..

"When did this happen? Who is she? What is her name? Why didn't you tell me about her before? I want to know all about this...NOW! You vill give me ze information!!!"

Brandt sounded infuriatingly calm. "She and I have known one anothaa for nine yeaas. Her name is Colleen Ann; she's called Annie, though."

Then...I had to ask him the question which I feared hearing the answer to:

"Do you love her?"

"Yes, I love her," Brandt answered. "When it's good, it's fantastic. When it's bad, it's haaible." His words lay there like a corpse.

When I could manage to speak, I asked, "Why didn't you tell me about her before?"

Brandt answered, "It had been ovaa. Then she called me laast week."

With dread in my heart I asked the next question...I had to. "What about me? Do you love me?"

After too long a pause, Brandt answered, "Well, I like you, and I respect you. If that's love, then I guess I love you."

"You like me? You respect me? For God's sake, Brandt, who are you talking about -- the woman you recently made passionate love with for hours, or your Rabbi?"

Brandt's answer was too much. It devastated me.

"You must have known I had a gil, didn't you?"

Between sobs I answered, "Yes; I knew you had a girl. I thought she was me."

"You aaa," Brandt answered. "But you and me, it's a fantasy. I mean we aaa so faaa away. How often do we see each othaa?"

"You're saying that what we did in bed never happened, that I dreamed the whole thing?"

"Of cosse you didn't just dream it." Brandt answered. "I mean, I'm confused about the whole thing."

"*You're* confused!" I wailed.

"Oh, Valentine, please, don't cry. Is it because of me?"

Why the hell did he THINK I was sobbing, because I'd broken a fingernail?! At the same time I admonished myself, "Valentine, your neediness! It's stultifying! What do you expect him to think of you, displaying yourself like this?"

Then, of all things, I asked, "Colleen?!" Emphasizing her name. "She's not Jewish, is she?"

"No, she's Irish." Brandt replied.

"COLLEEN, yet!" I thought. "Brandt can't run far ENOUGH away from his mother's kosher kitchen! I'll bet THIS one hasn't converted, which is probably why Brandt went back with her!"

As non-religious as I was, my preoccupation with the religious persuasions of Brandt's women was a puzzle to me.

You might be wondering why I didn't tell Brandt right then to take his insanity and to get lost with it. That's something I have asked myself, many times. I think an answer is, due to my awesome feelings of connection with him in multiple areas, I'd become too attached to leave. Today probably it would have been different.

Insead of leaving with my angst, I wrote two poems to Brandt which I was not certain that I would actually give to him. (I never did).

They were:

The Fantasy

"Fantasy. You say that's what we are.
You say it can't be real
with one who lives so far.

Fantasy.
I'm sure you're right.
It's not much of a sacrifice
to gladly give up this plight.

Fantasy.
So go now. You are so wise.
With you cardboard heart
and on your paper mache legs,
walk out of my insides.

It's fine with me.
Thanks for trying.
It didn't mean that much anyway.
Then why am I crying?

And perhaps more to the point…

Your Song To Me
You were a bird
I was a tree.
You flew down
onto my branch.
You sang to me.

When I spoke to you
you crapped on me
and flew away.

Fly back
and sing a different song
one day.

***

At that moment I was so deeply into the memories surrounding this part of history with Brandt to the point of reliving it, that when Cheng coughed I was startled. I had forgotten that he was sitting in the next train seat.

"So here I am, Cheng, three years later. Wouldn't you think a woman with two men supposedly in love with her should be getting something worthwhile from between the two of them! I only wish it were so! To steal Brandt's words, although I hate them because he wasn't describing our relationship, with him 'when it's good, it's fantastic. When it's bad, it's horrible!' Imagine a three-year roller coaster ride. That's been my relationship with Brandt. Whereas Richard's been so depressed that our relationship's been like a lifetime ticket to keep re-entering the haunted house- even though my life with him has hardly been an amusement park! Two men; lucky me!!" I sat there glumly.

The train had pulled to a halt at Coldport. Cheng stood, then offered me his arm, helping me to my feet also.

"Come," Cheng said, gesturing with his chin to the doorway. "Let us first leave the amusement park."

I giggled despite myself. Then I asked in a low voice, "So, what do I do now?"

"One thing to know and one thing to do," Cheng answered. "To know: Don't try to teach a pig to sing. It will only exhaust you and irritate the pig."

"The pig in this case is Brandt?"

"Metaphorically so, yes. Don't try to change him; it won't work." The train was so crowded that Cheng and I stood at a standstill in the aisle.

"You told me the thing to know; what is the thing to do? Get rid of both men?"

"Not necessarily change circumstances. Change yourself."

"MYSELF!" I exclaimed, feeling anger rush from me toward Cheng. "MYSELF!? But I already told you. Two impossible men are the problem! Why myself?!"

"Because," Cheng explained, "you are the only one you CAN change. Other people are merely messengers showing us who we believe we are. Once we re-estimate ourselves, they will confirm that change."

I opened my mouth to angrily protest but found that my anger had mysteriously disappeared, leaving me calm and open to consider Cheng's words. Was he correct? If I changed myself, would I then be able to have a great relationship with a man?

"How do I start?" I asked.

We had reached the stairs leading from the train down to the platform. With an athlete's agility, Cheng jumped down, then once again offered his arm to me. "You have already started," Cheng answered as I swung down to the platform beside him. "You have had great life experience. You meditate. You WANT change. Where is your car parked?"

I pointed, and Cheng walked me to the Porsche. Giving it a pointed look, he said, "Ah, we were into money, I see." Not knowing what to answer, I unlocked the door.

Cheng said, "Get in, Val-teen, and lock your door again." After doing so, I unrolled the window.

"I just want to know my next step," I told Cheng.

"Next step, you roll up your window and drive home safely."

Cheng's gleeful chuckles rippled through the night air like wind chimes. "Then, you come Thursday night to Dr. Cheng Ho's class at university. Last two classes of semester coming up."

"Last two? It doesn't seem the right time, then, does it?"

"It is the perfect time. Thursday I begin Dr. Cheng's Discourses on the Universe. Before was just The Preliminaries."

"Then, won't I have missed a lot? I mean, aren't The Preliminaries important?"

"Sure. However, you have already had them."

"I don't understand."

"You will," Cheng answered, already walking toward his car. Almost there, he turned around, waved and called, "See you in class, Building C, Room 111, Thursday, 7:15 PM."

CHAPTER NINE: DR. CHENG'S DISCOURSE ONE-
The One You Are Looking For Is the One Who Is Looking; Discernment vs. Judgment, and the Eight Magic Words.

A summary of all eleven Discourses is found in the section at the end of the book, "**Cheng's Summary Of The Discourses and Practices**."

"Oh, God, remove from our eyes the veil of ignorance, and show us things as they really are."

-- Jami

"Sometimes I lie awake at night and I ask 'Where have I gone wrong?' Then a voice says to me, 'This is going to take more than one night.'"

-- Peanuts, to Snoopy,
Peanuts Comic Strip

At ten after the hour I dashed into Cheng's university classroom, glanced around at the handful of students already assembled, then took a seat in the second row. Relieved that I wasn't late, I drew in a deep breath, noting how especially good the energy in here felt. After the turmoil of the studio and city at large, entering this room was like entering an - enchanted rain forest - was the best analogy that I could think of. I sensed much of that was due to where the people in this room were at, as compared with most. More curious than controlling, more seeking than striving, more into love than lunacy. I looked at each of them again, this time more slowly and carefully. I felt an astonishing sense of familiarity, and more amazing yet, even though I had taken a chair with vacant seats between the others and me, I felt a sense of oneness with them all. It was as mystereous as it was fathomless.

At exactly 7:15 Cheng appeared, seemingly carried through the doorway on a wave of palpable loving energy.

"Hello, Dear Ones," he called enthusiastically, throwing me an extra wave and pleased grin. Almost in unison we called, "Hello" back. Feeling Cheng's energy, I realized that he was the one most responsible for our enchanted forest.

Cheng, after taking a position standing in front of us, announced, "Welcome once again to Dr. Chengs Life School. So, this is our first Discourse class, as well as next to last class for the semester." There were several moans. "And," he continued, "also the next to last class here at the University." That part elicited shocked gasps. But Cheng reassured us. "Not to worry. After these two, we meet in February - at the home of Dr. Cheng Ho.

For months afterward we speculated over whether Cheng had left the university voluntarily or whether his academic superiors had told him to leave because his material was too unconventional. Consensus was the latter, but since Cheng offered no information and nobody wanted to ask, that remained an unanswered question.

However, that evening, my first in class, everyone was attentively riveted to Cheng. I noticed that although he had with him what appeared to be notes written on rice paper, he didn't refer to them. Since to my knowledge I was the only one entering the course at this juncture, at that moment I was having some uncomfortable feelings of being the new kid on the block. Sensing the others looking at me furtively with curiosity, I wondered why Cheng was being so rude as to not have introduced me to them.

Meanwhile Cheng, like a panther, slowly paced in front of us as he spoke, his eyes moving from one of us to the next until he covered each one in the room.

"First and most important, once again, the Discourses are not teachings Dr. Ho invented. I simply convey very ancient teachings from Eastern India in perhaps new ways for your modern times, teachings from what's called Yoga. Altogether, Yoga is a philosophy and methods by which an individual may become connected with Reality, with Truth, with the Self, with God - all terms meaning the same. The Bhagavad Gita, one of the greatest ancient Indian texts, calls Yoga, "The realization of the highest end." While Western psychology is still developing, coming up with new theories and discarding old ones, Yoga is a finished product. If one practices it correctly and consistently, results are assured. Not a religion, it is a true science which can be practiced by Hindu's, Christians, Jews and those of other religions and nationalities alike. In fact, every major religion has it's outer forms and it's esoteric forms, the latter secrets restricted to only a few; The Cabala and Jewish meditation is a good example of same. So, these teachings are for anyone who has felt the narrowness of wholly secular life and has hungered for the esoterically spiritual. The teachings are ancient, ageless, and all embracing."

"A Chinese teacher conveys truths from ancient India," I pondered, bemused. "I guess that makes as much sense as anything else in my life right now."

I refocused on Cheng's words: "These teachings, then, are based on a deep yearning we each share to be connected with Truth, so, knowing we are doing something ancient and authentic here puts us in a great tradition. The tradition of humanity; humanity aching to be free, aching for the light; longing to know that we are not separated, that we are by no means trivial, and that we are going home."

I looked around. Everyone was so still and quiet that I could not even detect breathing. I understood. I too could not move a finger nor utter a sound. That I had not been introduced mattered no longer.

Cheng continued: "Everything in these Discourses is to lead you toward the Truth, to your Self with a capital S meaning your higher Self, your God Self, to a new way of being, one delightful characteristic of which is total love for yourself and for all others."

"Each Discourse contains principles. The only way they are proved valid is through your own experience. You put them into practice in your daily lives."

Now from around me I heard exhalations of breath. Again, I understood. A great peace filled me as it obviously had the others; I felt atypical relaxation, as if somebody had slipped me something. I was becoming drunk on Cheng's words as they resonated with some inner wisdom that I clearly shared with each member of the group. Pulled as I was into a meditative state, I closed my eyes. But, there was to be no meditation just then. Almost immediately Cheng's voice boomed forth like the stereo system in the studio.

"EXPECT FAILURES!!!" he shouted out. Startled, I sat forward in my chair, somewhat frightened, somewhat amused to see that everyone else was doing essentially the same thing. "*So-called* failures," Cheng modified, now in a normal tone. "The only way that you can fail is if you fail to try." Once more the voice boomed, "BUT WHEN YOU TRY - IF YOU DO – YOU'LL EXPERIENCE MIRACLES!!! HOWEVER, I FOREWARN YOU. THIS IS NOT FOR SISSIES!"

The last sentence was delivered as Cheng stood over us, waving his short arms in the air. He looked like a Samurai. Then, just as suddenly his body and voice melted. Cheng remained that way for possibly a minute, then, like a ballet dancer, he made his way to the front of the room and took several swallows of water, then floated like a swan. Next he instantly turned his back to us and stretched; the swan had become a big cat. Again I sneaked a look at the others. I shrugged, shaking my head. Several of my fellow students returned the gesture. We clearly were all realizing something similar; with Cheng as our teacher, whatever we expected was not what we'd get. And that we had, indeed, begun a journey, possibly the most glorious and exciting one that we had ever had. But, it would be a bumpy ride.

Cheng turned to face us now, his face and demeanor alert yet serene.

"The first Discourse has much to do with DISCERNMENT AND JUDGEMENT. It has a sub-theme also; How To See Through People. And since the majority here tonight are women, this theme might also carry the sub- heading, 'How to See Through Men.' Allow me to remind you, regardless of how that sounds,that this Discourse is not for being against people but for understanding them, which leads to higher love for both sexes. To also remind you that these are not just Dr. Ho's beliefs rather those of the great masters of India. But not limited to them, rather are the beliefs of the Self -Realized masters of all ancient tradition, as recorded in ancient scriptures.

Discrimination, or Viveka from the Sanskrit, is necessary for living on this earth. To think that we should just be totally trusting of everybody we encounter is not only naively stupid, it's not even spiritual. In a later discourse I will be discussing the Bhagavad Gita at length. It is simply a great text of truth. It says, pertinent to today's Discourse, "one without a sense of distinction between good and evil is headed for ruin."

A woman raised her hand, but Cheng lifted the palm of his hand to face her, indicating for her to wait.

"So, I begin with a question," he continued. "Are we in a position to judge anyone or anything? No. In the East we have a saying, 'Nobody knows enough to be a judge.' However, we are always in a position to discern, to evaluate a person or situation, and we must. Now your question," Cheng said, nodding to the girl who'd raised her hand shortly before.

"I'm Hinda," the girl said.

I stared at her. She was beautiful. She glowed. She continued, "You're saying we shouldn't evaluate? Will you distinguish between evaluation and judgment?"

"Yes, definitely, and thank you, Hinda" Cheng said. "The following is the distinction: Judging says, since I don't like how this person behaves, this is a terrible, inferior person who is beneath me.' Discerning says, 'The way in which this person behaves is not something with which I wish to align myself right now.' So, judging is trying to discover a person's or thing's worth and finding it lacking. Discerning is asking if this is a positive force in your life at this time. Is that clear to you, Hinda?" Hinda nodded affirmatively. "And, to the rest of you?" Cheng asked us. We did the same. Cheng expounded, "When you judge you do something called characterization. This means that you decide what a person is based on several characteristics only, and thereafter fail to recognize the sum total of that person's being, because your perception filters out everything that doesn't fit your characterization of the person. Therefore judging is wrong, discerning is right, but discerning can be tricky. We may conclude wrongly. Because many bad people do good from time to time, while some good people do bad on occasion, we can easily be mistaken that the bad person who has done good, is a good person, while the good person who has done bad, is a bad person. This is how people throughout history have often evaluated inaccurately."

A girl began to speak, but Cheng interrupted her.

"Raise hand, I'll recognize you, then give name first, please, like with Hinda," he instructed. "In the East we know importance of discipline. If you raise your hand and are recognized before speaking, you will be speaking for the right reasons, because Universal Energy or the Shakti, desires you to share. Once a person is recognized, all the rest of you please put all your attention on the one's words. This gives the speaker, as well as you, more energy and clarity, so his/her words will have maximum power for common good. And,when we pay full attention to the moment, when we really listen to another person,then we become totally in the moment rather than somewhere else entirely as is usually the case. So when we give full attention to whatever is happening - when we really listen to a person who is speaking - we feel very real, very alive, very centered. We feel very connected, through and with them, and especially to our own core. They feel very cared about. Both really connect, so both really benefit. Now, your name please first?" he asked the girl.

But the girl had apparently had a change of mind, for she shook her head and mumbled something such as, "No...no...;" at the same time she waved away Cheng's acknowledgement of her to speak. Cheng nodded and said "Yes!" for whatever reason seeming pleased with this exchange between them.

Again I noticed the curiosity that when Cheng taught formally he spoke more like an American speaking English than like a Chinese man speaking English as was often true when he spoke with me one-on-one.

Cheng continued: "Each of us here is part of two entities: yourself, and the larger entity, the group. When you are in a relationship with one other person, there are three entities in that relationship; each of you is one entity, the relationship is the third. There is a constant moving back and forth of energy, or Shakti as they say in India - in my Chinese culture we call it Chi; every culture has a different name for it but it is the same energy - here I shall term it Shakti. Those who see auras can see that visibly. Kirlian photography which captures energy fields can demonstrate it. So in a relationship with another person or with any group that has come together for a purpose, if each of you stay attuned to the Shakti, you will know when the energy, so-to-speak, is in your court. When to contribute, when to listen."

A man raised his hand then and Cheng acknowledged him. "I'm Andrew," he said. "My question is, suppose I don't see energy?"

"You then just feel it," Cheng answered. "Everyone can learn to be attuned to it. Most are not, though. For example, in a group someone raises a good point. It is commented on, absorbed. Now there is no more to say on that at this moment. It is time to move on. However, that person is so enjoying the high of the attention that he's reluctant to let go. So, he beats a dead horse. Because his moment should have ended when the Shakti left it, he is no longer able to draw energy from the Shakti. That energy is now coming from his small self. Whenever that happens in anything that we do, we get drained and so does anyone with us at the time. Now let us return to that same situation and take a different possible instance. Where did that Shakti that left that person go? Perhaps it moved on to another person in that group yet that individual is reluctant to share, so withholds doing so. This deprives that individual, and the entire group, of the Shakti that could have been shared, as well as perhaps also useful information.

"Now, in most situations you will need to know when to stay and when to leave. So long as the Shakti is in the situation, it remains energizing and constructive. When it leaves, it is telling you that the encounter is over for the time being. To try to prolong that phone call or goodbye at the door beyond that point is draining and discouraging, because the Shakti is no longer sustaining it, only you didn't let go. Align yourself with the Shakti – you'll learn to feel it inside you like a buzz, a force, and elevation. Go with its direction."

"Those endless goodbyes at the door, I know what you mean," an auburn-haired slightly built man with a somewhat turned-up nose and freckles was speaking. "In my tradition, we call those 'Jewish good-byes.' Oy!" He made a face of mock distaste.

"Serge," Cheng admonished the man, "please in this class not to blurt out. To raise hand, get acknowledged, say your name and then your comment."

"I'm very sorry, teacher," Serge apologized.

"Very good then. But now that you have spoken, let us take an example for the teaching so far. Class, how many of you, until now, would have thought that Serge was Irish, not Jewish?" Everyone raised his or her hand. "Aha, yes!" Cheng said. "So remember, when discerning we cannot always tell a book by its cover."

"In any relationship," Cheng continued, "remember, you are connected spirits. Seek to connect, not control or be right. Remember, in every encounter you either promote connective spirit - C.S., or you get B.S; you *know* what *that* stands for. There no way around it. The ancient scriptures don't put it exactly in those terms," Cheng said with a giggle. "I Americanize to get my point across." The giggles from those of us in class matched Cheng's own. "So," Cheng continued, "in each interaction, decide if you want to be right or you want to be happy. Because if one person wins both lose."

As Cheng spoke I looked again at Hinda and couldn't take my eyes off of her. Aside from Cheng, she was the one with whom I was feeling the strongest connection.

Cheng continued, "We are of two minds. We evaluate incorrectly because often we perceive from the ordinary every day mind; here the eye wears a blindfold so sees only a part, thus is often deceived. For example, the most dangerous is bad which counterfeits as good. Even trained therapists and very intelligent people have been deceived by such. We want to come to perceive through our True Mind, our innermost essence of pure pristine awareness."

At this point the young woman who had changed her mind before raised her hand again. "Yes!" Cheng acknowledged enthusiastically.

"I'm Nancy," she said. "How can I stop being so gullible? I'm sick of my lousy taste in men!"

Cheng answered, "But you have very good instincts, Nancy. You began to want to speak earlier but sensed that the Shakti wasn't in it right then so reconsidered. You waited until you sensed that the Shakti was with you. And you were exactly right both times. Nancy, and everybody, here is one of Dr. Cheng's rules of life. In the first thirty minutes with a person, they usually tell you everything that you need to know about them. You just have to listen and to observe. But it gets even better than that. In China we say that our most accurate assessment of a person occurs during our first five minutes with that person; pay attention to that, as after that we get brainwashed.

"Your relationship with yourself has everything to do with your relationship with men, and with women," Cheng continued. "You know how it goes. You confidently plunge into a new relationship or activity, or do so after much forethought. You feel that you've finally taken the right road this time. Suddenly, there's a tricky turn or a dead end. The plan or lover shows a hidden side. Disappoints. Disappears. Self-doubt strikes again. Your confidence leaves. Only emptiness and pain remain.

"Let us now distinguish between the self – said with quiet voice, small letter s- and the Self, said with strong voice, capital letter S. The Self is your connection with the consciousness which pervades the universe, or with God if you wish. Connection with the Self is total absence of self-doubt. This means that we must discern not with the eye alone, which is often deceived. We must see also with the heart, the Self."

Serge asked, "Why is the eye deceived? I mean, an orange and a piano look different; I use my eyes and accurately discern which is which."

Cheng frowned. "Next time, Serge, please raise hand first and be recognized. Although you did not follow the rules, this time I will answer. Ah, you are an engineer, you see the orange and piano through scientific eyes. That is because you have no emotion about the orange and piano, is that not so? Emotion wets our window on the world. Have you ever tried to look out a wet window? Everything looks distorted. You will also have a distorted view of people by seeing them through stormy emotions."

"Such as?" Serge asked.

"Such as fear, fantasies of reality, desperate hopes, anxieties. Women, for example, you don't see a man as he is but as how you are. Then you blame him for how you are and get angry with him that you haven't changed, but tell him that it's him. Is there any wonder that confusion and pain result?! The Gita says that anger makes us misjudge a situation. That when angry we cannot distinguish between good and evil. So, we should eschew anger. Keeping our emotions clear we become increasingly lighter and more accurately perceptive."

I wasn't sure that I believed what Cheng had just said about relationships- or, maybe I didn't want to accept it. I thought to challenge him, then decided not to at that moment.

Obviously Cheng had read my thoughts, for he directed his next remark at me.

"We can understand our self by looking at what bothers us in another person. Many people fail to find the peace that comes from self-understanding. Why? Because they don't want to see themselves, their so-called faults, their fantasies. They fear losing their so-called present happiness. Well, remember this, Dear Ones: If you fear losing your happiness, you don't have it in the first place. You have only maya, illusion masquerading as happiness; the slightest wind can blow away that disguise. Happiness is higher, and deeper."

When I did speak it was not to challenge but to ask a question. I guessed I'd attuned to the Shakti which seemed to be guiding me to do so; a peculiar sensation. After raising my hand and being acknowledged, I said, "I'm Valentine. How can I tell when I'm seeing things from my Self, large S rather than my self, small s?" As I spoke I felt all eyes upon me.

"Everybody," Cheng interjected, "as you hear, Val-teen has just introduced herself to you. She comes from Long Island, works in New York City and because she has already had The Preliminaries she has entered the group at this point." I felt the group's attentive acceptance of me. I felt it elevate and support me. At that moment I realized that Cheng had known from the start that the group would accept me best if he did not single me out at the beginning, rather,he did so when I'd demonstrated that I was ready to become proactive with them. Obviously Cheng's timing, while not always conventional, was always correct.

"It's a sense of knowing, Val-teen," he answered my question. "Like returning to your childhood neighborhood. You know where that red brick schoolhouse is, that woods you used to walk through to get to the school, the one where all your parents marked your trail with blue paint on the trees. The beach that your mother took you and your friends to with the fresh water well at the entrance from which you all loved to drink."

I was once again totally astonished by Cheng! He was describing my childhood environment. Even as he spoke I could see that well with running water in the wooded area about one half mile from the shell pink pristine sanded beach itself. I could see us filling tin cups; I could taste the delicious pure, cool water passing my lips; I could smell the pine scent of the trees and see the blue paint streaks by which we kids risked braving the woods, walking to school. With those painted trees to guide us, some risk! It was a metaphor for how easy and idyllic my childhood had been. The universe had made up for that later!

"Nobody could tell you that beach went by any other name, nor deceive you about the wood's location, could they?" Cheng elaborated. "Similarly, when you know from your Self, when you live from that place of returning home, you will never again have self-doubt attacks. Your Self will tell you what is reality and what to do. Important to realize that my teachings are not for my students to *become* anything. Becoming is an illusion. I simply guide you all to be as you already are and always have been."

Once more I felt directed to raise my hand; Cheng nodded for me to speak.

"Valentine again," I said. "So, is it that the Self is just intuition or habit, not reasoning?"

"Your higher view is a combination of your spiritual wisdom and the mental alertness which is part of your Self," Cheng answered. "You will eventually just know your Self -the True Mind- decide from it, live from it. In that way you can never make a mistake, never doubt yourself again. You will simply hear what the intuition is saying and honor it."

Nancy again raised her hand and was acknowledged by Cheng.

"But how do you get to know and live from your Self?" she asked. Cheng answered, "Ah, thank you! That is what all the Discourses are leading to. Actual steps for accessing the Self will be covered in the next Discourse and in those to follow. First, further questions about what we have covered thus far this evening?"

Nancy had one: "But my boyfriend and I are totally different, not alike as you say," she argued. Good. She had saved me the trouble.

"On the outer level you may well be so," Cheng explained. "One is quiet, the other talkative. One drinks, the other is sober."

It was obvious by the startled look on Nancy's face that Cheng *was* accurately describing her and her boyfriend.

Cheng continued, "However, although the manifestations may be different, both of you have similar degrees of self-doubt, inability to be intimate. As you think so you feel,as you feel,so you seek, as you seek so you find,. You feel lost and lonely and are looking for a man to connect with. You will find one. He will be as lost and lonely as you. He will be your mirror, at least at the time that you meet. Like attracts like.

Anger is a dark energy. If you are an angry person, you attract other angry people into your world. An angry person lives in a world of angry people. Love is light energy. A loving person lives in a world of loving people.

Also, know this; the lessons that we need to learn we will experience the opposite of; if we need to learn not to be jealous, we will experience jealousy; if we need to learn generosity, we will live in a world of stingy people, and so forth. So be the change that you want to happen. If you want to see more compassion in the world, be more compassionate. If you want to see less hate in the world, put more love into it."

I asked, "I have a theoretical question (like hell it was!). I believe I'm a very truthful person but I connect with a partner who appears to lie to me. So, he *isn't* my mirror. How do you explain this?"

Cheng answered, "If you connect with such a man then you too are not as honest as you think." I felt my face fall, which Cheng did not fail to notice. "I am not saying that you deliberately lie to others," he added kindly, "only that you lie to or delude yourself to some degree. The man in question must take the lion's share of responsibility here for deception, as his kind of lies are worse; more calculating. Think of the sound of the word; unreLIEability. Every lie that a man knowingly tells to you, large and small, corresponds to a degree of unreliability. Each indicates some lack of character. A deceitful man is hiding something, e.g., his fear of intimacy, habits like drinking, gambling or womanizing which make having a good relationship with him doubtful, perhaps suppressed hostility, a secret pleasure in hurting people, perhaps his fear of seeing himself. Such a person has a broken spirit, and hides that as well."

"Should I, theoretically, then give up such a man?"

"You might, but not necessarily," Cheng answered, "But hating, crying or nagging won't help either, nor will vague hopes that things will change. Change yourself! Rise yourself above the mess. Your Self will know just what to do, when and how. You can come to let it show you."

Cheng's words unsettled me, but almost immediately thereafter his metaphor about not teaching a pig flashed into my head, making me smile.

"I'm Ginger," a woman said, after raising her hand and being acknowledged. "I'm really wondering why I'm here, listening to ways to become happy. I'm happy now. I've got it together already."

Cheng looked at Ginger through narrowed eyes, then replied, "I am glad that you are happy *now*. What about *later*? Everybody can keep it together for awhile. Permanence is the key. I've been doing this for thirty years and I don't have it all together yet."

I very much doubted that Cheng did not have it all together; I believed all of us in the classroom were having similar thoughts. But, Ginger had more to say.

"Cheng, you're right," she admitted, "It's very hard for me to admit this but I'm not going to grow by lying to myself further. I thought I knew what would make me happy, so I went after those things and I achieved them. I have a very successful career in sales, bringing me a six figure annual income. I also have a great husband who, incidentally, makes a lot of money too, and two lovely children. I have everything, yet I'm miserable. I get no sympathy from anybody. They say, '*You're* complaining! *I* should have your life!' Then I feel guilty because they're right, but I'm still unhappy. Why?"

"You have the plight of the rich women who "has everything" Cheng empathized. "The only one who has any patience to listen to *her* problems is her psychiatrist. But I understand very well. You still lack something; you just don't know what. Do you want me to tell you?"

Ginger's eyes grew huge, as she said, "Yes, please!"

"I will tell not just Ginger but all of you what you want," Cheng continued. "Dear Ones, all of you are feeling it. Restlessness, dissatisfaction. The majority of people are going to be feeling it increasingly; it will peak at the turn of the century, the Millennium. Material things will then not be enough. What you all want is YOU. To know and live from your Self. You think you want somebody to love you, but that is not so. What you really want is the experience of love. Most people believe that another person is required for this, but that's wrong too. It is fine to have that other person, although that is still always an intermediate step. Remember, the one you are looking for is the one who is looking. To the degree that we want love, we are unhappy. To the degree that we love, we are happy. One who knows the Self is more in love with everyone than the ordinary person is ever in love with anyone. This, then, is a blissfully happy person."

That was deep. I quickly raised my hand, got recognized and asked, "Then how does falling in love with another person fit in here? Does this mean there is no such thing, actually?"

Cheng answered, "There is actually the same consciousness as your own peering out from what appears to be another person. When you really adore someone, want to be with that person all the time and are never bored but supremely happy in his or her presence, this is usually experienced from afar or after limited contact. At this point we are still experiencing this person as Consciousness. We are opening up to that inner love, feelings of unity, closeness. However, the more that we get to know the person the more s/he becomes "the other" instead of "like us." It is fine to have a love partner, but unless love, peace and satisfaction come from understanding your Self, your love for any love partner will be short-lived indeed. You must seek Self before everything else in your life. Then let it see for you. That is perfect love, peace and protection. As the Gita says, "The knowledge of the Supreme One is pure bliss."

Hinda, after being recognized, asked, "If we find the Self now, must we still endure restlessness later along with the others?"

"That's such a great question, Hinda. We do not know when each of you will become Self-Realized, but on the continuum, you will incur a lesser degree of restlessness than the others will. And so you might help the others with theirs."

I noticed how when one person was called on to speak, the group consciously gave that person their utmost attention and interest. I could see that in their faces and in their body language. I strove to do the same by telling myself that at this moment nobody or nothing was as important as that person's words. As I did so I experienced wondrous feelings of peace and well being, along with authenticity. Just as Cheng had explained one would.

Nancy, after being recognized, offered, "Daily living is very difficult, though, when a person has nobody to love him or her."

Cheng said, "You mean you have nobody *else* to love you. Remember, you want the experience of love from wherever it comes. So, first, love yourself. When we love and accept ourselves it is so much easier for others to be uplifted around us. Give yourself a mental hug. You're trying to know the Self; that makes you very special. Make a 'Yes List' and if the items are constructive, make it a priority to give them to yourself one-by-one. Similarly, make a 'No List', of all the things which you are doing now which make you feel unhappy and unloved. One by One stop doing each of them. Expect some flack from others when you begin to say, "No, I'm sorry, I cannot do that," or "Yes,I am going to do this for myself." Without being rigid, once you have decided on these changes, do not turn your yeses into nos, or your nos into yeses when you do not want to. In this way you will come closer to having your needs met. Then, when another person who is right for you comes along, you will be able to love him or her without the anger, bitterness or needy demanding behaviors that come from having felt deprived.

There is the User Friendly kind of love where we sort of use the other person for our needs; that is love coming from our lower self; there is the Other Centered love in which we think mainly of the other person's welfare; this kind comes from our Higher Self. Love also requires wisdom, Dear Ones, meaning appropriate expression. Otherwise even with the most well-intended love, pain ensues. If we want so much to give to a person, to show that person a better way that we overpower her or him, that person might retreat or revolt; pain results. Dear Ones, in other words, there are ways to relate to a love, and to life in general, other than your present unhappy ways."

Serge said, "You seem to know what life is all about Cheng. I've been here all semester yet I don't seem much closer to that than when I came here. Is there hope for me?"

With great patience Cheng replied, "If you will raise your hand first, there is great hope for you, Serge." We giggled until Cheng gave us a look, which was unmistakably clear and immediately ended our laughter. It said, "Let whomever is among you without flaws laugh." Cheng then resumed, "But of course there is hope, or why would I be teaching you!" Cheng continued, "True love and true life are identical. Know what love is all about and you will know what life is all about."

"When?" Serge asked impatiently, then remembered Cheng's admonishment and raised his hand.

"How long did it take you to get where you are as an engineer?" Cheng asked.

"I don't see what that has to..."

"How many years?" Cheng insisted.

"Well...let me see...all together.. fifteen years."

"Ah, fifteen years to get where he is in career, yet wants to become a Perfected Being in one semester!" Cheng laughed good naturedly. Then he softened. "Serge's desire is good," he said. "What he wants to achieve is what these Discourses are all about. First, be as authentic as possible and appropriate in every encounter; wear no disguises. Keep asking yourself, 'Is this how I really feel, what I really want?' Do this by watching your thoughts, actions and emotions while neither approving not condemning what you see. Then, one by one, drop whatever is not the real you. Decent people will usually like what you are once they can figure out what that is. If you will be your true Self to the degree that you know it, that will make it much easier for good people to discern that. Deluded people might not like you whatever you do; you could turn yourself inside out. So, be true. We can keep up pretense for only so long. If we don't acknowledge our negative feelings as soon as we have them, they take on a life of their own. Every suppressed emotion causes suppressed energy. So be honest with yourself about what you feel and where you are. If you try to go for the light too fast instead of facing the problem, you'll be brought down again and again."

A woman raised her hand and identified herself as Mindie. Once recognized, she offered, "You are talking about putting yourself out there regardless of how it's received, aren't you? That's so hard to do, especially with a man I like whom I want to accept me."

"No, no!" Cheng corrected, "You don't really want to be accepted by a man, or by anyone else for that matter. You really want self-acceptance. You want to know from yourself that you are all right. You could have the approval of one special man or of ten thousand men, but if you lacked self-approval you'd remain empty. Approval from others is a poor substitute for the real thing, self-approval. For self-approval and self-love you must all stop identifying with your thoughts and actions, which are imperfect. Then you are on your way. When the ancient oracles said 'know thyself' they also meant 'love thyself'; the one follows the other. With true self-love we automatically love everybody else. So, that is where it must start, just as that is where it culminates."

Hinda got recognized once again and asked, "Will you please comment on self-love on the part of the people that you called bad people?"

Again Cheng was obviously pleased with Hinda. "You anticipated my next point! Excellent!" he exclaimed. "Really, there are no bad people. Only people vibrating at lower frequencies much of the time. It is their thoughts, motives and actions that are 'bad', whereas their Selves are just like ours: joyful, omniscient, wise, discerning, energized yet relaxed, spontaneous, peaceful, totally loving. Also, courageous, stable, loyal, patient, adaptable, tolerant, and let us not by any means forget enthusiastic; we believe that as we become adults we should be blasé; nothing is further from the truth.; being enthusiastic means being in God; enthusiasm in anyone, child or adult, is most contagiously attractive. And being capable of miracles great and small. So, all these to the nth degree. When I say live from your Self, I mean as much as possible live those traits that I have just named, for that is what you are. Then the lower tendencies will eventually drop away. But that will occur after the latter have become obvious to you, often painfully so. Again, I am not in any way advocating denying or failing to work on your feelings when necessary."

I scanned the faces of some of the group members as I examined my own reactions to that statement. Clearly, we were all experiencing various degrees of skepticism.

Little time to ponder that, however, for Mindie was again recognized. "I'm afraid to lose my boyfriend by being myself," she said.

"No," Cheng corrected once again, "No woman fears losing a man; she fears losing her feelings that he loves and protects her. Such sense of security is delusory. A manipulative partner controls by subtle messages that he or she will leave or you will lose something crucial unless you keep playing the game, that is, keep being manipulated. If you give yourself away to him, he will take you. A person who owns the Truth would say to such a partner, 'If those are your conditions, then goodbye.' Of course, you don't have to physically leave in order to stop the games, but don't be the manipulator either."

"How else, then?" Nancy asked.

"You just stop playing the game. In partner games, unless both play the game ends."

Andrew raised his hand and was recognized. "I assume you mean a female partner can manipulate too?"

Cheng answered, "Yes, very definitely; thank you for that."

"So," Andrew continued, "suppose my girlfriend gets that hurt demeanor each time I tell her that I have to work late?"

"What do you do when she does that?" Cheng asked.

"I console her."

"How?"

"I tell her I'm sorry she's upset. Offer to make it up to her - bring her a present, whatever. Am I wrong?"

"That depends on whether you are using work to avoid her or just doing what's needed to do your job well," Cheng told him. "If the latter, no, no, you are playing the game; doing what's inherent in your job yet apologizing for it. Better you name her game. Say, 'You sound hurt about this. It seems that you want me to apologize and feel guilty because I have to work. Is that so?' Do you hear me, Dear Ones? Name the person's game and often they too will get more real and honest, frequently immediately. But stay tuned in and respect needed boundaries. If they are too fearful of facing themselves they may get defensive; they may run away, literally or emotionally. So, be ready for those possibilities also."

Another man, Walter, was recognized. "My wife is extremely critical," he said, "and I'm having trouble taking it. Any suggestions?"

"Criticisms from others can be a wonderful way to know ourselves," Cheng answered. "We want to get enough in touch with the truth to have insight into the person's motives. Is your wife doing this just to relieve her own demons or because in those areas you really need correction? A foggy mind can't know. A mind in Truth knows almost immediately and acts accordingly."

Walter said, "I think it's mostly the former, although, maybe some of the latter at times. It's impossible not to be affected. We live in the same house."

"Not true." Cheng said, "We each dwell in our own places inwardly. Our inner, not our outer, location, is the source of our irritation, or our peace. The Bhagavad Gita says that we should be calm in the face of great provocation. That is the way of the true yogi. Move into a new place inwardly and do what is right outwardly. If she's being unjustly critical, also name her game."

A girl named Trenna who had been silent until now offered, "I've just realized something painful. I've a control thing with men." After a pause she said, "I don't know what my question is. I only know that what I'm doing is wrong."

Cheng answered, "Good for you for self-honesty. Dear Ones, this is a perfect time to emphasize that in our work together a mirror will periodically be thrust before your faces. You will see so-called flaws more clearly. This can be too painful to handle unless viewed correctly. So begin now to see these flaws as just your stuff. Unless you are already saints, you have stuff. Remember, you *have* your stuff, you *aren't* your stuff. See it, don't identify with it. In this way the journey will be less painful. Now, to answer you, Trenna, attempts to control are simply insecurities masquerading as necessities. You tell yourself it is for him, for the good of the relationship. People try to control others for one reason only. They feel if they give up control, there will be nothing to sustain them, nothing to hang onto life with, so that they'll cease to exist. Notice the pain, frustration and tension that you feel when trying to control anyone, then tell me if that is good and necessary. Of course it isn't either. Yet it is the biggest problem going on all the time between people, especially between so-called love partners. Being in Truth, in spiritual security, frees you from all that. We need to draw our energy from the Shakti of the universe, not from another person, and let the flow of that Shakti carry us. This frees us from those exhausting emotions and the ineffectiveness of trying to control another. You best control a partner by not caring to do so."

Mindie admitted, "I'm a man-pleaser and getting sick of it. This preoccupation of mine has made my career plans and every other aspect of my life suffer."

Cheng responded, "Pleasing others is another way of control, of assuring ourselves that we'll be loved. Only it doesn't work, does it, Mindie?"

Mindie, with tears in her eyes, whispered, "No."

"Please yourself, not a man," Cheng said. "This is for all of you. As I said before,make a list of everything that you're doing for others that you don't want to do. For example, saying 'yes' when you want to say 'no,' agreeing when you want to disagree. One by one stop them. One success leads to another. Not controlling, and pleasing yourself, sets you free, which in itself is very pleasing and attractive to all decent men. To all people."

Mindie said, "I'm with a man now who is very cutting. I take it because I don't know what else to do."

"You name the game," Cheng said. "If that doesn't work, you look at him and calmly but firmly tell him these eight magic words: 'I don't wish to go where you are.' There are two ways to handle any problem, with a man, or otherwise. You try to solve it, or you have nothing to do with it, which will end the problem. However, don't hide your eyes from reality. Face the facts, then you can pass beyond them. Work at living the Higher Truth and your problems will fade into the nothingness from which they came.

There is one magic formula for all problems. Feel the pain, seek the higher view, then take the high road in doing what can be done for you from that knowing. That will be the best for everyone. Use negative events positively. See each one so clearly that it is not apt to happen again. When you have painful emotions, use them constructively by knowing that if your emotion is painful, your action or reaction was wrong. Don't repeat it. When you've acted right, and reached high, you feel right."

Trenna said, "I believe what you say. I know I've been wrong. I just don't know what to do about it."

"Good!" Cheng exclaimed, to everyone's surprise. "We are always in one of three states: 1) we know what to do. 2) we don't know what to do and we know we don't know, like you, Trenna. 3) we don't know what to do, but we don't know that we don't know. With the first state we have no problem, exploring the second one can end the problem. Only the third one makes the problem worse."

Hinda asked, "What can I do when I feel I might be discerning incorrectly? As you said, people have been doing so throughout history."

Cheng answered, "Similarly, history will usually take care of that by revealing truth. The Bhagavad Gita tells us, 'patience is a great support for Truth.' Ever hear the expression 'time will tell'? Hasn't that often happened with the passage of time? You think a man is a nice guy but time reveals he's a cad. Science says one thing is so, twenty years later science proves otherwise. Since time is only one more earthly illusion, if we eventually see the Truth and learn from it, exactly how much time it took us to do so is relatively unimportant. However long it takes, constant searching for Truth in all thoughts and deeds is the right practice."

Cheng gave us a few minutes to ponder his last statement, then announced, "In a few minutes it will be time to end this Discourse, and time for you to get out there in your lives and to practice what you have learned. Let us first do a Dharana, which is Sanskrit for an exercise, to let go of control and to feel safe knowing we are connected to the One who *is* in control. Close your eyes. Feel yourself rising above yourself to connect with a stream of light. Now follow that light to its source, God. Feel that light also flowing to the one you are trying to control at that time. Now let go of any possibility of connection with that person through control, and relate to that person from your connection to the light and from your higher connection with him or her via the light."

The Dharana was powerful!

"So, in conclusion of this evening," Cheng said, "use that Dharana when in the situations calling for it. And, toss out the other mental junk one piece at a time, then start fresh. This can even happen with your present partner. You need not necessarily verbally share this with him or her. Unless your partner is vibrating at a similar frequency, she or he won't understand; you can speak with such a person about seeing things from a higher view and she or he will think that you mean looking out a window of the Empire State Building! I speak here of a mental, not necessarily a physical shift. However, the person who keeps scrutinizing and examining others for faults is tossed about in a sea of mental unrest. Remember, balance in everything. And, here is one further bit of wisdom from the Gita. When unable to distinguish between good and bad, concentrate on the duties that have been prescribed for you. Always remember this, Dear Ones. You are becoming a group of people who are conscious. That is power. For every form of power comes a greater responsibility for how to use it. As you grow closer to the light, you must become more responsible about how you use your power."

"So, you have homework," Cheng told us. "Make the two lists to help yourself. Each time that you give yourself something that pleases you, write that down on a pad. Each time that you stop doing something that displeases you, jot that down as well.

"As for the other points," Cheng said with a twinkle, "Don't worry about opportunities to put these to the test. When your spiritual teacher gives you a lesson, the universe soon gives you opportunity to do the homework. Knowledge unapplied is useless. Stay alert as the opportunities appear, and apply the principles from this Discourse. Knowledge unapplied is a waste, period."

Ever since the subject of personal love had been raised I had been aware of a burning question simmering in my mind. I hadn't asked it because I'd been unable to get clear on exactly what I wanted to know. Cheng was already clearing his desk to leave. I realized that I must ask my question and the time was now. I raised my hand. "Yes, Val-teen," Cheng acknowledged. I gave a furtive look around. My classmates, some already on their feet, looked surprised at the timing of my question. Only Cheng did not.

"Cheng," I asked, "you speak of self-sufficiency related to love. But if we don't feel any need for love with another person on an intimate level, what would be our motivation to seek it? Or, are you saying that we should not seek personal love, since self-love and universal love should be our goals?"

I saw those who had stood up sit down again. Obviously my question had hit a common nerve. Cheng looked at me so intently that I cringed. I felt that I had asked an ill-timed or worse, stupid question. Everyone was silent.

Then Cheng smiled like an angel. "Val-teen," he told me, "you have said the *most* important thing that has been said here tonight." As I felt all eyes upon me, I sensed my face getting warm and could imagine it turning a subtle shade of pink. "Val-teen, and everyone," Cheng proclaimed, "Wanting a satisfying intimate partner type relationship is a normal desire for most people; those of you who will want that should and can have it in time. When you have achieved a sufficient degree of self-love you will know the kind of need for a partner that will serve you, serve your partner, serve the third entity, the relationship, and serve your continued spiritual growth. You will be able to think beyond, "What do I need right now?, and even beyond, "What does he/she need right now/, to, "What does the third entity, our relationship, require right now?" A love relationship doesn't have to be labor, but love isn't leisure either. Love is work. I will say no more now because part of our work here is leading to your ability to experience this answer for yourselves. Let that be a primary motivator to move on in your spiritual journey."

As the class members floated out the door as if on a cloud, Cheng motioned for me to stay. When he and I were alone in the room he asked, "So, did tonight help you with Blandt and Richard?"

Cheng mentioning the two men together that way embarrassed me. Yet he'd done it so non-judgmentally that quickly my discomfort vanished.

"I hope it will," I told him, "Only, I didn't fully understand your answer to my last question."

Cheng smiled. His answer was filled with genuine sweetness and love. "That shows that you have much work to do, doesn't it. But we could expect that, of course. To see where we've gone wrong takes more than one night."

I then found myself honestly telling Cheng how interesting I'd found it to see him with a group, how very surprised I was at his fluency in English in the classroom, whereas alone with me he was brief and encapsulated. That more and more I was realizing how many facets there were to him.

"I'm realizing how perfectly those traits of our Self manifest in you, Cheng," I told him.

Cheng listened attentively, as always. Then, without any trace of ego or false modesty, he answered, "You have noticed this in me because you sense the same in yourself." I began to protest, but when Cheng raised a hand to stop me from doing so, I changed the subject.

"I'm delighted you'll be teaching from Long Island. That will certainly work better for me. I'll be able to go home and have dinner with the children first instead of running to class in New York right from work. But what about the others?" I asked. "I gather that most of them live in Manhattan or the boroughs. Will they come?"

"Oh, they'll come, when." Cheng answered.

"When?" I repeated. "When what?"

"When their pain gets too bad." Cheng replied. Then, gathering up the rice papers which he'd never looked at throughout, Cheng motioned to the doorway and asked, "Well, Val-Teen, shall we now share a taxi to the train?"

CHAPTER TEN: BRIGHT LIGHTS, BIG CITY

"Gained without effort, discovered like a treasure in my house, my enemy is to be appreciated as a helper on the path to Enlightenment."
--Santideva

"Many men have been just as troubled morally and spiritually as you are right now. Happily, some of them kept records of their troubles. You'll learn from them... just as some day... someone will learn something from you. It's a beautiful reciprocal arrangement."

--J.D. Salinger,
The Catcher in the Rye

The first signs of winters chill-when the crisp autumn nights give way to indigo skies, and when crickets and bullfrogs have ceased their concerts, so by contrast all is serene-always give my spirits a lift. I love November and December, in New York, to a point. That point arrived.

Monday morning, four days after Discourse One, a massive December snowstorm plummeted the East Coast. The day I'd begun working with Ernie he had given me his home telephone number, "fer emergencies." This morning at 5 AM I used it for the first time. He answered on the first ring, obviously pumped. "YEA?"

"Ernie, V.J. I assume the shoot's off today but just wanted to verify with you."

"Like hell it's off."

"You've heard the weather report?"

"Yea, snow. So?"

"Only surgeons, fireman and policemen – *maybe* - are venturing out today, Ernie."

"Add Ernie Ernest and company to da list. The shoot ain't on location. It don't snow inside the studio. We shoot at 10, see ya 9:30."

Ernie wanted me there; it appeared that destiny didn't. The Porsche wouldn't start. Desperately I remembered, "you are not the doer," from Cheng, and just told the Universe, "If you want me to get there, take care of it." To my amazement the Porsche engine turned over and took off like a truck. The trains were colossally messed up. There was no way I'd arrive by 9:30. With that realization I gave up *that* anxiety. Ernie would have to settle for whenever I got there.

Manhattan had been hit by the storm but not as badly as Long Island. In New York City, outside the cold winds and snow bursts bit my cheeks and Christmas Carols, which would have been lovely at a modulated volume, boxed my ears as they blasted from store speakers. Meanwhile, various bundled up volunteers, soliciting funds for assorted charities, incessantly rang hand-held tinny bells in front of department stores and on street corners. I put some coins in their boxes, at the same time mentally hearing Richard had he been with me. "How do you know where that money is really going?" In New York you were excited knowing Christmas was close and at the same time longed for January.

Another small miracle; I was in the lobby of the studio building by 9:15! In fact, all of us - crew, models, client, Janine and Dawn, the fashion editor and our stylist, respectively, Jayson, Ernie, seemed to arrive at about the same time. The small lobby was so crowded that the elevator had to make three consecutive trips to bring everybody up. On the ride up we dripped snow from our hats and gloves as we swapped, "My- perilous- trip-in" stories. I in fact remained on for all the rides, listening to and sharing, and was still in the studio at 9:30.

Since I'd met Cheng my small miracles had definitely increased. And, one huge one. For this job Ernie offered everyone time and one half pay and upped my commission 10 %. Ernie offering more money? Everybody involved became a believer in miracles.

So, outside a massive December snowfall was occurring. Inside the studio it was summer. For fashion, magazines work 3-6 months in advance. The crew got busy putting finishing touches on both sets which they'd built yesterday. Set one, a boardwalk at the beach with an ocean backdrop; here models in warm weather dresses would languish. Set two, sand and again the ocean backdrop; here models 5'9" and 110 pounds would be showing the average 5'2" 140 pound housewife how she - by buying any of these suits - could look just like them. In the past we all would have traveled to one of the Caribbean Islands, total expenses paid, for this type job. But the client was on austerity budget, so, fake sand and cardboard ocean.

Janine and Dawn began moving around the sets, as Jayson followed the models who looked less than ordinary in jeans and sweatshirts, toward the dressing rooms. After making certain that the client was comfortably seated with a cup of coffee, I went from Janine to Dawn and back, helping to get things ready. I really relished this part of my work. People had always told me that I have a feel for fashion and decor. From my elegant mother I'd inherited taste, learned to buy good things, and to never pay retail if I could help it. My style sense and feel for what goes together came from within; I don't think about it. Ernie had recently even suggested that we eliminate Dawn, because, he said, "You do it as good as she does." I answered, "I have many faults, but taking a job from a single mother supporting two kids isn't going to be one of them."

Typically the magazine fashion editor scans the market for appropriate clothes, usually from several locales. There are a mix of garments and accessories, so something unexpected can be added for extra dash. For this shoot, Dawn had lugged four big boxes of accessories to the studio, encased in plastic bags for protection against the snow. Those who had named this, and related fields The Glamour Industry obviously hadn't worked in it!

I went into the dressing room to help Dawn and the models dress, after which Jayson would do their make-up and hair. The illusion of make-up was essential. I found dressing the models a very challenging creative art form, often more difficult than it looks. Combinations which looked good on the hanger sometimes didn't on the model. If they looked good on the model, sometimes they didn't through the camera's lens. We had to experiment with different accessories, putting them on and taking them off again until it all fit together. When everything looked smashing for the camera, once the make-up and hairstyles were completed perfectly sometimes the total outfit no longer worked. Then further adjustments were needed.

The models were coming out of the dressing room, dressed, made up and hair done. The illusion, the maya of the models' presentation was complete. When I'd started in the business I'd see a model walk in for a shoot, plainness personified, and I'd think, "*She's* the model?" She'd disappear into the dressing room, then an hour later a gorgeous creature would slink into the studio and I'd think, "How did *that* girl get in here, fly in the window? I've been here the whole time; I never saw anyone looking like that walk in our door." Transformation! Women needn't wish they - or men their girlfriends - looked like the models; truth is, even the models don't look like the models. She might walk in beauty like the night, as the prose says, but only until the camera stops clicking. Then like the late August summer, she fades fast.

Once the model was made-up, dressed and accessorized, you had to decide what to take off. In a fashion shot, when the model isn't wearing jewelry or earrings it usually wasn't because the fashion editor forgot, rather because the clothes hadn't needed the embellishment. In fact, jewelry could have been a distraction.

Sessions couldn't be exactly planned, either. Mistakes happened; since we were working under deadlines and pressure, one had to improvise quickly. Today, for example, we were fastening a model's ponytail with an elastic band when the band snapped. A quick search for a replacement indicated that not in the entire studio, not in one of those four huge boxes of accessories, was there another elastic band. So, I fastened the ponytail with a brooch, and it worked. Next crisis: the shoes brought along, dyed pink to match a model's dress, were a size seven; she was a nine. Zarela wore a nine, so we borrowed her black shoes, which fit but looked nauseating with the pink dress. I got a flash. I placed a large pink pocketbook on the floor in front of the model's shoes, hiding them. It worked too.

Some of the clothes that we were shooting were actually cheap and in the shop would look tawdry. Our job was to make them look terrific in the print ads, with expensive accessories, creative photography, and lighting to die for.

Summer in December. Cheap clothes turned into designer-like creations with a mix of costly jewelry and scarves, camera and lighting magic. This was our work, creating and selling maya plus. So I worked all day in the studio under the fake August sunshine, then traveled home in the December freeze. Little wonder people in the business confused reality with fantasy. Would it have to happen to me? Had it already? I prayed not. Becoming more my Self, not deeper into maya, was what meditation and Cheng's teachings were all about.

At the moment, though, a problem on the set was what it was all about. The problem had a name. It was Stu. He was hanging around our set with nary a reason to be there, making caustic remarks, making things difficult for everyone, me especially. I was already pressured with the work itself, train delays and holiday crowds everywhere, plus shopping for Christmas gifts for the clients, a necessity which I disliked and found all too obviously devoid of what Christmas should be about. Every day I missed my children and couldn't wait to see them after work, yet got home only barely in time to put them to bed. Richard and I, in fact, both returned from work too spent to do much beyond grab something to eat and fall into bed.

I didn't need Stu to make things more difficult. I complained to Ernie, who was hardly helpful. He screeched in a stage whisper, "Stu's being a pain in the ass? So, what else is new! What do you want from me? He pays half the rent. Just tell him to fuck off."

"Ernie" I answered, "Please, your stage whispers can be heard in Hal Brent's studio; that's ten blocks downtown. What I want from you, since you asked, is, get a less lavish studio without such huge overhead and let Stu get a separate space." But as usual when I broached the subject, Ernie wouldn't hear of it. His and Stu's relationship was inexplicable. Like a couple in a moribund marriage, bonded together with nothing but velcro. Ernie's Hasselblad camera was at the ready. I took the first polaroid shot - I would do this instant photography to proof out the shots throughout - and once Ernie approved, the Balcar studio strobes went on, and with the light flashing into the umbrella, the photography shoot was underway.

After we finished the dress shoot, before the bathing suit models were to come on the set, Ernie called a twenty-minute break. I was dripping perspiration from the bright lights faking August-on-the-beach-at-high-noon. Beautiful models had just walked the boardwalk in the hot sun, looking cool and collected. Now they were wilting. Looks like the summer was fading quickly. Soon bathing beauties would bask on the sand, their faces upturned to old sol; fashion magazines seemed oblivious to melanoma; I was finding this rather offensive, since they set trends for people. I looked around for something cold to drink. We had only coffee on the set for which lately I'd lost my taste. I thought that might have something to do with meditation. I'd asked Ernie if we could have juices brought in. He'd answered, "Yea, sure," but juices hadn't appeared. I'd have to remember to take care of that myself.

I was headed for the rest room to get water to drink and some to splash on my face, when Stu intercepted me.

"Could you possibly leave the sets neat this time?" he snarled nastily.

His remark took me aback, seeing that it was as off-the- mark as if he'd objected to my bright red hair when in fact I'm brunette.

I always tried to leave the sets as neat as I'd found them, sometimes more so. Even then I was a more disciplined person than most; Willie had made the discipline part necessary, Zen had reinforced it. "What makes you think I won't?" I asked. Stu, giving a sarcastic laugh, snarled, "In two words, past performance." This uncalled-for nastiness made me angry. I was ready to really give it back to him when I remembered: "Cheng's homework time!" Well, Cheng had said without doing the homework little growth would occur. Besides, if I didn't do it Cheng would no doubt know, so I'd better go for it.

Attempting a calm tone, I asked Stu, "What exactly have I done that's bothering you?"

"Who has time to list it all!" Stu answered.

I told myself, "Stay calm…calm…calm… You can hate the action, not the actor." Then, in that calm, suddenly I knew exactly what was bothering Stu. It *was* something I'd done all right; something I'd done *right*. I'd gotten Ernie work; Ernie was busy whereas Stu was slow. I was responsible; I was the target. Maybe Stu wasn't consciously aware that he was playing this resentment game. Perhaps he believed that my twisting the telephone cord *was* his major annoyance.

I didn't feel like naming the game. I felt like telling Stu to go to hell. I mean, why even try with such an impossible person! Even if he did know the truth he'd never admit it. No Discourse would ever work on him. Still…I knew this was happening for a reason and that I had to try to react properly.

I took a deep breath, exhaled, and said, "Stu, you seem angry at me all the time. I know that isn't doing anything for me and I doubt that it is for you either. I doubt the phone cord is what's bothering you the most. Why don't you tell me what is?"

Stu was definitely momentarily disarmed. For a moment he actually looked vulnerable. Then his old manner returned.

"I *told* you what it's really about," he said gruffly. He was, as Cheng had forewarned, being defensive rather than facing his true feelings. Penetrate this rock? I'd do better hitting my head against a wall!

"You don't really know me" I answered. "Why would I take seriously criticisms about me from somebody who doesn't know me? Get to know me and you'll find plenty really wrong with me to criticize."

It wasn't planned, it wasn't calculated. But, it worked. Stu looked directly at me for the first time, momentarily bemused.

Then he slumped down on a chair and asked sadly, "Do you think it's easy, being slow this time of year?"

I'd never seen Stu so defenseless. I could feel his hurt. I felt empathy with him. I didn't know how to answer him without sounding solicitous or patronizing. Silently I prayed for direction. In a few seconds the words came and I listened to myself say them.

"Yes, I know how it is, not having what we want, especially when we see other people having it, when we're as good and smart and deserving as they are. It stinks. You're a good photographer, Stu. I don't know why you don't have work. I wish I could help, but obviously I can't go after jobs for you; I work for Ernie. If I can help in any other way, please, ask me." Personally, I felt Stu's rep was ineffective but I wasn't going to get involved in that.

I didn't have to. Several days later Stu told me that because I was so good at what I did, he had looked at his own situation and found his own rep lacking. So, he'd fired him. He wanted one like me. Did I know anyone? I promised I'd look around.

After that the change in Stu was noticeable, albeit gradual. He began by immediately getting off of my case, then started to listen to me and to respond sensibly. "Goodness me!" I thought, "It worked! It works! Thank you, Cheng!" I couldn't wait to tell the class, and Cheng especially!

We resumed the shooting and wrapped the shoot up on schedule without further delays.

I arrived home at night frozen and tired from the long day and the commute. The Long Island Rail Road didn't need a heavy snow to mess up; that evening that WAS the excuse. Next week it would be something else. I was just in time to help prepare and eat dinner with Essie and the children while hearing the daily litany of complaints; Willie had gotten into the Botto's (our neighbors to the right) driveway and thrown some of the gravel from it into their pool. Sammy had bitten another of the Nickel's (our neighbors to the left) children. For whatever went on in his dog-mind, ordinarily complacement Sammy had decided that any child gliding by our property on a sled deserved to be punished with a nip through his snowsuit leg. Richard had phoned to say he had a late meeting. He was working on one transaction as if his life depended upon it. Not that he'd told me much about it. That wasn't entirely fair. I hadn't asked. "I can't find the time," my ego rationalized. "You haven't made the time," my Self responded.

Once the children were asleep I called the neighbors to make necessary amends. First the Botto's. When I'd heard that Nick Botto was connected somehow with the Mafia, I'd thought, "Thank God!" I'd been told that they're the best neighbors. In fact, Mrs. Botto, whom I saw leaving for church most Sundays, had told me, "Your Willie is a blessing from God." While I would often differ with that opinion, I was grateful for her attitude. With Willie, understanding neighbors were not just a pleasantry, they were a salvation. Nick answered the phone and, predictably, told me to forget it; "that's nothing," he said. (In *his* life, probably so!) On the other hand, the Nickels, our "straight" neighbors, told me that if I didn't keep "that damned dog" inside our yard, they'd shoot him. I offered to pay their pediatrician's bill. They accepted my offer and quoted $125. $125? For what?! I felt they'd padded more than a little, but I wrote them a check for the full amount. Like Scarlet O'Hara, I'd worry tomorrow about covering it.

Once the children were asleep I headed for my bathtub. This was where I went for a retreat, where awarenesses unfolded, answers appeared. This time I'd indulge in a rare sybaritic treat, a luxury bath.

I poured bubble bath into the Jacuzzi. While the tub filled, I shampooed and conditioned my hair, pinned it to the top of my head, removed all the traces of make-up and city grime from my face, exfoliated it with an apricot scrub, then spread on a mud mask. I lit one candle and some incense. I didn't know anybody else who used incense then, but I'd unexpectedly found some in an obscure health food store in Manhattan. I loved it's sandalwood aroma in my rooms. Then, after dipping one toe in to test the water temperature, I climbed into the tub. I turned the whirlpool on, and with water up to my neck, luxuriated in the bubbly perfumed elixir swirling around my arms and legs. After twenty minutes, relaxed was not the word for me. I in fact felt myself on the verge of going into a meditative state, so I let out three-quarters of the water for safety, and told meditation to take me. But first, inexplicably my mind gave me thoughts of Brandt.

Our relationship recently had been warm and loving, which I attributed to Brandt and Annie having broken off theirs'. He'd told me that she'd been dumping all over him; he didn't want to take it anymore. I was glad. It seemed an equation. Annie dumps on Brandt, Brandt dumps on Valentine. I'd told Brandt, once they'd broken off, that while I didn't feel that in my circumstance I had the right to ask him for exclusivity, I indeed claimed every right to be told if he was seeing Annie again, or feeling serious about anybody else. In that way I could make an informed decision as to whether or not I should continue our relationship. He had replied, "I understand," which I'd assumed to be an agreement to my terms. Whoever had coined the term, "To assume makes an ass out of you and me," probably knew me.

I'd been meditating for about a half-hour when I began to get mental images. This was incredible. First, I saw a pretty blonde young woman swimming in liquids; in fact, she looked like she was drowning in them. Suddenly, Brandt appeared beside her and after struggling, managed to pull her from the water. Next I saw her with Brandt, in what I knew to be his apartment. I didn't understand the liquid part, but the rest was clear. The blonde young woman was Annie. Right then I knew that Brandt had taken her back again and wasn't planning to share that bit of information with me.

In that condition of feeling violated my meditative state vanished. I twisted the whirlpool knobs to off, nearly jumped out of the tub, wound a towel around me, and still dripping, ran to the bedroom phone and dialed the long distance operator. When she came on, I gave her Brandt's apartment number.

"Excuse me, Ms. Jordan," she answered. "Didn't you intend to make that collect?"

"Th…th...thank you, I did forget to do that. Yes, please."

Her voice *was* familiar. Obviously so was mine, to her. Incredible. After five hundred collect calls to Brandt since we'd met, even the operators knew me!

After about five rings I heard the receiver lift and a woman's voice say, "Hello." The operator asked if she'd accept the charges; she answered, "Well... I... guess... so." Quickly I interjected, "Thank you, operator, but I'll pay for this call."

I responded, "Hello," and asked, "With whom am I speaking?"

The woman answered, "I'm Colleen Ann. Who is this?"

Her voice was high, childlike, and tentative. After a moment I opted to say, "I'm sorry the operator made that error about reversing charges. I'm vice president of Four Our Children Incorporated. I imagine you know about the organization?"

"No, Brandt, he hasn't told me about it." Obviously they two had an intellectual relationship. Her I.Q. must consist of one digit.

"Oh. Well, then, is Dr. Mancino in?"

"No, he's at a meeting." How nice. Both Richard and Brandt were at meetings. Maybe Annie and I could have a girls-night-out!

"Do you want me to say who called?" Annie sounded like a six-year-old trying to remember the phone etiquette she'd been taught by the adult who was raising her.

"Mrs. Valentine Jordan."

"Does Brandt have your phone number?"

I thought quickly: "Probably he does, at the office."

"Is there a message?"

"None, thank you. Goodbye." Once we'd disconnected I rubbed my forehead into the receiver and realized the reality. Brandt may not have been home but he'd be going home…to Annie. Where was God! That night I wrote another poem.

COME TO ME IN SILENCE

At some hidden middle night,
I do not doubt
you'll come to see me again,
in solitude or silence.
And we will meet,
as we have met,
at a plane or at the end
of some new train of thought.

I do not expect
that we will be
exactly as before,
My smiling face like a Dresden cup
over satin with lace;
your face a frown away from being glad.

It will not be what we had

That we will grow
perhaps in different ways,
is a reality, quite sad.

I spent a miserable night.

The following day I threw myself into work at the studio. Brandt had broken my trust. He was toast. Although I knew it would be horribly painful, I'd better start right then getting accustomed to life without him.

That afternoon I had just finished speaking with the twenty-sixth client or perspective client of the day when the phone rang again; this would be number twenty-seven. I welcomed speaking with one more client like I would have welcomed a headache...which, incidentally was also entering the mix. Woefully I lifted the receiver and said "Studio."

"Hi, theeeaa. I heard you phoned laast night."

It was the first time that Brandt had ever called me, either at the studio or at home. We'd agreed how we'd do it. How dare he jeopardize my position by calling me here, especially now, considering everything? Now I was doubly furious. I just thanked God for the small favor that I was alone in the office when his call came.

"Is there something that I can do for you?" I asked, total ice.

"I... needed... to retunn youaa call."

"Obviously. But I don't need to accept it. Goodbye, Brandt."

"Valentine, please, don't hang up. It isn't what you think."

He sounded so vulnerable, so sincere. My higher Self said, "Valentine, you aren't going to believe anything he tells you, are you?" My small self told my higher Self, "SHUT UP!"

I asked Brandt, "Then, what *is* it?"

"Can I aask you something first?" Brandt said. "How did you know to call me when you did?"

So I briefly told Brandt about my psychic impressions after meditating while in the tub.

"I'll be damned!" Brandt exclaimed, clearly in awe. "You aaa an intuitive genius! This is incredible! I caan't believe it....!" The man was beyond words!

"Brandt" I snapped, "my intuition and what you think of it is hardly of the point!"

"Hold on," he interrupted. "I'm about to tell you what this is really about."

"Go ahead. I haven't had time to read any good fiction lately. I'll listen to you instead." I rationalized that under the circumstances God wouldn't disapprove of a little sarcasm.

"I'll ignoaa the unkind remaak," Brand offered. How generous of him. "I fisst met Annie at the hospital when she was a psychiatric aid. She wanted a singing careeaa. So I financed lessons and arrangements. But she blew it. She's a semi-alcoholic. Recently she called me foaa help again, which from Annie means money, always. This time I wouldn't give hea any. I'm just letting hea stay at my place until she can get a job and pay rent in her own apaatment again."

"Semi-alcoholic, she is? Is that like being semi-pregnant?" So Brandt was no longer giving Annie money. Now it was just rent-free accommodations in his apartment, sharing his bed. Alcoholism. So, that was what the drowning in liquids image during my mediation had been all about. Amazing. But return to the point, Valentine. I definitely didn't construe an "ex" girlfriend living in Brandt's apartment as a truly ex, non-serious relationship. It was a soap opera all right. "As The Stomach Churns." My stomach was doing just that. I didn't want to hear any more.

Brandt insisted, "I miss you, honey, *very* much. I *really* do. Annie's pathetic. Its ovaa between us. All I can mustaa up for hea now is pity. So I've let hea stay until she gets situated. Then I want to come be with you in New Yaak. February seems a good possibility; in fact, can we plan on that? A long weekend. Please?" Next I heard a strange sound. Could it be what I thought it was? I listened closely. Unbelievably, it was. Brandt was crying.

"After New Year, we can see," I said, trying not to melt. I staunchly hid my feelings from Brandt, but I couldn't from myself. I ached for him. I wanted to be with him more than practically anything else. I was captive; he had run circles around my heart.

When I got off the phone and went onto the set, Ernie looked at me carefully. "What's with you?" he shrieked. "Ya change in a phone booth?" Then, directing his remarks to the crew, he said, "She walks in here this mornin' lookin' like a wraith, and comes out of her office, now, glowin' like an angel."

That was what showed. What Ernie didn't see was the hidden inner part of me that was sinking. And that was even before I'd heard one of Cheng's Discourses which was ahead; go for what is right instead of what is merely pleasurable.

CHAPTER ELEVEN: DISCOURSE TWO- The Mind And Meditation

"Meditation is the breaking of contact with pain."
--Pantajali

"This human body is incredibly equipped to open the door to the subtle realms."
--Gurumayi Chidvilasananda

"Most people's inner worlds are so jagged and harsh, no wonder they won't go there," Cheng began. "They are experiencing only the self, not the Self. Meditation is the path to the Self. The technique of meditation is simple. Being with the process takes longer. Your minds need time to understand. There are many effective techniques of meditation. I shall now instruct you in one."

As Cheng finished his sentence he turned off the room's lights and lit a white candle in a blue holder shaped like a lotus flower. The candle's glow illuminated the blue lotus iridescently. It was so soft and shimmering; I thought it could only be an illusion.

"Remove everything from your laps, please," Cheng instructed. "Look at the blue light. At home you can simply visualize the color." There was the sound of objects being moved, followed by rustling noises while objects were being placed on the floor. "Now please sit with back relaxed yet straight and slightly elongated, as if a string attached to the crown of your head is easing you upward. Gently bring your thumbs and index fingers on each hand together. That is Chin Mudra. It assists your meditations." Although I was growing spacey, I forced myself to listen to Cheng's words.

"Place your fingers, in mudra, on the corresponding knees or thighs, palms down," Cheng continued. "Now, shut your eyes."

I glanced again at the blue light, then I closed my eyes gratefully.

"Visualize the shimmering blue light in a line about two inches wide, as if painted with brush strokes, moving toward your nose and entering it through your nostrils. As you breathe in, think the sound of the mantra 'Om.' Pause. Now paint the blue light going outward as you exhale through the nose, thinking again, 'Om.' Strive to make the blue strokes going in and going out somewhat equal in length.

"So, we shall meditate in this way for fifteen minutes. When thoughts come simply pay them little mind. Instead, just gently return to the blue light, your breath and the mantra 'Om'. After awhile you might want to leave the breath or the blue strokes or both of them out of it and simply mentally repeat, 'Om' at whatever pace seems natural to you."

I did as instructed. Soon I felt I was floating and eventually I lost all sense of time and place.

I heard a small gong sound, and Cheng's voice. "Slowly, when you feel ready, open your eyes." I did so, looked at my watch and realized fifteen minutes had indeed passed. It felt like two.

After a few minutes of silence, Cheng invited, "Now, your questions and comments, please."

Nancy raised her hand. "I had lots of thoughts," she said, worriedly.

"That is the usual monkey-mind," Cheng answered. "We expect thoughts. Simply let thoughts come and go without becoming involved in them, or see the mantra absorbing them as they come."

Next Andrew spoke. "Something wonderful happened to me which I can't explain. Suddenly, inwardly, I was flying. Wow, it felt so great!"

Cheng answered, "You transcended the mind, the self with a small s, and touched the Self. That's very good. You'll all experience similar in time. Just, don't try to *make* anything happen."

Trenna said, "I wish I'd felt what Andrew did, or anything like it. I just felt angry, so now I'm in a bad mood."

"As you meditate certain feelings will come up for all of you at times," Cheng answered. "That is the Prarabdha karma being burned out. But, I get ahead of myself. These are called kriyas. Kriyas are some of our stuff being eliminated through meditation. Latent tendencies, samscaras, our stuff, or the psychological conditioning as they are called in the Western world, except in ancient India they know that these are carried with us not just from this lifetime but from an accumulation of all our many lifetimes."

"Oy Vey," Serge exclaimed. "As if the ones from this lifetime aren't enough for me to deal with!"

Everyone laughed. Although I felt Cheng, too, was amused, he maintained a serious demeanor as he gently admonished, "Serge, your sentiment is understandable, yet to shout out in that way diverts attention thus dissipates the Shakti. Please try to remember to raise your hand!"

"I'm sorry," Serge apologized. Cheng nodded as in, "I understand," (the man had *patience*!) then continued, "Even if any of you are in a bad mood or if things seem not to be going well, everything is alright. We are living in the physical world where sometimes things happen as we would like and sometimes not. The magnificent truth is that none of that matters very much. It is all secondary to what does matter, the degree to which we know the Self. When so-called negative events bring us closer to that they are actually good; when so-called positive events take us further from that they are actually 'bad' for us. We can cultivate the ability of remaining light and happy regardless of what happens externally. Outer activities and involvements are vastly overrated as a determiner of our mental state."

Walter raised his hand, was acknowledged, and offered, "I believe what you just said is true, Cheng, because you're proof of that. I just can't fathom it for myself."

"It can be cultivated in everybody," Cheng repeated. "Taking responsibility for how we feel is the subject of a future Discourse. For now, let us return to your specific questions and thoughts on meditation."

Mindie was acknowledged and asked, "Cheng, I have no idea why my head jerked back when I meditated, almost like being pulled from behind. Do you?"

"Yes, Mindie, movements of the body are under the category of kriyas, physical ones. Something like water passing through a hose; when it meets with a blockage it has to push to get through, so the force of that pressure results in some movement. Something was being released. Very good."

I had a question. "I began meditation... before I came here, so I should know this by now..."

Cheng interrupted, "We all do better in sadhana, or spiritual practices, if we don't 'should-on' ourselves. You can't bully yourselves into enlightenment. Be the gentle witness rather than the critical self. Continue, Val-teen."

"Well, sometimes I feel like meditating for just a few minutes, sometimes for much longer and, truthfully, sometimes I don't feel like meditating, period. How much should my feelings be the determinant of when and how long I should meditate as opposed to doing whatever else I feel like doing at the time?"

"That is an excellent question because it pertains not only to meditation but to much else in life. It is also a tricky question. It depends on what's guiding your feelings in any situation. If the

Shakti is guiding us, the Self, doing what we feel we should do is perfect. If the samscaras, our stuff, called the ego in Yogic Philosophy, is guiding us, then it isn't good. You must be very honest with yourself about what's going on in you at the time. Ironically, meditation is one of the practices which will increase your ability to do just that."

"Also, I find myself feeling guilty when I don't get up early enough to meditate," I added.

"What's early enough?" Cheng asked.

"Oh, four AM."

"What time ARE you getting up to meditate?"

"More like five AM. Then I haven't much time; I have to leave for the train at six."

"Val-teen - and all of you – again, be disciplined, not fanatic. Don't be a spiritual-aholic. You all need to be balanced in all things in life. Don't do sadhana as if the more you exhaust yourself the better it is. We each have to learn how much and at what times meditation is best for us. The ideal of meditation varies with the person. You can meditate before you go to sleep, or when awakening. Some people enjoy meditating a long time, so an hour to them is nothing. Others can barely meditate for ten minutes. Eventually you'll be able to determine if you are meditating enough by your state when out of meditation. If circumstances and people are easily throwing you off, you probably need to meditate more. But if you start to feel spacey or ungrounded, you may need to meditate less. On the other hand, if you find your mind steady, if things of the external world are not disturbing you much, you are probably meditating the right amount of time for you. Some people who have meditated long in the past can now meditate for a few seconds and feel totally renewed. So it depends. We have to do it and stay tuned in. For you, Val-teen, it might work to meditate on the train. The Long Island Railroad could *use* some positive energy!"

I raised my hand a final time for that evening, and once acknowledged, offered, "Before I came here I meditated at the Mid-Town Zen Center. Their method was far more difficult. Could you comment?" Cheng answered, "Only explanantion is that different methods exist, that is all." I nodded.

Ginger raised her hand, was acknowledged, and asked, "About the mantra, couldn't I just as well choose an English word? I can't help being suspicious of what seems like mystical mumbo-jumbo."

Cheng said, "Concentration on an object is a necessary preliminary stage to take the mind deeper than all objects so as to unite itself with the Self, or pure consciousness. Certainly a variety of objects can serve that purpose. However, the Sanskrit mantra 'Om' is a vibration of the Self, of God. Such a mantra has all the powers of God, so when we immerse ourselves in it, it takes us to that place of the Self. It has certain vibratory patterns which can bridge the gap between our ordinary surface thinking and the awareness of the Self within us. So, while the mind can focus on anything, only certain words can qualify as mantra; they do that if they connect you with God. The 'Om' is the one basic sound, or totality of all sound. The Bhagavad Gita, once again, says that one should let the sound of Om resound in one's consciousness with each breath. So I use it here. There are other mantras. You may connect with another that's right for you at another time."

Cheng continued, "It is most influential, also, where a mantra comes from. I gave you this mantra as it was given to me by a great teacher who was authorized to pass it on to me, as I have been authorized to do so for you. Such a mantra, then, becomes chaitanya, or alive. Meaning you could find the same mantra in a book or some other throw-away way but it would not have the same power as a chaitanya mantra." Sensing our skepticism and confusion, Cheng added, "I know the Western mind distrusts some of these concepts, or then turns around and is too gullible. I can only ask that you trust me enough to do the practices so you can come to know, through your experiences, that Cheng gave you the truth."

Andrew said, "Most of the time during meditation I had awful thoughts. They really disturbed me."

"Those are mental kriyas. They are not unusual, especially in the earlier stages of meditation," Cheng replied. "But they need not annoy you; in fact, not allowing them to annoy you is part of the discipline. You can just see each thought as floating by like a cloud in the sky. Or, again, you can see yourself offering each thought up to the mantra and allowing the mantra to absorb it. As you continue, as your mind calms, the mantra will become more delicate and subtle. It will be like a top, which spins on its own, needing only an intermittent tap from you to keep it going. It will, so to speak, pass from your lips to your heart. The poet Saint Kabir wrote that the mantra did his meditation while he sat relaxed. Mantra is not only for formal meditation times. You can remember it always. Use it silently to yourself when you are walking, when there is chaos around you, when you are stuck in a long supermarket line. It will calm you down as well as those around you, although they may not understand why. Mantra used in such ways is called doing 'japa.'"

Andrew became acknowledged, then asked, "Will you define ego again, Cheng?"

"Gladly. Simply, the ego is anything that we identify with which is not real. When we identify with our thoughts, with our feelings, any time that we feel we are superior or inferior to any-one else, in other words, any bit of identification that we entertain about ourselves or about anybody else which is other than our larger Self, is called 'ego.'"

Trenna, once acknowledged, asked, "Is it best to meditate alone or with others?"

"Both," answered Cheng. "In addition to meditating regularly on your own, it is good to find other people with whom you can share your interest in meditation. A seeker needs satsang, a group of fellow aspirants, a support system. This keeps you going when you might otherwise be tricked by your own mind into stopping out of boredom, sense of isolation, or other so-called reasons for quitting. Also, meditating with others creates a group vibration, which makes meditation easier and deeper.

"Right now all of you here have this group and this way," Cheng offered. "People whose karma was not to be in this group might want to consult listings for nationwide meditation organiza-tions and for smaller meditation groups, and to try one. They can see if they feel comfortable there, but at the same time try not to waste too much time in the beginning evaluating one group or the next. The important thing is to begin. After, with experience, a person may decide to drop one group and go with another. But try not to jump from one to the other to the next. Just imagine trying to fly from here to the Orient by changing planes every half-hour! With any group it is important to suspend judgements, criticisms and doubts for at least three to six months. Unless of course you *know* far sooner that the group is bad news. We would hope your Self will guide you to only ethical, honest, qualified people. You have to start somewhere, so plunge in."

Nancy, after being acknowledged, asked, "What can I expect myself to be like from meditation?"

"Ah!" Cheng exclaimed with pleasure, "A most important question. With its answer always in mind, our motivation to con-tinue is more assured. As meditation continues, 'less is more.' We become totally content with less noise and sense stimulation of every kind." Now Cheng looked directly at me.

"One of my own teachers was silent for many years," he told me. "He communicated with a chalk board on which he wrote many phrases. He instructed me to do the same. At first it seemed just a game, but in time I saw the depth, beauty and value in it. First I started getting tired of writing such long answers, so I began to find simpler ways of saying things; this simplified my thoughts, so quieted my mind. Silence brought me great energy and clarity; we don't realize how much energy we lose in normal chatter."

Although I found that last information from Cheng especially fascinating, I had no idea why he'd singled me out to impart it to.

"Any more questions?" Cheng asked. There were none, so he went on. "Well, your questions thus far have captured very important points. To conclude this discussion I'll now encapsulate some other factors about meditation and its known results.

Your friends: As you grow, your friends will change. Your pull to turn to others out of need will dissipate. You may increasingly prefer to be with those who share your interests in meditation and related things, or to be alone more. Having friends who are on your path will not stop the drama and conflicts that people go through, but can throw a different light on them with your newfound perceptions. These type dramas are usually worked through relatively quickly.

Proselytizing: Don't. Of course, in the beginning you will ignore this advice. But after a while your need to convince others will also fall away. You cannot convince others that meditation is right, just as they can't convince you that it's wrong. Your own changes through meditation will be your strongest convincers.

Solitude: At some time during our Discourses please spend some time alone, be it a day, weekend, month. During that time you will do some intense inner work, which will accelerate your progress.

"Is meditation an escape from life? There are people who use it as such; they are copping-out. Meditation is not an escape from responsibility and the world; rather, meditation leads us into deeper appreciation of our interrelatedness with the world and with those in it - our family, friends, communities. It makes us more aware of our dharma, our right roles to fill. For example, one oriental teacher protested social injustices which was apparently his destiny; that isn't my particular role to play but evidently it was his. Whatever our right roles, or our dharma, meditation allows us to see it more clearly and to then want what we are intended to do. To do it enthusiastically and compassionately, non-argumentatively and non-angrily, as well as to not get carried away emotionally. See Ghandi as an example. He always tried to meditate and to remember God; even when assassinated his last words were to God.

Experiences through meditation: At times during meditation you will have intense experiences, feelings of agitation and feelings of deep peace. There will come the desire to try to repeat the "good ones," and to compare all future meditations to those. Don't do that, for that also becomes an attachment. You will also develop powers. We will discuss those in a future Discourse. Becoming attached to those takes you from your ultimate purpose, to fuse with the Self, with God. So you will be urged not to exaggerate their importance.

Oppositional states to meditation: The ancient texts list them. The major ones are tiredness and torpor, strong desires, distractions, agitations and worry, depression and doubt; the enemies, which will be the subject of a future discourse. Treat these like any distraction. Just make the effort to meditate. Of course, if you haven't been getting enough sleep and feel tired, at that moment you may need to take a nap instead; use discretion. Many of the distractions are the ego, which is not going to give up without a fight. A common ego tactic is to question your teacher or your method. Question your questions here. Even if your teacher were one of those rare ones wrongly motivated, such a person usually cannot hurt a sincere seeker. Examine everything, including your doubts, clearly.

Fears: Of losing control, fear that something will happen, fear that nothing will happen. I have seen people who had been very opinionated losing that quality and worrying that they were losing their personality, their strength. What was actually happening was that their so-called strengths were actually rigidity, whereas now they were developing the perception to see all sides, which is far preferable. With continued meditation your fears will pass.

Fewer Special Moments: The highs will become fewer as the rest of your life rises to met those highs. Before, the highs seemed so high because most of your life was so low. So, you may find yourself getting less of a rush from those things, which formerly gave you excitement. You will miss such excitement at times, but keep in mind, that excitement was simply high-level agitation. As more moments become richer, fewer become special. However, there will be periods during the transformation when the darker moments are leaving but have not yet been replaced by the lighter and richer. Keep meditating and be patient. That, too, will pass.

Confronting your Attachments: It is important to face all your weaknesses in turn, as painful as that can be. With continued sadhana, hopefully you will welcome that process. This is important," Cheng added. "Psychotherapy may be essential to work through awarenesses from meditation. Meditation helps us confront our issues, then therapy helps to obfuscate them. Few individuals can do that alone, and friends are usually not the ones to turn to; they lack sufficient objectivity and training. During the meditative processes, the help of a qualified psychotherapist is recommended, preferably one familiar with the meditation process. You can at times work through some of this on your own. However, when something happens and you feel a painful emotion, you can help yourself by trying to follow your pain back to its source, so you can better understand why it came up in the present moment.

New Energy, Old Habits: New energies will surge through you. Beware of using your new energy, charisma and the like gained through meditation for wrong reasons. Through meditation, you will indeed become more attractive to people. There will be intense periods. During those you may want to breathe more deeply, get more rest, watch your diet, do the yoga postures - all the above advisable at any time. Keep your sights on the highest so you won't take the energy and go astray with it.

Lightness: Meditation will gradually make you lighter. You'll want to giggle." Cheng punctuated that with a giggle, causing us to join in. "You will increasingly see the 'lila,' or the divine dances of life, and it will amuse you, like a crazy, comical, confused movie. That's wondeful, but be appropriate.

The Journey: In the West, you have little appreciation of the years of intense spiritual effort which brought the few to the top.

Christ's forty days in the desert; Buddha's years of intense spiritual work; the great Indian Saint Nityananda, who was said to be a born saint, however devoted lifetimes to sadhana before becoming recognized as a Siddha, a Perfected One. Asia has innumerable stories of those beings. Many of the greatest of those Ones then returned to the everyday world as a light for others, whether formally or otherwise. Such Bodhisatvas, Siddhas, Zaddiks, thus returned but were beyond return. Up until that moment, that liberation, there is some degree of suffering, some clinging, some emotional imperfections. When liberation is reached, that being is totally free. All is intuitive, spontaneity, clarity. All is love.

"That is the end of this evening's Discourse," Cheng announced. "Do your homework. Meditate. And please, before you leave tonight, read this."

With his last words Cheng began to hand every one of us a flyer. As each of us received ours we began to read it as instructed. Very soon many giggles of amusement filled the room along with murmurs of appreciation. The flyer said as follows:

Dr. Cheng's Signs and Symptoms of Meditation

✧ The signs of smiles on faces and laughter, considered especially strange, since often the causes of such symptoms of joy are unclear to the observer.

✧ The symptom of loss of interest in activities which one formerly enjoyed, like manipulation, relationship game-playing, as well as in formerly appreciated group sports like gossiping, backbiting, one-up/one-down games of competition.

✧ The symptom of a peculiar lack of fear in situations which the person formerly would have found fearful, and the majority still do.

✧ The symptom of unusual tastes, such as savoring (or at least being able to stomach) all kinds of weather, including "yucky" kinds, like slush.

✧ Rare combinations of symptoms such as being strong and sensitive at the same time.

✧ A diminishment of certain former signs such as criticalness and judgementalness, with a corresponding increase in other signs like finer discrimination and clearer perceptions.

✧ This symptom is perhaps the STRANGEST of all! Overwhelming sensations of love within, felt for everyone -- even for those one can't stand.

Please Be Forewarned!

The symptoms of meditation increase in number and degree as the condition progresses; they are felt to be irreversible. In that the syndrome is affecting growing numbers of people and the symptoms are highly contagious, it is felt that meditation will reach epidemic proportions soon.

At the bottom Cheng had written the following in smaller type:

Dr. Cheng Ho became interested in the condition of meditation having been personally exposed to it eons ago and seriously affected by it thereafter. His condition has intensified progressively, so that he must now be considered (for lack of a better classification, unfortunately) a "hopeless case." As a perfect indication of the way in which meditation affects a person, Dr. Cheng now makes the following statement about his condition: "I wish it upon every single person on this earth."

After we'd finished reading, we all turned to look at each other, smiles on our faces, everyone of us seemingly with the same thought which Ginger verbalized. "So you're also a writer, Cheng! My heavens, What CAN'T you do?"

"Not as much as each of you can once you get in touch more with your Self," Cheng answered. He then handed us still another paper.

"Now here are directions to the home of Dr. Cheng Ho, where I hope to see you all when we resume, February 15 at eight PM. A merry holiday to each of you, Dear Ones. Blessings."

I had one more question. I went up to the front of the room and asked Cheng, "When you spoke of silence and writing on the chalkboard, you directed your remarks mainly to me. Any reason?"

"Of course. There is always a reason," Cheng answered, his look penetrating deeply into my eyes.

"Well…what is it?"

"I don't know." Then, eyes twinkling, he grinned broadly, turned, and walked out of the room.

CHAPTER TWELVE: EXPECTING THE UNEXPECTED

"True mastery can be gained by letting things go their own way. It can't be gained by interfering."

--*Tao Te Ching*

"Everything in the universe is exactly as it should be. You need to learn to look at the universe and say to yourself, 'this is what I get. I'll accept it and enjoy it as it is. I'll work at changing what I dislike and then that will be what is'."

--Wayne Dyer

"Honay, we're gonna have an executive committee meetin," Wilson drawled. "Too much ta work on ta do it by phone. Since we're on austerity budget, can't pay ya'all's air fare. We're hopin'ya' all can come, but if not, we unnerstan, darlin"

"Air fare?" I repeated. "Where is the meeting?"

"Oh, damn, sorry, darlin', foolish me didn't even tell ya that, did I. It's in San Diego, California. Givin' our West Coast members a break this time."

"I'll get back to you on this, Wilson. I'll see what I can do. Goodbye." After that bit of news, I had to get off fast. Of all the states they could have chosen..!

I decided that my commitment to the organization couldn't depend on having my expenses paid. I'd go whatever the personal sacrifice. I'd put the air fare and hotel on the credit card and cut corners later to pay for it; God only knew where I'd cut from; I certainly didn't.

It was amazing what happened next. Once I'd committed to do the right thing whatever the sacrifice, there was little sacrifice. It unfolded this way. The next time Brandt and I spoke I told him that I was going to San Diego for FOCI. The interesting thing was, I had not planned to tell him that I was going to be in California. I was not even certain that I wanted to see him while there. I didn't want my attention diverted from the buisness at hand. Although I never mentioned finances in this conversation, Brandt asked if they were reimbursing my expenses; when I said that they weren't, he offered to pay for my plane fair and my hotel. Considering everything recently, I was surprised. Maybe this was because he felt guilty about how he'd treated me shortly beforehand. If so, it wasn't because I'd consciously *made* him feel that way. I don't know if this is bragging or complaining, but in my personal life I simply wasn't that shrewd. Anyway, although I didn't ask him to pay my way, I didn't turn him down either; I wasn't *that* stupid. Once again destiny was bringing Brandt and me together

San Diego was fun, flavorful, and fulfilling. We had hours of meetings and hard work, yet at Wilson's encouragement we also had some fun. That happened during the Saturday afternoon meeting which Brandt also attended. Wilson called a break so that we could go sight-seeing. Several points of interest were suggested. Of course for me there was no question; it had to be the San Diego Zoo. The Zoo won hands-down. All of us went together. To my surprise Brandt had never been there before either.

Well, I was enthralled! What a place! All the animals looking so happy in their natural habitats (other zoos would later copy that format, fortunately), while I, *out* of *my* natural habitat yet feeling very comfortable here, and Brandt, managed to take a small walk away from the others. We strolled, holding hands, in the spectrum of sun drenched colors in the nectarian San Diego climate, and visited Chester The Bear. We learned that there were over eight thousand different species at the zoo including odd ones like an Albino Koala. Awesome! We then rejoined the others and we all went to the Elephant Mecca. This totally thrilled me! I felt like I was in India.

One thing disturbed my mind, however. Ever since Brandt had offered to pay for my hotel room I'd wondered why he simply hadn't invited me to stay at his apartment and saved the expense of a hotel. I of course drew the only conclusion which made sense. Annie was still living at the apartment. Although this definitely bothered me, I kept my anger in check. I wondered just how long it was going to take Annie to "get situated." Well, at least now I'd get a chance to see Brandt's office. I couldn't wait. I had pictured him in it so often when we'd spoken over the phone. Finally it was about to happen.

That's what *I* thought! When I asked Brandt to bring me there, his answer was immediate. "That's not a very good idea, Valentine. Theeaa aa some very psychiatrically ill patients at the hospital."

"Are they running loose? I don't get it. I hadn't planned to socialize with your patients, so what has that got to do with anything?" I asked impatiently and not without sarcasm. "In any case, surely we could close your office door."

But I could not move Brandt from his position. "Just stop forgetting, Valentine," I told myself, "that your shrink boyfriend is strange. You'll be better off."

Instead, Brandt called for me at the hotel nights, took me for dinner, one night brought a friend and his date to the hotel for drinks with us. And of course there were the glorious times when Brandt and I were alone in the hotel room. Once after he'd called his office from my room, he left his pen on my bureau where I found it after he'd gone home for the night. I had nothing tangible from Brandt to call my own and wanted something desperately for those times when we were apart; somewhat guiltily, I decided to "forget" to return his pen to him. I placed it in my suitcase.

When Brandt drove me to the airport there was great gaiety between us. Whereas usually our partings were sad, knowing we'd be together again in February helped .

So, I sported a rosy glow as the plane lifted me upward, leaving Brandt and THAT life behind. I found it all easier to do when I was the one leaving. On the flight home I diverted myself from feeling afraid by thinking of Brandt, how he'd been especially attentive, focused and enthusiastic this time, and wondered why. It then occurred to me, with some amusement, that perhaps this had been the first time I'd ever seen him when he hadn't had jet lag!

* * *

I'd really been trying to live the Discourses, to live more my large Self. With Richard that meant attempts to be more patient and understanding of what he might be going through, giving that at least equal importance to what I'd been enduring. Cheng had been most helpful here. He'd pointed out to me that one possible reason Richard's and my "intimate relationship" had fizzled out had been because while I'd changed my actions toward Richard my thoughts toward him had remained largely negative. I'd had the right words but the wrong music, and on some level perhaps Richard had tuned into that and related in kind. "90% of what's communicated is below verbal level," Cheng had explained. After that talk with Cheng I'd made every effort to also monitor my thoughts about Richard, resulting in a somewhat improved relationship between us. I also took Cheng's advice to regularly try to discern not just what each of us individually needed, but what the

Third Entity, the relationship, needed as well. For example, at a particular time we might each feel like being alone but the Third Entity might benefit by our being together to communicate.

We even had some social life over the holidays, never easy with Willie in our lives. On those rare occasions when we did go out, our evenings usually ended prematurely once I called home or received a call telling me that Willie was "out of control." Still, I needed so much to get out and socialize that it was a worth a try.

So, we arranged an evening out with Bernie and Sallee-Mae. Not that they were exactly my idea of fun.

Richard and Bernie had been friends since their Brooklyn childhoods. Bernie being somewhat the older was sort of an older brother-figure. Their mutual devotion was fine to see. It had become obvious to me that their strong ties had past-life origins. Not that either of them would believe such a thing. I'd always liked Bernie, an entertainment lawyer with a great brain and engaging personality. His former wife Paula was what I considered a real person, as bright and personable as Bernie. We'd become close friends and a terrific foursome. Then one day Bernie shattered that by announcing that he was leaving Paula for Sallee-Mae, supposedly a secretary for one of the entertainment firms Bernie represented. Later he let it slip that she'd been a receptionist.

I was convinced that Sallee-Mae was something that I had done in one of my past lifetimes and was now paying for. She's doll-tiny - with a brain to match - except for her breasts; beside her I looked flat-chested, which was a feat. I recall, right after meeting her two years ago, asking Richard, "Is Bernie out of his mind, leaving Paula for that... that... that... I mean, we know she's stupid. Stupid alone would be good. She's also self-centered and inconsiderate." I also felt, although I didn't tell Richard, that she might be one of the "bad people" of Cheng's description. Taking a man away from his wife and seeing nothing wrong in it!

"Bernie says this is right for him. That's enough for me," was Richard's analysis of the situation at the time. That was so uncharacteristic of Richard, who was quite conventional and of all people didn't suffer fools gladly, thus a perfect example of the extent of his unconditional acceptance of Bernie.

So this snowy night before Christmas, as Richard and I were dressing to go out for dinner with Bernie and Sallee-Mae, I fell into nostalgia.

"I wish Bernie and Paula were still married," I sighed. "It was so perfect, all of us together. I wish I could see Paula now. I miss her."

"Well, you know she never liked New York except for being here with Bernie. It was natural for her to go back to her home."

Paula had come from and moved back to L.A right after the divorce. I wished when I'd recently been in San Diego I'd had the time and money to fly to L.A to visit with her.

"I wonder how she's passing her time there?" Richard said. A thought passed through my head. "Probably dating Brandt. Is there a woman in L.A. who hasn't?" I tried unsuccessfully to suppress a giggle.

"What is it?" Richard asked.

"Oh, really nothing." After giving me a second look, Richard sat down on the bed and turned his attention to putting on his shoes. Just then a flash of white outside the window caught my eye. "Richard!" I exclaimed, quickly flicking off the lamp. "Hold off on the shoes. You might want to wear your boots instead. Look outside, at the size of those snowflakes falling. How beautiful! I can't wait until we get out there. It will be such fun!"

"This is all we needed!" Richard replied. "Of course it will be fun, especially when we slide into a truck." He shook his head, adding under his breath, "The woman is crazy!"

"If you'd rather not go..." I looked at Richard hoping he didn't want to renege.

"No, we'll go," he said, resigned. Of course. Afterall he'd made a commitment to BERNIE.

"I can't imagine..." now I shook MY head, "Where Bernie's head was when he asked Sallee-Mae to marry him. I take that back. I CAN imagine where his head was..."

"V!" I think Richard was truly shocked. Then he laughed in surprise. "Is this what New York has done to you!"

We, Bernie and Sallee-Mae live on the north shore of L.I. Sallee-Mae had insisted on our dining at The Golden Dove, a restaurant on the South Shore in the town of Nissapqua, approximately a 45 minute drive for us in *good* weather. There are, by rough estimate, 500 restaurants on the North Shore, all of which Sallee-Mae had proclaimed unacceptable. Bernie, trying to avoid the long drive in this inclement weather, had pleaded, "How about the Schooner," a restaurant about a ten minute drive from our home.

"Nobody goes there anymore," Sallee-Mae had answered. "It's too crowded." Sallee-Mae *said* such things. She was the Yogi Berra of the Bimbos.

Bernie had explained his divorce from Paula to Richard by telling him that he hadn't wanted to remain married to a Jewish woman. "They're too pushy," Richard told me Bernie had said. Whereupon I had asked Richard with some rancor, "Did he mean pushy like when Paula worked two jobs while raising both children in order to put Bernie through law school?" So Bernie had married this lil ol' gentile gal from the South; his shiksa wife had then become an honorary Jewish American Princess to rival all!

Richard dutifully drove us, in what had become an ice storm, toward The Golden Dove. I realized that he could hardly see out the driver's-side window. Finally, an hour and one half later we arrived at the chosen place. "The Golden Dove," as announced by the gaudy bubble gum pink florescent sign in front of the place. Except there were flamingos, not doves, painted on the sign and statues of flamingos in front of the restaurant. I pointed to them, asking facetiously, "Where are the doves? Did they all perish in the storm?" I whispered to Richard as he opened the back car door for me, "I can't believe we drove one and one half hours for this place. It belongs on Broadway and Forty-Second street!" As Richard extended his hand to help me out, he admonished me, "Shhhh, not so loud. You'll upset Bernie." God forbid.

After the head waiter showed us to five tables consecutively, Sallee-Mae finally found one acceptable, directly beside the restroom. After we were seated, she went on with,

"Did y'all see this dah'lin necklace Bernie gave me?" (lifting off of her massive chest what must have been $50,000 of a gold chain encrusted with rubies and diamonds) "Ah picked it out maself," and about "This darlin' little jiffy poo salon where ah get ma hair done, To Dye For," - I began to think the location of our table appropriate; I might just have to throw up. The waiter came to take our drink order; I, who had recently lost my taste for alcohol in any form, seriously thought of getting sloshed.

After ordering a Perrier with lime, I listened to and watched Sallee-Mae coo and bat her eyes at Bernie; I guessed she wanted earrings to match the necklace. Meanwhile, she continually flashed her engagement ring, which they could have used at Kennedy to signal in airplanes; I didn't know how she managed to lift her hand. Through it all I thought of Casse, trying to picture her here reacting to all this. However, I'd learned not to put these two women together again ever since the evening that I'd tried a six-some with Casse, Albert, Sallee-Mae, Bernie, Richard and me. At the point where Sallee-Mae told Cassandra, "Ah don't need any PHW. You all actin' like men...", whereupon Casse had stood up and shouted out, "It's women like you who set our cause back two hundred years!" – I'd started to realize that it wasn't going to work.

I excused myself and went to the phone booth to check with home, for once almost hoping that Willie was in one of his crises so we'd have to leave. However, Essie reported he was "fine." Willie was nothing if not perverse.

Once back at our table I sat there in The Golden Dove in my simple navy silk dress, priding myself on being classy enough not to say it was a Harve Bernard. Also for not mentioning that my diamond earrings were from Tiffany's. Richard had presented them to me some years ago in their trademark blue box.

As I've said, I pride myself on my taste. After Richard had started to do well financially and we'd bought our home, Richard had wanted a decorator to help us furnish it. So he'd called in a well-known one named Billy who'd exclaimed, "When I get through, this will be a palace!" That did it! I'd told Richard, "Maybe you're a Jewish Prince, but I'm no Princess. I don't want to live in a palace. I want a home."

So, with protest Richard had fired the decorator, and I'd taken over that role, with Richard's support. We'd never stopped liking the results.

Richard was now looking at me as he used to.

"Look at Valen," he said. "Isn't she beautiful... isn't she sexy?!" He put his arm around my neck. I looked down, sort of pleased-shy, and said, "Please, Richard." I touched his hand.

"You two lovebirds," Sallee-Mae squealed, "I ain't nevah seen no couple so in love as you all." Then extra loudly, "An as ah told Bernie, ah bet you two has a mighty hot tahm in bed, too!" A couple at the next table dropped their forks!

"I'd say you're perceptive," Richard answered, winking, I was unsure at whom.

"That's enough, Rick," I said just loud enough to be heard.

Sallee-Mae asked, "What does perceptive mean?"

Thank God right then the waiter came over to take our dinner orders. Thus ensued the next ordeal of the evening. For a first course Sallee-Mae ordered vegetable soup, after first making the waiter assure her that it had alphabet noodles in it. (This caused me to wonder if illiterate people got the full effect of alphabet soup.) It then took her fifteen minutes to decide between the Veal Picata and the Clams Mariniere. This was a life-changing decision? She didn't even consider the Fettuccine Alfredo, probably thinking this was the latest Italian hairdresser.

While we waited for our food I endured Sallee-Mae showing us her diamond encrusted watch from Bernie while he was in the men's room (I'd wished I could have been!). Seeing Sallee-Mae's watch made me realize I'd forgotten to put my own watch on again after my shower. Ironically, Richard had left his home deliberately as it had been losing time; he'd meant to bring it in for repair. From this I saw a perfect opportunity.

"Sallee-Mae, what time is it?" I asked.

"Y'all mean right now?"

Was this happening?

My voice dripped with sarcasm. "Just at your earliest convenience." A quick look from Richard and my own poignant thought, "What if Sallee-Mae can't tell time?!" restored some vestiges of my compassion. For awhile Sallee-Mae studied her watch, finally looked up pleased and announced, "It's eleven-thirty PM." I resisted answering, "I'm glad you were specific, otherwise I would have thought it was AM." I said instead, "Oh my goodness. We have to get up so early tomorrow morning. We have an event. We'd better be leaving."

Richard, giving me a puzzled look, started to open his mouth. I kicked him under the table. "Mother and dad's annual holiday party, Richard *darling*. Have you forgotten?" I hoped Sallee-Mae didn't know that my parents were on a cruise to Alaska. (I wished *I* were. I wished I were *anywhere* else.)

"Oh," Richard said. "Anyway, we *should* go. It will take us at least an hour to drive home." He signaled the waiter for the check as Bernie returned to our table.

The weather had let up, so we drove home in less then one hour. After we'd dropped off Sallee-Mae and Bernie, we finally pulled up beside our house; Richard parked the car. Sitting there, we began to recount the evening together.

"You shouldn't have said that... about her figuring out the time," Richard told me, laughing, "But the entire thing was *so* comical..."

"He's YOUR friend," I teased. "I can't help it if he married somebody who can't tell time."

"She TOLD us the time," Richard insisted.

"Rethink that," I suggested. "We left the restaurant around 11:35 PM. It takes us around 45 minutes to drive home. We've been back here five minutes, approximately. Use your skill in math. What time would that make it right now?

"About twenty-five after midnight," Richard answered after a pause.

"Terrific calculation. But look at the clock." I pointed to the one on the dashboard.

"11:25?" Richard asked, looking bewildered.

"That's what I see, too," I agreed. "Now, how do we leave that restaurant at 11:35 and get home at 11:25? You believe in time-warps?"

"You know I don't. I give up. How?"

"Sallee-Mae couldn't tell the difference between 10:30 PM and 11:30 PM, that's how!"

"I'll be damned."

We both laughed until our sides hurt. "Well, it was a mistake in our favor. Extra time. I want to make love to you," Richard said. We kissed and with our arms around each other walked into the house, looking forward to what was ahead.

As we opened the front door we entered bedlam. The first sound that I heard was Brenna crying hysterically. Then Willie came darting by, jumping and screaming, totally out of control, with Essie on his trail. "What's going on here?!" Richard demanded to know. I feared the answer. In the next minute Brenna, hysterical to the point of muteness, came running down the stairs and into my arms. "Mommy, Mommy," she finally cried.

Once we were able to get Brenna somewhat calmed, she took each of our hands and dragged Richard and me to the back patio, directly under her bedroom window. Essie followed. There on the ground was Brenna's record player and probably twenty five of her other possessions, smashed, broken, scattered all over the patio in an unbelievable toy stew. I didn't need a picture drawn for me. Willie had gone on another of his rampages and thrown Brenna's toys out of her bedroom window.

As I wordlessly reached down to pick up the pieces of one of Brenna's records, I looked up at Essie and said, somewhat accusingly, "Over the phone you told me that everything was fine." Sobbing, Essie answered, "Senora, forgive... I want that you have…good time...I no wanted to tell you." I wondered what the neighbors had thought. This must have been quite a din! Then I thought of the very religious Mrs. Botto next door. She probably would maintain, " Your Willie is a blessing from God." Of course he was, and here was proof! Tonight God had splattered his goddamn blessings all over my deck!

Two hours later we finally had Brenna calm enough to fall asleep, and four hours later Willie, in exhaustion, fell asleep as well. By this time any thoughts of making love were destroyed, and that was the least of it. There had been a movie around at the time, The Exorcist. At times like these I felt I was living it. As always when Willie had these "spells," we were left confused, heartsick, exhausted. Richard fell asleep first. For quite awhile I just lied there, thinking among my thoughts –and I was shocked mainly that this one failed to shock me - "I wonder if I could kill Willie painlessly." Finally I began to watch my breath and after awhile started to feel that blanket of comfort from meditation envelop my being. Thus through meditation I went to the only place that I could find to escape from the endless angst and unbearable pain. My life was saved once again.

* * *

Then things settled down for awhile and Richard and I had some peaceful time, albeit short-lived. The first night that we made love after that incident, some time during it I found myself almost watching Richard and myself, and asking myself, "How *can* you do it, Valentine? Brandt, now Richard?!"

Immediately my answer came: "Brandt is 2,000 miles away, Valentine. He has nothing at all to do with your life here." Had I somehow managed to do to Brandt what he'd seemingly done to me? Put him somewhere up on a shelf, to be taken down now and then when it suited me? Cheng had taught us not to try to change others. "Change yourself," he had said. That meant I could not make Brandt's and my relationship balanced by forcing him to be more committed to me, only by being less committed to him. Would it work for me, with Brandt? I supposed that I would find out.

The holidays passed and along with them Richard's good humor.

CHAPTER THIRTEEN: FOR BETTER OR FOR WORSE; WAITING FOR THE FORMER

"A student pointed out obvious injustices committed against a Rabbi and asked him how he accounted for that in a world created by a benevolent God. 'Oh, that,' responded the Rabbi with a chuckle. 'Surely that is just what is needed by my soul.'"

--Hassidic tale

"Love is blind, but marriage restores its sight."

-George Christoph Lichtenberg

Discourse One had motivated me to put Connective Spirit into practice with Richard. Having had more than enough B.S., I was ready for C.S.

A cozy and romantic weekend at home alone together seemed the perfect setting. But when I told Richard my idea he looked at me like I'd just suggested we move to Vietnam. However, I finally persuaded him to ask his mother Glady to let Esmerelda and the two children stay with her for the weekend. I was grateful that fate had gifted me with that rarity, a nice mother-in-law, especially since my own parents lived down South.

Friday evening after work while Richard drove the children and Essie to Glady's house, I grabbed a hardly-worn red negligee from my closet, rushed with it into my bathroom where I turned on the shower. While under the spray I heard footsteps in the bedroom, meaning Richard had returned. I turned the water off, stepped out, dried off, rubbed body lotion all over my skin, brushed my hair, and put on the negligee. I glanced in the mirror. Satisfied that I looked appealing enough, I walked out of the bathroom into the bedroom and found Richard - asleep in bed. Attempts to awaken him were met with mumbles of "Tired, wanna sleep." I could have been wearing a trash bag. In a quiet rage I pulled off the negligee, threw on a cotton nightgown and went to bed where, unlike Richard, I slept fitfully.

In the morning the sun's rays slow-danced under the lightly drawn window blinds and swayed into my eyes, awakening me. I looked at the night table clock; it was 7:19. I stretched my right arm over to Richard's side and touched - the right side of our mattress. I looked over and saw a dent in Richard's pillow where his head had been. I did a quick search in the bathroom and all the other rooms in the house; no Richard. I looked in the garage; his car was gone. I panicked. "He's left me!" I thought. But I told myself, "Don't get confused. Disappearing isn't Richard's thing, it's Brandt's. Live in the moment; all will explain itself soon." So I forced myself to climb the stairs once again, to put on jeans and a tee shirt, make myself presentable and get on with the morning.

It was difficult to be calm but I forced myself, humming to the stereo as I fed the animals and let the dogs out into the newly fenced- in back yard; we had felt that more cost-effective and safer than continually paying neighboring childrens' medical bills. Next I changed the paper in the litter box. I was cleaning the birdcage when Richard opened the front door and walked in. With all the calmness and lightness that I could muster up, I made the brilliant observation, "You're back!," then added, "I was thinking of calling the Missing Person's Bureau." Richard didn't know how close that was to the truth.

"Went out for breakfast and the Times," Richard announced cryptically. Standing in front of me, he opened the Times and turned to the television page.

"You went out for breakfast on OUR weekend together!" I thought. But I forced a sweet smile. "What did you have?"

"A bagel and coffee." Richard walked into the den. Soon I heard the sound of the television.

The house looked like it usually did after the hectic workweek of this two-career couple who had ten children, counting Willie. I walked into the den and said, "Richard, maybe we could straighten up here together? Get it out of the way and then enjoy the weekend?" When Richard just grunted, I tried again. "Could we start by picking up the clothes in the bedroom?"

"Oui, Mon Capitaine!" Richard responded, saluting. Then, pleased with himself, he re-rooted his eyes to the set while his butt remained Krazy-glued to his armchair. Meanwhile, he intermittently scanned the Times business and sports sections. Then, perhaps realizing that he might be on thin eyes, he added, "I'm reading the paper now. I'll help you later," without lifting his eyes from the newspaper.

"Of course later," I said. "Why don't you join the Procrastinators Club of America? You'll love their Christmas party. They hold it in July." At the moment I found it additionally annoying that in anything about the house it was always, "What can I do to help 'you' – never 'us'." Did I alone eat, shower and sleep here?

I decided that since Richard obviously didn't share my enthusiasm for straightening the house, I'd try to get enthusiastic about what he was doing. After all, I asked myself, "Is your priority this weekend to connect with a husband or with a dustmop?" The answer being clear, I took a seat on the sofa adjacent to Richard's chair. Following his lead, I proceeded to glue my eyes to the television screen where a semi-attractive copper haired girl was running down a city street with a blonde male hunk chasing her, shouting, "Glenda, Glenda, it was all a mistake, all a mistake. Wait, wait."

"This show looks intriguing," I told Richard. "Has it been running long?"

Richard appeared incredulous. "It's a commercial," he said. "It's been on every ten minutes for the past six months. The world is passing you by!"

"Of course it is!" I thought. "All I do is take care of your children, commute to Manhattan every day, work for FOCI, a few other little frivolities, and I don't have time to watch TV! The shame of it!" But Richard had already given me a look of dismissal and was proceeding to click the remote repeatedly. I opted to say nothing. He finally settled on a mystery with a blonde woman protagonist. After some effort I got into it. Then I spotted one of my hair clips on the den carpet, and leaned over to retrieve it. It took me all of thirty second to do that, then to straighten up and look back at the television screen. In that brief interval the blonde girl had dyed her hair black and had acquired a Spanish accent.

"I don't understand what's coming down here," I told Richard. "I *was* following it, but…"

"Different movie," Richard said. "I changed the channel."

God, one didn't dare look away for a millisecond! I tried to get into this one too but since I couldn't, I kept trying to connect with Richard from time to time by commenting on things I did see.

"She's a good actress, isn't she."

"She stinks." Richard proceeded to click the remote again repeatedly. I thought of taking off all my clothes and lying on top of the television set, but Richard probably would just have asked, "While you're up there will you change the channel?"

I'd run out of ways to engage Richard's attention, and patience. I got up.

"Where are you going?" Richard asked. "Why don't you sit for a while?"

"Because I'm a woman. There's work to be done here. In my next lifetime perhaps I'll come back as a man; *then* I'll sit." I added, "I've decided that men should be the ones to breast feed."

Richard asked, "What are you talking about?"

"I think men breast feeding would be a perfect arrangement; men *like* sitting for forty minutes five times a day doing nothing." With that I walked out of the room and upstairs to our bedroom, where I put away some of our clothes that had been draped over our bedroom chair since last Wednesday.

By Sunday Richard's mood had changed. That didn't mean it was a better mood, just different. Choosing between Richard's recent moods would have been like deciding which I preferred, a black eye or food poisoning.

I hadn't thought I'd see the time arrive when Richard wouldn't want to make love with me given the opportunity; I saw just that, that weekend. I saw it on Friday, Saturday and again on Sunday morning. Sunday morning, before Richard had the chance to go out again, I told him that I was going to make us breakfast. During it I tried to have some meaningful conversation.

"More coffee, Richard?"

"No thanks."

"How's your corn muffin? Would you rather have toast?"

"Corn muffin's fine."

"You always did like them."

"Be better with jam, though."

"We have some."

To his credit, at least Richard got up and went for the jam himself.

"Where is it?" he called.

"In the pantry."

I almost expected him to ask, "Where's the pantry?" but no, Richard walked toward it. Thirty seconds later he called, "Where in the pantry?!!"

"On the right side, third shelf," I called back. After three minutes had passed and Richard hadn't yet come out of the pantry, I got up, joined him in the pantry and lifted the jam exactly from where I'd told Richard it was, which happened to be right in front of where he was standing.

"You can't leave me, ever." I said. "Without me you'd never find the toilet paper!"

Once we were seated again at the table, I drew a deep breath. "Richard, we haven't used our communication skills much with each other lately. I'd like to tell you more about my spirituality, you know, my meditation and Cheng's classes. I'd like to know how you feel about it all."

"Intriguing." Richard actually stopped spreading jam on his muffin long enough to make eye contact.

"Really! You feel an interest?" I was more than encouraged.

"I wouldn't lie. In fact, I belong to a spiritual group myself."

I could not believe this! It was clearly a miracle from God!

"Richard, when did this happen; what spiritual path is it?"

"It's called Jews for Moses. I guess it happened at birth."

I scrutinized Richard's straight face, whereupon he broke up and began to laugh hysterically. Finally, when he stopped guffawing, I asked, "Why do you feel my spirituality's something to mock?"

"You begrudge me a little fun?" Richard left the table, went into the den and put on the television set.

I sighed and proceeded to clear the table. I was loading the dishwasher when I heard Richard, from the den, shout,

"OHHH MY GOD!"

The man was in pain! Heart Attack!!! I rushed into the den, then stopped in my tracks as I then heard Richard shout again, this time to the television screen, "SHIT! WHO TOLD YOU, YOU CAN PLAY BALL!"

I turned back around into the kitchen to finish cleaning up.

That done, I again entered the den.

"Richard," I said, "It's nice out right now. How about we take a walk?"

"You crazy? It's freezing out!"

"Well, then, can we just turn off the set and talk for a while?"

"What about?"

"Nothing, really, I just..."

"You want to talk about NOTHING?" Richard looked genuinely puzzled.

"Not really nothing, Richard... I mean, we used to talk about absolutely everything. Why, now, does it have to be about SOMETHING? Won't you just talk with me?"

Richard's eyes never left the set.

"I'm watching the game now." I never would have guessed.

"I'll talk with you when it's over."

I became quiet. God forbid I should interrupt the Knicks! After all, Richard had promised to talk with me when they finished. I quickly calculated. The playoffs had been from October until about April. All I had to do was wait until May; then I might be able to talk with my husband.

I got up. "I'm going for a walk," I announced, then mumbled under my breath, "If I'm lucky I'll freeze to death."

Richard was right, it *was* freezing out. But I was not going to admit that to him. I'd keep walking. I didn't care. While I walked and shivered I reflected on this weekend. If my partner(s) was (were) truly my mirror image(s), I didn't like the reflection. Hadn't I better do some heavy house cleaning, not so much in my physical house but on my inner Being? I made a mental note to ask Cheng about this.

When Richard brought the children home that night I ran to hug them both. Willie looked so happy that I felt ecstatic watching him. Brenna, on the other hand, was sullen.

I kneeled down beside her and cupping her face in my hands asked, "Bree, what's wrong, pigeon?"

"Why did I have to sleep at Glady's?" she asked, looking away.

I was surprised. "I thought you liked sleeping there."

"Only without Willie? I don't like him sleeping in the same room. He makes noises like this 'Ruh…ruh…ruh'."

"Honey, I didn't know Glady put you two in the same room."

"She didn't. Daddy did."

"It figures," I thought. Glady had a day bed in her sitting room which would have been fine for Brenna.

Brenna interrupted my thought. "Why did we have to go there?" she asked. "Why couldn't we have been with you and daddy?"

I hugged her. "Daddy and I want to be alone once in awhile. Just like you want to be alone with your friends sometimes."

"Does that mean you and daddy aren't going to get a divorce?"

I was stunned silent. When I was finally able to articulate, I asked "Brenna, why would you think that?"

"Because you and daddy don't kiss anymore."

I tried for a light touch. "And how would *you* know *that,* young lady*?"*

"I used to see when you kiss. Now I don't. I feel scared. *Are* you getting a divorce, mommy?"

I gathered Brenna in my arms. Then I saw the tears in her eyes; my heart throbbed. Avoiding answering her question directly – and feeling guilty for it – I said, "I think what's happening is that daddy and I have…just been very busy and stressed lately. That's why we needed to be alone this weekend."

"So you could have time to kiss?"

"Something like that."

Suddenly Brenna was her delightful sunny self. "Then I'm glad I slept at Glady's," she announced brightly. "Even with Willie in the room."

I held my daughter tightly to me. To reassure her, and to hide from her my own tears.

CHAPTER FOURTEEN: DISCOURSE THREE- S.E's: Coincidences Which Don't Exist; And The Rescue Angel Squad

"It is not to be learned by world-flight, running away from things, turning solitary and going apart from the world. Rather, one must learn an inner solitude, wherever or with whomsoever he may be."

--Meister Eckhart

One evening a wise man said to his wife, "Let us eat some cheese tonight, for cheese enhances one's appitite and makes the eyes brighter."

His wife said, "We are out of cheese."

The wise man replied, "That is good, for cheese is injurious to the teeth and eyes."

"Which of your statements is true?" the wife asked.

The wise man answered, "If there is cheese in the house, the first one, if not, the second."

--Eastern Parable

Usually I find February on the East Coast about as uplifting as I would find touring the war zones of Southeast Asia. This February was typical; gray skies, ponds of brown slush everywhere splattering one's stockings and coat, and the holiday glitter replaced here and there with wilting wreaths on doorways. This February my world looked pretty. I didn't know whether to attribute that to eagerly anticipating Cheng's class resumption on the 15th, to pleasurably looking forward to Brandt's trip east at the end of the month, or to my accumulated meditations. I assumed that it was a combination of the three.

On the 15th I managed to leave work early. Walking into the train car to which I habitually gravitated, I was at first surprised to see Max sitting there. Then I remembered, this was his usual train, just not mine. Some people like Max *did* work human being hours.

We chatted about the mundane. What else could I talk about with Max, or with most people for that matter? I would have loved to talk about Cheng's classes, about spirituality, the topics that most interested me those days. But I had nobody to share it with except Cheng. Casse changed the subject; it frightened her. Zarela was interested, but there was no time at work to talk with her about this, besides at the studio there were always other people around. I saw the Cheng Gang—as we now called ourselves—in class only, so had little opportunity there. Every time I'd tried to tell Richard about my meditation, tried to explain to him what it meant to me, his reply - as you might have expected - was a joke, or admonishment that it seemed a rather self-indulgent activity on my part when we were having money problems. To Brandt, my spiritual activities were at best a phase I was going through; at worst, I feared he'd diagnose me psychotic. To paraphrase Cheng's remark, if I suggested to either of these men seeing things from a higher view, they'd think I meant looking out the window of an airplane! Max, too, was a conservative professional man. I felt that with him it would be the same.

As the train was approaching our station I began worrying about what excuse I'd give Max *this* time if he asked me to go for coffee. For once we were arriving home early together. How could I not spend that extra half-hour with him now when he asked? In reality, my schedule this evening was tight with priorities; to spend as much time as I had with Richard and the children before running out again to Cheng's class – something else that I couldn't tell Max about. Still, if he asked me for coffee I'd have to fit that in too.

I need not have worried about that. To my surprise, when the train arrived at Coldport for once Max didn't linger, in fact he seemed more rushed than I. "Got to go, Valentine, have an appointment," he said after helping me off the train. "See you here tomorrow morning."

I thought, "Max must have a date." Then I had a further thought. "Nobody glows like that from a mere date!" I couldn't resist. I asked, "Max, have you met somebody special? Could it be…are you in love?" When Max failed to answer right away, I looked deep into his eyes and saw stars dancing there.

"You are, aren't you!" I persisted, "You're glowing!"

Max smiled. "You're perceptive. Well, you could say that."

"Max, that's wonderful!" I felt genuinely happy for him. "I'd like to hear all about her."

Max said, "Maybe we'll talk about it some other time. Good-bye for now." And he rushed off. Well, goodness me!

Essie gave Willie a bath while Brenna helped me to make our dinner. I enjoyed cooking and household chores in the way of a woman who didn't do them often lately. Then, with the main course in the oven and the salad in the fridge, Brenna and I went upstairs together and chatted as I changed from my work clothes into more casual wear. As a working mom I needed to make the minutes with the kids count, but then I imagined that stay-at-home moms had to do the same.

After dinner I spent every second right up to the last with Richard and the children. Brenna didn't like it that I was going out again; there was no way that she could understand that Cheng's teachings were saving her mother's life. What she did understand, fortunately, was that in a half-hour her daddy was going to put her to bed anyway, and what she liked was that the weekend would soon be here with mommy home both days.

As for Richard, he didn't seem to care that I had to go out again. Although he'd made it abundantly clear that he thought Cheng's classes were a waste of my time. These evenings he seemed to prefer being alone anyway.

At 7:45 PM I arrived at Cheng's home, which turned out to be a darling little cottage. A poster board sign taped to the front door had printed on it in magic marker, PLEASE RING BELL AND WALK IN. When I did so, it was obvious that I was the first one to arrive.

I looked around the living room, inhaling the heady comforting aroma of sandalwood incense burning along with some other scent which I couldn't identify. Cheng was nowhere in view. His home was utterly charmingly HIM. The room, although small, contained three overstuffed loveseats, two armchairs and a couch, with floor cushions in bright silks spread out everywhere. It was amazing how it all fit without the room seeming crowded. Over the couch was a reproduction of a Persian tapestry. On an Oriental corner desk was a flowered tin box which complimented the tapestry's colors. I went over to examine the box and caught a scent from sea bark and petals nestled within. Beside the tin box sat the blue lotus candleholder that he'd used in class before. Just looking at it gave me a beautiful heady feeling. There were framed posters everywhere, each one, I assumed, catching the essence of a different one of the Discourses. There was an adjoining tiny kitchenette with breakfast bar on which were stacked mugs with painted-on flying seagulls. Beside the mugs was an assortment of Chinese teapots. The mugs and teapots went with the tapestry as if custom designed. Also on the counter were boxes of Oriental and herbal teas. Every part of the decor complimented every other part. I added "master decorator" to Cheng's numerous other talents.

I waited for Cheng to appear from wherever he was. When he didn't, I sat down on one of the love seats, sank into the cushions, and closed my eyes. From a stereo somewhere in the room an Oriental chant was softly playing. Without effort I almost instantly entered a meditative state. I remained there while hearing the doorbell ring, then another person entering the room. By the footsteps I could tell it was a man. Languorously I opened my eyes. I saw, in this order: brown loafers, brown slacks, then a brown shirt. I looked further up into brown eyes, and saw…

"Max!!" I shouted.

"Valentine!!" Max responded.

"What are *you* doing here?!" we chorused simultaneously.

Max gave me a huge bear hug which I returned while practically jumping up and down for joy.

"Max, is this your first time here? How did you know about Cheng? How long have you been... interested in all this?" The questions flew forth from my mouth. Max, like a good professor, said, "I'll answer the questions in the order asked: I've been in Cheng's classes since The Preliminaries. Cheng was my colleague at the university, remember? I've been interested in spirituality most of my life but actively so since my marriage began to fail."

"But I was at the last classes and you weren't," I told him.

"You were at those? Imagine that! The only classes I've missed. Surely no coincidence. You probably needed to ease into it surrounded by total strangers thus fewer distractions."

"But, you told me you were hurrying to a date with a woman."

"No" Max corrected, "*you* told *me* I was hurrying to a date with a woman."

"Wait a minute. Did you or did you not tell me you've fallen in love?'

"Yes, and I have, with my inner Self."

I felt myself growing angry. "Why didn't you tell me you're into all this? We could have shared so much of it."

"I'll give it right back to you, Valentine. Why didn't *you* tell *me*?"

"I see what you mean," I admitted, ashamed. Nobody blurted out about his or her spirituality in those years.

"We can take it from here, though. Isn't that great!"

Indeed, what a delectable miracle this *was*. Before I could answer, Max added, "And, there are others for us to share with. In fact, here they come." One by one our classmates trickled in: Serge, Nancy, Andrew, Ginger, Mindie, Trenna, Walter, and two people who hadn't been to the last class. Max introduced us; they were Jack and Felicia, a married couple. Hinda was absent. Trenna mentioned she'd gone out of town.

At exactly eight PM Cheng entered the room, dressed in a pair of blue silk Chinese lounging pajamas. Every other time that I'd seen him he'd been in his university attire of a shirt, tie and jacket. He looked very different tonight. His marvelous energy was the same, however, in fact intensified by his home ambiance.

"Hello, Dear Ones," Cheng greeted us. "Welcome to Dr. Cheng's old home and new classroom." His gleeful laughter echoed through the room, elevating me and - I could tell - the others. I had missed that laughter. I had missed being in the presence of such a happy person. Before meeting Cheng, I'd thought one had to be brain dead to achieve that state of happiness. The beautiful thing about Cheng's state was that even though I was far from having achieved it, he somehow made me know that it was attainable for me, too.

It was remarkable how Cheng could be simultaneously totally relaxed yet so very efficient and disciplined with his teachings. He eased us right into them, not wasting a moment, speaking fluently without notes.

"Tonight, I offer two topics grouped together as one," Cheng said. "Let us start with 'coincidences.' Dear Ones, nothing that occurs is coincidental, absolutely nothing! Every situation, every person coming into our life comes for a reason."

Cheng sat down and continued, "Let us take a look at our so-called 'problems.' Most people consider them, at best, nuisances to be eliminated as soon as possible, at second best they want somebody else to solve them. I wish neither for you. That way you would not grow. The only thing that makes us really happy is going within ourselves and thereby discovering how strong and powerful we truly are. Knowing that helps to release us from the prison of fear that most people are locked within. Because then we know that from within we can handle our so-called problems. Doing so is how we grow spiritually. Don't worry, if you are given big problems, it is because you possess big strength, thus can access the inner resources to overcome them.

"So, consider this game: pretend you are your own Rescue Angel Squad. Once there was a play, 'Stop The World, I Want to Get off.' Our game is, 'Stop This Life, I'm Stepping In.' The game is that at this point in time you have volunteered to step into your life because only you are up to the challenge of handling it in the best of all possible ways. In the future, there will be in your world a computer game termed Virtual Reality: you enter the picture and interact. Play this game now; step into your virtual reality life. The past doesn't limit you because you just stepped in; the future doesn't worry you; you are here to deal with now. So, you think of all the creative masterful ways that you can handle this life. Perhaps out of your difficulties you will later help others to go through similar problems more easily. In fact, that is perhaps one of the reasons why this 'problem' came to you; if you had not known about it through personal experience, you probably wouldn't have had the interest or the knowledge to help others. A later Discourse will be exclusively on dharma, your right action in the world, and, the way of a warrior."

Cheng stood again. "Back to the Rescue Angel Squad," he continued.

"At various times during this game of Stepping Into Your Life, things will be by turns fun, amusing, comical, smooth, painful. Sometimes challenges will arise. What kind of game would it be if everything were hum-drum? If all went smoothly, how long would you be 'up' for playing such a game? It is the human condition that there are challenges in the game of each person's life. So, we make our best moves and enjoy the challenge and the results."

In line with that I want to stress what I call "The Agony of Haves and Have Nots." Knowing this truth and practicing its antidote saves everybody untold discontent. This includes people who due to wealth or such life circumstances have available to them more choices than average, just as it applies to those people who due to lack of funds have few choices, to people who are trying to choose between several options, and to people who at the moment have no choice. I shall address each. The contentment antidote is the same for all the above. It is this; every choice has two sides -its advantages, and disadvantages. Many choices available; this may be one reason very rich people often get crazy, because even with almost unlimited funds nobody can have everything and do everything, since we are all, regardless of financial status, in a physical body with limited energy and time. Few choices available; you need a car, you know a Mercedes is out of your reach, so you try to decide which of two cars in your price range to buy. Or, you want to be in a committed love relationship but you have no choice because you haven't met anyone. If you have the advantages of having a new Mercedes to look at and drive, then you might have the disadvantage of worry that the attendant at the country club will scratch it. If you have to drive a moderately priced car, while you may not have the advantage of pride in owning a luxury automobile, you have the advantage that probably nobody will be tempted to steal it. Since every situation has its advantages and disadvantages, look for and focus on the advantages of the situation that you are in. If you are in a relationship you may have the advantage of companionship. If you are not currently in a relationship you may have the advantage of more time and energy to pour into that book you're writing without the conflicting need of spending quality time with a partner. See how The Agony of the Haves and Have Nots is illusory?"

There was no reaction from any of us for several minutes while we thought about it all. Then heads began to nod "yes" accompanied by, "Yes, I do see" and "Oh, that's good." "Wonderful. It is so simple and people don't think of it," Cheng concluded. "Use the antidote."

Then he went on. "Now I want to cover 'Coincidences which don't exist.' Carl Jung, the great psychiatrist, called it Synchronicity, or 'meaningful coincidences.' It is those seemingly unrelated events which are so uncanny. Synchronistic Events. S.Es. we'll call them. I think we can illustrate this phenomenon best by each of you thinking of examples of S.Es from your own lives, and then, if you wish, sharing one with us. Who would like to start?"

After a brief pause, Max raised his hand, was acknowledged, and related the following S.E.

"Early in my career as a psychiatrist, a certain man - I'll call him Bud - wanted me to treat him. I didn't think that he'd be a particularly interesting patient; at that time I wanted only so-called fascinating patients. Talk about being spiritually moronic." Max made a disparaging face, which Cheng mimicked to perfection. We all laughed.

"Well," Max continued, "I told Bud that I had no free hours for him. That was definitely an overstatement since I believe that at that point in time I had all of two patients."

We laughed again. Max went on, "Bud phoned me several times. 'Treat me, treat me,' and I answered, 'No hours, no hours,' and put down the phone, believing that was the end of it. Guess what? Every other place I went, I met Bud. I'd be walking out of a diner, he'd be walking in. 'Oh, Dr. Witkin,' he'd say, 'Treat me?' I'd pull into a service station, he'd be pulling out, would see me, roll down his car window and ask, 'Dr. Witkin, any hours open up for me?' Well, after this happened about five times, I looked up toward the sky - because that's where I thought God was, then - and said, 'Alright, if I meet this clown again, I'll take it as your sign and give in!" Sure enough, I walked into a stationery store the following day and the guy was standing there! Before he could say a word I asked him, 'Would Tuesdays at eleven AM work for you?'" We all laughed once more.

"Of course, once I began treating this guy I stopped meeting him on the street. All told, I think I learned more from that patient than from all my subsequent patients combined. The Universe knew that he and I needed each other, so obviously was not going to let me off the hook."

"A very amusing and perfect example, Max. I'm sure we all enjoyed it. Next?"

Nancy offered, "How's this S.E.? Scott, a friend of mine was visiting from New Mexico. He apparently tried to get in touch with me just before flying back, however we missed one another. I was very disappointed; he'd intended to give me his new unlisted phone number and his new address but we'd forgotten. The following day I drove into a parking lot. After searching a few minutes for a parking space, I saw a car pulling out and drove beside it. In the car was a friend. We chatted for a while. Then we said "goodbye," but just before she drove away she said, 'Oh, by the way, I almost forgot. I saw Scott Cantor just before he left town; he asked me to give you something.' With that she reached into her glove compartment and pulled out a piece of paper, which she then handed me. On it was Scott's address and phone number."

"A good example, these by-the-way happenings," Cheng said. "Anyone else?"

Felicia spoke. "Here's a short one. Jack and I were both so amazed. It was last New Year's Eve. We were driving home from a party, and you remarked, Jack, 'I wonder what kind of year we'll have this year.' Jack nodded in remembrance.

"Tell them, Jack," Felicia encouraged. Jack obliged. "Well, as Felicia told you, we were driving and asked that question. We then went under a small underpass. When we came out we heard a noise overhead, looked up and saw a blimp. On its side were printed in large letters the words 'GOOD YEAR.'"

"And," Felicia added, "It *will* be a good year. For one thing, we met you, Cheng. We're here together."

Everyone applauded, including Cheng. "I like that blimp story," he said giggling.

Andrew had an S.E to share: "Just last week I was driving in my car, feeling despondent and without faith. Then, at a red light, I looked to my left and there was a huge truck with the letters G.O.D painted on its side. Although I knew it stood for something other than the obvious, I needed that reminder just then. Wasn't that something!"

"I'll say! A sign from God, 'Hey, I'm here!'" Cheng responded, then continued. "Time as we know it is accelerating. People are going to be having increasing Synchronistic Events. You go to a meeting alone. Take a moment, attune to the Shakti. You will sit down where you should sit, and meet the person or persons you should meet. There will be teaching and learning here on both sides. Since spiritual growth is an uneven process, more than likely each of you will be both teacher and student. And remember, Dear Ones, the ancient Indian teachings tell us to talk about God to others as often as possible. It need not sound pious or religious, in fact, best it does not. We can give and receive spiritual teachings while talking about a baseball game, a movie, or the ballet." As Cheng said that I realized that he himself did exactly that. None of his seeming idle chatter at off-moments was without spiritual significance.

"A reminder before we close for this evening," Cheng continued. "Remember to meditate regularly. How many of you are doing so, Dear Ones? Hands please." All but Serge and Ginger raised their hands. "Good for you who are. What about you who are not? Reasons, please. Serge?"

Serge said, "I haven't found time. I know it's a poor excuse."

"We do not *find* the time for what's most important, we *make* it," Cheng said firmly. "Through meditation itself, we will begin to have more time for everything. Don't believe me. Do it and see. I will promise you that for every effort you expend in *any* self-discipline, you will reap ten times that in rewards. Ginger?" Cheng asked. "How about your meditation practice?"

"I guess I just am not convinced meditation does all those wonderful things; I'm not sufficiently motivated," Ginger admitted.

"I do not know how to motivate you further," Cheng answered. "So why don't you just not meditate until you can hear from the others how things are for them from meditation?"

"No, I'd hate to be left out. You just motivated me. I think you knew that about me, Cheng," Ginger said. Cheng's twinkling eyes were sufficient response. "But I just can't find the time to meditate in my busy schedule," she added.

Cheng's answer was firm. "Ginger, you've already told us that your work and other successes have not brought you contentment, so spend five minutes a day trying something which will. And Dear Ones, if anyone here has a life which doesn't allow five extra minutes for the Inner Self, that life is too crowded! So, uncrowd it. However, I suspect that for many of you not doing your practices is more a matter of ambivalence than a time-factor. Part of you wants to meditate in order to change, while another part of you wants not to meditate in order to stay the same. Such conflict of interests will cause a struggle within you. However, your strongest intention will win. That applies to everything. If your desire to sleep fifteen minutes more in the morning is stronger than your desire to meditate, the desire to sleep will override your desire to meditate. So, to do what is right for you requires focus and motivation. Therefore, your homework," Cheng concluded. "Three parts to it. One: Continue to go within, to meditate each day if possible; if you have only five minutes, that's what you use. Meditation is going to help you with each Discourse to date as well as with later ones; keep strongly in mind the results of meditation to keep you motivated when conflicting desires arise. Two: Practice being The Rescue Angel Squad for your life. Three: Be aware of, and have fun with your Synchronistic Events. We will have further teachings of how life is just a game anyway. You will have ample opportunity this month to practice this game. Go forth, now, Dear Ones, and play."

With that, Cheng jumped into the air, clicked his heels and bringing his palm repeatedly toward and away from his mouth, simultaneously issued a war-hoop. "Try it" he encouraged us. "It's fun. And it will loosen you up. You can all use that too." And so for the next ten minutes all of us war-hooped, jumped and laughed, looking like a Mel Brooks satire on a Western, until we were on the floor, hysterical.

CHAPTER FIFTEEN: BUT BEAUTIFUL

"I asked God to spare me pain. God said, 'No. Suffering draws you apart from worldly cares and brings you closer to me.'"

-- Author unknown

"All I wanna do is have some fun, I got a feelin' I'm not the only one."

--Sheryl Crow, from song *All I Wanna Do*

At the end of February Brandt came to New York.

This time was different. Divine, actually. With a few minor glitches.

The first glitch wasn't at all minor, in fact it was extremely distressing to me. It was that for the first time, in order to be with Brandt I had to lie to Richard about my whereabouts. Because I couldn't think of anything else to say, I told Richard that I was going upstate to a meditation retreat. Actually, it was the St. Regis Hotel in New York City.

The second glitch was, in retrospect, actually funny. In that era unmarried people didn't openly register in the same hotel room, so Brandt and I were registered as Dr. and Mrs. Mancino. However, we were, of course, arriving from different directions, so we'd arranged to meet in our room at about five PM Friday evening.

Having arrived a bit before five, I waited for Brandt in the room, periodically walking the lobby in search for him until nine PM. I began to notice curious hotel guests staring at me walking the lobby once more. "Surely," I thought, "they think I'm a hooker!" I later learned that Brandt was doing the same lobby scene, although only at the times when I was in the room. A Key-stone Cops comedy.

Finally, both Brandt and I thought to check at the registration desk, where we learned that both of us had been at the hotel all that time. Registration had put us in separate rooms!

"Get out of here!" I exclaimed when Brandt told me that he'd been looking for me just as I had for him.

"I just got here."

"Sorry. New York idiom."

That incident became a precedent. Every single time thereafter, every place Brandt and I registered and there were many such places to follow, Long Island included, registration put us in separate rooms! I could never figure out why or what that meant. Was it a repeating S.E. -- synchronistic event -- the universe moralizing?

In any case, the rest of the weekend was glorious. I had brought with me a red light bulb, satin sheets and incense. It gave our hotel room a special sensual patina which we found exciting. From then on I had red light bulbs, would travel, making cozy sensual love nests for Brandt and me in St. Regis', St. Moritz's and Sheraton's coast to coast.

This weekend we rode through the park in a horse-drawn carriage. I was so happy with Brandt beside me that I forgot to feel sad that maybe the horses were overworked. The universe even treated us to a light sprinkling of powdery snow, turning Manhattan into a truly enchanted island. We saw a Broadway show, ate at the best restaurants, had room service in the mornings. And we made marvelous love.

Sunday morning we took a cab to Central Park. During the ride I sat nonchalantly, but when I looked over at Brandt I saw such a terrified look on his face that I had to laugh. "Not accustomed to New York taxi drivers, hmmm?" I asked.

"Not any moaa. This doesn't scaah *you?"*

"Not really. Maybe that means I've been working here too long."

"Reminds me of a joke."

"I thought it might."

"Well, the story is a man dies and goes to Heaven's gates. St. Peetaa aasks him what he did on eaarth. The guy says, 'I was a Cabby in New Yaak City.' St. Peetaa' says, "Wondaful! Heeaas a silk gown and septa. Go right in.' The next guy on line steps up and announces real loud, "I was a Ministaa at St. Mary's Church in New Yaak for twenty-five yeeaas.' St. Peetaa tells the guy, "Good. Heeaas a cotton gown and septa. Go right in' The ministaaa says, 'Wait a minute heeaa. That taxi driver gets a silk gown and I, a ministaa, only get a cotton gown? How come?' St. Peetaa answers, 'Up heeaa we go by results. When you preached, people slept. When the cabby drove, people prayed."

One time during this visit Brandt became impatient with me. It was as we were walking to our hotel and a panhandler approached us. I automatically reached for my wallet and put a dollar bill in the man's outstretched hand. After the poor guy had walked away, Brandt admonished me, "Why did you do that? Let him get a job!" Sounded familiar!

I learned that both Brandt and I preferred fresh air to air conditioning (Richard always wanted the AC on; I usually preferred it off), hated violent movies (I walked out of the room when Richard watched them on television) and were night, not morning, people (Richard was a dynamo mornings; it drove me crazy). Brandt and I were compatible. In some ways he was like my male counterpart. I wondered if we were what are sometimes referred to as "soul mates."

Brandt told me about a book he was writing on autism. "Haad work!" he complained. "I wonder if it's wooth it!"

"Oh, Brandt, it is. It's needed. Finish it and get it out there."

This time with Brandt I opened myself to him on my feelings about Willie. He was a wonderful listener. He drew me out as nobody else had. I felt closer with him than with anybody.

Brandt said that he wanted to buy me a present. He wanted to open a charge account for me in whatever store I chose. I turned him down ("Fool," I would tell myself later), saying, "You brought me the only present I want. You." Brandt had told me how Annie was always asking him to give her things, and for money. It seemed she was kind of a gold digger along with all her other sterling qualities. I wanted to show Brandt that I wasn't that way. Thereafter he never offered me a gift of any tangible kind. I showed *him*, all right!

During that weekend Brandt phoned his children. I assumed it was Mary who answered. Brandt was very businesslike and cool to her as he asked that she put the children on the phone. Though I disliked myself for it, I felt glad for the frost between them.

When we had to part on Sunday afternoon, we clung to each other. I felt that I had two marriages; the close geographically distant one, and the distant geographically close one.

I knew that I was glowing when I arrived home. Richard saw it, too. "Meditation must agree with you," he said.

Although I'd vowed never to allow my relationship with Brandt to deprive Richard, it was over a week before I could make love again with Richard. While it was pleasurable, as I mentioned before I felt guilty, as if by doing so I was being unfaithful to Brandt. Strangely, I hadn't felt, when with Brandt, unfaithful to Richard. For a long time to come, that feeling was to prevail. With Brandt, my life was covered with honey.

Then the vinegar started to drip into all the areas of my life. The drops poured so quickly and consecutively that I was destined never to forget them.

To my shock and astonishment, one evening Richard announced to me that he hadn't paid the mortgage in many months. We had pooled our incomes, but Richard had handled our bills, an arrangement with which I'd been satisfied; I'd felt he, being a finance man, was better qualified with that than I.

"How could you have let this happen?" I implored.

"There just wasn't enough money to go around" Richard explained.

Thoughts came into my head which, unbelievably, made sense. It wasn't Richard's fault, nor mine. Things in my industry were not healthy either. Many clients had turned to illustrations for their ads rather than use more expensive photography. So, although with Cal's help I'd found an excellent rep. named Harry for Stu, and Stu was now my friend, these days Ernie AND Stu were sitting around more often than working. Ernie had even started taking his own portfolio around on appointments. He'd told me, "Why not? I used to rep for myself before you came along, and did it fucking well." Implying that I didn't?

I argued, "Ernie, economic times were different then. Now you won't get any more work for yourself than I will. Besides, if you take your book out, how can I make appointments?"

"I got more than one book. Take one of da oders," Ernie insisted, although he knew as well as I that the portfolio he was taking had the better pictures. It was as if suddenly my photographer was competing with me in getting work for him.

I'd felt upset enough about this to go see Cal in his studio one afternoon to discuss the situation. "You're right, V.J," he said, "You shouldn't tolerate that. Want to come in with me? I could find James another situation."

"You can't do that to James, Cal," I said. "And believe it or not, I still feel loyalty to Ernie. I'll stick it out for now."

"I'm very impressed with your integrity," Cal said. "Along with your guts." With voice lowered, he added, "I think these are two of the reasons I love you."

What had he said? Oh, but of course, he had meant love like for a friend. I looked at Cal's handsome face. He was sensitive and perceptive. I wondered how much he knew about me.

Casse, too, advised, "Tell Ernie to get lost, Val. Loyalty, my ASS!"

But I decided to remember Discourse Three and to step into my life and deal with the challenge.

When I told Casse and Cal that Ernie had finally agreed to stop taking his book out, they said I must be very convincing. I rather thought Ernie had convinced himself by running himself ragged yet not getting any more work than I had. Once he stopped doing that, business picked up some, but not enough. It was at about this time that Richard made his startling announcement.

"The bank has started foreclosure proceedings on the house."

I was shocked silent! Finally I managed, "You're kidding."

"Sure, I'd kid about this."

"What are we going to do?"

"I don't know, Valen. I don't know."

On top of all that, the biggest vinegar bottle content was about to pour down upon me. Richard and I were reaching a sad conclusion. We would have to find a residential placement for Willie. He was bigger now; our large home and back yard were no longer enough for him. He was as fast as a meteor. He'd begun to roam, to explore other places. On numerous occasions I'd had to call the police to find him. Once during a rainstorm I became terrified because he'd disappeared. Several hours later two policemen had brought him home (thank God!) in their police car. They said they had kept asking him who he was and where he lived. After driving around for an hour with nary a word out of him, he'd finally given them our address. I hadn't even realized he knew it! I assumed he'd waited until he got tired of riding in the police car, or until he could think of how to say the words. I worried that the next time we might not get him back. Brenna, who had started to become social, had expressed reluctance to invite friends over due to embarrassment over Willie's erratic behavior. I discussed it all it with Brandt, who said, "I think you should do it, Valentine. I believe when a person can't swim in the deep end of the pool, you put them in the shallow end and let them splash around."

Although Brandt's words held some wisdom they still hurt me. Was sending Willie away a conclusion that he'd never progress to the deep end? A giving up on him?

In any case, with the help of a very kind social worker we did finally find a school in Connecticut called Fair Lake, which seemed to have a staff of very humane and concerned people. The setting was beautiful. The glitch was, they were reluctant to take a child from out of state due to New York funding problems. However, as we were talking with the director, Richard noticed a decided family resemblance. Further conversation revealed that the director was a distant cousin on Richard's mother's side! Richard's family was small and its members loyal to each other. Thus, due to this amazing S.E, Fair Lake accepted Willie.

Sending Willie "away" affected me to such an extent that I can only approximate it in words. It tore something out of my insides, leaving a hole there, a gaping wound so huge that I was certain it would never heal, could never be filled. Emotionally it was like nothing I'd never experienced before; "despondent," "despairing," "distraught," "disillusioned," only begin to describe it. Richard and I, both suffering similar pain, were useless in comforting each other.

The Fair Lake social worker had asked me to let her bring Willie there without me so he could make a better adjustment; then we could come and see him in three weeks. I agreed to that arrangement, probably because I was too worn down to resist. I never again agreed to do that with any other facility for Willie. Even when an older child goes to college the parents take him or her. Why then, should Willie be sent without us? Who knew how much or little he understood about where or why he was being sent away from home to live with strangers? It was a rule which made no sense to me unless for the convenience of the caretakers.

I was at a board meeting, in Albany, N.Y., then alone with Brandt the day that they took Willie away. Brandt had made the arrangements for us two. I'd stay two days after the meeting ended, then leave with the other board members. However, I'd leave to check into another hotel in the city where Brandt was staying.

I arrived at the hotel on time. Of course Brandt didn't show up in the room. I called the desk and asked, "Do you have a Dr. Brandt Mancino registered here?" The desk clerk said, "Yes, ma'am." I sighed, smiled and asked, "Will you connect me, please."

In a moment, Brandt's sensual voice was on the other end of the line.

"Valentine, where ahh you?" he asked.

Suddenly all the tension of the past weeks demanding relief; I wanted to play.

"I'm home, Brandt," I said casually.

"Did I heaaa you say you're HOME!?"

"Yes, honey, I am."

"But... how... why?"

"I'm a bit behind schedule, that's all. Unfortunately, I had to miss the board meeting. Don't worry. I'll be in Albany in about five hours."

"FIVE HOUAAS! Are you kidding? We only have two days togethaa. Why five houaas?"

"I'm going to drive."

"Drive?? TAKE A PLANE, FOR GOD'S SAKE! It's snowing heavily. It could take you ten houaas to get here, and driving in this weathaa isn't safe."

"I hate to fly," I answered. That part was true. I white knuckled everywhere, as I had flying here to Albany.

"I know that," Brandt answered. "But you do fly, regardless. So, fly now."

"Brandt," I changed the subject. "Would you like to hear what I'm going to do to you when we're alone together in the room?" In detail, I told him.

"Naughty girl," Brandt said, his voice growing husky.

"I won't deny that," I answered. "I'll only guarantee it."

"Do you know what you just did to me?" he asked.

"I have an idea," I said. "Brandt, what room did they put you in this time?"

"212," he answered. "Why?"

"How long do you suppose it will take you to take your suitcase and get down here to room 111, where they've put me?"

"Why you... I'm going to come down theaa and smothaa you!"

"Is that what they're calling it in California these days? How long will it take you?"

"Five minutes."

He made it in two.

"Is it really you?" he exclaimed, grabbing me.

"It feels like me to me. Does it feel like me to you?"

"Oh, yes. It's you!

"Thanks. I was wondering who I was."

Somehow in Brandt's arms I felt everything would be all right..

Afterwards, I asked Brandt, "You called the desk, didn't you?"

"Not yet" Brandt answered

"Brandt, they'll charge you for the room." Was I, God forbid, turning into a wife?

Then I told him, "Brandt, I have a surprise for you. Everyone was talking about you at the board meeting. The members want to invite you onto the Professional Advisory Board. "With a little convincing from you?" Brandt asked, not looking totally pleased. "No, none was necessary," I answered. That was true. Brandt was very well liked by the board. Let's face it. Brandt was very likeable.

"Great, we can be together more often, at the meetings."

Brandt put his arm around me and looked into my eyes with great love.

I should have felt divinely happy at that moment, and in a sense I did, but I also felt some trepidation. Part of that concerned autism. I wanted to fully trust Brandt, this man whom I loved, as an autism expert whom I sensed would rapidly become increasingly known and influential. But he was very conservative and conventional, while I somehow believed some answers to autism would come from outside of the mainstream, Due to that, Brandt wouldn't even entertain looking for them.

I had to find some way to convey to Brandt how I felt.

"Brandt," I said, haltingly, "Sometimes when we think we'll find answers to a problem and look in unaccustomed place, we find them there. You might find some answers to autism that way."

"That's magical thinking," Brandt dismissed my idea.

Knowing Brandt's susceptibility, opposing him then in that area of his ego required more strength than I felt I had then. I grew silent on the subject.

Brandt believed one way and I another, but he, not I, was the expert who would be interviewed about autism by the media and others. Who would care what I thought? Well, at least I'd planted a seed with Brandt. At that moment I had the thought that if I could at all influence Brandt away from his negative positions on autism, perhaps God might approve of my sleeping with him, due to its fringe benefits for humanity!

At that moment Brandt looked at me and out of the blue implored, "Valentine, what's going to happen between us?"

"What do you mean?"

"Where do you think this is heading? I mean, can you suggest something?" He was beseeching me.

Taken by surprise, I answered what I felt. "I just don't know, Brandt. I really don't. There's Richard... there's Mary. Not to mention seven children, including Willie."

"I've been in limbo with my marriage for five yeaas," Brandt said. "I don't feel it's a situation I want to stay in much longaa."

"I'll have to think about everything," I told him, realizing that I'd never felt as confused and indecisive in my life.

I arrived home feeling even more unsettled and distraught. This was obvious to Richard. "Valen, is anything wrong?" he kept asking.

"I don't feel right" I kept answering. "It might be a virus." For two days I pretended that was what was wrong, until Richard said, "You can't keep going to work sick like this. I want you to make an appointment with a doctor."

To this day I can't explain what made me do what I did next. I only remember thinking, "He's right. I can't keep going on like this. I am not sick. I am just sick of it! Of the double life I'm leading. The lies, the deception. Sick of having everything that is nothing, and nothing that is anything."

Right then, before I could stop myself, I told Richard about Brandt. Despite myself the words just poured out. Theoretically, I would say that is something one should never do. Adultery is bad enough, but if it happens one takes it to the grave, one does not dump it on one's partner. However, since I really didn't have any intent of saying anything, perhaps in our case it was meant to happen for whatever reasons. I'm still not sure.

First Richard looked shocked. Then he became maniacal. He hadn't known a thing, he said. He grabbed my shoulders - he who had never laid a finger on me - and shook me. Only once. Then he moved to the other side of the room, fist clenched, muttering, "I can't believe I did that!" Next he shouted, "Why are you telling me now!!!??"

"I just couldn't stand it anymore. The dishonesty, the sneaking. It... wasn't me."

"Then who was it, Valentine?" he shouted "Have you asked yourself that?" It was a koan that I was to contemplate repeatedly at a later time.

"Why did you do it, Valentine?" he went on, shouting even louder.

"I...don't know," I answered, cowering.

"You don't know?" he repeated. "You were willing to sacrifice all that we have, your marriage, children, your entire life here, and you didn't even know *why* you were doing it?!"

"Richard, it wasn't planned. It happened." I managed. "I walked away from many men. This one I didn't. You and I weren't close anymore…"

"Then why didn't you ask for a divorce? I would have had more respect for you…"

"It wasn't that simple" I whispered.

"I don't know you. Not at all." I watched Richard, horrified, as he yanked a suitcase out of his closet and started throwing things into it.

"Richard!" I asked, panicked, "Where are you going!?"

"I'm making it easy for you. You go, run, jump, swing. Go fuck your doctor. From here on you won't have to sneak and lie anymore. I'll come home for the rest of my things tomorrow."

"Richard!" I called. "Please stay. I won't... see Brandt again, I promise."

As the door slammed my words echoed back at me.

After I'd wept for almost an hour, I pulled myself up. "Get a hold of yourself," I told myself. "You'd better. You're all you've got now."

The following day, Richard came back. "V," he said, "I was very upset last night."

" I don't blame you. I'm just…so sorry… I hurt you."

"I can forget it. We can go on like before."

As recently as the evening before, those words would have filled me with relief, but I'd had time with myself. I 'd been truthful with myself, now I would be with him. "Richard" I told him, "I can't forget. I haven't been happy in this marriage for a long time. I'm not blaming you. Just, I haven't."

"So, you want to go on seeing him, then?"

"I don't know, but this isn't about Brandt, it's about you and me, Richard."

Richard put his head in his hands. "I can't believe this is happening."

"I know. But unless it could be very different, it would be miserable for us both."

"I don't begin to know how to … make it different." Richard said. "Maybe we could try marriage counseling."

"I only wish I still wanted to."

BOOK II

THE INTERLUDE

CHAPTER SIXTEEN: THE ABYSS

Includes Discourse Four: The Most Concise Simple Rule For Assuring That Nothing Will Go Wrong In Your Life.

"When I think of myself,
You are not here."
--Ravidas

"My life is very complicated now. Can we please let things return to how they were?"
--Valentine

A week after Richard and I had sadly agreed to a separation, the bank announced they were going to repossess our house. I would have been frantic except that I'd had so much stress I was about out of frantic. What I did have was a lot of numb.

"We'd qualify for welfare assistance," Richard informed me.

"You want us to go on welfare?" This was somebody else's life, surely.

"No, but I'm giving you options. The other one is to ask for hand-outs from our family and friends."

"I don't want to do that."

"Neither do I. I can apply for welfare for us as a married couple since technically we are."

When Richard moved out he went to stay with his mother. Glady was a strong independent lady whom I liked and admired. She had an apartment in her home with a separate entrance currently without a tenant; Richard said that Brenna and I could move into it. Since the easy way isn't always the easy way, I declined and instead found an apartment in a complex called The Interlude. It was close enough so that Brenna could walk between it and Glady's house. I discussed it with Richard who agreed that's what would be best for her now.

I decided to have a garage sale, and (burying my pride) told my Cheng Gang. They all came to help. Although I offered to share the proceeds with Richard, he told me, "No, you keep it -- you did most of the work."

Richard and I together spoke to Brenna. We told her that Richard and I would be living in separate places for the time being, and that she'd have two homes instead of just one.

"Are you getting divorced?" she asked, between sobs. I felt my heart cracking into pieces.

"Honey, your mother and I are taking some times to work things out," Richard told her.

"You know," I added, "Like when you and your friends need time to cool off."

I took the apartment. I had to ask my parents for a loan to pay the security deposit and one month's rent up front. Richard and I were lucky. We had nice parents who respected boundaries so didn't ask a lot of pain-producing questions, rather by word and deed conveyed that they trusted us to work things out for the best. The apartment didn't take animals but I snuck in Tabitha and Sly. Richard took Jonah and Sammy.

The adjustment in space limitations to this tiny place after our large home was in itself enormous. The second adjustment was that the apartment was all brown, dark and dreary. I had neither the resources nor energy to change that.

I was especially worried about how all this would affect Brenna. First her brother gone, now her parents' marriage as she'd known it along with the only home she'd ever known. On the train I sought Max's advice on Brenna. He suggested that I just keep reassuring her that Richard and I loved her as much as ever, that our separation was not her fault, and about her two homes, just as I'd done. "You're loving parents, Valentine. Brenna knows that. That will give her security," Max assured me.

There was no room for Essie to sleep in the apartment. Besides, I didn't feel that I could afford to pay her salary any longer. I'd have to manage with sitters. Regretfully, I told her I'd have to let her go.

"No, no, Senora, I no go," she said. "You my family. I work for room and board." I was overcome by her offer. Glady came up with a solution. She had a finished room and bathroom in the basement. Essie could sleep with Brenna at Gladys; weekday evenings both could come to the apartment for supper with me. Brenna would alternate weekends between Richard and myself. I told Essie that I would not have her work for nothing, but if she could take some reduction in pay, I'd be grateful.

The first night that I stayed alone in the apartment I heard the place creak; I was sure there was an intruder. I realized I'd gone from my parents' home to living with college roommates, to Richard. I'd never lived alone. I had difficulty sleeping. It didn't help that the apartment was so damned depressing.

I thanked God for meditation, for Brenna (and that Willie seemed content and adjusted -- how I missed him!), for my work (bad as it had become, right then I needed the diversion and place to go), for my FOCI involvement, for my friends -- and, for Brandt.

I especially thanked God for Cheng's classes. I believed the one for this particular Thursday evening would be, for me, now, like a life raft to a drowning person. So when the evening arrived, I couldn't wait. Once we were all assembled, Cheng began to teach us Discourse Four.

Discourse Four: The Most Concise Simple Rule For Assuring That Nothing Will Go Wrong In Your Life.

"Dear Ones, change your mind and you change your life. The most important self-effort we can expend is in controlling our conscious mental activity. Our mental images cause emotional feelings, which sooner or later will create external conditions and experiences corresponding to the nature of the thoughts which we entertain.

"There is one law to follow which will assure that nothing will go wrong in your life. It is this: Think only thoughts which feel good, and refuse to think any which feel bad. In this way, even what appears wrong will work out right for us, because the universal forces will then work positively for us.

There was a psychiatrist named Viktor Frankl who was imprisoned in a Nazi concentration camp. Although there he experienced horrendous conditions, he decided that the one and only thing that the Nazis couldn't take from him was his attitude. So he chose to think about his experiences in the camp in the most positive way, as a constructive learning experience. He directed himself to think that he was there to observe human behavior; that when he would come out of the camp he could originate a new form of psychotherapy. And that is exactly what happened. Instead of just becoming a death statistic he survived to become a famous worldwide lecturer and teacher, helping many. Is your life as difficult as Dr. Frankl's was in that camp? If *he* could think positively in that camp, *you* can do so here on Long Island.

"If we continue to allow ourselves to think things that make us feel bad, we are inviting universal law to bring further difficulty and disruption into our lives. We are also depleting ourselves spiritually, emotionally, physically. If we refuse to believe that our thoughts create the nature of our experiences, then we will be burned again and again. It is important to realize the source of our pain. If we plunged our foot into a bathtub of scalding water, we'd realize the source of our pain and pull that foot out right away. No doubt we wouldn't repeat that experience; thereafter we'd test the water first. It is less obvious, but just as true, that the pains, the burns of life, come from the thoughts that we entertain which don't feel good. This is true for all people whether they know it or not, whether they believe it or not.

"There is absolutely no force or no thing which works against a person who thinks thoughts which feel pleasant.

There are karmas, things that we are going to go through. Karma will be the subject of a future discourse. We need to come into harmony with what is; then change is possible. For now, just realize that things come to us from the inside out, not from an unjust creator. The first step toward change is to recognize what is, next, to do what we can about it. The first and best thing to do is to think good thoughts whatever our situations. Our mind can see it as desirable and pleasant, rather than as undesirable and unpleasant. After the initial let down and reflection, you can think, "It is not a difficult time, it is an interesting challenge." You will find by experience that when your mind is at peace, you feel wonderful. On the other hand, you can be in the most perfect dream-job or beautiful relationship on the loveliest day, but if worry or anxiety disturbs you, your beautiful experiences become for nought. What we think about something is much more significant than the thing itself.

This caused much class reaction. Serge asked, "I get fired. From your perspective I can be happy about that?"

Nancy inquired, "My boyfriend acts like a class A jerk. I should think that's good?"

"You say it is ridiculous for me to tell you to think pleasantly about all your situations," Cheng acknowledged. "Maybe you can do it about situation A, but situation B? Impossible! Then imagine this: You go into a movie theater and you see a film in which a child is ill with a mother too sick to take care of her. The mother soon dies, leaving the father to fend for himself and the child. The father can't work and take care of the child, so poverty ensues. Then he too becomes ill. On and on it goes. Perhaps momentarily you get into it and feel sad, but then you leave the theater. You step out into a beautiful sunny day. Do you bring with you the sadness of the movie, or do you think, 'It's only a movie. Now I'm here in this beautiful weather, I'll enjoy the present moment?' If you are smart you'll do the latter. Are you thinking, 'But *that* was a movie. My life situations are real?' My Dear Ones, maya, or illusion, is just maya or illusion, however you experience it in your life. It *is* a movie. Remember Virtual Reality. Remember you've stepped into your life.

"If you are not choosing thoughts which make you feel good, you are very foolish. You are telling me that you cannot do that about certain circumstances because it would be inappropriate to think pleasant thoughts about those things? My answer to you is, who told you that you are allowed to think good thoughts about certain things but not about others, and who distinguished which are which? Were those persons very happy? Were they Self-Realized? If not, why would you want to emulate their habits, to listen now to what they taught you then? So try it; a Three-Week Pleasant Thought Diet. Each time that you find yourself thinking negatively, change that thought to something positive about the same situation. If you find yourself unable to do that, then change your thought to a positive one about something else entirely. Remember, the universe will rearrange itself to accommodate your vision of reality. But don't worry. It is not our fleeting thoughts which create our situations, it is those which we entertain. That is what the sages advised. Keep your mind calm and serene. The Bhagavad Gita says that one who is in perfect control of his mind has attained the highest yoga. So it is a discipline worth cultivating."

Serge, after being acknowledged, challenged, "Now, wait a while, Cheng. Suppose I wake up and I'm depressed, like today. I should feel good about that?"

"Exactly," Cheng affirmed. "We want to learn to flow with whatever is happening, whether we believe it should make us happy or unhappy."

"I should be uplifted that I'm depressed? Or calm over being agitated? Or happy that I'm sad? That's nonsensical!"

"Not nonsensical, Serge; *of* the *senses.* Choose your words carefully. Language has power. Notice your language -- I am depressed, I am agitated. *You* are not depressed. Depression is just a mental state you may be *having*. It's just a bad feeling. Your Higher Self is unaffected. Take a positive attitude about your unpleasant feelings, like 'This sadness is burning through something that I've had in me for eons!' We can even think, 'Oh, depression, how interesting,' or 'Sadness again, how dull.' If we don't get obsessed with why a bad feeling is there and don't dwell on it, it won't stay around long."

"I can't relate to this," Serge said adamantly.

"I know," Cheng said "Only a person doing Sadhana, spiritual practices, begins to find this a viable idea. Others are incredulous over the suggestion that circumstances of our life need not affect us. This becomes increasingly clear as we become more in tune with the Self, as it will for all of you. Happiness then arises naturally from just flowing with what's happening."

Max, after being acknowledged, asked, "From your perspective, Cheng, how does psychotherapy fit in here?"

Cheng answered, "Very nicely, actually. I was about to make that clear, so thank you Max for bringing this up now. What I've said so far tonight doesn't imply that it is unimportant to validate the pain that we feel. To do so can be most important. If we deny our unpleasant feelings and thoughts believing we are too spiritual to have them, they will come back to haunt us at the most inopportune times. Yes, every unacknowledged unpleasant emotion does suppresses our energy flow to some degree. We can shed some light on our patterns and their origins and then move beyond them. Here is the program: We examine our feelings, examine what's going on in us, make changes or take action if warranted, move on. There psychotherapy can help enormously. We also want to be appropriate with others. We don't tell somebody who is suffering, 'Your pain is only an illusion.' We can empathize, not sympathize. Ultimately, our present experience is all that is relevant. The present moment is alive with beauty and possibility. We need not relate to it in old prescribed ways. We can bring new perception and actions to it, and change it totally.

"Another thing: It is important to distinguish between the two kinds of thought waves, the good and the bad. Here an important discernment is necessary. Once again I remind you, a thought wave which seems negative or unpleasant may in fact be positive or good; the reverse is also true. For example, a pleasurable thought wave might be negative if it is a lustful thought which will cause addiction and jealousy. Or a painful thought wave, such as feeling sorry for somebody unfortunate, might be good if it teaches us compassion or motivates us to help people. Eventually - and this seems strange to Westerners - we will want to be able to look through, not at, even our most positive thoughts, knowing that regardless of how good they are, they are not ultimate reality. The truly Great Beings, as compassionate as they are, are always calm in mind, because they see God in everything regardless of how stressful, wrong and sad circumstances seem. Therefore, unlike many well-meaning people working for good causes who become, as you say, 'bent out of shape' while trying to do good, these Great Ones remain calm and happy no matter what, because they know the circumstances are not reality. Now, your questions."

Again I raised my hand. "I have one."

"You may ask your question, Val-teen."

I felt everyone's attention on me. I asked, "If I had a very painful realization about a person in my life, as terrible as it felt would that, then, be a good thought?"

Cheng's eyes penetrated mine. "Yes, Val-teen," he answered, "because it is good when we perceive a situation accurately even if our perception is temporarily painful. Hopefully that awareness will lead to changes in our thinking, behavior and perhaps even in the circumstances themselves."

I nodded. Cheng had given me a great deal to think about. He asked, "Are there further questions?" There were none, so he continued. "Be a bit detached from what is occurring in your life. There will be challenges, delays, restraints. Again, feel about your life that it belongs to another person, that you stepped in as the Angel Rescue Squad, as the best one to handle the challenges of this particular life; to do the best with what's happening at present. To mope, become immobile, or to envy those with 'better circumstances' is defeating. It also makes no sense; we have no true idea what others' lives are like; we see only the iceberg tip; *they* might be envying *you.* Also remember that it is never necessary to let others' words make you feel badly or to cause any negative reactions in you. Just as you are selective - I hope - in what foods you allow to enter your body, be discriminate and selective in what words you allow to enter your being. If we remain optimistic and cheerful in even the most difficult circumstances, these circumstances will change for the better most quickly. And, the quickest way to make your troubles disappear is to laugh at them when in the throes of them." Seeing our disbelieving looks, Cheng added, "As you say in this country, 'don't knock it until you've tried it.' Increasingly, our outer life will reflect our positive and cheerful attitude.

"So" Cheng concluded, "your homework is the Three Week Pleasant Thought Diet. Begin now. If after three weeks you want to go back to thinking thoughts which make you feel badly, then be my guest. But try the three weeks first."

Thus concluded Discourse Four. Cheng then invited us for tea and conversation with each other. Then, after inviting us to stay on as long as we felt like it, he disappeared behind a door into another room, which I assumed was his bedroom. While I think we all wished he had stayed for our after-class chat sessions, I believe we realized that as always Cheng had been aligned with the Shakti, which had finished its work through him for that evening. Had he stayed on and milked it after that, that would have dissipated the Shakti, something Cheng was never guilty of.

During tea, I told Max, "You look so happy. Little wonder I thought you were in love."

Max answered, "As I said, I am, Valentine - with my Large Self, with God. You know how people are when they just fall in love with a person. They glow, they laugh, their eyes shine, they behave lovingly toward everyone. Because they're happy. Those truly connected to spirit are one thousand times that."

I thought about some of my teachers at Pathways, about Cheng, and even Hinda; every time I'd seen them they seemed to be as Max had described. "Yes," I answered, "I have noticed that."

I can't express in mere words how exquisite it was to have friends to share all this with. And we class members *WERE* friends. More than that, we felt like family.

We left Cheng's house that night vowing to begin doing our Three Week Pleasant Thought Diet homework, along with all the homework of the previous Discourses. Felicia and Jack had missed Discourse One and Two, so Felicia had phoned me prior to the class to get a copy of my notes. Now, as I handed them to her, she said, "The homework from just those two Discourses is a tall order." She then quickly added, "Let me select a pleasant thought about *THAT*." After a moment's silence, she offered, "How's this one? At least my Discourse homework will keep me busy and out of trouble." She smiled, proud of herself.

"I wish I could say the same," I mumbled.

Wilson's drawl over the phone was unmistakable. "It seems time to strengthen the Eastern Area, don't you think, darlin"? he said.

"I agree" I answered. "Maybe even tri-state"

"Good with me. You'll arrange it, darlin'?"

"I'll do my best."

"Valentine, you ah a peach. Get back to me soon, ya'all hear?"

Many phone calls later a four day regional meeting in Albany was arranged.

Richard agreed to take Brenna for the entire time.

Brandt's book had been published. He was going to bring me a copy. I wanted to bring him a present, too.

At the studio I was pondering what to get Brandt that would be special and which I could afford with my very limited funds. "Afford?" I scoffed. I was barely making my expenses to commute and related, but hanging in because everyone said the industry would improve soon. Whether or not that was wishful thinking, I chose to believe it.

At that moment the phone rang. It was Cal. We touched base at regular intervals.

"Have you moved, V.J?" he asked. "I tried your number at home. The operator said it was disconnected."

I'd not told anybody in New York about Richard and me, although The Cheng Gang knew. And of course Casse and Albert knew. They had taken our separation hard. "YOU TWO?!" Casse had cried out. "What's left now about marriage to believe in!"

"Yes, I'm in an apartment now," I answered Cal.

"With Richard?"

"No. We're living separately at present."

"I see. They didn't give a forwarding number."

"I know. Richard didn't want me to be pestered by calls about his business. I'll give you the number though." I then did so.

I realized that Cal wanted more details, but I didn't feel like getting into it right then. I had something else in mind. Hearing his voice had given me an idea for a gift for Brandt.

"Cal," I said, "There's something I have to talk with you about."

"What?" Cal asked.

"I can't do this over the phone. When can I see you?"

"Well, you want to come here for lunch? I'll order in from the place on the corner. They make a great pastrami on rye."

"I don't eat meat, Cal. I guess you'd better get me peanut butter and jelly."

"Yuchhh!" I could imagine Cal making a face.

"I'll be there in twenty minutes."

Cal gestured me to a chair while he extracted our sandwiches from a bag and straddled a stool. "I told them" he said, "under penalty of deportation, 'do not let that peanut butter and jelly touch my pastrami.'" Cal made an exaggeratedly disgusted face. "Which wasn't intended to be a dirty line but sounds like one. Now, I'm VERY curious about what you have to tell me. So shoot, pardon the pun."

"Actually," I said, "I want *you* to do the shooting. Cal, do you remember not long after we met, you wanted to do some nude testing work with me?"

"Sure I remember."

"Is your offer … still… good?"

Cal's eyes widened as he leaned so far forward on his stool that I thought he would tip over.

"Are you kidding? Of course it is. You want to do it?!"

"Yes, Cal. I have a few conditions, though. It has to be totally professional, we do it this weekend, and I get a copy of the prints, along with the negatives, within a week. Can you give me all that?"

"Sure, but…"

"I trust you that nobody but you will ever see the originals."

Cal's pleased expression turned to a frown.

"You know that. I'd just like to ask one thing. Why?"

"Why what?"

"For years you refused - now suddenly you want to pose nude and you want to right away. Why, V.J?"

"Must I answer?"

"No, but I'm hoping you will."

"Alright- I decided I wanted pictures of myself to show my grandchildren. Will that do?"

"You got grandchildren already? So you're not going to tell me why."

"No."

"Alright then, V.J. You've got all the conditions you asked for. How's tomorrow night at 6:30?"

"Perfect."

My God, I was actually going to do it!

I thought fast then. These needed to be the best. What else? Make-up and hair, naturally.

At our studio the next day I located Jayson and asked if he could make me up for photographs that I was going to have taken. After thinking for a minute he said, "It's tight today, but. for you angel, yes. How about five tonight?"

" Couldn't be better! I thank you so, Jayson. I can pay you something every week until I've paid your fee," I offered. "Would that be acceptable?"

"That is *not* acceptable. Who mentioned money?" Jayson insisted. "Its my honor to do your face."

At five that evening I sat in our studio as Jayson prepared to do his magic. "I can't wait," I told him. "You are the best."

"A slight exaggeration," Jayson answered, "but, only slight. Sweetie, what will you be wearing for the shoot?"

After a rather long pause, I answered, "Nothing…much."

"Dearest, puu..leeze. To do this right I've got to know the color of your outfit."

"Flesh tones" I offered. "Is that close enough?"

Jayson appeared distressed. "Pardon my French, but why would you want to look like shit in beige, not that YOU could, but why not iced pastels or vivids for you? Beiges on someone as spectacular as you are boring."

I gave up. "Jayson" I whispered, "these are nudes."

"Nudes. Oh, my!" Jayson gulped. "I take it all back. Nude on you will be far from boring."

"Jayse, one thing… please don't tell anybody."

"Don't ever worry about that with me. When you grow up gay in the 50's in the South as I did, you learn how to keep your mouth shut." After a moment's reflection, Jayson added, "Honey, you look so gorgeous, the guy who gets these will lose his breath."

When Jayson was finished I had to concede. I looked beautiful.

When I arrived at the studio, Cal had arranged some wineglasses on a small table and Stan Getz played softly in the background. Cal took a bottle of Chardonnay out of the studio refrigerator and offered to pour me some. "It'll relax you," he said."I'm relaxed enough," I answered nervously. "I don't drink on a job."

Cal, shrugging, poured himself a glass.

"Can, can't we please get started?" I asked, fidgeting.

"I'm ready."

I just stood there as if I'd never been on a set in my life.

"You can go into the dressing room and put this on." Cal handed me a drape cloth.

When I came out, the set was dim except for a key light. The stereo now was playing Paul Desmond on the sax. I took my place on the no-seam and reclined. I had a sudden flashback of the facilitator at Pathways, telling me how to take my clothes off. "You just do it," he'd said. Certainly I'd come a long way since then - or had I? Quickly, I removed the drape and tossed it in Cal's direction.

Cal sighed and whistled. "Ba-by -- you are even more gorgeous that I imagined."

"Cal," I admonished as firmly as I could manage in my vulnerable nakedness, "You promised you'd keep this professional."

"I am. You're a knock out! That's my professional opinion. Do you want to change your mind about some wine?" he added, sipping his.

"No, Cal, let's get on with it, and I suggest you cool it with the wine yourself. This is a job, you know."

"I'm going to do my best," Cal said and coughed. "You're very -- ah -- distracting."

An hour later we were finished. Cal turned off the key light and put on a small lamp. Then he brought the drape over to me. I stood up and reached with my hand to take it from him but instead he draped it over my shoulders. As I started to wrap it around me, suddenly Cal's hands were on my shoulders.

"Oh, don't cover something so beautiful," Cal whispered sensually. The drape fell to the floor as Cal kissed me, or attempted to.

I wheeled around, forcefully pushed Cal away, and then, because I couldn't think of what should come next, I asked, "Have you an inkling that the photographer-model professional line has become blurred at this moment?!"

Cal didn't say anything. "Fine!" I intoned. Then, surprising myself as much as Cal, I lifted my breasts upward and toward him, saying "Take a good look, then! You will see that these are my breasts, they are no big deal, then we can get on with it. I'll split, you'll print my pictures, I'll pick them up."

In a husky voice Cal responded, "Your breasts ARE a big deal."

I picked up the drape, tossed it over me, ran into the dressing room, threw on my clothes, and without another word, left.

Considering, it would have been easier to ask Cal to mail me the pictures, but because I didn't want nudes of me in the mail, early the following week I went to the studio to pick them up. Clearly, Cal had chosen the best from the contact sheets. The seven he'd selected were lovely. I raved about them, pretending that nothing had happened here between us the week before. But nothing that I said or did could really mask the awkwardness.

Finally Cal said, "V.J, I'm sorry about last week, really. I'll be honest. It wasn't the wine talking. It was how I feel. The wine just made it easier to say. I'm sober now and I'll say it again. I've never known a woman like you. I can't get you out of my mind."

"Cal," I answered, "my life is very complicated right now. Can we please let things return to how they were?"

"I'll try," Cal answered, "For now. I just want to know-who's the guy whose getting---my pictures?"

"I don't mean to be blunt, but does the phrase 'None of my business' ever enter your mind, Cal?"

"I'll try to keep things…as you want them, for now," he answered.

I looked at Cal's expression. I felt awful. He was smitten. Why had I failed to pick that up earlier rather than later, thus putting both of us in such a position in the first place! Besides, was I crazy? Here was Cal, gorgeous, sexy, successful, interesting and sensitive, a good person, crazy for me, and local. He and I would have at least made some sense. But then a phrase came to me: "If the heart always made sense, then it would not be the heart."

Cheng came to mind. "If this is a movie, Dear Teacher," I mentally implored him, "Show me how to avoid the sequel!"

Interestingly, Cheng's next Discourse was to be on karma.

CHAPTER SEVENTEEN: DISCOURSE FIVE- Karma

"Ingratitude causes most of the miseries of our life."
--Gurumayi Chidvilasananda

"God gets pissed if you don't notice the color purple."
--Alice Walker, in The Color Purple

"You all have some knowledge of the doctrine of karma," Cheng said. "But, not much." He punctuated the latter with his giggle, so infectious that we all had to join in. "Let us now rectify that," he continued, "Dear Ones, you are God, every one of you." I became extremely attentive, sensing that the others were doing the same. "We are not our body, we are not our thoughts, we are Consciousness, God, Universal Intelligence -the Self- call it as you like- inhabiting this body. Truthfully, the only thing inside each of us is God. Do we know this? Most of the time we do not. Our senses are attuned to the vibrational frequency of the physical universe. We then relate to the world from that vibration, hence believing this external world is reality.

"This notion that we are somebody separate from God must go. The process of uniting with God, Consciousness, our true Self, is called Sadhana, or spiritual practices. When the final goal is achieved that is called Liberation, or Self-Realization. To attain Liberation is our reason for being here in this body. Indeed, in this body is the only place that we CAN attain it.

"What does all this have to do with karma? Karma is the law of cause and effect; 'As you sow, so shall you reap', operating over a span of many lifetimes. Sometimes karma operates obviously. For instance, a person worries and eats poorly, then gets an ulcer. Or, a person murders another, is apprehended and gets the electric chair. Without exploring moral issues about capital punishment here, it is obvious that this murderer reaped what he sowed. Cause and effect.

"On the other hand, we all know people who *don't appear* to be receiving their due. However, since everybody does receive his or her due, here is *non-obvious* karma in operation. Example: A man murders another man whom everybody considers a wonderful person, yet the murderer isn't indicted. The murderer thus appears to have gotten away with the crime and to live happily ever after. Or take a reverse situation; a wonderful woman helps everybody;

she herself is very poor; despite her goodness, most of her life she struggles to make ends meet. Isn't this unfair? No, it is not, because the law of karma is irrefutable.

Let us look ahead to possible future lifetimes of this murderer and this wonderful woman. Perhaps the murderer, many lifetimes hence, has evolved into being a really good man; however, he is "senselessly," in quote marks, murdered. Everyone who knows him exclaims, "Why HIM, who never hurt a fly!" "How senseless!" But in fact it makes perfect sense because in a prior lifetime he murdered a very good man; he had to evolve to becoming a very good man himself before BEING murdered. And the woman who treated everyone so well but experienced terrible luck, in some future lifetime falls into wealth and is very much taken care of. People say, "I work so hard and look at her; *she* doesn't lift a finger and gets everything handed to her. Life isn't fair!"

"You see, Dear Ones, when it appears to us that life is totally unfair, that is only because our vision is far too limited. Any questions thus far?

I raised my hand. "Does this mean a person who has big problems in this lifetime did very bad things in previous lifetimes?"

Cheng answered, "We must understand that we have hopefully been evolving over each of our many thousands of incarnations, or lifetimes. We have all done some, as you said, bad things. I would prefer the term wrong actions as well as right actions in prior lifetimes. Some of our problems we brought over with us, so to speak. They are karmic. You might say that we came here to solve them. If it is a great problem, this means you have great inner strength to solve a great problem. It is probable that you waited to choose such a life until you evolved enough to have that great strength. Then by solving this problem or these problems you make much spiritual progress in this incarnation. You finish up a karma in one lifetime, or even in just several years out of a lifetime, which you'd otherwise have had to go through multiple lifetimes to achieve."

Hinda asked, "Does that mean that nothing bad ever really happens to us, because solving problems helps us get free of karma in the fastest possible way?" I gazed at Hinda's glowing face, this woman whom I increasingly admired for her countenance, poise and profound understanding.

"Excellent question!" Cheng exclaimed. "Yes, once again, what seems good and pleasurable might not be spiritually good for us because there is no challenge; we would tend to coast and not grow. On the other hand what seems awful might be excellent for us for the opposite reason. We must trust the law of karma."

Andrew, once recognized, asked, "So, whatever happens to us is our karma?"

"Absolutely," Cheng said. "There is no way anything could get into our life even for a second if it were not karma. There may seem to be accidents or mistakes or chance encounters, but nothing is an accident or mistake, Dear Ones. Absolutely nothing. When you drive your car on the road, every other driver on that road at the same time, the person ahead of you in line at the supermarket and the waitress assigned to your restaurant table, are people you have karma with; people you've met before, either in this lifetime or in previous ones. Of course those examples were relationships of the most casual sort, but they existed."

Felicia got recognized and exclaimed, "That makes life very exciting for me."

"And so it should, for all of us!" Cheng replied with equal enthusiasm.

"What about husbands and wives, lovers and friends?" Felicia wanted to know. "Did we know each other in other lives?"

"Always," Cheng answered. "In the case of a couple who relate easily without much conflict, we can assume they developed that ease by being together and working out their major problems together over many past lifetimes. So this lifetime they came back together not so much to work out their problems with each other but perhaps to do something together to help others, or to just enjoy one another peacefully; they earned it."

Nancy, recognized, asked dryly, "You mean there are such couples? Where have I failed!" We all laughed, Cheng included.

Then Cheng continued, "Conversely," (here he looked pointedly at me) "couples at odds have an opportunity to work out their problems together as a means toward their growth. They came together to resume where they left off in a prior lifetime. I can think of nothing more lofty than to grow spiritually through a relationship."

"Now, getting deeper," he said, "where does karma come from then? From ourselves. We create it through our words, thoughts, and actions."

I raised my hand again, and after Cheng acknowledged me, said, "I just have to ask this. If a couple came together to work out their problems, does that mean they should remain together no matter what, and if so, what about the many separations or divorces?"

"That is a worthy question which I do wish to answer now, Val-teen, because it relates to all life- challenges as well as relationship ones. Whenever there is a challenge, we have to discern whether it is a barrier or a stepping stone. Is it there as a stepping stone for us to work on this challenge, thereby elevating ourselves, and if so for how long do we do it and when do we stop? Or, is it there as a barrier telling us it is in our best interests to move away from the person or situation toward another direction, and if so, when and how? There is a vast difference between staying with something and elevating ourselves versus staying and rendering ourselves unconscious by repeatedly knocking our heads against a stone wall. Again, Viveka. Sanskrit for discrimination."

Cheng paused, took a sip of water, then continued. "This type discernment is needed in all life areas; a difficult relationship; a job we don't like; trying to help a resistant friend or relative; working for a cause."

Serge raised his hand. "I think my students have declared this a question/answer period," Cheng offered, his laughter cascading upon us. "Very well, let us go with the Shakti. Discourse One, remember? Your question, Serge?"

"How do we tell if it is a barrier or stepping stone?"

Cheng grinned. "THAT question is THE question, well worth interrupting my great train of thought! How do we know what is best about anything, in any instance? Well, we must realize there is one thing that everybody will always give us and we won't even need to ask. What is that one thing? Money? Hardly! Their car? You know not! Their time when you need help? Forget it! What is that one thing, then?"

"Aggravation?" Serge offered.

Cheng laughed. "You are close, Serge. Their advise! They'll give that one thing willingly. Not that it is always good advice. Not that they always know what they are talking about. Not that their own lives are in such great shape that they can advise you about yours? Not that they're Self-Realized. Does that stop them? Of course not. So, what do you do? You can listen and consider what they say. In fact, if you don't at least listen - not necessarily interminably - to a seeming bore or a fool, you are a fool yourself. Since God works through everything and everyone, it could be

God telling you something through that person at that very moment. Pay particular attention to something somebody says out of context which leaps out at you. On the other hand, it could be their ego talking, thus worthless to you. To know whether to keep listening or to excuse yourself, to take what they say seriously or to discount it, you stay tuned into the Shakti. You ask God. God can answer in many ways. It might be a definite voice within. It might be an outer sign, such as the examples that I just gave where another person speaks truth. An S.E. For instance, you feel moved to put on the radio or TV for no particular reason, or to open a certain book. The answer to your question jumps out at you.

"Now," Cheng told us, "I will teach you how to go within to recieve answers from the Self about what is right in any situation. It is called Contemplation. The actual meaning of To Contemplate is, "to be in the temple," to make sacred. In contemplation the most magical, beautiful and rewarding things happen. Contemplation is the invitation of the sages to go where the mind is dissolved into its own divinity. This method is far from unapproachable. All the Great Beings have affirmed it again and again from their manual of human experience. The technique is very much like meditation, however I make the following distinction between the two; contemplation is going within for direct problem solving, whereas meditation is just going within. Contemplation, like meditation, is an essential ability to cultivate. Uncertainties, all those, 'What should I dos?' followed by all those, 'Should I haves?' are merely mental gymnastics which consume your energy, frustrate and further confuse you. Contemplation, like meditation, has to translate into practical results to be of value. When successful they do just that.

"If you had to pick just one tool to develop this spontaneous intuition, ongoing, regular meditation would be it. Secondly is Dr. Cheng's Three Step Contemplation Process. Pay close attention, as I shall now give it to you: There are two movements in our lives, extroversion and introversion. We shall employ both here."

<u>Extroversion, Step One: Clarify your question, phrase it clearly. Only in this way can you receive a clear answer.</u>

We want to be certain not to eliminate this essential step.

What exactly do you want to know? Choose one question or subject at a time, not many.

Extroversion, Step two: Draw a circle in the middle of a sheet of paper. This represents your problem or question; call it your Central Issue, or C.I. Write down your insights, outside of the circle. Allow in, without censorship, every thought related to this C.I., every characteristic, pro or con. Pro to the right, con to the left. Connect each thought with a line to the circle, to the C.I. Increasingly relax as you write; you will then begin to write aspects of this C.I. which hadn't previously occurred to you. Free associate, as Max would say. Now, read all that you've written, and then think about it for up to fifteen minutes. Realize that not only does your conscious mind have viewpoints, so does your subconscious mind; the two may be out of alignment with each other, which causes you conflict. You can further assume that both may well be somewhat out of alignment with the Truth; the voices from our Self are often muted by the voices of our ego, also called our subconscious conditionings or again in Sanskrit, our samscaras.

"So in doing this process you might have insights into this ego, this past programming, which have been distorting your thinking. Especially your mega - negative experiences, your karmic pains, shocks from the past, this lifetime or other ones; those type experiences most distort our present reality."

Introversion, Step one: Relax your physical body. If very tense, first tighten each physical part to the point of quivering, then relax it completely. Now breathe slowly in and out through the nose until you feel calm. You may use the phrase 'God responds', or whatever you like as long as it isn't the same phrase or mantra that you use for meditation. With each breath, 'God responds' as you breath in deep, 'God responds' as you breathe out long. When you feel very quiet within yourself, ask your question clearly. You can do that aloud or mentally. Then rest into yourself and listen. You might get answers, thoughts, ideas, and solutions. When you get difficult or confused answers and feelings, you can ask, 'I don't understand. Where is this feeling from?' It might be from the Self, from God, or it might just be something that was festering. Sometimes the revelation might come, 'It isn't quite time to know this. Keep cooking as you have been."

How can you know that an answer is from the Self? Your conviction. It will be a strong feeling. You know that it is right as you know your name, and it will be in line with your spiritual teachings. If after awhile you get nothing, you just affirm, 'God, I know that you are going to give me an answer.' Then you end that contemplation session and go about your business. However, you can also do the next step.

Introversion, Step 2 While still within ask for a sign, a Synchronistic Event, an S.E, to occur in your outer life.

Remember, there are NO coincidences. Example: You have a job offer from both a bank and an insurance company, and are trying to decide which to take, if either. You ask for a sign. Maybe two days later you are sitting in your living room in a rare moment of repose. Your child runs in. (If you have young children, you know *how* brief moments of repose are), switches on the TV, runs out of the room with nary a glance at the TV screen. As you, shaking your head, reach for the remote 'off' button, the station clicks into commercial and you hear, 'at our bank your money never sleeps,' or such jargon. And that *might* be your answer, to take the bank job. Finally evaluate both of your Extroversion and Introversion answers to help you decide. Again, your answer might be, 'it isn't time yet'."

Serge, after raising his hand and being acknowledged, asked, in an agitated voice, "That MIGHT be the answer? After all that work, it MIGHT?! I can be that confused without doing sadhana, thank you! I mean, how long will it take for the *mights* to become *absolutelys* ?"

Our laughter was met by Cheng's disapproving tone. "You laugh as if Serge's problem is not also yours!" he scolded. "Serge, and all of you, are burdened with Feyurga Snay. You know Yiddish?"

"My bubbe -- my grandmother -- used to say that. It literally means 'Yesterday's snow.' But how did YOU...?"

"Yes, yesterday's snow," Cheng affirmed. "Gone. Melted. Nothing you can do about it. Very few of your thoughts – I mean this for all of you - are tuned to the present. Most of your thoughts are about what happened yesterday, last year or lifetimes ago. Sadhana will help you tune to the present, to know which voices are from the Feyurga Snay (meaning the ego) or from Truth, from God. To know that is why we do these practices. So that when God shows up to tell us something, we'll be home. Now I'll go on with the amazing, important subject of karma.

"Karma, the doctrine of cause and effect, is as scientific as the laws of any proven science; however, for the general scientist of today to try to 'prove' karma scientifically would involve factors beyond his present comprehension. To attempt it would be a futile waste of time. Suffice it to say that we have evidence that all our experiences are of our own creating, therefore, this should motivate us to want to ascertain ways to create good effects.

"Generally speaking, karma is divided into four kinds, as follows.

"One. White karma. This produces happiness.

"Two. Black karma. This produces pain.

"Three. White and black. This kind brings us both happiness and misery.

"Four. Neither black nor white. This kind produces neither pain nor sorrow. The fourth kind is desirable."

I was feeling unsettlingly puzzled. I raised my hand, was acknowledged, and asked, "You mean, we aren't supposed to *Feel* anything?"

"Great question, Val-teen," Cheng enthused. "Of course to be in an inert-state way would be undesirable. But in a totally healthy state there is no particular feeling of either pleasure or pain and that is desirable. You should come to understand this increasingly. It is the state of a saint."

I sighed. I was increasingly realizing that any time my ego told me all this was simple to grasp, I was reminded that it was anything but!

Cheng continued. "Karma can fructify in this very birth or in future ones. Similarly, karma manifesting in this lifetime may be from seeds sowed earlier in this lifetime or past lifetimes.

"There are three other main types of karma. Type one, technical name, Prarabdha; Type two, Sanchita; and Type three, Kriyamin.

"I will explain each to you.

<u>"Type one, Prarabdha Karma</u>: When we mention karma this is usually the kind that we mean. In a word, unavoidable karma. It is something that just happens which you didn't make happen. Like an arrow shot from a bow, you can't stop it. It is the karma created in the past from this lifetime or former ones. Some examples are: a birth defect, the family you're born into, your gender, your eye color, certain predispositions of your nature. Again, we can't usu-

ally change this kind, but we can deflect it. We are free from Prarabdha karma when we undergo it cheerefully and with detachment. It can sometimes be mitigated or changed by the Grace of a Great Being." I looked up, ready to ask for clarification, but Cheng shook his head 'no', saying, "You'll understand this later, also." I did remember Cheng having mentioned the term Prarabdha Karma to me once.

"Type two, Sanchita Karma: This is the karma you have 'in the bank' - stored up in what Freud called 'the unconscious,' and the ancient Eastern sages call the Shushumna, the unconscious not just from this lifetime but from all of our lifetimes. Sanchita karma is seeds waiting to sprout unless we do something to burn those seeds. Spiritual practices burn the seeds or nullify them. In that way, we don't experience it, or experience it in a watered-down fashion. For example: Perhaps there is something difficult which we were destined to experience for many lifetimes, but by doing spiritual practices and living a good life, it lasts only for a brief time. We were destined to have an accident in our car and do, but are uninjured, or not seriously, or somebody rams into our car but when we are not in it. Once as a very young man I had a car accident, and while recovering I saw visions of many angry, nasty women whom I would have had to marry had that accident not occurred; karma, the seeds of which the accident burned out. Believe me, seeing that, I realized the accident was next-to-nothing!" Cheng laughed heartily.

"Meditation, other spiritual practices, selfless giving, helping others, doing our work with dedication, love - all help to burn our Sanchita karma. Sometimes, if we are doing spiritual practices, a horrible feeling comes up during the practices or during life itself. That is Sanchita karma being burned, something we would otherwise have had to go through much more profoundly. As I mentioned once before, that is called a kriya.

"Type Three, Kriyaman Karma: This is our deposit-in-the-bank-or withdraw Karma. Our present actions and thoughts, our free will, create subtle impressions to become Sanchita karma, eventually Prarabdha karma. A series of virtuous actions cancels out a series of vicious actions. Example: In a past lifetime you stole $400. In this lifetime, you gave $400 to charity. It is like two waves, one going away from you and somehow removing $400 from you, another coming toward you somehow bringing $400 to you.

Serge asked, "How do we know, for example, that in a past lifetime we stole $400, so that to compensate we can give $400 to something worthy in this lifetime?"

"Great question! This class really *thinks*!" Cheng exclaimed with a wide grin. "We don't necessarily need to know about stealing in a past life, although as we do sadhana past life remembrances will come to us. What does occur, Serge, is that with Sadhana we'll get feelings to do the right things, e.g., if you feel a strong desire to give a friend $400 out of the blue yet can find no reason for your urge, you can rightly assume it's past life karma prompting you to balance the scales.

"This Type Three Kriyaman Karma is the karma totally under our control, Dear Ones. We need to truly understand this much now: what we think, say and do now is determining our future life-conditions. Understanding that, we will assume far more responsibility for how we live every moment in the here and now. Serge might even decide to get acknowledged before speaking, "Cheng smiled, then continued.

"Eventually, we will experience that we are not 'doing' anything.' We just see whatever happens as the dance of life. You have heard the phrase 'live in the moment.' To the sages a lifetime is a moment. When the scriptures tell us to live in the moment, they mean accept what comes and make the best of it, thus you will live your life very well."

Serge asked the question that I was thinking: "Are you saying that if somebody treats us terribly we have to take that treatment because it is our karma?"

"Not at all," Cheng answered. "I am saying that we should do the loving thing. Often, the loving thing is not the sweet thing; people get confused about that. To allow a person to act badly toward us is not loving, for they are creating karma by doing so, as are we for allowing it. So we might first try to gently stop the person;perhaps by naming their game. If that doesn't work we might have to do so more strongly. Dislike the action perhaps, not the person. The Great Beings sometimes 'get angry,' but it is not out of ego, being out-of-control, or a desire for revenge; it is out of love. Motivation is key."

Hinda asked, "So asking God what to do is a good practice for creating a good present life and good future lives?"

"YES INDEED!" Cheng proclaimed. "And to do it on-site, as you say or think. Most of you who believe in God are rather good at talking with God when you are in the forest alone or on the beach. But trees and sand don't give us too much trouble; it is *people* who do." We all laughed at Cheng's humorous wisdom. "Ask *when* you're *in* situations or before you enter them if you know ahead. Then you want to ask God, 'Handle this situation perfectly.' Try it when in an argument with your partner. Say or think, 'God, I know that you are within us both and leading us both to perfect action.' Your argument will end instantly. If you don't believe me, try it the next time you're in an argument." Cheng added, giggling in delight, "But don't deliberately start an argument to try this out."

Nancy got acknowledged and asked, laughing "How did you guess that I was thinking to do just that, Cheng?"

"I don't know" Cheng answered between giggles.

Then he resumed seriously, "If you did something dumb, hurtful, or wasteful, realize that, see that, contemplate that, know that, make amends if appropriate. Just don't waste time and energy guilting, let us call it. It happened because it was supposed to happen."

Andrew, after going through the usual protocol, asked, "This makes me feel like a robot. Where is *my* responsibility here?! If I feel like stealing, do I just do it because it was supposed to happen anyway; it was my karma?!"

"ANOTHER EXCELLENT QUESTION!" Cheng enthused. "Your karmic map doesn't control you. In fact, the more that you do sadhana, your spiritual practices, the less it controls you. We are destined to experience certain things. What we do with them is sadhana. Those who *don't* do sadhana are the ones most inclined to act like robots, usually taking the course of least resistance, doing what is easiest although not best, handling events in the lowest possible ways. And they say they don't need spirituality because they want to be free! They are about as free as a murderer imprisoned for life. Every event, whether seemingly good or bad, is good or bad by one criterion only. Does it bring us closer, or further away, from Truth, the Self? Seen this way, an accident could be great for us while a big promotion could be terrible for us. The idea is, don't be attached either way."

As I sat listening, a peculiar thing started happening. I felt a buzz of energy inside of me. It began at my feet, moved upward to my head where it became stronger. It then compelled me to speak. It also told me what to say. I recoiled. I didn't want to say it. My reasoning mind told me to say it would be too disruptive, too sad, too personal. But the Shakti would not let me remain quiet. At that moment, the Small I stepped aside and watched and heard my Self. This was the first of what would become many times that this happened to me; it was fascinating and frightening all at once. I did not want to speak but I was being practically made to do so, with only the vaguest idea, if that, of what I was going to say.

So, I began to speak and can only explain that at the same time that I was speaking I was also listening to myself to hear what was coming next. "As you know, Cheng," I heard myself say, "I have what the world would call a tragedy in my life. My son Willie is with autism. It's considered one of the most serious developmental disabilities, and the most difficult to cope with." I heard some surprised gasps. "I am attached to it. Sometimes I hate it." I felt the tears begin to roll. I was appalled! I heard myself next say, "Sometimes I feel I can't go on." Then I became silent. I was surprised that the part of me which wasn't aghast was very calm and serene. The room was without sound as if uninhabited. I then realized that somewhere while speaking I had risen to my feet. Doubly appalled at this realization, I sat down quickly.

Cheng's voice, when he answered, was total love. "Your feelings are natural. Spiritual people feel guilty for their human feelings, but that is a big mistake. Although we are all God, we *are* all human."

Nancy got acknowledged and asked, "Come on, Cheng. Isn't that ego to think I am God?"

"No, Nancy," Cheng replied. "It is ego to think we are not, that we are separate from God."

I let that sink in. Then I asked the most profound question in my life to date. "Does it all mean that whether Willie is autistic or not, whether one day he is no longer autistic or remains so, doesn't really matter? That all that matters is that Richard and I do our best for him and that he does his best? Does it mean it doesn't matter whether or not the scientists find a cure, but it does matter that they do their work sincerely and honestly, with egos aside, for *their* growth as well as to help autistic people?"

"You have the gist of it, Val-teen," Cheng said. "Thank you! That was a perfect example of seva, of selfless service with non-attachment to the results. And a perfect reminder that for each of us it is the journey rather than the destination which counts the most."

It was at that instant - and this apparent self-indulgence really appalled me - that I heard myself blurt out my deepest guilt and pain. "I wish I knew... what I did... to bring autism upon Willie. It must have been something terribly wrong!"

"Of course you did something terrible," came Cheng's surprising answer, but then he softened and continued, "I repeat: In the course of all our previous lifetimes we each have done things 'terribly wrong,' as well as things 'marvelously virtuous.' Again, often if one has many large burdens in one lifetime it means that one is a very strong evolved person to shoulder them all. Often before coming here such a person made a decision to take care of a lot of stuff in this one lifetime in order to make great spiritual progress. Such a person could be a great yogi burning up the last of that stuff."

"You mean, Willie could be a great yogi?"

Cheng gave me a direct stare. "Yes, Willie, for ONE person," he responded.

What did he mean? That I could be one too? No use asking Cheng to answer such a question. I might as well get the cow to jump the moon. Which no doubt Cheng would say *is* possible.

My musing was interrupted by Cheng's next words.

"Dear Ones, here is your homework until next time," he said. One: Practice accepting your karma cheerfully. Once again, when you complain and get very heavy and serious about things, you sustain those situations indefinitely; you create more similar karma. Try laughing at your troubles and watch them dissipate. Laughing is the highest, but if you can't manage to laugh at your troubles at the time, right then at least practice floating above your problem. Then handle it in such a way that later will do you proud.

"Two: Whatever is happening, remember, in the entire span of your existence-eternity-this will last only a moment. There is practically nothing we can't tolerate for one moment. Train your mind to desire what the situation presents.

"Three: Check out your every thought, intended word, and action. Ask yourself if they are motivated by love; if not, do not say, do or continue thinking that thing. Always remember, Dear Ones, that the Great Ones call this world Karma Bumi, the Land Of Karma simply because they know that although often it may seem like hell here, it is really greater than heaven. The reason is; only here have we the opportunity to learn the greatest lessons thus to evolve to the highest. As that great Indian epic, The Bhagavad Gita explains, a soul stays in heaven only until merits earned on earth are exhausted, then returns here to continue the process. So, that is the third part of your homework.

"And now, Dear Ones," Cheng announced, "Class is ending, tea is beginning."

Felicia poured me a cup of mint tea while the others gathered around me. Max, with his arm around my shoulder, asked, "Valentine, Valentine, why didn't you tell me about Willie before? Maybe I could have helped you."

"I didn't feel I could... until now," I answered. "I didn't even want to now, but the Shakti made me. Do you think maybe before tonight I wasn't supposed to ...make it easier for myself?"

"That's profound," Max answered.

"I still don't understand why I had to dump on everybody tonight like I did," I said, feeling shame. "I mean, it is MY own problem, not all of yours..."

Mindie interrupted. "Valentine, stop right there!" She said it with a firmness which coming from her surprised me. "You spoke tonight with such honesty and simplicity in your tone and demeanor. I'd never seen you that way before."

"Yes," Trenna agreed. "I was elevated, and beyond."

They felt elevated by my pain? "I don't understand," I said.

The following morning on the train I sought clarification from Max. "I felt so embarrassed. I acted like a fool," I lamented.

"To the contrary, Valentine," Max explained patiently. "They always saw you as so strong and all-together. You look like someone who has everything. Of course, nobody does. We each have our own crosses to bear. But people do tend to perceive people like you as I explained. Last night, when you showed them that you hurt, you gave them permission to hurt, also."

"Max," I admitted, "I don't feel strong now. I feel I'm collapsing suddenly. I feel like last night I lost part of myself."

Max, touching my hand tenderly, said, "No, Valentine. Last night you found a part of yourself. You felt what it's like to be a whole person."

"I felt fragmented when I spoke about Willie last night, Max," I told him. "But it was a comfortable fragmentation. Does that sound too crazy? One part of me was the speaker, the other part of me the observer watching it all unfold."

"Not at all crazy," Max answered, smiling." That is what the ancients called 'witness consciousness,' Valentine. An experience of being in this world but not of it. Of not being the doer. You allowed the Shakti to tell you exactly what to do and when, then you obeyed it. By doing exactly what you were intended to do, you benefited not only yourself but also all of us. Last night, Valentine, you were a powerful teacher!" Max concluded.

At Max's words, it clicked within me! Letting go and letting God *gave* us power, it did NOT take it away.

CHAPTER EIGHTEEN: RESOLUTION

"Those who haven't seen the Self and who haven't tasted its bliss, desire sense objects and relish them."

--Jnaneshwar's Gita

"Pansy's so pretty Violet's tall.
How can I choose? I love them all."

--From the song, American Beauty Rose

Of course a possible future with Brandt had entered my mind, but it was only after he asked, "What's going to be with us, Valentine?" along with Cheng's Discourse on karma and on dharma - doing what is right – that I started to think seriously about this. So, I began contemplating the question. First externally. On paper I did the Extroversion Contemplation. I was crazy for Brandt, no doubt about it; those times when we were together I'd lie beside him in bed at night, enthralled, feeling ecstatically fortunate to have found such a love. The sexual chemistry was awesome; I respected his intelligence, his accomplishments, and his place in the world. We'd discovered that we were compatible, had mutual interests and had fun together. He must care for me deeply, too, or he wouldn't have as good as proposed. What more could two people want? On the debit side, Brandt's track record with relationships was poor. But; he just hadn't met the right woman before; with me it would be different. This was too good, too worthy, too sublime to merely continue playing house long distance.

I also contemplated it internally with the Introversion Contemplation and finally one night I prayed for a sign. Several mornings after that I decided to take a bus to the studio. For some reason I felt impelled to get off a few stops before my usual one and to walk the rest of the way. On the face of things that made no sense; I was already late for work. Neither did it make sense, once I got off the bus and began walking, that I decided to stop at a bookstore. Standing outside the door I firmly told myself, "Browse another time!" Yet I felt strongly drawn inside and gave in to the urge.

It was a small bookstore with the books pristinely arranged on the shelves as if a customer had never touched them. I found the organization and dimly lit ambiance inviting. I walked around until I came upon the spiritual section, a very sparse few shelves tucked in an obscure corner; typical in bookstores then if indeed they had a spiritual section in the first place. The books here, like in the other sections, were carefully vertically arranged. Curiously, however, one small book lay horizontally conspicuous on the shelf in front of the other books. I lifted it and began to thumb through. Soon my eyes nearly jumped out of my head! It was a book about reincarnation, specifically seeming to consist of many case stories about couples who had known each other in past lifetimes, then had become reunited in this one. Hurriedly I bought the book, then rushed out the door and on to the studio.

That evening after I'd driven Brenna and Essie back to Glady's, put Brenna to bed, read her a story and kissed her goodnight, I returned to the apartment. I removed my work clothes, put on my robe, propped some pillows up against my headboard, got comfortable on my bed, and then eagerly opened the book.

There was a remarkable prelude! It told about a man living in the 1800s who'd been bitten by a rattlesnake, who would have died if an Apache woman had not found him and nursed him back to health. They fell in love and spent the next forty years together until he was killed in a flash flood. It continued, "They didn't see one another again until one hundred years later in their next lifetimes, in 1972, when they met at a party in Los Angeles." The prelude ended, "They were born again to be together."

Chilled, I sat upright so quickly that the book slid off my lap onto the floor! I was recalling Brandt's words the night we had met; "We've known each other 100 years." The reference in the book to Los Angeles and to 1972, the year Brandt and I had met, was equally astounding. Two S.E's, Synchronistic Events, certainly! I lifted the book from the floor and as I read further I found that there were many other startling "coincidences!" I first scanned the pages where the book had opened in falling; my eyes went immediately to this passage: "A man named Brandon walked into the party with a beautiful girl named Valerie. He was from Boston, Val from New York. They were involved together in special education." I turned to the adjoining page and saw mention of a man named "Richard Mancusi;" Richard was, of course, Brandt's middle name, while "Mancusi" was darned close to Mancino. As were "Brandon" and Brandt. "Val," well, it was too amazing, as were the references to "special education" and to Brandt's and my respective hometowns.

The chapters that followed were fascinating case stories of couples who'd felt an immediate attraction upon meeting, and were then hypnotically regressed back to previous lifetimes together.

Cheng had taught, "Nothing is a coincidence, absolutely nothing." I put the book down and rubbed my eyes. Could it have been any clearer! Obviously, my sign from God that Brandt and I had been "born again to be together." Perhaps the reason I'd told Richard about Brandt and me – something I'd never understood – had been to pave the way? And wasn't Richard's and my separation, then being evicted from our house, part of it too? An inner smile spread through my body. I'd tell Brandt at the conference that I could now answer his question about our future; I was ready to make a real commitment to him and to our relationship; now there was nothing standing in our way.

***

The conference was perfect. Brandt and I sat side-by-side at the dais, a very public spot with the attendees seated in front of us seemingly scrutinizing our every move. As a boring speaker droned on, I moved closer to Brandt and whispered in his ear, "I wish we were in bed instead." Brandt moaned, "Did you have to do that to me *now*!" Then we both tried to publicly present ourselves as seriously interested in the speaker's words, such a major acting feat that we nearly cracked up in the attempt. By the end of that segment we were just plain giddy. Out of nowhere Brandt asked me, "Why can't Nixon be circumcised?" It took me a few seconds to realize that it was a joke. Watergate and that entire political scandal had been upon us. I began to giggle before the punch line, saying. "I don't know, tell me." "Because" Brandt offered, "There's no end to that schmuck." He looked at me expectantly. After several seconds I had to admit, "I don't get it." Brandt, patient to the point of patronizing, asked, "Valentine, what does schmuck mean?" "A total asshole?" I offered somewhat timidly. "No, but you're close," Brandt said. "In Yiddish a schmuck is a penis." "Is it really!" I said with total sincerity. Brandt asked, shaking his head, "Are you SUAA you'aa Jewish?" At that moment he sounded uncannily like Ernie and Richard combined.

It was during the first morning of the conference that Brandt said, "Chales Ott, my book editaaa, lives nearby; he and his wife have invited me foaa a late lunch. I asked him if I could bring a friend. Would you like to come?" Would I *like* to? Try to keep me *away!* Except for that time in San Diego when we'd had drinks with Brandt's friend and his date, and at FOCI functions, Brandt and I had had no social life together. This would be a perfect beginning of that. "I'm thrilled to come with you," I enthused, "but when do I see the book?"

"When we return to the room laata, I'll give you an autographed copy - among otheaa things."

At Charles' home we had a socially lovely time and a fish dinner which I was minus-enthusiastic about - I had found myself veering away from flesh foods - but ate out of courtesy to the host. By the time we arrived back at the hotel at 6:15 I was feeling odd. Odd rapidly changed to terrible, terrible to sick-as-a-dog! By the third time I'd dragged myself out of the bathroom after vomiting, I sat down on a chair, feeling as humiliated as I felt rung out. Brandt, however, was wonderful. "Probably some food poisoning," he said. "The fish tasted a bit peculiaaa to me." I rather felt it was my vegetarian mind/body purging me of the flesh-food. Whatever, after awhile I stabilized, but in the aftermath I was very weak and tired.

Brandt asked me if I felt well enough to receive my present. After I feebly nodded yes, he handed it to me with great fanfare. Although at the moment I was too foggy to focus properly, at Brandt's suggestion I turned to the inside cover and read, in his hand, "To Valentine, with my love and respect."

"Oh, Brandt," I said, kissing him, "I'm so proud of you. And I love your inscription to me! I can't wait to read the book. But I feel so ridiculous and embarrassed about tonight."

Brandt couldn't have been sweeter. His answer was to gently take the book from my hand and to place it on the night table. "Don't be foolish, I'm a doctaa" he said. "Theaa's plenty of time to read. For now you should sleep." He led me over to the bed, encouraged me to lie down, and covered me. "Theaa's a meeting at seven thaaty for the Professional Advisoay Boaad. I don't have to go if you don't want me to..."

I wanted to say, "Please stay. We've had so little time together." But then a montage flashed through my brain of all the movies I'd seen of famous men doing important work; Abraham Lincoln, Albert Schweitzer, John Kennedy, the list went on. And what were their wives doing? They were all saying, "When are you coming home? You're never home." Women like that made me want to throw up more than the fish lunch had. I'd never say such things to Brandt. I'd never said such things to Richard. In fact, I realized, it had been Richard who had more often said them to me.

"Brandt, honey, of course you have to go to the meeting. They need you there," I told him, being the heroine to the hilt.

Brandt's pleased look delighted me. He was probably thinking, "This *is* the woman for me, she's so great, so supportive of my important work." He pulled a piece of paper out of his jacket pocket. He began to pat his pockets, then to look at me in the manner of a man who had things handed to him. I'd best start things off right. "There's a pen right there," I told him, nodding at the night table. After a slight hesitation Brandt put down the phone, walked over to the table, lifted the pen, jotted something on the paper, then walked back to me and handed the paper to me. "This is the numbaa of the room wheaa I'll be if you should need me. Sleep, then in an houaa ordaa tea and toast from room seavice. By then you'll be fine." He arranged the covers around me and kissed me while taking the paper out of my hand and placing it on the night table.

My own in-house M.D. I felt so nurtured and protected. But I'd almost forgotten. "Brandt," I said, "I have a gift for you, too. Will you get it please? It's in an envelope in my suitcase."

Brandt, after retrieving the envelope, asked, "Something you wrote?"

"No."

"What, then?"

"Guess."

"Give me a hint."

"Alright, but only one. Let me think. Well... after this you'll be able to see me in a whole nude light, how's that?"

Brandt appeared to ponder for a second, then ripped open the envelope and pulled out the photographs. I watched, thrilled, as his eyes grew wide. "My God!! These are beautiful." Then his face darkened somewhat. "Who... took these?"

"A photographer, a professional."

"How old is he?"

"I don't know, about your age. For him, this is just a day's work," I white lied. This was cool! Brandt was jealous. Seemingly appeased, Brandt stayed a few minutes more to rave about the pictures. "Nobody will evaa see these but me," he promised. "Now sleep." He kissed me again and left.

Feeling deliriously happy for a sick woman, and doubly delighted because now I had a legitimate gift from Brandt, I fell asleep.

When I awakened about an hour later my nausea was gone and my headache mostly a memory, just as Brandt had predicted. He was *so* intelligent. As I switched on the bedside lamp to call room service, my hand accidentally brushed the piece of paper that Brandt had given to me. My eyes followed it as it floated onto the blanket. I lifted it to throw it into the wastebasket; in so doing I noticed that it had reversed to the opposite side which had something written on it also, in Brandt's handwriting. I read it; "Suggest J.B. for PAB."

What did it mean? Albeit with the aftermath of a still fuzzy head, I forced myself to think. PAB was, of course, Professional Advisory Board, the one Brandt was on. But what the hell was a J.B.? On instinct I picked up Brandt's book, turned again to his inscription to me, smiled, then looked at the front cover where I plainly saw, "Edited by Brandt R. Mancino, M.D and Jill Bernstein, Ph.D. I quickly turned to the biographies on the back cover. Dr. Bernstein, it seemed, was a clinical psychologist who worked with Brandt. SHE WAS J.B.! This apparently was a memo from Brandt to himself, which he'd intended to take to the meeting or, had he?

As I held the book I began receiving mental images of Brandt and J.B. together and *not* just doing scientific research! I started feeling myself get queasy and have temperature fluctuations, this time not due to the fish. I let my head fall back upon the pillow.

I remember back to my moments of denial then; "There's a perfectly innocent explanation for this, otherwise Brandt wouldn't have handed that paper to me, he would have hidden it." Only later could I ask myself if it wasn't more likely that Brandt had deliberately handed me that slip of paper because on some level he'd wanted me to know about him and J.B. And to answer myself, "Yes, very likely!"

My first impulse was to call Brandt at the number that he had given me, my second impulse not to. I ambivalently wanted to see him at once yet never set eyes upon him again. Throughout our relationship I'd made only one important stipulation: "If you meet somebody else just tell me." Brandt was a wonderful listener, something I could not claim for Richard, but I was starting to wonder how much of an asset that actually was in our relationship.

He'd been professionally trained to listen and there was carry over. So what? He obviously did not respect my wishes and sensibilities. Bottom line, Brandt did whatever *Brandt* felt like doing whenever *Brandt* felt like doing it.

I began to put things together; Brandt's inane excuse in L.A when we'd returned from San Diego and I'd wanted to see his office; "There are a lot of psychiatrically ill patients here." *Of course* he hadn't wanted me to come there. J.B was there! Probably Brandt and she had been together on his office couch while I'd been at the hotel. And, how the hell had he dissuaded *her* from attending that conference? By telling *her* that there would be, "Many psychiatrically ill patients" *there* too? Certainly he'd thought of something convincing or crazy to tell her, God only knew what, and what did it matter? I felt numb. Then feeling returned; I became incensed.

Brandt returned at 8:30 in a most expansive mood. Obviously the man thrived on meetings as well as on women, many of both.

Have you ever had an absolutely dreadfully agonizing scene from hell with another person, so bad at the time that if anybody had witnessed it and laughed you would have slaughtered them, because to you nothing about it was remotely funny. But years later you looked back upon it with ambivalence; partly amused thinking it should be in a slapstick comedy movie, partly humiliated knowing that you'd let any other human being bring you to that? That which happened between Brandt and me in the next half-hour qualifies for the above.

"Heeaa you aaa!" Brandt announced from the doorway.

"Thank you. I was wondering where I was."

"Well, you look *much* betta." Brandt remained exactly on the same spot, smiling widely. Then, as his eyes swept the room, he added, "But, I don't see any tray heaaa. It looks to me like you didn't ordaa youaa tea and toast."

"Thank you, Columbo."

Brandt peered at me cautiously, his smile fading. "Is something wrong?" he asked, continuing to stand in the doorway, starting to look as if he'd rather be anywhere else.

"You noticed," I retorted. Brandt shuffled in place. Just looking at him shot feelings of fury through me. In a chilled controlled voice I told him, "If you're coming in, please do so and shut the door." Brandt did so.

From the moment Brandt shut that door you would have thought I'd never heard of Dr. Cheng Ho, the Discourses and especially of Kriyaman karma, type three! In a voice akin to the wicked stepmother of *Snow White and the Seven Dwarfs* I screeched, "You want to know, Dr. Detective, why I didn't order from room service as you prescribed? Because I'd already had more than I could stomach of *your* type medicine!"

Brandt's face was as inscrutable as Cheng's often was. "What's going on?" he asked innocently.

I waved Brandt's book in the air like an evangelist shaking a donation basket. "That's exactly MY question to YOU!" I sputtered. "What's going on between… between… you and…and… this… Bernstein… woman?"

"What do you mean?"

"What do *you* mean, what do *I* mean?" I dashed over to Brandt and stood facing him. I was barefoot so had to stand on my toes to meet him eye-to-eye. "Is English your second language?" I hissed. "Then I'll go more slowly this time. I asked you, 'What's going on with you and this Bernstein woman?'"

"Dr. Bernstein and I are reseaach associates." Brandt emphasized each word very much as I just had, making me even angrier.

"That's all?"

Brandt didn't answer.

"For how long have you two been *research associates*?"

"About two and one half yeeaas."

"Two and one half years yet you never once mentioned her to me!"

"Don't you have co-wokers? Have I expected you to tell me the names of everyone *you* inta act with?" Brandt asked, sounding so reasonable that I wanted to deck him.

"Maybe because I don't INTERACT quite as YOU do! Are you having an affair with Jill Bernstein?" I demanded to know. When you hear Brandt's answer…and I swear this is exactly what he said…I ask you to remember that this was the seventies, before President Bill Clinton was even heard of.

"That depends upon youaa definition of affaaia."

"I thought the meaning of the word affair was quite clear."

"According to my definition, Dr. Bernstein and I have not..." Brandt began, but I cut him off."Dammit, Brandt, stop playing dictionary with me!And will you also stop that *Doctor* Bernstein shit!" I hissed. "I'll say what I think and you answer with the truth, fair? I think there's been a lot of intellectual screwing going on between you and JB (I emphasized the letters). You tell me, now. HAVE YOU BEEN FUCKING HER??!!"

"Valentine, I've neveaa heaad you use language like that befoaa. One of the things I've always admiaad about you has been youaa class, youaa being a lady, youaa not speaking like a longsho aaman. I have appreciated that quality so greatly in you..it's what I like...."

"You think at this moment that I give a shit what you like?! You haven't answered my question. Are you and J.B lovers?"

Then Brandt delivered his answer. "Dr. Bernstein," he offered, with an amazing amount of dignity, considering, "is a woman I've had intacosse with a few times."

"A woman you've HAD INTERCOURSE WITH A FEW TIMES?! INTERCOURSE WITH A FEW TIMES!" I kept repeating it to convince myself that he had actually said it. "What am *I*, then? *Also* a woman you've HAD INTERCOURSE WITH A FEW TIMES!!??" I heard myself shouting as if my lungs had a will of their own. I feared they might burst.

"Of couaase you are not," Brandt said. "Please stop shouting, Valentine," he pleaded. "Some of the othaa confeance attendees heeaa on this floor could heaa us."

"You think THIS is shouting?!" I shouted. "WAIT 'TIL I *REALLY* START SHOUTING. THERE'LL BE ENOUGH PEOPLE OUTSIDE THE DOOR TO CONDUCT A HEART TRANSPLANT OPERATION!"

"I don't think theaas anything to get so excited about," Brandt offered.

"OF COURSE YOU DON'T," I boomed. "THAT'S BECAUSE *YOU* HAVEN'T BEEN TRYING TO HAVE A RELATIONSHIP WITH YOU! YOU KNOW VERY WELL THAT ALL I ASKED OF YOU WAS THAT YOU TELL ME IF YOU MET SOMEBODY ELSE; THEN I COULD AT LEAST MAKE AN INFORMED DECISION ABOUT US. YET THIS HAS BEEN GOING ON FOR MORE THAN TWO YEARS WITHOUT ANY INTENTION ON YOUR PART OF TELLING ME, AND I'M SUPPOSED TO TAKE THIS IN STRIDE? YOU LIAR. YOU LOUSY BASTARD LIAR..." Brandt's eyes followed me as I flew across the room, grabbed the incriminating memo where it lay on the bed, dashed back to Brandt again, all the while no doubt looking like the Kitchen Witch in flight.

"NOW TELL ME ABOUT THIS!" I demanded, waving the paper in Brandt's face.

"What?" Brandt asked, like butter wouldn't melt in his mouth. The man was cool, give him that.

"We're back to English-As-A-Second-Language Class once again? Answer me directly, Brandt. Were you going to nominate this... woman... to the Professional Advisory Board?"

"Yes."

"How COULD you?!"

"Because it's right."

I did not believe him. "Right!!?? For WHOM??! You're hoping to convince me that for you to bring this person onto the PAB, into FOCI, OUR thing together, because she sleeps with you, is right?! So that then you can have sex with her here, like you've been... with me? Don't even try it, Brandt."

Brandt's voice, when he answered, was quiet, too quiet. What he answered was inconceivable, even from him. "I don't have to have sex with her heeaa, like with you," he said. "I can have sex with heaa any time I want to."

Suddenly I was like a puppet come to life. For one thing I was realizing, as much as I could analyze it at the moment, that I was more threatened by Jill than by Annie. Annie, though no doubt beautiful was, as Brandt had intimated, "not the brightest star in the sky." Brandt did like intelligent women; he'd been married to two medical doctors. But this J.B, in addition to no doubt being pretty (*unlike* Clinton, unless a woman was a head-turner Brandt wouldn't even look at her), probably also had an I.Q way up in the stratosphere. And something else...

I asked Brandt, "J.B's Jewish, isn't she?"

"Yes."

The ultimate, the Jewish thing again. "I want to understand this," I silently implored. " Why does J.B being Jewish make me feel better than if she'd been Christian?"

It must have been a strong prayer, because no sooner had I pleaded than I was there. In my childhood, in the Christian neighborhood where I had been raised, the only Jewish child in my school. My family wasn't what anyone would call "very Jewish." They were classy, they blended in, the Christians accepted them. Except, in school I stood out. I had dark brown hair and olive skin while the entire blonde Marybeths and red haired Maureens surrounded me. And I stood out again when everyone else had a Christmas tree and I couldn't, because "what would the rabbi think?"(We never went to temple nor did the rabbi come to our home, so how, I'd wondered, could the rabbi think anything?) I was so embarrassed to live in the only house without a tree. Had I felt inferior to the Christian girls because I was different, and had the inferiority feelings stayed within until Brandt came along to being them forth? Had Brandt's women, then, become a barometer of my self-esteem? Highly likely.

The thought of Brandt propelled me again nastily into the present, so that I became like a plug pushed into an electrical outlet. The current was surging through me; I was powerless to turn it off. I flew to the other side of the room and lifted Brandt's book from the bed. Brandt, watching me, appeared frightened, as if he couldn't decide whether to escape from the room or get *me* to a psychiatric unit.

I threw his book at him. "You are very fortunate, Dr. Mancino," I shouted as Brandt ducked, "that I'm sick tonight so weaker than usual. Otherwise I'd punch out your lights right now. I have my brown belt in karate, you know."

Brandt eyed me skeptically. "AH!" I shouted, "You don't believe me?!" I ran toward him, lifted my foot in the air while I jumped as I'd seen Bruce Lee do in countless films, and kicked Brandt square in the shin. I howled in pain as my bare foot hit his hard calf muscles. Brandt didn't even cringe.

After my foot stopped stinging terribly, I informed Brandt that I'd just written a song in my head, "It's especially for you. Should I sing it?" I asked.

"Certainly," Brandt replied, looking relieved, flattered, and puzzled, in that order.

In a voice hoarse from vomiting and screaming, I sang, to the tune of "Old Macdonald Had A Farm..."

"Brandt Mancino had a harem,
S-C-R-E-W. (I spelled out the word)
And in that harem he had some chicks,
S-C-R-E-W.
With a redhead here,
And a brunette there,
Here a wife, there a blonde,
Everywhere a chick chick.
Brandt Mancino..."

"SHUT THE HELL UP! NOW!" That from Brandt startled me into silence. I'd never before heard him raise his voice. "I RESENT THAT IMPLICATION!" he shouted further.

Although I was intimidated by Brandt's uncharacteristic shouting – or uncharacteristic as far as *I* knew - I recovered from that rapidly. "But do you deny it?" I asked, staring him down.

Brandt answered in a once again modulated voice. "It isn't like you present it. I've always been very selective."

"OF COURSE YOU HAVE!" I shrieked. "You see a woman within fifteen feet of you, and if she has a pulse you SELECT her!"

"I deny your accusation-"

"Which one?"

"All of them; such as that I'm insatiable..."

"In Satiable? In Mary, in Annie, in Jill, in Valentine, why *not* in Satiable?!"

"That was nasty," Brandt offered.

"And so undeserved? Do forgive me."Once Brandt had told me,"you have the curse of the beautiful woman." I hadn't known what the curse was. Now I knew. The curse of the beautiful woman was Brandt! Had I been plain he wouldn't even have given me a second look.

"Where does this leave us?" *That* question from Brandt made me stare at him in utter amazement. To even ask such a thing after what had just ensued, he'd have to either be very isolated from the reality of his impact upon others' feelings, or believe that I would tolerate completely unacceptable treatment. But then, why *wouldn't* he believe that I would? By remaining in the relationship regardless of whatever he had thrown my way, *I* had *taught* him that I *would*.

Well, not one moment longer! "You ask where this leaves us? It leaves me no longer willing to be a member of your goddamned harem, Brandt!"

For a while neither of us said anything. Finally I spoke again. "So, if you like Jill better, have her."

"You mean CHOOSE between the two of you?!" Brandt sounded as incredulous at my request as if I'd just asked him to jump out of a plane without a parachute. (I was tempted!)

"I apologize for my nerve." Under the circumstances it wasn't difficult for me to muster up a little extra sarcasm.

"So, you want to say good-bye to the whole thing, is that it?" Brandt's tone carried the hurt of one who had been wrongly accused. He was turning it all around.

Looking back, I realized that Brandt had always been an expert at Kafkaesque illogic, at turning everything backward. When I hadn't known he'd been married twice before, according to him that wasn't his responsibility; afterall, he'd told me; I'd forgotten. Forgotten, my foot! When I'd gotten angry with some of his totally unacceptable behavior, he'd advised me that I was over reactive. When I'd intimated he'd lied to me about other women, he'd suggested that I was just full of fears. More often than not he'd even convinced me that it *was* me. *Love* at first sight, I'd called it? Try *lust*!

"Yes, I do want to say goodbye to the whole thing," I told Brandt. "I find you a despicable person. I can't imagine why I ever thought I was in love with you."

Brandt looked at me, I thought surprised, remaining silent. "But before we part, I want you to hear how I feel right now."

"You feel upset," Brandt offered in his best psychoanalytical manner.

"Upset is the least," my words poured out. "I feel betrayed. The only reason FOCI exists is due to the tears, sweat and blood of many parents like me. True, you and I did meet through FOCI and have been here together. You found *me; you* came after *me; I* wasn't looking. Not that I take no responsibility for what you and I have done. That probably was morally wrong and for that I am responsible as much as you are. But I've still put my heart and soul and muscle into this organization. The truth is, I somehow thought our relationship was noble. You've just shown me that it was no more than a cheap lay." Brandt started to protest, but I said, "*I'm* talking now. Remember this, Brandt. FOCI's meant as a lifeline for our kids, not as a giant playground for doctor colleagues to rub their bodies together."

Brandt looked down. "I promise you this last thing," I added. "You put that Bernstein woman on the board and other people will know why, and that will be the *least* I'll do about it!" I then realized that I was still holding the notepaper with the incriminating "J.B for P.A.B" message in my fist. Slapping the crinkled paper into Brandt's hand, I told him, "Oh, here; this belongs to you."

"What am I supposed to do with this now?"

"I so much appreciate you asking. I suggest that you just take it and shove it up your ass!" Brandt appeared somewhat in shock; I imagine that sometime during this evening it had started to occur to him that the, "Goodness me" girl had gone.

Numb and spent, I felt my body crumble. "I want you to leave now, Brandt," I told him.

"Leave?"

"Yes. Please. Just go."

Brand kept looking at me beseechingly as if expecting me to change my mind, but I stared back at him, remaining silent. Then, even though Brandt was paying for the room, even though his return flight was not until the following evening – so I had no idea where he'd go in the interim and couldn't have cared less - he put his few belongings into his suitcase and walked out of the room, closing the door after him.

With Brandt gone, stillness blanketed the room like fog over the Manhattan skyline.

I sat on the bed for a while, my mind churning. "Well, Dr. Cheng Ho, what's in THIS that's positive, HMMM?! Excuse me, teacher, but I can't think of one damned thing." In fact, aside from things regarding Willie, I'd never before felt such heartbreak.

Then I crumbled. There I was, "the woman who had everything, men falling at her feet," curled up in a ball on a hotel room bed in a strange city, weeping inside myself but externally unable to utter even one small cry. It then further occurred to me that there in a city of so many people, if anything had happened to me right then nobody would know; I hadn't exactly announced before coming here, "In case you want to reach me I'll be at the Excelsior Hotel" . Only Brandt knew I was here and I'd sent *him* away.

Since I couldn't move, I stayed in that fetal position for what seemed a long time.

I'd come to Brandt full of love and belief - God forgive me my innocence - that Brandt had wanted to love me in return. Then tonight naivete had crashed to earth and broken its goddamned neck. Suddenly I realized that Brandt *had* given me something. The knowing to never again give to a man with my entire body, mind and spirit. To never trust a soul.

CHAPTER 19: HELL-ON-WHEELS

"To say it briefly and clearly so that there may be no doubt: God in His faithfulness gives each man what is best for him."
--Meister Eckhart

"Trouble keeps overflowing the retaining wall of philosophy."
--Robert Frost

July 1977. The newspaper headlines were filled with Son of Sam's latest killings. Son of Sam was actually a man named David Berkowitz who was killing people because, he said, a dog was telling him to. Manhattan was going crazy with fear. To bring it even closer to home, Son of Sam seemed to be targeting young women with long brunette hair and light colored eyes. Women in New York City of that description were understandably panicking. Some were cutting their hair short and/ or coloring it blonde or red. Me? I don't mean to be facetious or to trivialize the tragedies of the people's loved ones that were being killed in this travesty. But in my state of mind the Monday morning after that weekend with Brandt, if I'd known where Son of Sam was I'd have gone and stood in front of him, flaunted my long dark hair and batted my green eyes at him, thereby inviting him to kill me.

It wasn't that I was crazy or out of control that morning. I knew exactly what I was doing. Being Hell-on-Wheels. A deliberate bitch. I should have been wearing a tee shirt, "I hate everybody and you're next." My usual polite feminine manner had flown-the-coop, leaving me a combination of Casse between weddings and Marie Antoinette. Again, you would have thought I'd forever been Cheng-less; a part of me was enjoying this karma-creating chaos, although "enjoy" is a peculiar word for the frenzy that I was feeling *and* creating. All day I was one of those bad things that happen to good people.

I'd started my day by being short with Brenna, impatient with Essie, and as for Richard, I'd had not one civil word for him. I was about to leave for the train when Brenna began to whine, "My throat hurts, Mommy." After taking her temperature and finding it 101 degrees, I hurriedly called Doctor Sayler, the pediatrician. When the nurse answered, I told her who I was and announced that I needed to talk with the doctor. "DOCTOR can't come to the phone," she said officiously. "And why *can't* DOCTOR come to the phone?" I inquired, equally so. "DOCTOR is busy" she answered with finality. "REALLY!" I rejoined. "So, DOCTOR is busy, How INTERESTING! I'm busy TOO. My husband is ALSO busy. My children are busy. My dogs, my cats and my birds are busy! I haven't checked yet this morning but I believe my FISH is also busy! What does THAT have to do with anything? Put Dr. Sayler on the phone...NOW!"

Sayler was summoned to the phone immediately and agreed to see Brenna almost that quickly. In a short while he looked down Brenna's throat while eyeing me with trepidation, said he didn't think it was strep but took a culture to make certain, and prescribed rest and aspirin for that day. As soon as we returned home Brenna, her sunny self again, was deep into the couch cushions and the TV. I left for work. Of course by then I was quite late.

When I finally climbed onto the train I saw Max seated ahead of me and remembered that this was his day to go in late. I took a seat away from Max, pretending not to see him. When he "found" me I refused to talk. Let him blame it on P.M.S.

Then a taxi driver didn't go the way I had in mind from Penn Station to the studio. Actually, his way would have gotten me there the following Tuesday. I made no attempt to be my usual tactful and reasonable self with the driver. Rather, I screeched, complained and bitched. When the driver refused to comply, I threatened. And when that didn't work, I ordered him to stop the cab immediately, cursed at him and jumped out. He began to shout at me, "Lady, you no pay... you no pay." I shouted back, "YOU no go in right direction. You BET your ass I no pay!" At that he jumped out of his cab and began to chase me, shouting something in his foreign language that I was lucky not to have understood.

Before that maniac could catch me, I ran and flagged down another cab; we took off just as the driver of the first taxi caught up with me and shook his fist in front of the cab window. Then I realized this driver was going in the wrong direction. It gets worse. I asked the driver to turn around at the first possible opportunity. He did what I'd asked, taking us down a street where, as it turned out, ten cars and twenty large trucks were double-parked. The truck drivers were unloading merchandise. I called to them out the window, "We can't get through; you've got to move!" The minority of the truck drivers who bothered to respond at all looked through me like glass. I shouted at my driver, "*Do* something!" He did; he shrugged his shoulders, then sat there. He appeared unconcerned about the predicament. Once I looked closer and saw his meter ticking I realized why he was so calm, whereupon I shouted, "That does it!" And jumped out of that cab without paying him also.

This driver, too, began to shake his fist at me, appearing like he, also, was going to come after me. He didn't, though. I guessed he'd taken a look at me - by then I was probably close to foaming at the mouth - and decided it was best not to mess with a lunatic.

I went to the nearest bus stop where I could get a Number Two bus, which would take me within a block of the studio. Nobody else was there. After I'd stood alone for several minutes a woman walked over and positioned herself beside me, looking everywhere but at me the way strangers at bus stops, elevators, and in cashier lines do. A second later, though, she turned to me and asked, "Is this where the Number Two bus comes?"

"Yes!" My answer was curt.

"You taking the Number Two?"

"Yes!"

"How long ago did the last Number Two bus leave?"

"Do you think I stand here all day?" I inquired, raising my voice an octave.

The woman, looking puzzled, took a few steps backward. I in turn took a step toward her - it was a weird dance - and bellowed in her face, "Is this DIFFICULT? How the HELL should I know WHEN THE LAST NUMBER TWO BUS ARRIVED! IF I'D BEEN HERE THEN, DON'T YOU REALIZE I WOULD HAVE BEEN ON IT INSTEAD OF STANDING HERE LIKE AN IDIOT WAITING FOR THIS ONE?"

The woman cringed, shrank a few inches, and turned her back, whereupon the Number Two bus appeared. The woman held back until I'd boarded, carefully watching which seat I was headed for, then obviously avoided sitting anywhere near me. In fact, I not only got a seat all to myself but one for my handbag as well. I guessed it had something to do with the manner in which I'd stomped down the aisle. People in New York City learn to duck the dangerous. This made me even more stressed; I was running out of people to choke.

However, once I was seated an overwhelmingly painful feeling of loneliness came over me. It felt so terrible that I first tried to deny it, but then, remembering Cheng's teaching that one way to deal with uncomfortable emotions was to really get into them, I made myself really stare down inside and feel those awful feelings. "Oh, I'm lonely…sooooo lonely!" I inwardly moaned. At first it felt terrible, then the feelings began to abate slightly. I remember thinking, "Is it working, could this be?" and continued the exercise. After perhaps five minutes an interesting thing occurred. Not only had the feelings vanished but also the bus made a stop, a few people got off including that woman I'd met at the bus stop, and a few others boarded. One of them, a worn-out grandmotherly looking woman, took the seat beside me. After a few seconds she turned to me, sighed deeply and began to vent to me, "It's so good to be on a bus alone. It's the only time I ever am any more. Otherwise, it's my husband, my grown children, and now the grandchildren, always there expecting something from me." She sighed deeply and smiled as she repeated, "It feels so good to be here, alone."

***

I contemplated the sea gull. He was so beautiful in flight, so free, and yet purposeful.

After a while Cheng spoke. "So?" he asked softly.

"Oh, I'm sorry, I must have drifted," I answered. "This tea is excellent. What kind is it?"

"One of the same kinds you have had here many times," Cheng responded. "So? You came here to talk about tea or something else?"

I put down the mug with the painted sea gull on it.

"Oh, Cheng!" I moaned. Then I broke down into sobs. Cheng reached over from beside me on the couch and touched my shoulder. "Good," he said. "You'll feel much better."

Once my crying had subsided Cheng asked gently, "Tell me?"

"Where do I start? It's everything." I wailed. "My entire life's turned upside down. Richard and I are separated, and there's Brandt, who seems very happy to have me in his life plus anyone else he fancies. My apartment is dingy and depressing; I hate it. I miss Willie."

"Talk about Blandt first," Cheng encouraged.

"What can I say? He's a long distance man who has had the perfect arrangement with me, it seems. He gets laid and he gets left alone."

Cheng smiled. "You will find that many men are long distance men. Brandt, however, is unique even in that category."

"Was there something I failed to do about that, Cheng, I mean the women?"

"Of course. You could have followed him around putting Saltpeter into his food." I actually looked to see if Cheng was serious. "Val-teen, don't be ridiculous. You could do *nothin*g about that. Where is Blandt now?"

"Who knows? Probably on interstate flight to avoid prosecution. What bothers me most, Cheng is I got definite signs from the Universe that he and I were given a green light to go forward. How do you explain that?"

"You saw the green light but failed to read the road signs," Cheng responded. "It's common mistake. Your signs confirmed that you and Blandt have strong attraction and past life bonds. They *didn't* say you'd end up together, although you might. Just not now."

"How do you know that?"

"Two reasons. One, Blandt is right now - forget the doctor's white coat - like a drug addict sneaking down dark alleys for his fix, just Blandt's drug is women."

"Definitely a hopeless case, then? You're saying he doesn't love me, he never has? That he was never my soul mate?"

"Certainly not hopeless. People can change. Everyone has good qualities. Blandt loves you in the way that he can, but so what? He doesn't get involved. About the soul mate thing, well...maybe he could have touched your soul. But he wouldn't. So what good is that, either?"

"You said there are two reasons. What's the second?"

"It's that you, Val-teen, are not yet ready to be in relationship with *any* man. Not until you come into right relationship with yourself."

"So we've identified the problem," I said glumly. "Now what?"

"Identify the problem, don't identify with it, then you do something worthwhile about it. That applies to everything," Cheng offered.

"Tell me what I do now," I implored.

"I don't know."

"*Naturally* you don't. Why do I even ask! Oh, God, why are you doing this to me!"

"Ask the Universe and it will answer you," Cheng said

"Sure it will! It's certainly steered my right so far!"

I'd almost forgotten about my experience on the bus,with the woman who had no opportunity to be alone, which I now related to Cheng. "Very interesting!" Cheng said. "Isn't it!" I agreed. "What does it mean?" Cheng answered, "Obviously once you went with what was, the universe stepped in to help you by showing you the opposite of your present situation. The Agony of Haves and Have Nots, remember? A sign for you to thank God for your blessings."

"I'm not sure I can muster up much gratefulness about my life right now, Cheng. But this time you gave me an answer. I'm grateful for that, at least. Thank you."

"You're welcome."

Do you feel that nothing further should have had to happen to a person within any 72 hour period? I would agree. Yet something further did happen. Have you guessed that it was not something good? You are right again; it was not something good. It was something marvelous. Also magnificent, mysterious and divine. I thought of it ever after as, "The Taxi Shakti Miracle."

At around six the following evening I finished my final appointment, a showing of Ernie's book to an art director at an agency at Sixth Avenue and 42nd street. It was raining lightly, just enough to mess up the city sidewalks. I decided not to return to the studio, rather to walk the short distance from there to Grand Central Station where I knew there was a taxi stand area. If I were lucky I'd nab a cab to Pennsylvania Station and take a train home from there.

I arrived, quite wet, at the Grand Central taxi stand area, whereupon I had an epiphany; it would take more than luck to get a taxi this evening. It was rush hour and raining, a lethal NYC combination. Many people, as wet as I which only exacerbated their poor humors, stood crowded ahead of me around the taxi area where taxis were arriving and departing regularly. Each time a cab pulled up, the people pushed and shoved one another to get to the front and grab that taxi.

I stood in place wondering what I wanted to do. I knew I didn't want to walk the ten blocks to Penn Station in the rain, nor to go be a sardine in the subway at commuter hour. Nor did I want to play this crowd's nab-the-cab game, especially knowing that I probably wouldn't get a cab anyway; these past few days I'd stopped believing in miracles.

I wondered if I'd lost my drive and will. I stood there contemplating that possibility; within a few minutes I heard within me, "You have not lost your drive and will, only your drive and will for destruction." I was, to say the least, surprised at that interesting message. If that was so, when had all that happened to me? To my knowing all that I'd had lately was aggravation, no bolt out of the blue transformation toward enlightenment. Yet an odd relaxation and - I must say – contentment was spreading through me.

I then sort of calmly walked toward where the people congregated - and right past them. About fifteen feet beyond them I stopped, and stood. I didn't know why I was doing this yet didn't question it.

I was there only a short time when I sensed the stir of the crowd indicating that a taxi was approaching; the people were again shoving to get close to the curb. But, this taxi didn't stop at the stand. It drove right past it and stopped - directly in front of me. From my peripheral vision I saw the crowd starting to hustle to where I was. I was stunned into immobility.

Then everything came in fast forward. The driver, rolling down his window, yelled at me, "You, lady. GET IN!" I rushed toward his cab, yanked open the door, scrambled in and slammed the door behind me. Only then did I glance out the window and see at least ten angry puzzled people peering in at me.

"Where to?" the driver asked.

"Penn Station."

"You GOT it."

He threw on his meter, took off like a bullet and we headed down Seventh Avenue in silence. But, I had to know.

"Driver?" I asked.

"Yea?"

"There were so many people out there. What made you take me and not any of them?"

The driver appeared to be thinking. Finally he answered, "Well…you see…. it's hard to explain. Let me put it dis way, lady. YOU was the only one who didn't look greedy."

Even with that wonderful and perhaps significant experience, maybe even partially due to it, the following day I became very sick.

I'd awakened feeling ill in a way that I never had before. It was very peculiar. I was weak, dizzy, and emotionally and physically vulnerable, with strange symptoms in my head, chest, in fact in almost every part of my body. I in fact felt I was loosing control of my body, which was very frightening. At work I almost passed out.

Richard, upon seeing me the following morning, declared, "Valen, your face is like chalk. I'm taking you to a doctor." I said, "I don't want to go to a doctor." Richard insisted, "You *have* to go to a doctor." "Richard," I managed, "We aren't - for all intents and purposes –married now, so you don't *have* to fight with me."

However, I acquiesced. That doctor lead to two more and a week's hospital stay, where they did test after test with every result negative. That fact actually made me feel worse. If the doctors said I was fine, why was I feeling wretched? A very nice doctor asked me questions about my life, then offered, "Mrs. Jordan, this has to be due to stress. You appear to be suffering from exhaustion. You must slow down. You need much rest, sleep, good food, and a quiet atmosphere. I'm going to keep you here for another week, and then I want you to promise me you'll rest at home for another month."

"A MONTH!" I wailed to Richard. "I couldn't possibly do that. I can't afford not to work!" Richard answered, "You'll do it. Somehow we'll manage financially." I must say he was very supportive. My friends supported Richard's and the doctors' position. However, I lamented further to Cheng, "Cheng, I haven't time to take a month off to loll around!"

"Interesting, how people don't have time to take care of themselves but they have time to go to the hospital," Cheng mused. As usual he was effective in a way that all the others combined had failed to be. I gave in.

Everyone was supportive. Richard visited every day. The Cheng Gang came often, and of course Cheng himself, sneaking vitamins, power drinks and healthful snacks into the hospital, while whispering angrily, "Look what they give her to eat -- jello! People are supposed to get BETTER on..sugar and gelatin?" Casse came, Stu, of all people, Cal, of course Max, the studio people, And, Sallee-Mae, also. Ernie phoned - once.

In the hospital I had a bed beside a window, looking out onto the lawn and trees. The view was strangely comforting. I realized that I couldn't remember the last time I'd rested. Until then, my idea of taking a rest had been to stop doing whatever thing I'd been doing and to move on to doing another thing. I was a busy woman. Now suddenly I could only sleep, eat the good food my friends brought me, look out the window, meditate, and contemplate. Of course here I began to understand the message via that woman on the bus. You *are* alone, love-interest wise, anyway, so use it; it's not for nothing. I could try, at least. When Cheng had told us to spend some time alone I hadn't planned on this way, but I hadn't done it other ways, so maybe…

Somehow I had a feeling that stress and exhaustion was not really what was happening to me. I just could not put my finger on what it was.

Sallee-Mae visited. "Honay," she said, "Ah can't wait until you-all get outa he ah. But am sure you-all can't either." Glumly I admitted to her, "I'm in no hurry to get back to my bleak apartment. It's prettier here." The following day she returned with a huge Fendi tote full of pictures of rooms she'd cut from decorating magazines. "Here. Ah know lookin' at some purty rooms will perk y'all up," she said. We did that together, each of us pointing at which cheerful rooms we liked best. One had pale peach walls and a color scheme of violets, purples, pinks, light blues, muted greens, sand and cream. I could have moved right in. "I just love these colors." I told her.

"Honey, then you look at this picture and imagine yourself livin' in that place. It'll make ya' feel good."

When Cheng heard what Sallee-Mae had advised, he agreed. For the rest of my hospital stay I did just that. It did make me feel better. Sallee-Mae was right, it was elevating. She must have been talking with Cheng. When I saw her again I asked her, "Doctor, when will you hang out your shingle?" "I ain't got no shingles" Sallee-Mae answered, straight-faced. "Once I had shingles, in my left leg. Ow, I don't never want shingles again!" I smiled, shook my head and put my hand on top of Sallee- Mae's. I kept it there for quite awhile.

Finally the doctor told me that I was to be discharged the following morning with my promise to rest at home for a month. Everybody expressed concern in one way or another.

For example, Max. He said, "You shouldn't be alone in your apartment your first few nights home. What if you should pass out? I'll come stay with you and watch over you." I answered wryly, "Of COURSE you will!" Max hurriedly added, "I'll sleep in the other room, I promise."

"Max, what kind of watching over me could you do from the next room?" I asked, amused. "Thank you, but I'll be fine." Richard urged me, "Come back to the house for a few days. Glady fixed up the storage room near Brenna's room as a guestroom. Brenna will love it if you come. After that, if you want to I'll bring you back to Interlude." That last sentence about Brenna did it. I agreed.

Despite the love and concern from everyone, that first day out of the hospital I felt very depressed. I had begun to wonder what attention from men counted for in the long run. More on my mind then was the first conversation by phone that I'd had with Ernie once out of the hospital. Although he'd told me that my position with him was assured when I was ready to return, I didn't totally trust him. In all my life areas I didn't know where I stood. I felt displaced. And, I missed Willie just dreadfully.

That evening I was lying on the bed in Glady's new guest room, drifting, when I suddenly went into a kind of fog. I remember feeling, "If I should fall asleep now and never awaken again that would be all right with me," and being shocked at that thought. Everybody else's life, for better or worse, was going on without me whereas mine had seemed to have come to a dead halt. There just didn't seem much to live for.

Suddenly, I felt myself floating. A second later I heard Willie calling me. I remember thinking, "But Willie's in Connecticut. How can I be hearing him from here?" The very next minute I was up on the ceiling, looking down at a small body on the bed below. For heaven's sake, I WAS THAT BODY - except I wasn't because *I* was up at the ceiling! I continued to look down at my body with total disinterest. It meant no more to me than had it been a discarded raincoat. I was up here. The raincoat was laying on the bed down there. Actually, that was exactly how it was. My body was below but all that I was, all my awareness, my totality was up there at the ceiling. I was no less alert or real than usual. In fact, I was more so.

Then, I began to think that I could move, and as I thought it, I did. I began to float. I started to want to tell somebody about this fantastic thing that was happening to me, and with that desire I floated right through the wall of the bedroom (didn't even have to open the doorway, for Heaven's sake!) down the stairs and into the dining room.

Richard and Bernie were sitting at the table discussing a joint business venture. I left that room and floated into the room where Brenna was sleeping. She looked so peaceful. I blew her a kiss, then floated to Connecticut to look in on Willie. Willie looked fine too.

I then flew back to the dining room of our home.

The men had a box of Ritz crackers on the table and a jar of peanut butter with a butter knife sticking out of the jar. I smiled to myself. Richard's idea of gracious entertaining! I called to Richard, "Look up, I'm here." When he didn't respond in any way, I began to realize that he couldn't seem to see or hear me, although I could see and hear him and Bernie perfectly.

Then it hit me! "Am I dead?" At that, I became frightened, and with that limiting emotion, in what seemed like seconds I found myself floating back up the stairs, through the bedroom wall, and then smack back into my body. I "came to," if that is the word for it, with a hard thud. Then I became aware of a feeling of heaviness from being in body again which was decidedly unpleasant compared with the out-of-body state I'd just come from. I remember thinking, "This being alive stinks," and being somewhat delighted at that realization, but primarily very depressed at being back in my body.

I remember lying there awhile in a mixture of awe and confusion, needing to reorient myself. After a while I got up and went downstairs (the usual way!) to the dining room, where Bernie and Richard were still discussing business. After we'd greeted each other and they'd asked how I was feeling, I told Richard, "You aren't going to believe this but about one half hour ago I was in here watching you - from the ceiling."

Richard stared at me, then said, "For once you are right. I *don't* believe you." With that he walked over to me and put his hand on my forehead.

I had to laugh a little. "Rick, I don't have a fever and I'm *not* hallucinating! I had an out- of-body experience. I'll prove it to you. There's no food on the table right now, correct?"

"Correct," Richard answered, "but..."

"But before you had crackers and peanut butter here, with the knife sticking out of the jar. Isn't that so?

Turning white, Richard nodded yes.

"I saw it while I was up THERE before." I pointed to the ceiling.

Richard's jaw dropped, his eyes widened and he could have just seen a ghost – which in a semi-sense he was now seeing, I thought, amused. I could see him on the verge of freaking out.

Bernie came to the rescue. "It is possible, Rick," he interceded. "I've read about this type of thing." *Bernie* HAD? I was very surprised. Remember that this WAS only the 70's. People whom I'd thought I knew were amazing me lately.

It was predictable that Richard might make a joke at this juncture; he didn't disappoint us. "While you're flying around, V, why don't you fly down and get the mail," he cracked, pointing out the front window to Glady's then uninvitingly ice-covered long drive leading down a slight hill to her mailbox.

Richard persuaded me to remain at Glady's house for the rest of the week. "You might be handy to have around when we need somebody to fly to the grocery store for milk," he explained.

That night I had a peculiar dream. I saw a dark skinned man's face in front of me, perhaps Indian. He had the most compellingly exquisite eyes. He was saying a name to me, which sounded something like, "Cal" Then he gave me a message and transmitted to me unbelievable love. After that I fell into the deepest most peaceful sleep I'd ever experienced. When I awakened, try though I did I could not remember what he'd told me.

When the week ended I knew it was time to leave. My car was still in the parking area at Interlude, so I asked Richard to drive me back there.

As I opened the door to the apartment, Richard stood aside allowing me to enter first. My eyes widened and then I flopped down on the couch and just stared in disbelief.

My apartment had been transformed into the picture in that decorating magazine! All the walls had been painted that same peach tone. The slipcovers on the couch and chairs were a floral pattern in the magazine room's peaches, pinks, blues, greens, violets, and creams. The kitchen cabinets, those awful oily and scratched brown ones, had been painted a muted green to blend in with everything else. Our crystal vases from the other house were everywhere, filled with fresh flowers. Flower pots with mums and violets and greens abounded. We walked into the bedroom. I exclaimed "Ohhh!" It had the same color scheme. There was a white quilt with lace trim on my bed and matching lace curtains on the window slightly framed by drapes in all the rooms' colors. Decorative pillows in all the colors were on the bed in arranged abandon. The bathroom was equally delightful. Somebody - Stu, I later learned - had some violet carpeting they'd used for a shoot, which he had fit in my bathroom as wall-to-wall, covering the ugly chipped tile floor. Two sea gull pictures from Cheng were on the walls. I later learned that Dawn, our stylist, had overseen the entire project.

It was all like being in a gorgeous garden. I loved it!

I looked at Richard. He said, "I have to admit it's remarkable, also that I'm not responsible for any of it; decorating isn't my forte. Your Cheng people did it, also Sallee-Mae, Cassandra and some of your people from work. They were finishing it the night of the afternoon you got discharged from the hospital, one of the reasons I took you to Glady's. Only one of the reasons."

I learned that the men had painted the walls, while Sallee-Mae had sewn all the curtains. Later I asked her, "YOU SEW!" She answered, "What did y'all expec, Valtan? Thar was eleven of us kids when ah grew up. We was so po', we had no inside toilet. Ah had to sew ma own clothes or go naked."

I learned that Casse, who for days later admonished me to, "stop this crap and get back with Richard where you belong," had contributed the plants. The flowers were from Cal. Max had paid for the bedroom accessories which Sallee-Mae had selected. Later I told Sallee-Mae, "This is one advantage to living alone. I could never have had such a feminine bedroom living with Richard," Sallee-Mae answered, "You're wrong. A man likes his office to look masculine, not the bedroom he shares with a woman. A woman involved with a man should always have the MOST feminine bedroom. Men love it, just like they love women to wear feminine nightgowns and undergarments."

So much for my "discernment" that Sallee-Mae was one of the 'bad' people and also that she was stupid. I now understood that there are all kinds of smart. Sallee-Mae knew things that I needed to learn. It seemed my appraisal of her was just one of my recent mis-evaluations. Then, my mention of living alone lead Sallee-Mae into a diatribe about how Richard and I, a perfect couple, *must* reconcile. I was growing tired of hearing it from everybody although I appreciated the concern. *They* had not lived in our house.

My friends visited me often, bringing healthful treats and uplifting conversation. Sallee-Mae brought chicken soup, chuckling as she opened the lid, "Here, proof that ah *have* converted ta Judaism!" Hinda didn't visit, though. For whatever the reason, next to Cheng she was the one I really wanted to see the most. I'd heard she was out of town. Cal was on location but he called. Ernie didn't visit. I was not eager to see *him* per se, just concerned that he had been so distant and wondering what that said about my job with him.

Cheng visited the most, continuing to give me herbs, vitamin-packed drinks, and hands-on healing. He had me visualize myself running on a seagull-filled beach, becoming strong and energetic. He told me, "Visualization works, often miraculously. Remember, you visualized living in a beautiful apartment and it happened. It is like the song says; 'when you wish upon a star, makes no difference who you are. Anything your heart desires will come to you." It *was* a miracle that my dingy dungeon had become this enchanted place. Cheng also encouraged me to meditate every day.

Richard took exception to these forms of treatment. "Cheng Ho is not exactly the Mayo Clinic, Valen," he admonished me. "If you're still sick, stop fooling around with witch doctors. Get another medical opinion." I told Richard, "I'm getting better. Everything will be alright, I know it." He didn't look convinced, but I had the same innate feeling that this would soon be over that I'd had throughout about my illness being something other than stress-induced.

My improvement took time, for as one symptom would abate, another would take its place.

I asked Cheng, "Is this psychological?"

Cheng replied, "I shall quote to you from Robert Adler, an experimental psychologist from the University of Rochester. 'There is no such thing as psychosomatic illness. To say there is suggests there are some diseases that are not psychosomatic. All disease is influenced by psychological factors. Emotions speak through our bodies. The only question is, which ones are speaking?' Somebody is suffocating in a relationship. Then do they have respiratory problems? Feeling crushed in their job? Do they have a car accident wherein their chest gets crushed? Digestive problems? What aren't they digesting about other parts of their life? Heart disease? From what are they heartbroken? Arthritis? Where's the rigidity in their attitudes?' You have forgiving to do, Val-teen, not least of all yourself. I want you to make a list of ten or more ways in which you are not honoring yourself."

"And then you want to see it?"

"If you like. Primarily I want you to study it and then to begin honoring yourself in those ways that you now are not."

The following day, before I could begin my list, I developed what was perhaps my strangest symptom yet, and the most frightening. Every time I had even the semblance of a negative thought I'd get something akin to an attack in my chest and head, the intensity of which nearly knocked me to the floor. As this continued to reoccur, I found that the only way I could prevent it was to monitor every thought to make certain that no negative ones slipped through, and when they did anyway, to banish them instantly by positive thought substitution. Until then I'd believed myself to be a positive person. I'd had no idea just how many negative thoughts I had. The above continued all morning until I'd had all I could take. Petrified (what if this lasted the rest of my life?), I phoned Cheng.

The phone continued to ring for a rather long time. My heart sank. I was about to hang up when I heard the receiver lifted off the hook followed by…

"Cheng Ho here. And, you are?"

I sighed with relief. "Cheng, I thought you weren't home. I'm so glad you answered."

"I was going to an appointment. From outside I heard the phone ring, so I came back in."

"Cheng, please go ahead, then. I don't want to keep you from your appointment."

"Why not? Appointment was with you. See you soon."

Uncanny Cheng.

It seemed I'd hardly put down the phone when Cheng was at my door. I barely let him enter before I told him everything. He was not fazed by anything that had, or was, happening to me.

"You are being catapulted into an extreme sensitivity, showing you how greatly negative thoughts harm every one of us," he explained, "Just, most people are not given such a cause and effect learning opportunity. They suffer the effects of negative thinking just as greatly, or more so, but without this graphic a demonstration they may fail to realize the connection between those negative effects and their cause - negative thinking. Remember Discourse Three? You are getting homework for it. You are so lucky!"

"Oh, surely. I've been feeling so lucky all morning I've wanted to hide under a rock! What about my out-of-body experience? What was *that* for?"

"That was to help you realize the limitlessness of your True Self. Of all of our True Selves. To stop identifying with your body and your thoughts."

Then I had to ask the question as much as I feared the answer.

"Cheng, did I die?"

"I don't know." Cheng smiled benignly

"Oh Cheng, common, this is important!"

"Perhaps not as much so as you think." Cheng's tone was nonchalant to the utmost. "There is no such thing as death as you mean it, so why does it matter? We die many times in each incarnation. You died to something, that is certain, and were reborn into something else, something very good. Don't mind the challenge of the homework, Val-teen.. Real teachers and healers often get a heavy dose of that. So when they teach, or heal, they *know* the Truth through the only real way that we can know anything, our own experience. You are, in fact, being your own laboratory rat."

I didn't argue, just groaned, "Well, teacher, will you go a little easier on the homework? I'm not sure how much more of this kind I can handle right now."

Cheng's answer to that was, "Make your list of ways that you fail to honor yourself. Then you meditate. Ok?"

As usual he left before I'd had time to ask all of my questions, most importantly, what had he meant by that "real teachers" remark? I hoped I'd remember to ask him the next time. I began my list: "I fail to take enough time for myself," I wrote. "I believe in people long after they've shown me they're undeserving of it..."

Later that afternoon the phone rang. The voice on the other end was lovely and familiar, yet at first I was unable to place her.

"Valentine, it's Hinda," she identified herself.

"Hinda! I'm so happy to hear from you! When did you get

back?"

"I didn't. I'm still in India. I just had a feeling I should connect with you now. How are you?"

"India? Nobody told me. Well... uh... not that great." I tried unsuccessfully to encapsulate the experiences of the last three week, then said, "I don't want to bother you long distance with this..."

"But, please do."

So, between crackles and silences through the India to New York phone connection (technology has since improved) during which we alternated in asking one another, "Can you hear me? Did you hear what I just said?" I managed to give Hinda a run down.

"I think I know what's happening with you, Valentine," she offered. "I believe your chakras are opening and very fast. That accounts for your major symptoms these past weeks."

"Chakras? You mean I'm not sick?"

"No, not really. Oh, I agree you've also overdone it, are run down and need rest," Hinda answered. "But please realize that when the kundalini - that is, the inner Shakti or energy - rises through the chakras and opens them, often many impurities are expelled. Sometimes these can be felt - in the form of negative thoughts, events, even in mild forms of latent diseases all of which could otherwise have manifested more seriously later. In Sanskrit such occurrences are called kriyas, remember the term? While for whatever reason you're having an especially rough awakening, what's happening to you is wonderful, Valentine. Your biggest problem with it was that you didn't understand it."

"Does Cheng know about this type thing?'

"Cheng! Of course! *He* taught me."

"Then why didn't *he* tell me?"

"Cheng has a perfect sense of timing. I'm here now, aren't I?"

"You mean Cheng asked you to phone me now?"

"Probably, although not in a verbal sense. Valentine, when I return I'm going to explain much more about this. Meanwhile, be very kind to yourself. And God Bless, my friend."

Actually, even before that phone call from Hinda I had begun to suspect that something strangely wonderful was happening with me. The realization had begun with that taxi experience followed by the out-of-body experience at Glady's house. Since, I'd felt lighter. Not as light as when out-of-body but lighter than I'd ever felt before in my body. I was feeling a greater connection to my core, to the entire universe. For the first time in my life I was actually... happy. It was ironic. I'd recently lost my home, my marriage, my son, my lover, and for all I knew my job would be next. I *should* have been miserable. I tried to wonder if some of my newfound joy was due to my beautifully refurbished apartment, which I realized I now liked being in better than I had my former house; the latter had a black, red and otherwise dark color scheme; now my taste ran to the pastels and bright colors. As I myself grew lighter, I was more drawn to lighter things. Then I realized that while the cheerful apartment had certainly helped, I'd begun to feel these periods of absolute joy even before I'd known the apartment had been redecorated.

The next time I saw Cheng I told him about my seemingly incongruous happiness. "EXCELLENT," he exclaimed, patting me on the back enthusiastically. "Now you know what I mean when I teach that happiness comes only from inside ourselves, not from anything external. When *you* teach it, it will be the only kind of teaching that's meaningful, from a teacher who has actually experienced that state. People do not get from us mostly our words but our state of being. The perfected teachers actually give to their disciples just from being in their environs. The words they speak are only cake-icing. Our True Self IS that powerful, which is the partial subject of our next Discourse. We have not had classes lately because we voted and everyone agreed that we wanted to wait for you so you'd miss nothing. You want us to have it here at your place next Thursday?"

"Oh, Cheng, you can do that?"

"Sure, why not? You think the tea is too heavy for me to carry here?"

"Cheng, I'd love it, thank you!"

"Then so be it!" Cheng assured me.

"Cheng, I have a question."

"I am sure that you do. Go ahead then."

"Cheng," I said, "the other day you mentioned something about the kind of teacher I'll be. I don't understand; I'm not going to BE a teacher of *any* kind. Unless you meant that in some way each of us is a teacher to each other? That must be what you meant, hmm?"

"Sometimes you talk too much," Cheng answered. "It sounds like you haven't meditated yet today, yes?"

"No. I mean Yes, I haven't," I meekly admitted.

"Then meditate now. See you tomorrow."

The next instant Cheng was gone. I hadn't even seen him open and shut the door.

CHAPTER TWENTY: DISCOURSE SIX-
Living Our Dharma: Doing What Is Right Vs. Doing What Is Wrong Or Merely Pleasurable

"It is better for a man to do his own dharma imperfectly than another man's dharma well."

--Bhagavad Gita

"What is good or right to do may not seem as appealing as what is merely pleasurable. That is why Commandments or laws of living have been given to us. If they weren't difficult to follow, we wouldn't need them in the first place."

--Cheng

"It's unda control," he answered. I waited expectantly for Ernie to flesh that report out a bit; a reasonable expectation, I thought; it was *my* work, too. When he failed to do so, I asked, "Ernie, have you found a replacement?" Then I steadied myself for his response. I'd learned that while asking the right questions doesn't guarantee receiving right answers, not asking practically guarantees that we won't. It had taken me over thirty years to learn this?

"Replacement FER WHAT?" Ernie's voice boomed.

I cringed at the sound of it. "Not for WHAT. For WHOM. For ME."

"Ya gettin' PARANOID now?"

Ernie was calling *ME*, paranoid? Interesting. Cheng had told us, "What you most want to fix in somebody else is what you most need to fix in yourself." Or as Max would say, " A classic case of 'projection,' as we call it in my business."

A few seconds after that Ernie screamed, "TALK LOUDA, V.J, I CAN'T HEAR YA."

I actually hadn't said anything; with the stereo blaring it wouldn't have mattered either way. At the top of my lungs I yelled into the phone, "I'M JUST ASKING IF YOU WANT ME TO COME BACK WITH YOU."

"SO, THAT'S IT. YOU WANT TO QUIT BEIN' MY REP."

"NO, I DON'T. I JUST NEED TO KNOW IF *YOU'VE* MADE OTHER ARRANGEMENTS SO I CAN MAKE MY PLANS." I tried for a calm tone, difficult while shrieking. Had I really shouted like that every day at the studio? And I'd had to wonder why I'd been often hoarse and frequently fatigued?

"YOU WERE WONDERIN' IF I WANTED YA' BACK?" Ernie shrieked. "WHAT ARE YA, A JERK?"

The stereo was quiet at the moment. "Yes," I answered in my normal tone, "But not as big a jerk as I used to be."

"A 'cause I want ya back, ya schmuck," Ernie bellowed endearingly. For a minute it seemed that things between us were as they used to be. "When ya think that'll be?"

"I can't give you an exact date today but promise I will soon."

"OK, KID. KEEP ME POSTED." The stereo was again at full tilt. "WORK CALLS, TALK TA YA."

I heard Ernie hang up; I frowned as I did the same.

Was I paranoid about this or *was* Ernie acting strange, that is stranger than usual? For instance, I pondered, was it unreasonable for me to have expected Ernie, somebody I'd worked with closely, to have called me during my illness to ask how I was? Since I'd been home Ernie's calls had been conspicuously absent, except for that one transparent call when he'd asked about me but clearly had really wanted to know where some of our prints were. All that left room for speculation; was Ernie really looking for another rep? Loyalty wasn't considered prevalent in the so-called glamour industries. Perhaps Ernie had lined up a replacement for me. Paranoid, my foot! I'd ask Dawn and Zarela to keep their antennae up and to report anything suspicious back to me.

I felt dispirited. How had I ended up closely entwined with three men - Richard, Brandt and Ernie - different type involvements though they were - who had let me down? And among those, two, Ernie and Brandt, whom I'd begun to feel that I could trust about as far as I could throw, respectively, the entire BRD Advertising Agency and all of UCLA! Richard had once told me, "What do you care how Ernie feels about you? Just be professional and keep your guard up." Brandt had once advised, "Just be smaat. Forget about being nice." Once again Richard and Brandt were in agreement without knowing so. It seemed men have a better faculty for emotional disassociation at work, whereas we women typically make little families there and often stay on longer than we should.

I peered at my watch, a Movado that Richard had given me five years ago for no special reason; he had always been generous that way. It was 6:15. I was excited that this was Discourse night. Cheng and the gang were due at 7:15 yet I wasn't close to ready! Cheng always stressed that orderliness and cleanliness were essential in spirituality. I'd start by straightening up the place, then myself. I began to dash, then, realized that here it wouldn't take so long; one room of our former house had been the size of this entire apartment. I slowed down. Living in a postage stamp *did* have its advantages. Again The Agony of Haves and Have Nots.

More quickly than I would have imagined I'd made the apartment spotless, showered, and dressed neatly while for comfort in baggy style jeans and a white tee shirt. I had just made a braid of my hair, fastened it with an elastic band, and was about to apply some make-up when there was a knock at my door. With my still unapplied tube of foundation held mid-air in my hand, I froze.

Two sharp louder raps followed the knock. I looked at my watch, then felt a sudden chill. Cheng and the gang weren't due for another hour. Cheng would not consider arriving this early; it was no less dharmic to arrive too early than too late. Cheng was always exactly on time. I felt my breathing quicken as the knocks continued. I had to go to the door and get to the bottom of this, whatever it was. I walked toward it with my hands visibly shaking, stopped in front of it and in a quaking voice asked, "Who's there?"

"Cheng Ho here."

Confused but sighing audibly in relief, I yanked open the door.

"Greetings." Cheng, bundled in a red knit scarf and hat, looking like a Chinese Santa, adroitly alighted onto my tiny foyer, pointing with his chin to a tapestry bag that he was carrying, one of several he used. "The tea," he explained. "I go put it in the kitchen." He offered no explanation for his earliness. "You look great," he observed.

"Are you kidding? I'm not quite ready…I wasn't expecting..." I stopped, not wanting to make Cheng feel that he was unwelcome at any time. "I only meant… I haven't put my make-up on yet. I look like a ghoul."

"On the contrary. You have such an inner glow of health and happiness; you can leave the make-up off tonight. Look better without all that crap if you ask me."

"Crap?" My spiritual master had said, "crap?" I shook my head. "So, I can put this stuff in the kitchen now?" Cheng asked.

"Of course. I'm sure you'll find my kitchen without difficulty. Take two steps ahead, you're in it."

"Stop being apologetic about your present home," Cheng admonished, frowning. "When the guru is very pleased with us he takes something away. Let the guru do what has to be done to heal the ego-disease. You formerly defined your worth by your possessions. You are temporarily scaled down, the better to focus on your true worth; to prepare. As we sort out our belongings we sort out ourselves. No amount of stuff will be enough until we are enough. But remember this world is a play, the play of consciousness. So money, by definition, is only play money. We are playing Monopoly."

I hadn't a clue what Cheng was talking about regarding the guru and preparing. Preparing for what? Yet his money analogy intrigued me. "You mean, don't take money seriously?"

"Right. Don't worry or be heavy about it. Ever! Worry and heaviness increases any problem. Worrying about anything deprives us of that very thing. Just be light about money as well as every other challenge and play the game the best you can. Lightness and faith attract good. Know money will come, then you'll always have enough money. More than enough."

"This sounds like great stuff. How do I get myself to believe it?"

Cheng grinned. "At first you don't. You just do it. That way you'll find out it's true. *Then* you'll believe it. Remember, that is so for all that I teach you."

"Yes, I remember. I'll try."

"If you say 'try,' you won't. Not *try*. *Do*."

"Yes, yes, do is what I meant. Cheng, what do you mean by me preparing for something? And what's this about some guru, out of thin air?"

Cheng started to hum as he began to remove some boxes of tea from the carton.

"Cheng?" I repeated. Cheng's hum grew louder as he deliberately looked away. Suddenly I'd become invisible.

"Cheng, I asked you a question," I persisted somewhat irritably.

"I know. I heard it." Cheng busied himself arranging the teas on the counter. "The others will be here any minute," he added.

"You aren't going to answer me, are you?" I asked. More humming. "A needless question," I muttered.

I glanced at the Movado. The gang wasn't due for another forty-five minutes. Why had Cheng said they'd be here any second? Why had he arrived an hour early? He was, from A to Z, an enigma. At moments such as these I felt I'd never known anyone as exasperating. "Cheng," I said, "It's only 6:15."

"On *your* watch, yes," Cheng replied, "There it will also be 6:15 when the class ends tonight. Your watch stopped."

In retrospect, it should have been obvious to me that the Movado minute hand hadn't budged since I'd looked at it earlier. My observations had become skewed. Such things happened around Cheng's Shakti. My watch stopping was something else, some sort of Cheng's weird magic? I didn't like it.

"What's the mysterious thing with the watch, a new trick?" I asked him, beginning to get angry.

"Not mysterious," Cheng answered. "You need to change the battery. It's dead."

I peered at my watch, then at Cheng, shook my wrist, then looked at him again, shame-faced. "It was working just this afternoon," I lamely excused myself.

"I know. When that battery goes it goes just like that, without forewarning, like the Shakti often moves, sudden and unexpected. Requires alertness at all times."

Quite awhile ago I had realized that Cheng never made small talk regardless of how it might seem. Every word, every observation was to teach something; everything that occurred was a teaching session. He spoke only for some good purpose or he was silent.

Aloud I said, "Damn! Thc battery for this watch – it's the Renata battery, if you please - costs $44. Right now I can't afford Richard's presents."

"Then right now..." Cheng began, reaching into the tapestry bag, "...wear a Cheng present." He took out a silver-toned Timex and handed it to me. "THIS keeps good time and the battery's long-lasting," he said.

"Thank you, Cheng." I removed the Movado, placed it in a kitchen drawer, and put on the Timex. I realized I'd never seen a watch on Cheng's wrist. "You don't wear a watch, Cheng?" I asked.

"Not much," Cheng answered. "The Shakti is smart. It figures out the details. It does it automatically and perfectly. And," he added with a grin, "it doesn't need batteries." He nodded to the Timex. "Keep it as long as you need it," he offered meaningfully.

***

The sight of Cheng's fellow students occupying every seat and every inch of floor space in my tiny living room filled me with tremendous satisfaction. I had a realization. My former home, although by comparison materially lavish, had been spiritually impoverished. I wouldn't have believed it possible back then, but I was so much happier *here*! It was true after all. I'd believed it theoretically but experiencing it was something else! Things *don't* make us happy.

Cheng began: "This is Discourse Six, on our dharma.

"One of the most important things in life for each one of you to determine is your dharma, as the ancient Indian sages termed it. It is your unique and appropriate forms of expression in the world. Doing what is right, what is in harmony with *your* Truth. It includes, but is not limited to, your work in the world. It is also your moment-to-moment action. This changes; you must keep tuned-in. The great Indian epic, The Mahabharata, states, 'The root of happiness is dharma.' And the Bhagavad Gita states that Yoga is the performance of duties to the very best of one's ability according to one's knowledge, skills and aptitude. If something is worth doing, it is worth doing as well as we know how.

"Regarding our work per se, we can all do many things. However for each of us there is something, categorically speaking, which we can do especially well. These are our natural talents; abilities developed during previous lifetimes which came relatively easily to us here, although we may still require and benefit by further training. Often these natural abilities were evident when we were small children, before adults told us that we should do something else entirely. Unfortunately that too often happens. So, think back to what you were drawn to as children. If you don't remember, if possible ask your parents or others who knew you as a child. Here may well lie important clues to your dharma. And of course use the three-step process for self- discovery, also.

"Additionally we must make distinction between what is good and what is merely pleasurable. The flesh is always fighting with the spirit. That's why laws of life such as the Commandments were given to us. If laws of living weren't often difficult to follow we wouldn't need them in the first place. What is good or right to do at any given time may not feel as appealing as what is merely pleasurable. But in the long run doing what's good and right will lead to joy, whereas doing what's merely pleasurable will lead to misery - often long lasting misery. When what we're doing is gratifying and purposeful, it is usually dharmic."

I thought of Brandt.

"Be forewarned of a common serious error about dharma," Cheng said. "Copying. You see a friend very happy at some work and/or raking in a great deal of money, for example, thus you decide, 'That's for me,' and you get into that work, too. Only for you maybe it doesn't work. Maybe you aren't successful at it or maybe you are but you feel unfulfilled in it. Why? Often, primarily because while it was your friend's dharma to do that kind of work, it was not yours. Don't copy, or at least before you even consider copying, do the contemplation processes that I've taught you: Go inside to ask, 'Is THIS *my* dharma? Also ask yourself the following important question. 'If I won the lottery tomorrow, would I continue doing my present work or something like it?' If the answer is 'yes,' you are probably doing your work dharma. If it's more like, 'Are you kidding, I'd be out of it in a heartbeat!' then you are probably not doing your dharma, at least not correctly. Then further ask, 'Considering I would want to remain in this work even if I were very rich, would I change anything about how I do this work; if so, what?' If you get answers for changes that you'd make, consider making those changes now or make plans for doing so."

Mindie, after going through the acknowledgement process, said, "I believe my work IS not my dharma but right now it's my income, so I can't change my occupation. What do you suggest?"

"An excellent question," Cheng enthused. "Practicalities enter in for most people, not just you, Mindie. So keep your present work for the income while you plan and prepare for your dharmic work once you come to know what that is, through study, specialized training, whatever is required. It is our responsibility to help others with our dharma. God not only helps those who helps themselves, God also helps those who helps others."

Walter asked, "But what if I don't want to be in a helping profession?"

"Every profession becomes a helping profession," Cheng responded, "if you are coming from that place of happiness and love. The Bhagavad Gita tells us that rituals, fasting and sacrifice cannot bring about self-realization in the way that right performance of one's duties can. So, when you do your dharma from the heart, from your moment-to-moment kindness to others, you do help people whether you are an engineer, a cleaning person, a doctor, a professor, a train engineer, or an actor. The Bhagavad Gita says that work is seldom wrong. It is our perception of work which makes it appear wrong.

Max offered, "When you mentioned actor it made me think of one of my patients, a famous comedian. He complained that he made thousands laugh but inside *he* wasn't laughing; he was miserable."

"Then in truth he was a hypocrite, not a funny man," Cheng said. "A comedian who is sad inside might make people laugh for the moment, but he can't really uplift anybody. We can't elevate people beyond the degree that we ourselves are elevated, it's a universal impossibility. What fortunate dharmic work you have, Max, to help this talented man to become really happy. Think of all the thousands of people he will really uplift once that occurs; you will have jump-started that process!"

Serge asked, "You mean I could remain an engineer and help people? I wouldn't have to change my profession?"

"Yes, if engineering is your dharma. I repeat, when one is happy in one's profession and transmits that, then whatever profession a person is in becomes a helping profession. A cook who is happy and full of love automatically transmits that joy into the food. Dear Ones, be aware of eating so-called 'health foods' prepared by those just doing business but lacking love. On the other hand, ordinary food can become most beneficial when cooked with loving hands and hearts. It even tastes more delicious. Since we can't always be certain about our food, I recommend praying over every food before we eat it. Something like a silent, 'God, I know this food will be used by my body in the most beneficial ways. Amen' will suffice. Or repeating "om" eleven times will work. Either raises the food's vibrations and makes that food better for us.

"Yoga tells us of the three qualities of action. Rajas is that which causes desire for good results and is frustrated without them. The rajasik worker works for selfish gains, thus will ultimately experience sorrow. Tamas is that which is purposeless and haphazard. One must not be a tamasik worker, one who is careless, lazy and a shirker by nature. Rajasik work will only bring you sorrow while tamaski will engulf you in darkness. Sattwik is doing our work without any attachment to the results. We are urged to be sattavik in our work. So if you wish happiness, make your deeds sattwik. Also remember the trap of more, more, more. Yoga says the path to hell is paved with greed."

Serge, remembering to first get acknowledged, moaned, "Oy, you are giving us a lot of terms to memorize here, Cheng!"

"I don't care whether or not you remember the terms as long as you remember the disciplines themselves. We can no more live daily without self-discipline than your cars can run without gasoline. Even the great sages must practice discipline every day of their lives. We hear so much about control. *Birth* control, *rent* control, *environmental* control. As we approach the year two thousand and beyond we'll be inundated with even more controls –*gun* control, *violence* control. We're increasingly preoccupied with outer controls. What about *self*-control? If each person exercised a little more of that then we wouldn't need most of the other controls."

Mindie waved her hand excitedly. "An amazing coincidence that before you used the example of a restaurant," she exclaimed. "I've been asking God to tell me what's my right work and had begun to think about starting a vegetarian restaurant."

"COINCIDENCE, Mindie?" Cheng asked.

"No, sorry. I know, there aren't any coincidences. More likely my answer from the Shakti about my dharma?"

Mindie looked at Cheng expectantly. He remained silent. She continued to look, he to remain silent. Clearly, she wanted his confirmation about opening the restaurant. Just as clearly, he had no intention of giving it. I was amused. I'd been there.

"Well, DO you think it's right for me, the restaurant?" Mindie persevered.

For a few seconds Cheng appeared to be considering her question thoughtfully. He then answered, "I don't know." And stood, expressionless.

Mindie was obviously becoming frustrated. I felt my emotion changing from amusement to anger. What *was* this anyway? It was important for Mindie to know whether or not the restaurant would work, or she could risk a lot of money that she could not afford to loose. Wasn't life difficult enough without Cheng's games? He *had* to know the answer to her question. What would it have cost him to tell her at her moment of need?

His actions here were unsettling me enough that I was about to speak up, but I didn't have to; as soon as I had that thought, Cheng spoke strongly, yet with great compassion.

"I disappoint you," he stated, looking at Mindie but in some mysterious way making me know that the answer was as much, or more, intended for me. "You would rather I said, 'Yes, OPEN the restaurant, it IS your dharma. Start next Tuesday. Word will get out that from your food NOBODY ever gets indigestion, so in two months people will be coming from all over the United States and from three other continents.' You want to hear that?"

That brought some giggles, however not from Mindie, who looked like she wanted to cry, nor from me who was identifying with her plight. "Don't laugh," Cheng gently admonished the rest of the group. "You all want absolute answers from me as much as Mindie does. I don't want you to blame yourselves for that anymore than I want you to blame yourselves if you indulge in gossip, eat too much ice cream or overindulge in any sense pleasures. All can be temporarily comforting. It's human for it to happen."

Trenna asked, "Then it would seem that you disapprove of psychics who tell people what to do and make predictions?"

Cheng replied, "I do not disapprove of anyone. I do what is necessary. It's what I want you to do as well; make evaluations. Discrimination, Viveka. Remember that lesson? Predictions and directions to others may be in order on rare occasions by rare individuals who are SO clear within that the answers are primarily coming from the divine rather than greatly tinged with their own impurities. It takes a very long time and much inner work to be rid of all of those impurities, but the great paradox is that if you are diligent in your practices – and this applies to every person – then the amount of progress that you can make toward self-realization in a day, week, month or year is amazing."

Then Trenna dared to ask an unexpected question. "Are *you* one of those... rare people, Cheng?"

We all sat perfectly still, wondering how Cheng was going to answer. He did not flinch. "Me?" Cheng repeated, giggling. Then he became more serious. "I will tell you this," he said. "While psychic development often accompanies spiritual evolvement, psychic people are not necessarily spiritually evolved. They may or may not be. Psychicness of itself is a power, a magic, a siddhi. We will be studying about siddhis in a future Discourse. A psychic person may have developed that ability in a prior lifetime yet may have yet to learn the great lessons regarding scruples and correct use of power. Be discriminating and diligent about whose words to trust. This is a tough one, I warn you, because some of any particular person's words *may be* from God whereas some other words from that same person decidedly could be from their ego instead. We all have the inner omniscient teacher. Developing that connection, that discriminatory power, through meditation and the like should be our priority. Remember, a great teacher is always intent on showing you your greatness rather than his or hers."

After everyone had left, I brushed my teeth, relieved that there was no make-up to remove, put on my night cream, which- wonders- disappeared totally and non-greasily into my skin just as the ad had promised, and got into bed, for once glad to be alone. I had much to contemplate. About my dharma, my right action in the world, and about viveka, my discrimination. About how others - Richard, Brandt and Ernie - fit into that, if at all?

* * *

I was walking down a familiar corridor, cold, dark and cheerless. I felt as repelled by its gloominess as I was attracted by its familiarity. My footsteps echoed off of the cantilevered walls. It was so uninviting here, so isolated. I longed for a person, a solitary soul.

I heard voices in the distance, murmurs, really. My pace accelerated as I was magnetized to the source of the sounds. I turned a corner into another misty, dark and gloomy corridor and walked down it. At the end I jumped, then froze, petrified.

Standing there were three shadowy figures dressed in black, murmuring to one another something that I could not hear. I moved closer, for somehow, although I couldn't hear their whispers, I knew that they were talking about me. Now I was upon them. I called out in a friendly way, "Well, hello." But it seemed they could neither see nor hear me. Now they stood facing each other while moving in a circular fashion as if on an automated huge Lazy Susan. Then all at once their voices became audible. As each moved to a certain point on the sphere, his face became lit as if a spotlight held in front of his face illuminated it briefly. I looked at the first one to approach this light, his whisper becoming louder. "She's a fool," he said. "She doesn't know an angel from me, the Devil incarnate." As his face became illuminated I gasped! He was Ernie. As the panic built in me, Ernie - with a face like a ghoul - turned into the darkness and the next person lit up. "I can use her and abuse her and she doesn't know the difference. I'll have my fun with her, then discard her," he said. It was Brandt, with the face of the devil!

I started to hyperventilate. I tried to run but my legs wouldn't move. I realized that if I didn't get away now these men would destroy me. I had but one hope. Cheng! "Cheng! I need you, come to me," I shouted. I waited to see him at my side, and when he didn't come to me, I was ready to die. Then I heard his voice. "Yes, Val-teen, you called me. I am always here for you when you call." Feelings of calm and relief spread through me. I couldn't yet see Cheng but he was here; I would see him soon; I was safe. The spotlight illuminated the next man. When I saw this face I began to shake. It was Cheng, wearing the most evil menacing face of them all! "See, Valentine, things are seldom as they seem," he said, followed by the most ugly laugh that I'd ever heard. Whereupon the three men put their arms around each other like in a football huddle and joined together in evil laughter.

I screamed.

I awakened from the dream shaking and soaked in perspiration! Just as I'd been after the train dream, only worse. I didn't remember having dozed off.

I laid there for several hours, shuddering and thinking. The train dream had taught me to expect, accept and heed psychic prophetic dreams. This one, too, was a warning. A warning about Ernie and Brandt I could understand. But Cheng!

Well, why not Cheng? Cheng who sometimes seemed too good to be true? I told myself, "Viveka, discrimination, remember

Valentine! A Chinese man comes out of nowhere, gives you no background on him, nothing, his only claim to fame being an article in the National Inquirer, of all places. He invites you to a class at the university from which he's summarily dismissed with nary a word of explanation to anybody, and starts teaching in his home. At first he's all love and kindness and nurturing. But, then what? He becomes mean. Supposedly knows everything but tells nothing. Look, how he tormented poor Mindie tonight. Her entire livelihood's at stake yet he wouldn't give her an inkling of what to do. Hadn't he withheld important answers from me many times too! And why? Because, damn it, he didn't *know* the answers! Were we all just so vulnerable that he could get away with deceiving us? Did he get his power by keeping a roomful of hopefuls dangling from his strings? And lately his stupid talk about me teaching and then that guru nonsense! Well, talk about dumb, I'd been it! Other men may have duped me; that was bad, but only you, Cheng, did it in the name of spirituality; *that* was unconscionable! And unpardonable!"

Fury seeped through me! Well, no more, Cheng, no more! I wanted to go to his home and confront him immediately, but when I got up from the bed I found I was too exhausted to move. I'd sleep now and take care of Cheng in the morning. Then that would be that.

I slept fitfully, however, and by five in the morning I was wide-awake.

CHAPTER TWENTY-ONE: DISCERNMENT

"A seventy year old man complained all the time. Nothing could please him. Suddenly he changed, becoming optimistic and hopeful. He was asked what had made him change so much. He replied, 'Well, all my life I've wanted to be contented but never was. So I've decided to be contented with being discontented."

--Indian parable

"We make ourselves happy and we make ourselves miserable; the effort is the same."

--Carlos Castaneda

At 5:15 AM I was racing the Porsche through Coldport's then deserted local roads at 70 miles an hour. By 5:35 I was at Cheng's door, pounding hard on it with my fist, intermittently leaning unrelentingly on the bell. After seemingly hours, although it was probably more like five minutes, I heard movement inside. I put my ear to the door. There was some rustling, then Cheng's voice near the door. "And, you are?"

"Why must you ask? Aren't you omniscient?" I yelled, continuing to press hard on the doorbell.

The door opened and Cheng stood there in his doorway in a red silk robe with Chinese design. Despite my behavior and that I had obviously awakened him, he spoke to me in the kindest and most loving manner. "Val-teen, good morning! I'm about to make some tea. You will join me?" He looked the epitome of pleasured to see me, his outstretched arm welcoming me in. His graciousness under the circumstances made me feel contrite and ashamed. But only for a split second. I was sick of being taken while being so understanding about everybody's crap. Been there, done that, finished!

As I stomped across Cheng's threshold I replied, "You can skip the tea, I'm not thirsty." Cheng's arm pointed me toward the livingroom and to a soft armchair. "Sit down, please," he invited. Ignoring his offer, I cut right to it.

"Who *are* you?" I demanded to know.

"I'm Cheng."

"Very funny. I mean, who the hell *are* you?" The gruffness in my voice surprised me.

"Who do you think?"

That did it! “THAT IS EXACTLY WHAT I MEAN!” I shouted. “*THAT* IS WHAT YOU *DO*! You claim to be a guru. Then w*here* did you become one and what did you *do* to become one?”

“When did you ever hear me ‘claim to be a guru,’ as you say?”

“Well, I...”

“I never did, Val-teen.”

“Then what gives you the right to teach me?”

“Because I was intended to be your teacher and you came to me. When the pupil is ready the teacher will appear.”

“Parables! But... you don’t even look like a great teacher, nor do you act like one.”

“Good, then I’m doing my job.” Cheng grinned.

“SEE?! There you go again! IF YOU’RE A TEACHER, WHY DON’T YOU TEACH, FOR GOD’S SAKE! One and one are two. Dick and Jane. See Dick run. *That’s* straightforward, that’s not playing head games. Instead…instead of what you do - answering the simplest questions in the most ambiguous terms or not answering in the first place!”

“Why do you think that is so?” Cheng asked.

“Why is it so that somebody doesn’t answer questions? Let me think. Could it be because they don’t really know anything?” My sarcasm and scorn practically dripped onto Cheng’s rug.

Cheng gracefully seated himself cross-legged on a cushion on the floor, then pointed to the cushion beside it. “Please. You must be tired from standing. Sit,” he offered. I instead defiantly plunked myself into an armchair. This placed me in the awkward position of being seated somewhat above Cheng with him looking up at me, his gaze seeming to penetrate my face like a loving laser. As I looked away in discomfort, my eyes glimpsed Cheng’s decor-symbols of peace and joy that had always concurrently elevated and calmed me. I quickly averted my eyes to the ceiling.

“Go on,” Cheng directed softly.

“I had a dream last night. Ernie, Brandt and you were like the devil, each of you laughing sinisterly about me. Its meaning was obvious.”

“So, tell me the obvious.”

After mentally fumbling for words I finally sputtered “Look, put it this way. I once read that a Washington call girl with wealthy high profile clients said this: 'there are no great men. There are just men.'"

"That call girl was wordily-wise but not spiritually -wise. She lacked the understanding that one, whether man or woman, who has realized one's own Self IS great. That there have been men and women throughout time in every culture who have achieved that greatness. The potential for it is inside every person. On this subject, best to listen to Dr. Cheng, not call girl."

"You're telling me that you're one of those Self-Realized people?" Again I looked toward the ceiling.

Cheng said, "Two can talk better by looking, Val-teen."

I forced myself to look at Cheng, my expression, I knew, still fierce.

"I realize people have disappointed you," Cheng said kindly. "Perhaps mostly men. But you must learn to discriminate. Not to lump me with them. That would prevent you from doing what you are here to do, this time."

"And, that is…?"

"For you to know, soon," Cheng answered.

I exploded. "I AM OUT OF PATIENCE! So, FOR YOUR INFORMATION, TEACHER, I ALREADY KNOW WHAT I'M HERE TO DO THIS TIME. I'm here to raise Brenna as well as I can, and to make things good for Willie and in so doing also for those like him. I'm here to go back to work with Ernie, if he'll still have me, and to earn enough money to put food on the table and to pay my rent and utility bills, and if I'm really lucky to perhaps have a bit left over. Because maybe in your exalted state you can live without all that but my children and I can't. THAT'S ALL. DO YOU HEAR ME? And maybe I'm also here to one day find a man whom I can love and respect and who can love and respect me because he has an idea what love and respect *are*. That is what I'm here for and that is enough, thank you!"

Cheng sat silently, looking at me kindly.

"Well, what do you think of *that*?" I challenged him.

"I agree that you are here for all those things except maybe one, and I feel you left out a few things."

"Surely it would be a time-waste for me to ask you what that one thing, and those few things, are," I snickered.

"You got THAT right," Cheng giggled.

"PLEASE! No more!" I pleaded, slapping my forehead with my hand in exasperated.

Gently Cheng took the hand with which I'd hit myself and patted it lovingly as he invited, "Val-teen, will you meditate with me for a short while?" For the first time that morning I let my gaze meet his and rest there. How could he be so unwaveringly kind to somebody who had just acted as I had? It was making me angry that I could not make *him* angry. "Meditate NOW? What will THAT do in all this?" I shot back cantankerously.

"It will clarify your mind so that you can hear my words instead of your fears. Trying to communicate through heavy emotion is like trying to communicate when under the influence of alcohol or drugs. Everything gets distorted. Now hear me clearly, Val-teen. Your dream this time was not prophecy or reality, at least not the part about me. All emotions are energy of one kind or another. Your fear has been predominant lately, thus your dream was a projection of that negative energy."

I set my jaw and sat silently. As I averted my glance away from Cheng's compelling eyes, my eyes once again fell upon the sea gulls. This time I did not look away. Soon I began to have those calm joyful feelings. My jaw unclenched, I slid onto the floor cushion beside Cheng and fell into a deep meditative state.

* * *

"You meditated for an hour," Cheng said. That was hard to believe, since it felt that ten minutes at the most had passed. I looked at the Timex that Cheng had loaned me; it was 7:00 AM.

"Better by far *now* to talk," Cheng said. I tried to conjure up my former anger at Cheng but it just wasn't there. Instead, I felt a great desire to remain silent; to just listen to what Cheng had to say.

Cheng picked up on that. "The man you wish for you can have one day," he told me. "There *are* good men, Val-teen. You just haven't magnetized such a man yet. There hasn't been anything developed in your consciousness to attract one."

"So, you're saying neither Brandt nor Richard will ever be right for me?"

"No, that is not what I am saying. I am saying that at present you can not know whether either will or won't. Often when we change ourselves those we relate with change also…or, everyone moves on. It's one of those magical mysteries of life."

"So if I change but they don't?"

"Then there can't be any real relationship between such a two, even if for some reason they stay together. Such unions are sad unions of people who are a couple without a relationship."

Both of us sat quietly for a few minutes. Finally, Cheng broke the silence.

"Val-teen, the time has come for you to have one-on-one lessons. I offer it; of course you are free to accept or decline. If you decide to accept, you will continue with the class Discourses too, that is, if you wish to continue those also."

"Private lessons in what?"

"Your further inner development, for knowing the Self."

"Where would they be held?"

"Could be here, or at your place."

"I can't afford private lessons."

"Did I ask for money?"

"Why would you do that?"

"It is what I'm intended to do, this time around."

At that moment I had a flashback of something Cheng had said the first time he and I had spoken over the phone. "Your lips, Val-teen...Val-teen, you are really something." Waves of cynicism spread through me again. 'There are no great men, only men.' Right on, call girl!

Almost immediately Cheng responded as though I'd voiced my fears aloud. "I repeat. Your call girl forgot one thing. When one realizes the Self, that one IS great."

I looked at Cheng carefully and asked, "You are telling me you are Self-Realized, aren't you?"

Cheng smiled a smile I knew well, and answered, "You are a very beautiful and feminine woman. Perhaps the men you have known have confused lust for you with love. It is understandable that they make moves, as you say. I will not lie and say I have always been devoid of such thoughts about you myself, but I can promise you that I will never act on them; Michael won't let me."

"Michael?"

"The Archangel Michael. He's my spirit guide. He is always guiding me, as are my gurus."

"He's here now? They're here?"

"Yes, and have been whenever I've taught you and the others." Cheng looked deeply and penetratingly into my eyes. "Valteen. I love you in the highest way. Now, you can believe that and stay with me until I finish what I'm to teach you, thereby entering into the possibility of contentment, or you can walk away right now and stay as you are. Which will it be?"

"Maybe…I could take a break from all the lessons. Maybe…next year…I'd be more ready…we could discuss it…then?"

Cheng's gaze was steady as he answered firmly, "No, Val-teen If you leave now, you won't be given this opportunity again in this lifetime. At least not with me."

Although I found it difficult to speak I had one more important question. "Why do Michael - and your gurus, whoever they are-want you to further my self-discovery now?"

"So that you can know your dharma soon."

"You don't think I do?"

"Not totally."

My answer came quickly like one telling the dentist, 'stick the needle in now and let's get this over with.'

"When do we start the lessons?"

"I thought next week?"

"Fine," I said weakly.

"And by the way, soon you go back to work."

"With Ernie?"

"Of course. Do you see any other bird on the hand, as you say in the West?" Cheng giggled. "Indeed an apt phrase; your Ernie, he *is* a bird alright."

For the next several minutes Cheng and I giggled. Then I asked, "So, working with Ernie IS my work dharma then."

"I didn't say that. You'll decide."

"Why does that non-answer from you not surprise me?" I faced Cheng then. "I'm dreadfully sorry for barging in on you so early this morning and for the terrible things that I said to you. I'm so ashamed. If I hurt you..." My tears flowed copiously as my apologies poured forth.

Cheng made a gesture of dismissal with his hand as he handed me a tissue. "Oh, not to worry. It was expected, not disdained. As I think back, this was nothing compared to what I remember once doing to Michael, and a few times to my living teachers. Tell Ernie you'll be back next week. Then this week get some rest."

"Suppose I'm not strong enough to go back next week?"

"You will be," Cheng said. "Just a bit vulnerable, is all."

"A real answer, from YOU?" I exclaimed.

"Get some rest," Cheng repeated, "You'll need it with that guy."

"You're making work with Ernie sound so appealing I hardly want to make the call," I answered. Then I got a thought that struck me so funny that I began to laugh uncontrollably.

"Yes?" Cheng asked.

"You *know* why I'm laughing. You know everything about me."

"Tell me."

"Alright. Now that I'm going to be your serious student, you know that when I go back to work in New York I'll need to protect my virtue. Since protecting virtue seems to be Michael's dharma, can I possibly borrow him?"

"Michael," answered Cheng gleefully, "is downsizing; he doesn't want to take on such big assignments." Cheng giggled, I contagiously joined him, and then my magnificent teacher and I lost ourselves in laughter until the tears came.

CHAPTER TWENTY-TWO: PRIVATE LESSONS

"It would be wonderful indeed if a group of persons should arrive on earth who were for something and against nothing. This would be the summun bonum of human organization."

--Ernest Holmes

"New things lie in store for the earth, and one of them is us."

--Marianne Williamson in A Woman's Worth

Life moved on with the old and the new, yet the old had assumed such a new quality that the line between the two became increasingly blurred. Whether I ventured out into frost-glistened streets or snuggled at home in a plush comfy robe, life was getting interesting.

My private lessons with Cheng were phenomenal. I approached each one like a kid standing before the Big Tornado, dreading what was ahead and at the same time unable to wait to get on. They were indeed the ultimate roller coaster! The teachings were remarkably vastly multi-faceted; energy (hands-on) healing, uses of herbs, principles and applications of homeopathy and other natural medicines.

Then the lessons became progressively deeper as the concentration shifted to studying and applying the knowledge contained in the ancient scriptures. This entailed going far beyond subject matter. It meant having to face myself again and again through the often painful peeling and peeling away of layers and layers of my ego. At the time that I'd met Cheng I'd believed that I'd already had the most difficult experiences of my life; I'd been wrong! Cheng's teaching of me qualified for that honor, trust me! I frequently thought I'd have a heart attack! At least I came to trust that Cheng wanted one thing from me only, my spiritual development; he would never inappropriately take advantage of our situation. Thank you, Archangel Michael!

I gradually came to realize that Cheng was a far greater being than he'd let on. I saw that he knew everything, or close to it, yet was so humble that he preferred to be thought ordinary. For instance, he rarely made predictions but when he did he was always right. A case in point was his prediction that I'd return to Ernie the following week; I did so. The reason I knew that this was Cheng's accurate prediction rather than some random remark he'd made which I'd then tried to actualize, was this; after Cheng had told me that it would happen I'd in fact strongly resisted it; it happened despite me. Like this...

Friday afternoon, several days after Cheng's prediction, I received a call from Ernie.

"Rememba Steve Rhadman?" he'd asked.

"Who could forget him?" Rhadman was a client I'd brought in last year with a small job which had nonetheless been like manna to me then; Richard and I had used my commission check to pay our mortgage that month. Beyond that, it would take Alzheimer's to forget Rhadman. God forgive me for saying it, he'd been our most egotistical, irritating, control freak client ever. "HE JUS CALLED!" Ernie shrieked. "HE WANTS US FER ANODA JOB, BIG ONE THIS TIME. I'D ER... LIKE YA... TA BE HERE FER IT."

As I caressed my outer ear, comforting it from the shock of Ernie's shouts, my answer came instantly. "No thank you! Rhadman behavior on that small job nearly put me in the hospital. Since I've now actually been in the hospital, this time he'd put me in the graveyard." But I was curious. Why did Ernie, who had no doubt produced shoots in my absence, need me there now?

I asked, "Why ME, for THIS, NOW, Ernie?"

Ernie's voice was sheepish. "Becuz, Rhadman said... the only reason he's usin' us is... you. Be here, please?"

Ernie, practically begging me? That was something. "Ah, so!" I thought, Cheng-like, except Cheng didn't talk that way. Cheng had said I'd feel vulnerable for a while. "Think like they do,"Casse had often advised. Alright, then, I'd be going back with that edge and to a big paycheck. Ernie offered the final convincing argument: "If you'd turn down money now, not only doesn't your elevator reach the top floor, its cables are also broken!"

"Alright," I said, "tell Rhadman I'll call him Monday from the studio and set everything up."

* * *

Monday morning when I walked out of the elevator into the studio, on the wall facing me where it couldn't be missed, was a big, "Welcome Back' sign. Soon everybody came over with greetings. Then on the set, perhaps most touchingly of all, along with the usual Danish and coffee, was fruit juice and herbal tea (supplied, I later learned, by Zarela and Jayson). Ernie kind of milled around the little party trying to look appropriate but giving off vibes of hopefully-this-will-end-soon, then- let's-get-back-to-the-important-stuff.

Once I contacted Rhadman we had a week of planning/production before the actual shoot. I set about doing everything needed, consulting with Ernie only when necessary. His B.A.Q- Being Aggravating Quotient- seemed to have risen. When Casse called to inquire how I was doing my first week back, I told her just that.

"It's not just Ernie," she said. "Desmond, too, is being a royal pain in the ass. Business has been off since last year, they're worried, and it's our fault. Period, end of sentence."

"I'm finding my patience being tested. How do you put up with it?"

"Easier for me than you because even in this business with more pains-in-asses than practically anywhere else, the star pain-in-the-ass is Ernie. He's known for that in the industry, always has been."

"Oh, thank you so much for enlightening me before I hooked up with him."

"Did you need to make money?"

"What's THAT got to do with….?"

"I repeat. Did you NEED to make money?"

"I heard you the first time. Of course, but what's that got to do with…?"

"HAVE you made money?"

"You know I have..."

"The catch is, Ernie's a money-making machine type pain-in-the -ass. Would you have gone with Ernie and made that money had I told you before the extent of his pain-in-the-assness?"

"Casse, that isn't the p..."

"The answer is, 'No!' You would not have. Wouldn't having earned no money made you even more miserable by now than being with Ernie is making you? The answer to THAT is 'yes!' I rest my case."

"May the witness now step down from the stand?"

The surprising thing, and definitely new, was that while Ernie was perhaps more obnoxious than ever, I truly wasn't as affected. Despite Ernie and all the pressures of this job, I seemed to be maintaining an even temperament.

The first day, due to Rhadman's constant presence on the set, we started having problems. First, we began to run very late. Rhadman was on his power trip. His continuous corrections, orders and insistence in controlling every aspect of the shoot were pissing everybody off. They were pros, whereas Rhadman had no technical know-how. The crew knew that he had no right to be directing things except that he'd claimed that right because he was paying for the ad. They had no respect for him. Due to Rhadman's behavior Ernie was becoming increasingly upset with me. He urged me into a corner away from the set and stage-whispered, "Why din't ya "tactfully suggested" Rhadman stay away. Ya could have subtly arranged it!" Ernie's stage whispers were the volume of the loud speaker announcements at Shea Stadium only more discernable.

I put a finger over my lips to "shush" Ernie, then quietly whispered, "You mean hire a hit man? Rhadman doesn't know from subtle."

Then things started to become interesting. I found myself, while participating fully, at the same time standing aside and watching everything, seeing it in a new way. For example, for the first time I was realizing how shoots with models were a jumping event. This began to amuse me. Rhadman would complain about a model's lipstick, so the shooting would stop and Jayson would jump in and fix make-up. Fifteen minutes later Rhadman would complain that the model's dress was wrinkled, I'd ask Dawn to fix it, she'd jump in, steam the dress, then jump out again. It was a regular aerobics class. I was surprised to find myself, with so much at stake, with an almost uncontrollable urge to laugh. A small laugh escaped. Ernie shot me a dirty look. So I squelched it.

When I later described all this to Cheng he reminded me of one of his teachings, when he had explained that times like this would occur. "What is it that's watching?" he'd asked. "Myself?" I'd answered. "Yes, it is your Self, capital S, the witness, observing. Watching life as if it's a play, this so-called witness-consciousness, is the state of the saint in the world. It will happen increasingly. Your amusement at the play was the inner joy bubbling over. That will happen increasingly also. When it started happening to me, I used to go into my room, close the door so nobody would hear or see, then dance and sing. We have to act appropriate, you know. We do not want Val-teen laughing at funerals or at other serious places like photography shoots," Cheng said, with a wink of his twinkling eyes.

At 2:30 Ernie called a break. I hurried to the rest room.

My bodily functions also seemed to be differently unpredictably. "Is this part of enlightenment, or weak kidneys?" I'd wryly asked Cheng during one of our lessons. "It can very well be part of the cleansing process, kriyas, removal of the samscaras," Cheng assured me. "A good rule of thumb is, if one has doubt see a doctor, however in your case, now, one is not needed."

Once we'd regrouped on the set, Ernie casually tossed his bombshell. "V.J, I don't know if ya heard. We're gonna break at five, order suppa in, resume at six and work da night shoot fer as long as it takes to wrap this up."

I was chagrined. The plan had been to wrap it up around five, therefore I'd promised Brenna that I'd be home early to take her to McDonalds! "I can't stay tonight," I told Ernie.

"Why, ya din't take off enough time already?"

I noticed Rhadman was missing. He had probably left for the evening. That, at least, was a blessing. More important at the moment, it was as if Cheng was within me advising me, "Stay calm." Was this how it was for him with Michael or his gurus which he'd alluded to as always being with him? For the first time I believed I was beginning to understand.

"Don't tell me yer sick, AGAIN!" Ernie added.

All eyes were on me as I heard myself answer quietly, "No, I'm not sick. It's that I promised my daughter I'd have dinner with her tonight."

I'd never heard anything so still on a set.

Finally Ernie spoke with a smirk. "I'm afraid yer gonna hafta cancel that important dinna meetin'. Everyone's agreed. Rhadman took a break but he's due back any minute now. Okay, quiet on the set." Thus he dismissed my predicament.

I began to feel a buzz of energy inside of me along with a command, "Don't let this go! You must speak up now." I opened my mouth and it came out. "This is unfair."

I watched Ernie. His face was starting to get red. I glanced at all the others. They were following Ernie's and my exchange, their eyes moving right to left repeatedly like fifteen sets of Ping-Pong balls.

"You knew there'd be nighttime work and location shoots when ya took this job," Ernie said combatively. "A course, if this job don't mean nuttin to ya...." His implication was clear; now that I'd gotten Rhadman hooked, if I didn't want to work on this, fine, just *try* to collect any part of my commission. Otherwise, stay tonight. I had a mental image of a paycheck flying out the window. Momentarily I felt frightened. But overriding that I just knew that it would not be dharmic for me to buckle under.

"Ernie. Could we take a minute to discuss this privately?"

"We're DISCUSSIN' it now; there ain't no secrets hea," Ernie's voice challenged me.

All right, then. As gently as I could, I answered "Yes, we did agree that I'd work nights and locations, and, as you know I have, many times. However, advance notice was part of our arrangement."

"So, I gave advance notice. Was it my fault you was in the can? Look, I got a kid too, so what? Ya gotta orda yer priorities."

"You've also got a wife; right now I envy you that." (I very much felt like adding, "Although I don't envy your wife"; probably thanks to the inner Cheng, that part remained unexpressed.) There were some chuckles from the crew and staff. "Ernie, I'd gladly work tonight regardless but I made a commitment to my daughter. She's missing me lately; I can't do that to her."

"SO, YOU'RE SUGGESTIN BECAUSE OF YOUR KID WE LEAVE THE JOB UNFINISHED?" How Ernie's throat must hurt at the end of each day! Everyone else remained still and carefully attuned.

"Why don't we just tell Rhadman it will take another full day's shooting? We've done that with other clients many times."

"Rhadman ain't other clients. What makes ya' think he'd pay fer that?"

"Maybe because he caused the overtime and he knows it."

"So, we tell him that? You want that we never see or hear from him again?"

"Rhadman?" I answered. "Absolutely; doesn't everybody?" My answers were just coming effortlessly; in a way I was actually enjoying this. So, evidently was the entire crew. Having suffered

Rhadman all day, they broke out in a collective roar.

Ernie was not one to admit defeat. "You'll get us anoda client if Rhadman trows in the towel over this?"

"An easier one? NOT a problem."

Everyone laughed again.

The phone rang. Ernie answered, then, covering the mouthpiece with his hand, said, "It's Rhadman. He says he'll be an hour late."

"Why don't you tell him now?"

"*You* wanted it, *you* tell him," Ernie ordered.

So right there in front of everyone I took the phone and did so, while the entire crew plus Ernie leaned in unison into the phone along with me. When I got off, Ernie shouted, "SO??"

"So, he said yes, he'd rather not work nights anyway."

"Get outta here!" Ernie muttered. "That guy neva agrees to anything somebody else suggests first. What are ya, a witch or somethin'?"

"More likely something."

"Make da' announcement," Ernie ordered.

"Anyone who prefers to work tomorrow rather than tonight, raise your hand," I told them. Ernie interjected, "I didn't tell you to ask that..." Even as he spoke all hands went up. "Good" I answered, "then see you all here at eight AM."

Ernie, himself an honorary member of the Control Freaks Society, would have the last word. "I dint hire ya ta work bankers hours, ya'know" he said snidely. By then I was out of speech, but Jayson wasn't. He jumped in. "Banker's hours, Ernie? Do you *know* how many hours V.J puts in for this studio!"

Ernie smirked at me. "Don't worry. You're beautiful when you're overworked."

"Aha." Jayson responded, "so *that's* why she's always beautiful!"

Ernie bristled, then stormed off the set. A few minutes after that I heard him get into the elevator. He had left for the night.

I looked at Jayson, the crew, everybody and humbly said, "Thanks, guys." Jayson winked, "Any time, princess. You were fabulous!"

The women's reactions were especially very positive.

"Thanks, V.J, I got two kids myself."

"THAT A WAY, V.J."

"Go, Girl!"

I felt a new sense of power. I had to call Casse and tell her about it before leaving.

To my chagrin Casse was anything but congratulatory.

"That was the MOST unprofessional thing I've EVER heard," she admonished me. "Bringing Brenna into your work situation was a cheap shot. We are working here in a man's world, Val. At our jobs we do not wave our children around like an American flag! A man wouldn't do that"

"But we're *not* men, Casse. If we don't bring up the children and our special issues, who will? So, if women haven't done that yet maybe it's time we did."

"You've got to play by the rules, Val!" At that moment I wondered which of us was liberated.

Yet once I was on the train, mulling over Casse's words, I began to second-guess myself. What had I just done? Suppose it cost me my work with Ernie. Since word traveled fast in this industry, maybe it would cost me my career in it altogether?

I was concerned enough to rush into the bedroom the moment I got in my door and to call Cheng.

"How do YOU feel about it?" Cheng asked.

"Apprehensive."

"Why?"

"Because Casse said with this type behavior I'll jeopardize myself in the industry."

"How did you feel about your behavior before she said that?"

"That it was right."

"How did you know that?"

"It's hard to explain."

"Explain anyway."

I thought for a moment. "Well... like the words were on a buzz in my body and pushing to be expressed, like it would take all of my control not to say them, yet not so because I was overly emotional or out of control in any way. It was like I had to do what felt right and that felt right. I felt it in my heart and my gut."

"Exactly! EXCELLENT!" I could almost feel Cheng jumping up and down, pleased with me. "Those feelings you had were your

Self showing you your dharmic action in that situation and giving you the courage to act upon it! Now, let us look at this from an External Contemplative perspective. Ernie pulled a night shoot on everybody without notice. Surely there were others there who found that difficult. You had promised Brenna time together and felt it would be wrong to disappoint her. Ernie tried to walk all over you but you would not let him, meanwhile offering him and the crew a viable alternative. So, on both levels it feels right. Therefore, why have you still doubt?"

"I think because Casse disagrees. She's been in the business longer than I so she's more of an expert."

"That may be, Val-teen," Cheng said, "But she's only an expert on her own opinion. Is she Self-Realized? The less Self-Realized people are the more they offer their opinions like the gospel. Val-teen, I applaud you. Don't ever sell your soul for a hot dog"

Hearing those words, I thought, "I love Casse but Cheng's more spiritually evolved than she is. Hell, just about everybody is." I told Cheng, "Thank you...thank you *so* much!"

As Cheng's words, "Never sell your soul for a hot dog," reverberated in my head, I thought, "Hot dog! My God. Brenna! McDonalds!" I took off my suit and tossed it onto the bedroom chair, threw on a pair of jeans and a tee shirt, rushed down the stairs and into the livingroom.

Brenna was sitting watching Television. "Mommy!" she exclaimed, looking up at me.

"Ready for your Big Mac, honey?" I called. My daughter's huge smile as she ran into my outstretched arms was my final seal of approval for my actions at work that day.

CHAPTER TWENTY-THREE: DISCOURSE SEVEN- Non-Doership And Dharma

"Oh, Arjuna, if you think in terms of reality, you are not the slayer nor can there be a slain... Though the body may die, the Self does not. After casting away worn out bodies, the embodied Self takes on other new ones."

--Jnaneshwar's Gita

"Easy karma is what your culture will one day call an 'oxymoron.' Karma is never easy. We came here to know the Self, not for a perpetual day at the beach. Accept your karma with a light cheerful attitude."

-Dr. Cheng Ho

At 7:30 PM promptly Cheng began this evening's lesson:

"In this Discourse I shall go into detail about a text I've previously made slight reference to, the Bhagavad Gita. This is one of the most famous ancient Indian texts. In it is contained every answer to life and to of all creation. In that lies the greatness of the Gita. You should all read it.

Basically the Bhagavad Gita teachings take place on the battlefield of Kurukshetra. This is obviously a metaphor. Life is at risk here, just as all of us risk slow death out of ignorance. Two warring clans, the Kauravas and the Pandavas of which Arjuna is the ace warrior, face each other. Krishna has agreed to be Arjuna's charioteer, guide and advisor, although he himself will not engage in the actual fighting.

"And so Arjuna is, at least initially, resolved to fight the Kuauavas. But, as he surveys the enemy and sees within it members of his own clan, his resolve crumbles. The thought of fighting his own kin, let alone possibly killing them, repulses him. He tells Krishna, who symbolizes God, that he wants to renounce this duty. Haven't we all been in such a position many times!

So, consider the scene: The battle gongs are about to sound. The Kauravas, greatly outnumbered by the Pandavas, are relying on their hero Arjuna's well-known prowess to win the battle. Yet Arjuna, who can't face the mental anguish of what's ahead of him, is begging to be absolved of his responsibility. Although Krishna gently reprimands Arjuna, cajoles him and exhorts him to action, Arjuna remains adamant. So, Krishna explains to him the supreme philosophy of life and work. These gems of common sense, pure inspiration and sound immutable principles are the heart of the Bhagavad Gita."

"Why does Krishna want Arjuna to fight?" Serge blurted out.

"Serge," Cheng gently admonished, "Next time please raise your hand. However, this time I shall answer regardless. Krishna wants Arjuna to fight because Arjuna is a soldier. His dharma, or right action, is to fight. Krishna goes on to explain to Arjuna that each of us is a form through which God gives to others via our dharma. That in this world we must act unselfishly out of service, in a non-attached way, offering whatever we do to God. That being regular in the performance of our duties ensures our salvation. He explains to Arjuna that we want to see all our good actions as coming from God, flowing through us. That we must understand, as Krishna had to, "I am not the doer."

Andrew, after being acknowledged, said, "I don't understand not being the doer." The rest of us nodded in agreement.

"Not being the doer means it isn't good for us to allow ourselves to think, '*I* will do it,'" Cheng explained, "Rather, we want to just concentrate on doing our appropriate thing at the appropriate time without being attached to any particular results. Therefore, non-doership is an *inner* shift of awareness. It is a private matter between us and God. We still act dharmically. We give everything we have. It is even all right to think, 'I act,' but not to think 'I act this *well*,' or 'I act this *badly*.' In other words, we need to be sattavik workers, remember? Act while not being the owner of the results, not taking the credit or blame, not putting value judgements on our acts, as in, 'this is great,' or 'this is terrible.'"

Nancy, once acknowledged, asked, "I still don't understand. It sounds like you're saying we should act yet act like we're not acting?"

"Non-doership is actually non-identification with the body and with its actions," Cheng explained. "Try this homework: When you are walking, watch yourself. Did you teach your body to walk when a toddler? Do little animals teach themselves to walk? No, humans and animals usually just get up when nature intends. Therefore, observe yourself walking and realize you are walking without 'you' doing it. Indeed *you* are not doing it; your *body* is. We identify that we *are* our body but that is just a convenient form of reference. We need to break that identification. Through meditation, and all the tools I'm teaching you in these Discourses, you can."

Mindie, after being acknowledged asked, "So Krishna advised Arjuna to go out and kill people!? And you're telling us that's right action?!"

"Not just to kill people, Mindie, but to go fight. The motivation behind an action is key. A surgeon and a murderer might both use a knife but hopefully the surgeon's motivation is to save a life whereas the murderer's motivation is to take one away. The Pandavas were an evil vicious army, causing great havoc. They had to be stopped. Arjuna, a soldier, was there; it was his dharma, his destiny to be there, to fight the evil army. Krishna goes on to explain to Arjuna that in doing this fighting he should not identify with the enemies' bodies or with his own. We have had so many lifetimes, he assures Arjuna, and ahead we have eternity. "Nobody is killed, nobody dies," he tells him. He makes it clear, however, that understanding the eternity of all life certainly does not make it right to just go around killing people!

"Sometimes in our own lives" Cheng continued, "we are put in situations where it becomes obvious that somebody is doing something wrong, that we were placed there to intervene. So, once we correctly discern that we should intervene, we just do it, nothing personal intended. We might consider every wrong-doing a minus; a minus is darkness. Any right action is a plus; a plus is light. We need not hate a minus in order to oppose it, in fact, hating brings us pain. Wanting rightness non-judgmentally, which is the attitude that God wants Arjuna to have, is different than hating evil. We want to help bring in the light rather than hate the darkness."

Walter got acknowledged. "Why didn't Arjuna know his dharma?" he asked.

"For the same reasons that most of us get confused," Cheng answered. "However, Arjuna was an astute student as I hope you each are. Although he did not always know what to do, he was intensely open to learning. He pleaded to God to teach him. Then he *listened* to God, as we must. Before each of us came to this earth plane we made an agreement about what we'd come here to do, however we don't necessarily remember that when we get here. So Arjuna asked God what he should do, and God told him about the immortal Self, and said, 'Go out and fight! Get on the chariot and concentrate on fighting. Don't be attached. Don't get intoxicated or repelled by it.' If we know we are the immortal Self, we are able to perform right actions without attachment."

I raised my hand and once acknowledged, asked, "How does this non-doership feel?"

"Good question," Cheng said. "Ever have this happen? You were doing something in life yet you felt like you were not doing it, like you were moving and talking or otherwise acting effortlessly, as if cresting on a wave. It was just all happening perfectly, seemingly without your effort, without either forcing it or holding it back?"

I nodded, "Yes, I have felt that, not - often- but I have. How do we get more into that state?"

Cheng answered, "Lord Krishna gives four ways:

"One. Defer all actions to God.

"Two. Follow God's instructions.

"Three. Be non-attached to the results. God's delay is not necessarily God's denial. All will come in its own time if it's right.

"Four. Act without the fever but give yourself no-holds-barred to whatever you do. Then the astonishment of non-doership will ensue.

"So," Cheng added, "our dharma is our platform, the path through the world by which we rise to our utmost. Dharma is literally the law of correct action and behavior, the foundation and support of your life. It is in clusters. So, it means righteous action, our ethical behavior at each moment, our path through the world, and our highest state of knowing the highest truth."

"But," Andrew said, "Arjuna didn't like his dharma."

"True, like many of us at any given time," Cheng answered. "We are given tasks and experiences, we are drawn to some things which are natural to us, there *is* a path that's right for us. Yet at times we have all thought we should be doing something else. Anything else. But, not so fast. Just remember, that it is through God that we turn karma into dharma because dharma is God expressing the cosmic love through us. Your dharma is whatever God has given you to do in this moment. It will lead you to your great destiny. And, it's always changing so we have to stay tuned in. It requires great discrimination and appropriateness and self-respect to follow one's dharma."

"Now, Arjuna was sort of going through an identity crisis," Cheng added.

"I can empathize," Serge moaned. "My question is two- fold. Where does free will enter here, and how can we know when we're doing our dharma? Is there hope for me in all this?"

"Fantastic question!" Cheng actually jumped a few inches off the floor to show his enthusiasm. "And if you want to see me jump even higher from joy, Serge, please, from now on first raise your hand and be acknowledged. If you will do that, then there is great hope for you."

Laughter filled the room. Cheng, amused-stern, glared at each of us as he asked, "The rest of you act perfectly?" All laughter ceased. This man had *patience*. I would have punched Serge weeks ago! Cheng continued, "Yes, we have free will. Certainly we don't *have* to do our dharma. We *can* create something else. However, when we choose to perform our dharmic responsibilities even when they are difficult, contentment results. Essentially, then, doing our dharma makes us feel good. So, you see Serge, Arjuna, like yourself, was having an identity crisis. At that moment Arjuna didn't like his life. He wanted somebody else's. We all feel that way at difficult times. Remember, the highest dharma is to ask ourselves, 'Is this good for everybody?' That is the dharma which transcends all others, when we stay focused on God. So, don't necessarily tear down your thatched cottage to live in a mansion just because your friend does. That way you could find yourself without shelter."

"And so," Cheng continued, "I would like you to practice watching not only your bodies but also observing your minds. We can do this by watching all the thoughts that come and go without getting into or owning any one of them. We flow on the crest of that wave. We want to do similar with the emotions. Observe them without being the one who feels them. Then an interesting thing happens. The mind slows down. If we do that sufficiently, the mind will actually stop. When the mind stops we experience the bliss of the Self. The definition of bliss is our inner love fully realized. In this way, we enter paradise."

I raised my hand, was acknowledged and spoke. "If we do that will we then become spontaneous, in the flow?"

"If you do that some very interesting things will occur," Cheng responded. "For instance, we may be conversing with somebody and suddenly feel as if we're listening to a taped conversation coming from us; something on that order. When that begins happening it might scare us, like in 'God! I'm hearing myself speak but I don't know what I'm going to say next! I'm out of control?' Exactly! That's the whole idea, and the ideal. We've believed that in order for everything to turn out right, we need to control. Is that true?"

Cheng looked around. When nobody responded, he went on, "We've controlled for too long and look where it got us. When we stop controlling and things work out even better, what a relief! It is how the great beings, the Self-Realized live. It is what I am teaching you to achieve."

"Our personal life is a karmic movie," Cheng continued. "We can, in fact we must, dynamically participate. We are the *active* witness."

"So, like Arjuna, we want to face life as a warrior. It is not our true nature to be weak, timid, and passive. When an obstacle appears, normally we retreat, cower, whimper or gripe. But our lives are *designed* to have challenges. There is no other way that we can learn our true nature. If we go through our days meekly, hoping that nothing will go wrong, that everyone will be agreeable, that we won't make a mistake, then we will become extremely dissatisfied with ourselves and with our lives. If we live that way we will, because of the nature of the mind, think that our dissatisfactions and frustrations are due to our environment. In truth they emanated from our fearful cowering attitude. Inner strength is an integral part of our nature wanting to be expressed. If we actually face a 'terrible thing' courageously, we discover the strength inherent within us. Then, having experienced our true nature, we can face the rest of our lives with courage and wisdom. This self-awareness brings enormous happiness. Put a miserable person in paradise and s/he will probably feel uncomfortable there. But a person who discovers his/her own heroic nature will be in paradise wherever s/he is.

"So, how do we get there? First, we accept our karma with a light cheerful attitude. Laugh in the face of difficult circumstances. Fake that if you have to; at first, guaranteed, you *will* have to! Laments of 'Oh, poor me,' 'Oh, this is so terrible,' give energy to and prolong the situation. Remember, we are each actors playing our different roles."

Trenna raised her hand, was acknowledged and asked, "So, some of us have easy karma and some don't, and we should just accept that?"

"Easy karma is what your culture will one day term an 'oxymoron'. The two terms are contradictory. Karma is never easy. We came here to know the Self, not for a perpetual day at the beach. This life is difficult for everyone. It may not seem so, but appearances are deceiving. We don't *really* know what it's like for anyone else. We should take the attitude, 'This is my karma, let's see what I can do with it.' Then step into your life, remember? At that point change may be possible."

Felicia got acknowledged. "Are you saying" she asked, dubiously, "that we should all wish to have difficult lives because that will make us happy?"

"I am saying," Cheng responded firmly, "that the easy life doesn't build much except in the material sense. I am saying, don't feel you're unlucky if life has handed you many difficult challenges. Few people had the courage to choose such a life before coming into it. Few have the grace to be able to wipe out so much past karma with one big blow."

Serge raised his hand. Cheng, in mock-shock, exclaimed, "Serge, just now you have given us proof that indeed *anything is* possible! Your question, please!" Serge grinned, then grew serious "It's just that…Arjuna's work makes mine seem…so…useless."

"Why, Serge?"

"An engineer's work's unimportant compared with Arjuna's, fighting to save the lives of many good people."

"You are mistaken." Cheng told him. " If we are searching for something 'important' to do we are just kidding ourselves. The meaning of life lies in the inner hero, the inner enthusiasm for the challenges of life. With this right understanding, whatever we do, even the most mundane task, is meaningfully important. Nobody has to be appointed to a position in order to help others. But people don't understand that. So, especially as we approach the year 2000 and beyond we will see many manifestations of that misconception. Computer programmers will want to leave their professions to become massage therapists. Aeronautic engineers will want to become acupuncturists. *The*y want. Did they first contemplate what *God* wants for them? Ask them why they want to just toss all their talent and expertise away and they'll moan, 'I want to do work that will help people. In this career I am not helping people.' Who, then, will be left to be computer programmers and aeronautic engineers? If everyone were always the rake who would be the leaves? Every profession is a helping profession when one's work is done with love. Leaving others with a good feeling is the most we can do on this earth."

Cheng concluded, "We are all in this play, this maya, together. The ultimate goal is not to achieve good karma but to become free from karma, to achieve oneness with God. Remember, do your homework, specifically, practice watching your body, your emotions and your mind."

"So ends tonight's Discourse, Dear Ones. Blessings!"

CHAPTER TWENTY-FOUR: REVELATIONS

"The eyes of the blind shall be opened and the ears of the deaf shall be unstopped. Then the lame shall leap like a deer and the tongue of the dumb, sing."

--Isaiah

"Only when one is ready to peer into the darkness will they be given the gift of light."

--Unknown

"Give them free rein of the house. Let them have a ball. What's a home for but people?" So Glady said before leaving for Atlantic City with her Seniors' Club. So with gratitude we did hold Brenna's birthday party at Glady's house, as well as a birthday dinner there the next night with just Brenna, Richard and myself.

"Why can't we have my party at McDonald's?" Brenna had pleaded, but simple economics prevailed; I could be more thrifty at home. I told Brenna, "Next year McDonald's... but look, McDonald's doesn't have a big yard to run around in and a fish pond to look at your faces in." The birthday party was successful, fishpond reflections and all.

As was our private birthday dinner. The menu, fashioned and mostly prepared by me with some take-out from Richard, was fresh fruit, salad, french-fries, pizza, chocolate ice cream and left over birthday cake. The first two items were my attempt to build healthful eating choices with Brenna. The rest was my bribe to her for eating the first two.

It was a good night. Brenna was definitely happy and Richard appeared so too. I'd seen changes in him in that direction. Brenna did issue one complaint.

"Why do you work? I want you to stay home, Mommy."

"I work so you can eat."

"I'm not hungry."

It felt nice being a quasi-family on our child's birthday, even though I was well aware that it *was* quasi, that one person was missing. I missed Willie. My yearning for him was a constant emotional tugging in my heart. Mitigated somewhat lately by reports from the school that he was doing well, which Richard and I had also surmised when we'd visited him together two weeks earlier. As usual he had good caring people around him. Cheng would say "his fortunate karma." But who knew what Willie felt, his needs at any given moment which he was unable to express, whether or not he was lonely for us? Who knew what he thought of us for sending him away, and of himself for having to go away? I lived with that ache. Did people who didn't have to appreciate their good fortune? Had I, before it had happened to me? The obvious answer to that question made me realize that failure to appreciate our good is perhaps one of the greatest tragedies of life. Anyway, knowing about karma and that maybe all of us were "gaining karmic points" for our difficult circumstances, helped, as did "stepping into my life" as a trouble-shooter.

We put candles in Brenna's leftover cake.

"Go ahead, Muffin," Richard repeated, "Make your wish and blow out the candles." "I wish," Brenna said fervently, her eyes closed, her face radiant, "My mommy and daddy would be married again." "We ARE, Brenna, we just aren't living together," Richard answered. "I mean the kind of marriage where you sleep in the same bed," Brenna clarified.

There was an awkward pause, after which I said, "But Brenna, your daddy and I would have to want that or it wouldn't be good for him and me. You'd want it to be good for daddy and me, wouldn't you?" "No," Brenna answered with childhood candor. "I just want it."

Once Brenna had gone to bed, Richard asked me, "Sit with me in the den for a while?"

One lamp burned and the TV murmured quietly in the corner.

"I don't remember you playing the TV so softly," I offered. "A big change in Richard Jordan?"

"No. Mother tells me I still play it too loud. I just lowered it now so we could talk."

"About what?"

Richard walked over to sit beside me on the sofa. "I've been thinking about us. Val?"

"Yes?"

"I'd like us…to get back together. I love you, Val."

"I know that. This isn't about love, Richard. Nine days out of ten we weren't happy together. When you weren't being unreasonable when we were so-called together, you were somewhere else entirely. I tried. Maybe not enough or correctly, but I tried. I was the loneliest married woman possible. I met another man, became involved, told you, you were furious and crushed and you had a right to be."

"I don't blame you. That's over."

"What do you mean, you don't blame me, that's over? I violated your trust, broke our marriage vows before you, God, and myself yet you don't blame me, Richard?! How could you not? For God's sake, get in touch with your feelings!!"

"I am now more than ever. Then I wasn't. I was a zombie."

"Still, lonely or not, I have to take responsibility for my actions then."

"Well, that's all resolved in my mind. It wouldn't matter to me now."

"It matters to me. I can't be with you, or anybody else, until it's all resolved in my mind."

"You still... see him?"

"No, not for quite a while. But he's still in my head."

"I see. Well, you heard Brenna. There's her to consider, too."

"I know. I am."

Richard put his arm around me. "Stay tonight?" I shrugged him off.

"Why the hell not?" Richard asked. "I knew you before you were a virgin."

It was tempting. Sex had always been good between Richard and me, and it had been a long time since I'd been with anyone. I was growing tired of going to sleep alone every night and waking up that way. So, as Richard had just asked, why not?! But suddenly it was like Cheng's voice inside of me admonishing, "No, Valentine!" I was astounded! Was this the kind of thing Cheng had meant that he had with Michael? Part let-down, part relieved, I told Richard, "My lower self wants to, but my Higher Self won't let me."

"Well, get that last one out of here!" Richard offered.

Then remembering it was Richard to whom I was talking, I began, "I'm sorry. What I meant was..."

"You don't have to explain. I understand."

"You do??!!"

"Yes, Valentine, I do understand you lately, and that's what worries me. Maybe that means we belong together now?"

"Sort of a melding of mantra and mezusah?" I heard myself joke.

"Hey, that's pretty good!" Richard exclaimed admiringly, then laughed. "Even though I've been no more dedicated a Jew than I've been a Hindu. "Come on," he said, "I'll drive you home."

When we stood at my front door, Richard again looked at me expectantly, whereupon I gave him an explicit "no" look. "Don't worry," he acquiesced with a light kiss on my cheek, "I realize you don't do anything on the first date. Well, sleep well."

"You too, Rick."

With a semblance of a wave Richard turned and walked away. I stepped inside my apartment, quickly shut the door after me and locked it. Then I walked to the livingroom and looked out. I saw Richard walk slowly toward his car, then turn and look at my apartment door. Two lone figures, one looking in, the other looking out. After awhile he got into his car and drove away.

***

"Max," I said, "Your work intrigues me, really."

It was the following morning. "Delving into minds," I went on, "Finding what makes people tick, fixing them up."

"I don't fix anybody up," Max corrected gently. "Just try to help them fix themselves."

"How do you combine what you were taught in medical school with what Cheng teaches?"

Max smiled, trying to steady his coffee cup after spilling a few drops on the seat. "You should be a therapist yourself. You ask such astute questions."

I tapped a finger on his cup. "*You* could fix *yourself* by going lighter on *this,*" I admonished. "Keep this up and Juan Valdez is going to name his donkey after you!"

"Why do you have to be so right about me?" Max asked, laughing. "I *should* clean up my food act. You're fantastic. It would be so good with somebody like you at my side. Valentine, you have, as Henry James wrote in Portrait of a Lady, 'a general air of being someone in particular.' A creature unlike any other. And you amuse too. Little wonder you are, and always will be, beset by admirers."

Ah oh! I'd make light of it. "Well, at the moment *I AM* at your side so if you're serious about your food act, let's start." I took the styrofoam cup out of Max's hand and put it under the seat, laughing. "We'll dump it in a garbage can when we leave the train. Let the can have a caffeine fit!"

Just then Max's thigh brushed mine. "Max?" I asked myself, "HOW long will you stay in Naive-City!?" Why hadn't I seen this coming?

When Casse and I had been in college together she had told me, "Attracting men (only I think then she called them 'boys') comes so easily to you. You're like honey to bees. I, to the contrary, have to hold on with both hands. Tell me, is that FAIR?"

Then I hadn't known what to answer. Today I would have said, "Maybe in this lifetime I am honey and you're mustard. So what? Don't pray to be surrounded by bees. The more there are the greater your chances of getting stung!" Why, I wondered, would any woman want many men attracted to her? All she should hope and pray for is that one man whom she could love and trust, one worthy of her love and trust and capable of returning it. In the man department I was beginning to feel like the poor little rich girl!

Which brought me back to Max. Here was a wonderful person in a solid profession, a man I respected and could share spirituality with. He was quite well adjusted, seemed to adore me, and I couldn't have loved him more - as a friend. He would have been perfect for me except for the small factor that, for me at least, there was no sexual chemistry. As Cheng had inferred, if we all were attracted only to those partners who were good and right for us, life would be much easier. But life didn't work that way.

I felt the thigh thing again from Max. I moved my leg away, toward the window.

"Tell me, Max," I asked, "About East meets couch, but on second thought let's leave couches out of this."

Max, never one to press or at least not until today, again sounded professorial as he answered, "It's good you bring this up because it's a subject I've been grappling with lately. Before meeting Cheng I practiced Vipassana, insight meditation. Insight drifts from one awareness to the next to the next without attaching to any. It sort of resembles free association in psychoanalysis, so it was natural for me."

"What do your patients think of your two worlds?"

"They don't know." Then, seeing my surprise, Max added,

"Essentially I've been hiding in the Hindu closet, wanting to emerge, yet hesitant."

"Why????"

"Professional survival. In the seventies I told a colleague from Harvard that I meditated with a mantra. His answer was that he saw no difference between my mantra repetition and the behavior of some of his obsessive patients."

"But, this is the eighties... times have changed....."

"Somewhat, but I'm not sure sufficiently. The American Psychiatric Association, the APA, takes a negative view of meditative techniques in therapy. Recently I heard a psychiatrist here in New York, an APA spokesperson, say that perhaps meditation quiets people down but so does sitting in front of a Knicks game on TV and shouting one's lungs out. They just don't understand meditation. If I should appear to them irrational or irrelevant, I'm taking a big risk with my career."

"Max, it's such a shame that you can't help your patients with meditation!"

"To the contrary, I could not help *but* to do so. For one thing, being a meditator has helped me to understand my patients' silences. I can often see more than their words can convey, because sometimes feelings are too profound for words to suffice. I have a framed poster on my office wall: 'If you don't understand my silence, you won't understand my words.' It's my creed. I can just be with a patient now versus having to do something. Meditation has allowed me to suspend judgement of them, as of myself."

"How else has meditation helped you treat patients?"

"Some therapists feel spirituality and Western psychology have different goals and should remain separate. I disagree even when I don't verbalize it. Both schools agree that suffering is a part of our existence. Freud, though, believed that with extensive and successful therapy human suffering could be reduced to 'ordinary misery.'"

"Ordinary misery?! That's all Freud aspired to?! But, that's terribly limited!"

"Precisely. Western psychology to me is like the old medical model. On one hand there is a serious illness, on the other hand the ordinary state of health, which is if you're not having a coronary at the moment or terminal with cancer but are filled with aches and pains, that's as good it gets. Eastern philosophy adds a third possibility, wellness. In psychological terms, living in happiness and joy. That is not something my profession has been able to conceive of to any great extent."

"Go on," I encouraged, fascinated.

"Therapy comes to a point when something is exposed," Max answered, "Some crack in the armor. Realizations. Some inability to love, something empty or hollow inside, like narcissism."

"You mean self-involved, obnoxious people?"

"Narcissists are generally people who feel empty, hollow or unauthentic. Meditation gives one a way of working with such people, because meditation fills the empty places in each of us."

"For everybody, regardless of the seriousness of their psychological problems?"

"Another important albeit complicated question," Max said. "Psychotic people would, I believe, have to meditate with very close supervision, if at all; with a tenuous hold on reality to start with meditation could prove too fragmenting. Personally, I'd be interested in doing a study to discover if meditation could help sociopaths change."

"What's a sociopath?" I quickly added, "I'm sorry that I'm so uninformed."

"Apology unwarranted," Max assured me. "I don't know much about your modeling business either. Sociopaths are usually very smooth seductive people. Typically they go in and out of people's lives like a hurricane, leaving chaos and destruction behind them as they move on to the next victim with hardly a backward look. Sometimes, later, they return."

I felt a chill start within me. "Go on," I said.

"Well, they usually attract people to them because they dazzle. They are charming and compelling personalities with promises of drama and excitement."

"What's wrong with bringing some drama and excitement to life?" I realized I was being somewhat defensive.

"Per se, not a thing, in fact, in itself it can be nice. Not every exciting person is a sociopath. You certainly aren't one yet you're exciting. However with a sociopath one pays a high price for such excitement. Sociopaths are also extremely manipulative. When they speak they appear to be baring their souls; in fact they are chronic liars and users. They are very good about reading other people, their insecurities and desires, so while their words seem dripping with truth often that is far from the fact."

Although my inner chills were spreading, I had to ask more.

"How can a person tell when somebody's a sociopath?"

"Not easily," Max said, "Because they're so good, sometimes even experienced therapists are fooled. But if you get close enough to one sooner or later you will experience outrageous behavior. Sociopaths, depending on the degree of their affliction, lack the normal emotional abilities which most of us have, enabling us to feel what we do feel in relationships. They simply don't hold themselves accountable in the way that others do. There's an emptiness within them which permits unethical behavior that would be unthinkable for us. Sooner or later one who relates with a sociopathic personality will note behavior which contradicts how that person has professed to be. Part of their manipulation is often to keep the other person off-guard by implying that what that person has perceived about them is a product of the other person's imagination or hang-ups. They create suffering in the life of anyone who trusts them."

My body felt stiff as I dared to ask, "Are sociopaths ever in important positions?"

"Frequently. They are often found in politics, they are in medicine, business, the entertainment industry, you name it. Professionally and personally such people are users. Since they have the charisma to charm and the intelligence to dazzle, yet lack the ethics, morality and caring not to hurt people, they can step on heads and toes and climb the career ladders most freely. In love relationships they can be extremely good artists of seduction."

"So, they don't feel?" I shivered!

"They don't feel guilt but they do feel shame. You see, their entire lives are built upon pretense, so it follows that their biggest fear is being exposed. When caught in their acts of enormous lies or manipulation they become like hunted animals. They move away fast. In fact, they move fast in everything."

I gulped and steeled myself before asking my next question. "What are the women like who end up in relationship with these men? Sick, too?"

"Not necessarily," Max answered. "Unfortunately, a person who is a giver often ends up with a partner who is a predatory taker. She should take responsibility for her situation, however."

I was remembering one of Brandt's first observations of me. "You're so giving." I had felt that was his unadulterated appreciation. Had it, rather, been his cold appraisal?

Max continued, "Think of these people as homes gorgeous on

the outside but inside minus furniture. They've learned well to mimic human emotions, but actually they are empty shells."

I became very quiet. Finally Max asked, "Any special reason for your interest in the subject?"

"Oh," I stammered, "Just that I have a friend... who seems... like she's involved with such a man. What would you advise her to do about him?" I really said that.

"A traditional therapist would say that there is only one thing to do with such a person. Run as far away as possible as fast as possible and never look back. That would surely be a no-risk way to deal with such a man. Yet you and I know, V.J, that everybody has a Higher Self that is every bit as perfect, as good, as ethical and desiring of doing right as the next person. If sociopaths could be motivated to try some of the Eastern methods, who knows what they might uncover? If their conscience and natural sense for ethics could be uncovered intact, think what this would do in all areas of life. Greater ethics in politics, in research, in medicine, in relationships. It could be awesome."

I had to ask one further question. "Are sociopaths womanizers?"

Max smiled. "Not any more that diabetics are asthmatics," he explained. "The two are separate conditions although one person *can* have both. A womanizer's background often includes a very powerful, controlling mother. As an adult, then, his womanizing is a ferocious campaign showing that he, the weak small boy, is now the powerful man -in- control with women now depending upon *him.* Women are soothing, calming distractions when he feels most anxious. The warm bodies help him to escape his own feelings, to go to where all is beautiful and safe. He can benefit by meditation along with a Twelve Step Program, as can any addict."

I remembered that Brandt had gone to California to, 'Get away from my mothaa.'

"I hope you'll get to do that research," I said in a small voice.

I'd asked the Universe to clarify things for me about Brandt. Had God just answered? If so, could Brandt change? The answers Max had provided had raised further questions, obviously.

Max's next words interrupted my silent musings. "Let me offer one last thing, Valentine. If we allow ourselves to love somebody and possibly experience the wonder that love can bring, we have to take a risk of possible loss and pain. There's no other way to love. Never regret having taken that risk. For as Mahatma Gandhi so succinctly put it, 'A coward is incapable of exhibiting love. That is the prerogative of the brave.' A man who has your love, V.J, is the most fortunate of men.'" Max then gave me a poignant look and added, "I just wish it could have been me."

What was I supposed to do with that? The dharmic thing would be to set Max straight now, kindly yet directly. This wasn't easy. I prayed, took a deep breath and then spoke. "Max, I wish that man could be you, too. Because you're one of the most intelligent, honest and caring men I've ever met. The unfortunate part is that for me the chemistry isn't there. It's no lack in you. It just isn't."

"Exactly the same is true for me, about you," Max answered.

"I'm sorry. I don't understand."

"I too respect you and love you for all the reasons that you just said you do me. I too, then, wish the sexual chemistry with you were there. But it's absent for me also."

"But, how could that be!" I exclaimed.

"Are you so presumptuous to assume that every male in the world wants to get into bed with you?" Max answered with uncharacteristic irritation.

"Well, no…of course not, but….you're giving me mixed messages. You've been coming on to me since we met. Then here tonight you played kneesees with me. Now you're telling me you're not attracted to me?"

"I haven't been coming on to you, I've been admiring you, Valentine. I'm truly sorry if I did anything to make it seem otherwise. As for the rubbing of knees, I didn't deliberately do that – the Long Island train jostles a lot. About my saying I wish it could have been me, well, I do. But the chemistry isn't there, never will be, and wishing won't make it so."

I felt totally embarrassed and more than slightly perplexed. I'd seen Max look at me with such love. He'd asked me out. How could I have misinterpreted? Meanwhile, at this moment he was looking at me with an expression that I'd never seen on his face before. Then he said it.

"Valentine, I'm gay."

Max spoke so simply that at first I thought that I'd misunderstood. I looked at him for clarification… something.

"Yes, Valentine" Max said, "The Hindu closet wasn't the only closet I've been hiding in for far too long. Your friend Max is a homo."

The impact upon me of Max's words propelled me somewhere way out into the stratosphere; although I would have opted to remain there indefinitely rather than return and have to respond, the fates didn't so decree. Therefore, within a matter of I can't say how many seconds, I was again consciously seated beside Max, hearing him say as if from up in a cloud, "I understand how surprised you are."

Oh God, what was the best response here? I finally turned to Max and said, "Surprised is not exactly the adjective I'd use, I'm…" Damn, was that the best I could do?

"I understand," Max said, "you're very uncomfortable about me. Let's talk about your discomfort."

"I'm not uncomfortable."

"Come on, Valentine, don't lie to me. I think you're very uncomfortable"

"No, I'm not. I have a lot of gay friends. Jayson at the studio and I couldn't be closer. And there's also…"

"I hear you have lots of gay friends. Hairdressers, make-up artists, creative people."

"What are you getting at?"

"As long as they're in work where it's alright to be gay, that's fine. But someone who goes to work in a suit and tie like me, now that's different, isn't that correct, Valentine?" I shivered. It wasn't just Max's startling revelation. It was his manner now, very different than usual, that was unsettling me. "Isn't that right?" Max pushed.

"I would not say that's right at all…"

"Have you ever known a doctor or other professional man like me, prominent in this kind of field, who is gay, Valentine?"

"Actually…no…"

"I thought not. Well, Valentine, I'm not crazy about being gay any more than at this moment you're crazy about me being gay."

"You mean, you don't like…being as you are? I asked.

"Valentine" Max answered, "If an intelligent reasonably intact person – and I give myself that- were offered a choice between being straight or gay, do you think I'd decide, 'I'm going to choose to have to hide and cover up and yes, deceive, because if I don't I'm handing others a weapon to ruin my career, perhaps my entire life? Even put my safety in question'? Of course I would have chosen to be straight. If I'd had the choice." " I think," Max added, "It would be best for us to discuss this further with Cheng present."

The following night that meeting with Max, Cheng and I took place. Here I found and expressed my feelings about it all. First, anger. "Why didn't Max tell me about this before?" I asked Cheng.

Cheng said, "Ask Max, not me."

I turned to Max. "Well," I challenged, "why didn't you?

"Why didn't you tell me earlier about Willie?"

"That's different!" I snapped back.

"*Is* it?" Max challenged.

"Why is it different?" Cheng asked.

I couldn't answer.

Cheng's gentle questioning then took another turn. "When did your gay friends at work tell you they're gay?" he asked me.

I answered, "They...didn't have to. I could tell, I mean, it's just...obvious...accepted."

Max responded, "But with me you couldn't tell so you feel deceived?"

"I guess so," I admitted

"It's alright," Max said kindly. "I understand."

"I understand too," Cheng interjected firmly," but it is *not* alright." Max and I looked at him, surprised. "Val-teen," Cheng continued, "until you can completely embrace people who are not typical, how can you expect people to completely embrace people like Willie?" I hanged my head. "Further," Cheng went on, "if you cannot right at this moment fully accept Max, right now you don't fully accept Willie, whatever you may think."

"That can't be true!" I protested, hearing a sob escape from my throat.

"It can't be anything *but* true," Cheng insisted. "The world is your mirror."

"Cheng, please, don't do this to her," Max pleaded, reaching out a hand to me, but out of my peripheral vision I saw Cheng put his palm face up toward Max, indicating to him to back off.

Nobody said anything for a few minutes. During that interval I faced a painful truth. I had blamed Richard for not fully accepting Willie's differences, yet I hadn't either. I had simply been better at covering up. This had to be the most painful lesson that Cheng had ever given me. At that moment Cheng added, "And mostly, those who have any degree of non-acceptance of others have not fully accepted themselves."

I began to sob. Almost at once Max and Cheng were on their feet beside me, Max with his arms around me, Cheng holding my hand. In between sobs I managed, "Why are you comforting *me*? *Max* is the one who should be comforted. Max, you've not only had to hide your spirituality, you've had to hide being gay. How hard it's had to be for you."

Cheng said, "For you too, Valentine. To whom much is given, much is expected. True humility is understanding that everyone has a story just as sad, poignant and dramatic as ours."

I looked at Cheng first. "I'll totally accept Max" I said, then turning to Max, emphasized, "I really will." Back to Cheng, I added, "and Willie too. I know I'll get there."

Max said, "Ultimately we'll both be alright, Valentine." Then he kissed me.

"Yes, you two have a lot in common," Cheng said. Then he began to giggle so outrageously that Max and I just stared from him to each other. "So, count your blessings, Val-teen." Cheng explained. "Max is gay and I'm celibate. Talk about feeling safe? How lucky can a girl get!" His giggles accelerated infectiously, so that soon all three of us were laughing until we felt our sides would split.

The following week Max asked me out for dinner and I said, "Yes."

Over our entrees Max said, "Do you realize this is the first time I asked you out for a meal when you accepted?" Between bites of my pasta and vegetables, I nodded. "You...feel comfortable with me now?" Max asked

"Yes, more than ever. When did you realize, Max?"

"Difficult to answer. I was in deep denial for years. Consequently my marriage turned out to be a farce."

"You're sorry you married her?"

"Yes and no. No, because out of that marriage came my boys whom I can't imagine life without. But, I do regret having deceived and hurt her. She deserved better."

"You didn't do it deliberately"

"That depends on one's perception. It's something I'm in process of working out."

"How did you cope with it when you realized that you were gay?" I wanted to know.

"Not well at first. As I said, I was in denial for years. Even after I'd come to terms with the reality, I was deeply depressed about it for a long time. I prayed to God every day to make me heterosexual. When that didn't happen I felt that God had deserted me because He disapproved of me being gay. At that point I became almost suicidal."

"Goodness, that must have been hard. How did you come out of it?"

"After awhile I came to the realization that since I had not made myself gay, then it had to have been God who did. Therefore, since God's made me this way, he has to approve of and love me just as I am. I took that to be the answer to all of my prayers to God to change me. His answer was that I am perfect just as I am. I still didn't know why God made me gay, nor do I today. However, realizing that God had his reasons allowed me to stop questioning and to get on with my life. Something very good came out of all the pain; my turning to spirituality."

"That's just beautiful. Have you anyone special in your life, Max?"

"Not now. I'm not ready yet. One day, hopefully."

"I guess we're kindred spirits here, too." I said. "There have been times that if I could have I would have turned to women. I just don't have that in me."

"Exactly," Max agreed. "You could not choose to be gay any more than you could choose for Willie to be autistic. It's the Parabdha karma.

For the very first time I wished that I didn't have to go to my private lesson that evening. Cheng picked that up the moment I entered his home.

"You didn't want to come tonight, did you."

I was always so taken aback when Cheng read me that way that either I couldn't think what to say or my answers came swiftly and honestly, without pretense and often, to my chagrin, without tact as well.

"No. I would have preferred to just be with myself," I admitted.

"Why?"

"Oh, to get some directions, some truth. There's so much to digest, you know?"

"Truth?" Cheng repeated. "You mean, to allow your thoughts

to circle like one of those old records on a turntable, spewing around the same old material. And that's what you call truth? Because of your present confused mind, to turn to your own understanding to find direction would be insanity. That is not being with yourself. Here is being with yourself."

"You're right," I said, then asked, "Cheng, is Brandt a sociopath?"

"What kind of a question is that for me? You think I'm a shrink? I don't know."

"I should have known you wouldn't tell me," I pouted. "You have all the wisdom and answers. Can't you, just this once, make things easier for me? Then I can know what to do about things. Hasn't this week been difficult enough for me?"

Cheng's eyes became like an eagle's, strong and unwavering. "Most people know what's right to do," he stated. "They just fool themselves that they don't know so that they can continue to do what's wrong. You have all the answers within you, Val-teen. Which brings me to tonight's lesson. So, let us begin this time with meditation."

I was thought-out, confused-out, talked-out. I wasn't going to resist allowing the mantra to take me to a quieter deeper place. At first the thoughts came. "Maybe I should have gone to the bathroom before starting?" "Maybe I should have eaten more, I might get hungry." (Great material, my mind!!)

Eventually my breathing deepened. Suddenly I was in my dream, only it wasn't a dream. I was walking down a corridor with high windows. The floor was of stone. I was a young nun in a Catholic order, in Italy. I was feeling my feelings on being there. For the most part I hated it. I disliked the cloistered structures of this place, found the dogma terribly distasteful and the monks cold.

Then I saw myself sitting with one monk in residence. His name was Father Marsello. He was my teacher and I revered him. He was wise, kind and knowledgeable about the esoteric subjects which he taught me. I was a bright, eager student.

In this lifetime Father Marsello was Cheng!

At that realization I went into oblivion until sometime later, when I opened my eyes to the sound of Cheng's gong.

After a while I said quietly, "Cheng, remember once you said that you'd tell me what we'd been to each other in a past lifetime, unless I discovered that for myself first?"

"Yes, I do."

"Well, I think I just saw it."

"Go ahead," Cheng encouraged. So I related what I'd seen. "The amazing thing, Cheng, is that as it unfolded I just knew that it was a past life we'd shared."

"Exactly," Cheng answered. "That is how it happens. It is for that very reason that I don't usually advise people to deliberately try to see their past lives. Through regular meditation individuals will see all they are intended to see, past, present, and future, when they are intended to. Your recollection of that past life, as far as it went, was accurate."

"What do you mean, as far as it went?"

"Let's leave it at that for now."

I sighed. I knew it was useless to probe further. Well, what I had gotten was incredulous enough. I wouldn't be greedy. "So, here we meet again," I said.

"Have you thought any more about your dharma?" Cheng queried. I felt rather hurt that he had changed the subject as if our mutual past life wasn't worthy of further discussion. Immediately Cheng said, "Not a different subject, the same subject."

"What do you mean?"

"I'm going to retire, Val-teen."

"When?!"

"When I've finished delivering all the Discourses"

I was shocked and dismayed at Cheng's announcement. All my hidden abandonment issues surfaced and slapped me in the face.. "Oh, NO Cheng!! You can't, I mean you are needed. WHY??"

"It will be time," Cheng said simply. "After the Discourses I'll have done the teaching I was intended to do this time around. My dharma in that area will end."

"What will you do after that?" I gulped.

"Not much," Cheng answered, giggling gaily.

"But you can't just leave everybody that way. Who will teach the next students?"

"Hopefully, my successor."

"I never heard about a successor."

"It wasn't the time."

"Well, who is he?"

Cheng's answer absolute paralyzed me with shock as well as fright. "Not a he. A she. You," he said.

"You're saying… you've chosen ME as your successor? Come on, be serious."

"I am being so. That is my wish, if you want it of course. In that past life that you just recalled, after I died who do you think carried on the teachings for others?"

"ME!?!"

"You got THAT right."

"Then... then," I stammered, "Once was enough!"

"Tell me your reservations," Cheng encouraged.

"All of them?" I asked, my fire returning. "We'd be here a week. How about the obvious one to begin. I'M NOT QUALIFIED TO TAKE YOUR PLACE!!"

"How so?"

"Let me count the ways? I'm not as wise as you, I'm not as knowledgeable, I don't have your experience..."

Cheng giggled. "When I started I didn't have my experience either."

"You mean we're to repeat our past life when I took over for you? Well, I must have been far more evolved in that lifetime."

"You had done many spiritual practices in that lifetime, yes, and in many others. Then where do you feel all that evolvement went?" Cheng asked.

"Look Cheng" I said, "All this is fine for you. You just have to stand there and look Chinese. But me, a Jewish woman, teach Eastern wisdom? They'd laugh me out of town, and rightly so."

Once again Cheng showed himself to be a match for any situation. "If *you're* Jewish," was his rejoinder, "then *I'm* in a Yeshiva, so stop it already with using that Jewish stuff as an excuse for not doing what's right, or else I'll sock you with my yarmulke."

That stopped me in my tracks for certain. "Alright," I said meekly. "But if your reason for giving me the private lessons was to be your successor, then I think you should have told me that before I agreed to them." I looked at Cheng for an answer and got an expression instead. "I know. It wasn't time yet."

"You got THAT right! Give them to me now. Your other reservations. Start with yourself. How do you feel about yourself these days?"

I thought for a few minutes before answering. "I feel, well, like I'm making more peace with my mind, which I suppose is valuable, isn't it?"

"Invaluable!" Cheng proclaimed. "Our minds are like lakes during a windy day, turbulently full of the cares and worries of daily life. But, once we dive deep enough, through meditation, contemplation and the like, we come to that central serene core. That large Self, that real you is the best friend you'll ever have, Val-teen."

"I have times of that, Cheng. Times when I know I've accessed a universal form of energy, when I'm on-purpose in my life. I'm more blissful then and so contributing bliss to others. I'm more understanding and forgiving at such times. But then my problems bring me down and I lose it."

"Join the rest," Cheng said, giggling.

"But not you, Cheng. You don't forget. Isn't that true?"

Cheng did not answer that question, but this time I didn't mind, because instead he then gave me one of the most profound and meaningful teachings he yet had.

"Let us talk about your son, for he is certainly most apropos here," Cheng said.

"Willie's on my mind most of the time, Cheng. I know it's karmic, but I can't stop wondering what thing I could have done that was terrible enough to bring this on."

"I know. Val-teen," Cheng said, "There are other members of our class who have all so-called normal children. For example, Max and his former wife have two, Ginger and her husband have three. Then there are people like you who haven't had that seeming blessing. This may appear to be the greatest tragedy that could befall a family. Yet it can bring out some very unusual and desirable characteristics in such family members. They often become more giving, loving, and sharing, more insightful, with extra tolerance and forgiveness in difficult situations because they can understand everyone. You will notice, surely, that those are all the traits that I am here to instill in my students.

Child rearing with your first child was different than for most people. You had to watch your little son struggling and straining to grasp what other children learned naturally and quickly. You had to watch him make the same mistakes repeatedly, sometimes not under his control, other times deliberately, as he struck back at a world that was so frustrating and frightening to him."

How did Cheng know!

"Val-teen, have you ever thought of God as the parent of so-called disabled children? We all are that. Oh, we can walk and see but spiritually we are slow, deaf and blind. We learn with great difficulty and even then don't use what we've learned. God must stand by and watch us be self-abusive as you've had to with Willie. Although with us it might be through food, booze, drugs, sex, you name it. We're every bit as self-destructive as he is at times. Can't you, Val-teen, understand more than anyone else in the class how God must identify with the frustrations and patience of those who care for so-called disabled children? Just like you do with Willie, God must rejoice in even the smallest signs of our progress. Like you with Willie, God understands our moods, our lapses, our stubbornness to give up what we know for something new even though better. God knows when to be firm, when reassuring."

I could not speak. Cheng continued.

"Jesus, like all Great Teachers, had to face the fact that his disciples could absorb only so much at a time. He was patient and gradually revealed Truths. As he said, 'I still have many things to say to you, but you cannot bear them now.' Like learning disabled children, we forget what we were taught and have to go back and learn it again and again. The apostle Paul wrote in Hebrews 5:12, 'For though by this time you ought to be teachers, you need someone to teach you again the first principles of the oracles of God; and you have come to need mild and not solid food.' But God is patient and gradually reveals truths to us."

Finally I could speak a sentence. "It sounds like you feel as Jesus was. I feel that you are such a Great Being."

Cheng's answer was puzzling. "In your lifetime you will meet such a one. It will be something you've earned and will change your life profoundly."

"Cheng, is there something written somewhere that my destiny is to succeed you?"

"We have free will."

"Good, then my free will, won't. Oh, Cheng, I'm immensely flattered and honored, but maybe I don't think as highly of myself as you do of me. I do have work, and I do make rather good money at it. Why not leave it at that?"

"Do you recall the story of Arjuna with Krishna?"

"Yes, how could I forget it?"

"Jesus, too, often had to face the fact that his disciples were blind to the real meaning of their calling. He would tell them that they were spiritually deaf and blind. He warned his disciples about the leaven of the Pharisees and of Herod by saying, 'Why do you reason because you have no bread? Do you not yet perceive nor understand? Is your heart still hardened? Having eyes, do you not see? And having ears, do you not hear? And do you not remember? When I broke the five loaves for the five thousand, how many baskets full of fragments did you take up?... How is it that you don't understand?'"

"You're saying that you feel this way about me?" I asked, ashamed. Cheng didn't respond.

"I feel such pity sometimes for Willie, Cheng," I said.

"'As a father pities his children, so the Lord pities those who fear Him,' David wrote in Psalms 101:13. However, God's pity is constructive. As a parent of a so-called disabled child, you know that your understanding of his differences cannot interfere with your expecting the best for him and from him. God, too, has high expectations for each of us and never gives up on helping us to become all that we are intended to be. God always knows that we can progress and helps us to see beyond our present difficulties."

"Willie does often resist doing what's best for him" I said.

"As does his mother. She wants to keep selling photography rather than doing her dharma."

Although it hurt to hear all that, I was at the same time once again very impressed with this sage from China. His knowledge and wisdom was so universal.

"I am Chinese, you Jewish, so-called, yet the Truth is Truth from wherever it comes," Cheng said, once again responding to my thoughts. He then continued his metaphor.

"Your son needs to be encouraged to keep going. It requires utmost patience. Similarly, we who are spiritually disabled can be thankful that God is patient with our little steps. Spiritual progress, Val-teen, is as hard won as is Willie's progress. But the breakthroughs are incredible! Like when Willie and we finally get something. It was such moments that Job meant when he said to God, 'I have heard of you by the hearing of the ear, but now my eyes see you.' God must have rejoiced. His spiritually blind son was beginning to see! Take full advantage of the advantages and opportunities that have come your way through this child, Valteen. He is a great soul who has brought you to God. You must understand the day when everything with Willie will be 100 percent right. You know that time will come for all people with so-called disabilities."

You keep saying "so-called disabled, Cheng. Why?" I asked.

"Alright, I will tell you." Cheng said, "Although you are not ready to quite digest it, it will benefit you to hear this now. I say that because I do not think children with autism are sick. I think they are beings from someplace else."

I tried to quietly ponder Cheng's theory. Finally I said, "You know, Cheng, often I've referred to Willie as my child from Mars. I've also noticed, and it isn't just me who has, that all children with autism are unusually beautiful."

"Absolutely" Cheng agreed. "Do you know any other "disability" about which that can be said? One would think that your Western doctors would look closely at these things and conclude, 'Hey, something else is going on here.' Not yet, but in time that will come."

"Still, I want him to talk, Cheng, so he can tell us what he believes, feels, when he hurts."

"He will do so," Cheng said. "He will speak in a new way. It will be most profound and controversial for a long while, but as people progress spiritually it will be understood and accepted. Great interest will occur in the world about these differently-abled people called autistic.

"You mean people will want to know about them?!" I asked incredulously.

"That's an understatment!" Cheng answered. "Wait until we approach the millennium. A month won't go by that there won't be something in the media on autism. The media doesn't present material unless they know that the public wants it. People will begin to sense, then, that through autism and other people who aren't typical, they'll access keys to many mysteries about themselves and the world itself."

"That's hard to believe," I answered.

"Mark my word," Cheng said.

It was all becoming too much for me to absorb. I needed to change the subject somewhat. "Cheng" I said, "you spoke of Jesus becoming impatient with those who didn't recognize their calling. Is calling like dharma?"

"Yes."

"Were you talking about me, then? Are you frustrated with

me?"

"I have learned not to rush things," Cheng answered.

"Good. Then you'll have time to find somebody else to take over your teaching?"

Cheng said nothing.

"Are my private lessons over, then?" I asked, frightened of Cheng's answer.

"Only if you should so decide," he replied. "Otherwise, my heart is in continuing. There were not nor are there strings to my teaching you. Just know there is an end to every string."

"Whatever *that* means," I said "I don't know about string, Cheng, but at times, with you, I've been at the end of my rope."

"I know." Cheng smiled.

"I don't want to stop the teachings."

"I know that, too." Cheng broke into a huge toothy grin.

"Of course you do," I said, smiling back.

* * *

"You're quiet this morning," Max offered.

"Do you mind?"

"Not at all. I feel flattered that you're comfortable enough with me."

"Thank you, Max."

Again we were on the Long Island train. I'd been watching the scenery float by; trees, small buildings, telephone wires. Like the things of our life, here and gone, but we were still totally here.

"Max," I asked, "Do you mind if I meditate for a while?"

"Mind? A great opportunity; I'll meditate, too."

At first there was just thought, interspersed with quiet and peace. Then all at once I saw myself. I was in a costume play. I was an actress. I had just finished performing with my leading man. We took a curtain call, then the curtain went down. I called him Laramar but I knew him to be Brandt in this lifetime. The director walked over and told us that this had been an excellent performance. I called him Casard, but recognized him as Richard. It was around the sixteenth century. So, my ease before the camera had come from that past lifetime as an actress! Amazing how all the pieces of our lives fit!

The scene progressed. I was pregnant with Laramar's or

Brandt's child. He did not want me to have it. I would not abort the child, so a boy was born. I abandoned him backstage, hoping somebody more suited to having a child would take him and raise him properly. Casard, or Richard, loved me, but I left with Laramar, although I got the feeling we never married. My leaving broke Casard's or Richard's heart.

I came out of meditation abruptly, rubbing my eyes. Just then I felt a hand on my shoulder. "Hi," a man said. I looked up into the face of Serge. "Hey, sit down," Max told him, pointing to the seat opposite us. "What are you doing, joining the commuter track?"

"Could be, who knows?" Serge answered. "I have a job interview in New York. Maybe pursuing my dharma, you could call it."

"That's wonderful, Serge," I said.

"Hey, I've got something to tell you. I had a dream, about you, Valentine. It was so strange. No coincidence that we met here, obviously."

"Want me to leave?" Max asked.

"No, we might need your shrink ability here to interpret," Serge said. "Alright with you, Valentine?"

"If it's a clean dream, Serge, wonderful," I said. "You see, I know you."

"Clean indeed," Serge answered, "The only dirty thing in this story is a rather dirty baby."

I froze. "What do you mean?"

"It went like this," Serge said. "I was meditating. Probably I fell asleep. Suddenly there I was, backstage on a stage production or something. It wasn't here. It seemed to be another era. You were there, V. J, acting. You looked a lot like you do now. There was a man acting with you, somebody I've never seen in this lifetime. I was a technician of some kind. You all left, and I darkened the stage. I thought I heard a baby crying. So I went backstage and damned if there wasn't a baby lying there on the ground, wrapped in newspaper. His face was all smudged but he looked familiar. He had a beautiful and sort of wise look. I took him in and cleaned him up. I have the feeling I raised that child. Isn't that weird?"

I tried to catch my breath and once I finally did, I took out my wallet and pointed to a photograph. "Did the baby look anything like this?" I asked.

"My God!" Serge exclaimed. "That's him. That baby had the same face. Who IS this?"

"Willie. My son."

"My God!"

"My sentiments exactly!"

"I think," Max said, "You tapped into a past life with Valentine, Serge."

After that none of us spoke much. But when Serge got off at the stop before ours, I asked Max. "Could it be? Was the child in that lifetime Willie? Had I turned my back on him in a prior lifetime? Was THAT why he returned to me as such a strong challenge to my ability to love unconditionally?"

"It seems probable. You appear to be pooling into a great deal of information suddenly. Which reminds me. How are your lessons with Cheng coming?"

"With difficulty. But I wouldn't want to give them up. Although sometimes I wonder, 'Why would any sane person put themselves through this!'

"Of course it's painful. It's the destruction of the ego."

"Did you know Cheng wants me to succeed him as teacher?"

"No! But that's wonderful!! And you should!" Max exclaimed.

"I can't ever imagine feeling qualified."

"After I'd graduated from medical school and finished my residency, I saw my first patient. I felt totally unqualified."

"After all that schooling and more degrees than a thermometer?"

"Valentine, an actor makes his first substantial movie, but before that he studied, he was in plays in the boon docks which nobody came to but his mother. Finally he's acting in this movie with big-name actors. What is he thinking? 'I belong here'? Hardly! For quite some time he's thinking, 'What am I doing here?!' There are days now when I feel the same way in my profession."

"You, after so many years in practice!" I asked incredulously.

"Valentine, the only people who feel totally qualified all the time are complete idiots with huge egos. Certainly not a job qualification for Cheng's successor."

"Cheng says I did spiritual study and practice a great deal in more than one past life"

"Oh, I have no doubt you're an angelic old soul" Max responded. "For one thing, otherwise you would not have been given Willie."

"I don't know if I believe that, Max. I know mothers who have abandoned their so-called disabled children. I know how difficult it can become, but to abandon one's own child! You call that angelic behavior?" Max replied, "Those women simply don't know they are angels. They have identified with their problem instead of their true worth, so they believe they can't cope. By the way, if you judge them you're judging yourself. Remember Cheng's teaching on that. And what Serge revealed."

***

"I'll have the breaded veal chops, baked potato with sour cream, and chef's salad," Casse said.

"Chef's salad, hmm. On a diet, I see?"

The waiter looked at me inquiringly. "Well" I said, scanning the menu, "please bring me the sprout salad with garbanzos and lentils. Can they leave the egg out?" The waiter nodded. "Good, and do you have whole grain bread?" A "Yes" nod again. "Good, I'll have that also. That will be all for now."

"You've got that, haven't you?" Casse asked the waiter. "Eye of a newt, toe of a frog, hold the mayo."

"Excuse me, ma'am?" the waiter asked her, stone faced.

"Don't mind my friend" I told him." She's being funny. I'm explaining that as you probably couldn't tell." The waiter blinked, then walked away.

Casse made a face and offered, "Lunch with you has been an experience lately!"

"Lately? When was the last time, two months ago?"

"I'm having lunch with Auntie Mame."

"I'm not Anti-Mame, I'm all for her."

"The way you eat lately, too months apart is enough! Sprouts! Yuck! Which brings me to the subject of my sex life."

"Sprouts remind you of your sex life?"

"Everything reminds me of my sex life. Val, the truth is I'm finding other men *very* appealing lately. There's this gorgeous art director. I've been thinking...what would the harm be?

Casse expounded. After listening for awhile I said, "I'm concerned about you, Casse. Truthfully, I can't see any worthwhile man finding your demeanor attractive. You've emulated the worst traits of men; cursing, combative, overkill aggressive. Men still like women who act different than they do, who act like women. Think about it. Are you physically attracted to a man who acts feminine? The reverse is just as true. I think you've confused social roles with private ones. Why can't we be like women and still advance ourselves?"

"Moralizing, or judging?"

"Neither. I'm talking about what happens to people, women especially, who use bodies only for momentary pleasure. Sharing bodies should be the last step, not a preliminary. Sex needs to warm the heart and soul, not just the flesh."

"No seduction?"

"Of course seduction. But with feeling behind it for the person, not deceit and manipulation."

"Honestly, V.J," Casse said with a disgusted thrust of her chin, "I think that oriental guru you have is turning you into a monk altogether. I guess all those rishis and swamis and whatever the hell else aren't ever horny."

"Have you ever heard of the Kama Sutra?" I asked.

"It's a book, isn't it?"

"Yes, Cheng introduced me to it. Vatsyayana, a nobleman, sometime between 100 and 4000 A.D wrote it for the nobility of India. Kama in Sanskrit means love, sensual pleasure, sexual gratification. Sutra means expression. While the Kama Sutra was aimed at men, as women then were very much subordinate to men, it also stresses female sexual gratification. It considers that part of 'the work of a man', and gives explicit instructions. It advises if the Kama Sutra information is followed, the love that results will last 1,000 years."

"1000 years!?" Casse's eyes became moons. "That's 999 years longer than most of my relationships last! I must borrow your copy IMMEDIATELY!!"

"I don't have one. I've never read it."

"You haven't read it? What have you been doing all these years!"

"Doing what comes naturally, as my memory serves me. It's been a long time since I've been to bed with a man."

"I didn't mean that. I mean, what have you been doing with your Chinese teacher?"

"Studying lessons from The Bhagavad Gita, Raja Yoga, Shiva Sutras, those texts."

"That's all?"

"Hardly. We've been working on my blockages, and…"

"Forget that" Casse interrupted. "Go back to that Bhaga..whatchmacallit. What does that say about sex?"

"Nothing specific really. I think we're born sexual as well as spiritual beings and sex, like everything else, can be a fundamental expression of our Godliness. Cheng says Taoists honor each other before making love by actually saying, 'I honor you.' Whether we say the words or not I believe we should make love only with that attitude. Anything less dishonors us and affects us pervasively and negatively."

"You really aren't having sex with anyone lately?" Casse asked. "I can't believe this. The goddess hasn't been asked?"

"Oh, I've been asked. I'm just waiting until a God asks me. I've chosen to be celibate until sex can be an expression of rightness, with the right man, shared effort and mutual dedication to the relationship. Otherwise it disowns a woman's female self and only brings tragedy."

"Shit, at that rate you'll have to wait forever" Casse said." But I must say, some of what you have said makes sense, I'm impressed."

At that moment the waiter reappeared. "Will there be anything else?" he asked.

We shook our heads 'no,'so he put our check down and left.

To tell the truth, I was also impressed with those words, which had seemed to flow from me so easily. Cheng was right. We had only to allow, and to listen.

CHAPTER TWENTY-FIVE: DISCOURSE EIGHT- Yoga; The Eight Disciplines By Which Permanent Happiness Is Achieved, Part One

"Yoga is the breaking of contact with pain."
--Bhagavad Gita

"The majority of Western psychotherapists do not help their patients to achieve the union of perfect yoga -without which they will never be happy."
--Max Witkin, M.D.

"This part of our teaching will be in two parts. In tonight's Discourse I will present four limbs of yoga; in the next Discourse the other four.

"First, the term yoga. What does it mean, anybody?" Cheng asked, adding, "I explained this before."

Andrew, after raising his hand and being acknowledged, answered, "It's a kind of physical exercise. My sister took a yoga class at the high school continuing ed; I once saw her practicing the exercises."

"Andrew, and class," Cheng answered, "It is common for westerners to equate yoga with the physical postures. How many of you have believed that?"

Probably three fourths of the class raised their hands.

"The physical postures, called asanas, are only one aspect, or one limb of yoga, a very important aspect which I urge each of you to establish as a regular practice. However, yoga per se is much more far reaching than just the postures. It is actually a doctrine said to have been handed down from prehistoric times. Yoga actually means 'yoke,' or 'union' in Sanskrit. It is a method of spiritual union, a scientific means given to us by the ancient Eastern sages to achieve perfection."

Max raised his hand, was acknowledged, and offered, "If I may I'd like to draw a comparison between Western psychology and yoga."

"Please do, Max," Cheng encouraged.

"All right, then. In Western psychology we are talking about something unfinished. There is no real general agreement regarding which therapies are most effective. New ones are continuously being tried and older ones abandoned. However, yoga is finished."

"That is correct, Max," Cheng responded. "Yoga is a true science in that the ancient sages of Eastern India tried and tested these disciplines, or limbs, for centuries. If practiced as taught, the results are guaranteed, not speculative. Can you think of a further difference, Max?"

"Readily! The majority of Western psychotherapists do not help their patients to achieve the union of perfect yoga, that is, to unite with God. Yet a famous colleague of mine, Henry James, once said, 'Psychotherapy is fine, but without the spiritual your patients will never be happy.' He was correct. Through traditional therapy I might help my patients to make an adjustment on the psychological level to a certain degree, to a degree with which I'd be very dissatisfied."

"So you use yoga with your patients, Max?" Cheng asked.

Max's face fell. "I have to be careful in introducing the concept of God into my practice, not to be considered irrelevant, to say nothing of irreverent, by my colleagues."

"How well I know," Cheng offered, "but yoga is so essential. The Bhagavad Gita even says that through yoga we eliminate pain and suffering. Is there anybody here who would mind that?"

Serge's groan, followed by his remark, "How *soon* can we have it?" spoke for all of our feelings.

"Excellent question, Serge," Cheng answered. "However, *please* follow the rules - be acknowledged first. Getting back to your question, 'how soon?', how about within the next second?" Cheng remained quiet as did we. He clearly had everyone's attention. "Theoretically, there is not a single reason why any one of you should not achieve enlightenment immediately," he continued. "God IS within us. How far must we actually go to reach this God? After all, we walk further in our homes each morning before we even start the day; it is true, is it not? So why *not* in an instant? It is our past karmas and our samscaras, literally, our past impressions from this and many previous lifetimes, which usually prevent rapid self-realization. Yoga eliminates those impediments to perfect Truth, to uniting with God. 'How long will it take?' you asked, Serge. For any one of you it could be hours, days, weeks, months, lifetimes. I cannot tell you how long. I *can* tell you that no effort at yoga is wasted; the more we apply ourselves, the sooner we shall succeed.

"The limb of yoga called meditation, or dhyana, is one we have already studied in Discourse One. Please continue it daily. It is most important.

"The limb of yoga called postures is also most important," Cheng continued. "Earlier tonight I referred to the postures as asanas, a word that actually has two meanings; the mat upon which a yogi, or practitioner of yoga, sits, and the postures themselves. Here I would like to introduce the suggestion that each of you obtain a small white wool blanket to sit upon when meditating. It might be obtained from a wool sweater or a larger blanket, cut down;or knit it from scratch if you're handy, just, only *white* wool will do. This traditional requirement is still helpful today in containing the meditation energy and furthering your practice. Posture is very important in sitting for meditation. When the mind becomes still in meditation, a spiritual current, called kundalini, rises up the spine. A straight back will facilitate this passage. Remember, a maladjusted body is reflected in a tense, restless mind. Look for a good hatha yoga teacher; that is most important for this discipline."

Andrew raised his hand, was acknowledged and asked, "Cheng, how big must this asana be?"

"Not very," Cheng answered at once. "Just big enough to cover your ass."

After a startled moment we all tittered. As a teacher, this Cheng was expert at holding our attention.

"A third limb of yoga is Pranayama, control of the breath," Cheng continued. Prana actually means the vital energy which we draw into ourselves from the universe, and is primarily obtained through breathing. Calmness can actually be obtained through deep steady inhalations and exhalations; conversely, mental agitation and despondency are accompanied by rapid, shallow, uncontrolled breathing. This must be done sanely, however. In the west people have misused induced hyperventilation for a 'high.' That is an abominable abuse of prana. We will save the last half hour of this class for an exercise in Pranayama, followed by meditation.

"Lastly, for tonight, a fourth limb of yoga, concentration, or Dharana. There are many Dharanas, or exercises in ways to know

God. I would like to concentrate for you here on some of those which result in extraordinary perceptions. My reason for stressing these is not because such extraordinary perceptions, or powers, are important; they are not. It is because regardless of everything that the sages learned and teach, regardless of everything that I impart to you, unless you experience something you will have your doubts. So, I offer these Dharanas to you.

Seat yourselves as for meditation with head and neck in a straight line. Now concentrate on the tip of your nose; in time, you will smell wonderful perfume. And/or, concentrate on the tip of your tongue; you will develop a supernormal sense of taste; concentrate on the middle of the tongue; a supernormal sense of touch will ensue. Concentrate on the root of the tongue; there will come an extraordinary sense of hearing. So, if you're inclined, try these on your own; as long as you wish, for however long it takes; they will prove to you that anything is possible to one who concentrates, who disciplines the mind.

"We will now do that exercise in Pranayama. Please be well advised that there are highly advanced Pranayama exercises which have no place in your life now. Their indiscriminate practices could lead to serious mental disturbances. The kundalini power is not to be toyed with. The following, though, is a harmless breathing exercise which calms the mind. It can prepare us for contemplation and meditation. Please, watch me. Then you will do it with me."

Cheng said, "This is called Alternate Nostril Breathing. I will demonstrate." He breathed in through his nose as he held up his right hand. He closed his right nostril with his thumb. He then breathed out through his left nostril. Then he breathed in through his left nostril. Then he closed off his left nostril with his pinky and ring finger. He breathed out through his right nostril. Then he breathed in through his right nostril, after which he closed his right nostril with his thumb. Finally, he exhaled through the left nostril. Now Cheng said, "Alternate Nostril Breathing is a natural tranquilizer to the central nervous system. One can do five to ten rounds at one sitting. Now, will you all please do this exercise with me."

I did the exercise as Cheng directed it, and found myself growing peaceful.

Cheng continued, "A concentration that I really love for going beyond sorrow I now offer you. You may use this as an alternate method of meditation. It is concentration upon the Lotus of the Heart. The ancient yogis believed that there was an actual center of spiritual consciousness located between the thorax and the abdomen, in the form of a small house within which is a lotus flower. They instruct us to enter there and meditate. This is a helpful method of meditation as it localizes for us the Inner God. We enter that small house or shrine whenever we desire, and there we are safe and beyond sorrow. We can do this at any time in our daily lives as well. An alternate effective way is to concentrate on any divine form, symbol, picture or idea which is holy to us.

"Thought-substitution, as mentioned in an earlier Discourse, is a related practice in controlling the mind.

"So, you see, Dear Ones, yoga is outstanding for its breadth of vision and its universality. And, as you shall discover as we explore the other four limbs of yoga in Discourse Eight, yoga is very liberal and lenient as well. Yoga never says 'you must do this,' rather it says, 'It has been proven that if you do this, this will happen, whereas if you do that, that will happen;' *you* decide what to do."

"This concludes Discourse Eight," Cheng announced. "See you next week. Until then, Dear Ones, remember to breathe. Blessings."

* * *

Later that night, when I was almost asleep, my remembrance about my past lifetime with Cheng in the Catholic order continued.

I am walking again down the same corridor as before, this time full of fright and fear. I walk a long while until I come to an open courtyard. Many people are assembled there. I move somewhat through the crowd, then I stop and look at something - as much as I'm able to see it through the crowd. I look away, horrified. Then I scream.

A large hand is on my arm and a man is asking me to come with him. Not ungently, he is guiding me away from the crowds. I am hysterically uncontrolled. He leads me into a room which appears to be his office. He pats my shoulder. He is explaining to me that what happened had to be. "There are rules which must be observed or an entire system could break down, with dire consequences to the church." He is dressed like Father Marsella. He, too, is a monk, higher up in the hierarchy, though. His name is Father Lladro. He tells me that he understands my feeling of loss but that I must realize that this was for the highest good, and primarily that I will be saved; he will make certain of that.

Then I came out of it. Hurriedly, I phoned Cheng. "Cheng! I just saw that life that we had together again."

"Tell me," Cheng encouraged.

"Cheng, first, there was something that happened in the courtyard that I didn't see, something that upset me terribly. Do you know what that was?"

"Yes," Cheng replied, "and correction, you did see it. Your mind just didn't let you remember. They were burning me at the stake as a witch."

"BURNING YOU AT... *WHO* WAS?"

"The higher church authorities."

"WHY?!"

"I'd broken the rules. I was known in the order as well versed in the metaphysical arts, which I was allowed to practice but only on male persons in power. However, I took a risk and taught you, since you were so gifted and interested. They disapproved on two counts; you were only a nun, not in a power situation, and you were a woman. Women were not to be given such knowledge. That was handing them the devil's tool. So they killed me that way," Cheng said nonchalantly.

"You sound... very casual about it."

"Why not? Oh, it's not the greatest way to die, for certain, but after the varied ways, the moment of death is the same for everybody, so how much does it matter? And you see, we're here again anyway."

"Yes, THAT is pretty wonderful."

"By the way, you were scheduled for the same fate as I, but Lladro stepped in and interceded for you."

"So he intimated. But, why?"

"Your family was wealthy, so could donate to the church. Also, Lladro felt you could be useful. He was greatly interested in your spiritual knowledge and metaphysical abilities."

"Like today," I said. "Cheng, in this lifetime Lladro is Brandt, isn't he?"

"That is correct."

I drew in my breath, and finally exhaled. "*Did* I teach Lladro spiritual things?"

"I, of course wasn't around. The burning was the end of that lifetime for me. I looked down on you, though; you did try to teach Lladro. He wasn't very good at it, however."

"Like today?" I giggled.

"Some things don't change," Cheng agreed. "Lladro also saved you because he liked you."

"You mean, we were...?"

"Lovers? No, not in that lifetime. You both took your vows seriously and wouldn't break them. You also felt a bond and attraction to *him*. He did save your life. You owed him a great debt which you were never able to pay back in that lifetime. That's why in this lifetime you felt that you owed him." Cheng was correct. I had felt that. "By the way, you had one other great friend in that lifetime, a very kind Mother Rosetta, a Mother Superior who helped you. She had been British nobility who had given up everything to join the order. In this lifetime she is a he; Max."

I just sat there, digesting it all. Little wonder Max's speech was so formal at times, that he was so nurturing to people, and in the perfect profession for him. Finally I said, "Life makes such sense when we can see something of the larger picture." Then I thought something else and began to laugh.

"Tell me," Cheng encouraged.

"Brandt... a monk!" I giggled. "And, celibate? What was he doing this time around, making up for lost time!?"

"You could say that," Cheng answered, seriously. "And the fact that you and Blandt spent an entire lifetime where physical culmination of your relationship was denied, explains the tremendous sexual attraction this time around."

When I said nothing, Cheng added, "Interesting you had this experience now. Spontaneous remembrances of our past lifetimes is a Siddhi, a power. We'll be having our Discourse about those before long."

CHAPTER TWENTY-SIX: DISCOURSE NINE-
Yoga: The Eight Disciplines, by which Permanent Happiness Is Achieved, Part Two

"The yogi practices temperateness of word and action."
--Bhagavad Gita

"Formerly, so much of my life was spent on expediencies,
Doing things I hated doing but felt it necessary to do.
Feeling this way reduced my capacity for effective work
and there was little health and wholeness in me. Through love
(spirituality) I have discovered I can integrate thought,
feeling and action into that power of singleness and truth."
--Joseph Chilton Pearce

Cheng sat before us, eyes gleaming, back erect.

"We begin this evening with a fourth limb of yoga, the various forms of abstention, called Yamas. They are five basic rules of conduct: Abstention from harming others, from falsehood, from theft, from incontinence, and from greed. We shall take them individually.

"Abstention from harming others, or Ahimsa, means we are to live so as not to cause harm or pain to others by either our thoughts, words or deeds. This means to try to cultivate love for all and to see God in everyone."

Serge, seemingly agitated, raised his hand, was recognized, and insisted, "Let's stop right here. Are you telling us that we should see God in... for instance, Hitler? *Approve* of his actions?"

"Serge, you are talking about two different things," Cheng answered. "Seeing God in a person is one thing, approving of that person's actions is another. All people have God within, yet all people's actions are not always God-like. We know that from personal experience, don't we, Dear Ones?" I saw a few heads hang.

Cheng instantly picked up on the collective reaction.

"Please, no guilting. Yoga asks us to observe our actions with a degree of detachment, somewhat like a scientist looking at a specimen under the microscope. The good scientist doesn't look through his microscope and react, 'Oh, this is 'horrendous,' or 'oh, this is stupendous!' The good scientist thinks, 'This is interesting,' or just, 'This is.' Then she or he asks, 'Let us see what, if anything, we should do with this.' Yoga suggests evaluating one's thoughts and actions similarly, using the following guideline. 'Does this add to or diminish the path to my enlightenment?' Remember that every choice that you make moves you closer to either your lower self, that is, to darkness, or to your Higher Self, that is, toward the light. You decide toward which you most wish to move; make your choices accordingly.

"So, abstention from harming others means we help others but we do not help others to do wrong. However, I would temper this somewhat. As with Arjuna, a soldier in battle might have to fight. If we find insects or other so-called pests in our home, to leave them there would be unsanitary. We might, then, have to set a trap or use a spray, to help these creatures make their transition to the other side.

I cringed. "I know Valentine. I do not swat a fly; I open the door and urge it to fly out. However, with tiny insects and rodents sometimes we have to think on the hierarchy ladder. If there is no other way, human health conditions must come first. Anyway, what occurs for us when we follow this Yama? Yes, there *are* payoffs for following each. So, when we have renounced violence in our thoughts and actions, we create a certain atmosphere around us. It is a huge power. In such an atmosphere all anger and violence ceases to exist. Animals and people too, become non-violent and harmless in our presence." I remembered that I couldn't remain angry in Chengs presence. "There is a test for whether non-violence is present: it is jealousy. So long as any exists in the heart there is not yet perfect Ahimsa."

Cheng paused briefly, then continued. "Our next Yama is abstention from falsehood. In other words, ideally our thoughts, feelings and actions should correspond. So our words and thoughts must be truthful, in conformity with the facts..."

A bunch of hands shot up. "Yes, I predicted I'd get a big reaction on this one. Let us hear from somebody whom we haven't heard from in a while. Mindie."

"I can't imagine practicing this Yama," Mindie insisted. "Yesterday I had lunch with my friend Mirabelle who was wearing a new dress in the most loathsome color and style. I thought it horrible. How could I have told her that?"

"Important point, Mindie," Cheng answered. "Did you tell her?"

"Of course not! I would have hurt her, maybe even lost her as my friend."

"And yoga would say you did the correct thing," Cheng responded. "Yoga says we must be careful not to hurt others by saying something cruel even when true. Yoga says if the truth would hurt but do no good, remain silent. Now, what is the benefit, the gift that comes to the essentially truthful person? When a person gains control of truthfulness he gains power over the truth. He no longer has to 'obey' facts; facts 'obey' him. For example, he will say a thing and it becomes true. He can tell a person that person is well and that person becomes well. He can bless a person and that person is blessed - even if that person didn't deserve blessings."

"HOLY SHIT!" Serge exclaimed.

"Serge, you will please observe decorum," Cheng admonished. I furtively glanced around the room and saw guarded smiles. Cheng, on the other hand, had made his lips stern, however I detected a grin wanting to emerge.

"I apologize," Serge offered. "It's just too... I mean, are you *kidding*!"

"I'm not here to kid, as you say, with the truth. This is truth, Serge. The powers we obtain as we perfect ourselves are real, awesome and clearly stated in the ancient yogic literature. There are yogis who have achieved them. These powers, once obtained, are always to be used for the good, of course.

"Next Yama," Cheng continued. "Abstention from theft. Now you might all be thinking, 'he can skip that one. I don't steal.' But within the yogic definition, *do* you? This Yama against theft doesn't only mean not stealing somebody's wallet or merchandise out of a store. Harboring any feelings of covetousness toward anything or anyone would also be stealing within the yogic definition. We want to remember that nothing belongs to us, it belongs to the world. We are merely borrowing from the world. So, we want to borrow no more from the world than we really need and to make proper and full use of it. Wasting is stealing from the world. Spraying excessive window cleaner to a window when two sprays would have sufficed is wasteful stealing. Discarding foods that could be good leftovers is another form of stealing; ingenuous meals can be made of left-overs. Making a long-distance call on another person's phone without their permission is stealing. Copying pages from a book which is copyrighted or copying commercial audio and video tapes, is stealing. Keeping your homes cluttered with things which you don't use or care for, instead of giving them away to somebody who might make use of them, is stealing."

There was another collective groan from the group. "I know, I know, you have all done some, probably all of these things."

Andrew raised his hand and was acknowledged. "In theory this is well and good," he said, "but in the real world I couldn't have gotten through graduate school without photocopying book pages. It would have been prohibitively expensive to buy all those books."

Cheng was nodding even before Andrew had finished. "I understand, Dear Ones, that everything in these Discourses is simple but not easy. Ideally, they should be followed without exception; practically, they won't be. But when you remember the benefits that come from this Yama, non-theft, you'll be motivated to at least attempt to follow it as best you can. So here it is. That benefit is... wealth. Yes, you heard me correctly, Dear Ones. Wealth is attracted to those who practice non-theft. The reverse is, according to the laws of karma, if you 'steal' five dollars worth of phone calls, you'll lose at least five dollars elsewhere. Maybe somebody will spill coffee on your shirt resulting in a six dollar cleaning bill. So you have to spend the money regardless, plus the inconvenience of trips to the cleaner, and the guilt."

Serge said, "In other words, the goblins gonna get ya, if you don't watch out."

Cheng, looking chagrined, said, "An interesting metaphor, Serge, however you have been guilty of theft. You have stolen my time because you spoke before following the rules." Serge hit the side of his head with his hand, exclaiming, "Damn, I'm sorry," then his hand shot up, all this simultaneously, causing us all, Cheng included, to smile.

I did a quick self-analysis. Had I practiced non-theft? Certainly I was honest on the job, never having padded my commissions with Ernic as some other reps. did. But I thought of the recorded cassette tapes I'd copied. I remembered all the perfectly good left-overs I'd discarded in the garbage when Richard and I had been together and affluent. I thought of the instances during those same times when I'd left too-large portions of dinners in restaurants without bothering to take them home, and more stupidly and wastefully, had ordered too much food when I hadn't been that hungry in the first place. Had I done none of those things, would I have by-passed our recent money problems? I didn't know the answer to that, but I certainly could try to improve now. I looked around and sensed my classmates were having similar thoughts and resolves.

"Don't waste anything, including time," Cheng added. "Such as if you're on an airplane and know you need that time to meditate but your seat companion needs to chat, you might have to say, 'Excuse me, I must catch a nap' or the like. In another instance the dharmic use of your time might be to talk with the stranger. So we use viveka, or discrimination about our use of time as well as in all other life situations."

"Next Yama is abstention from incontinence," Cheng continued, thus keeping our attention with a vengeance. "Sexual activity, thoughts and fantasies use up much of our vital force. When that same energy is conserved it is transmitted to others like light or heat. In the Orient it is felt that abstinence is essential for a great spiritual teacher." Cheng looked at each of us in turn. "Not many of you aspiring at this moment to be great spiritual teachers, eh?" Laughter filled the room. "I will only say to each of you, use balance. If you do, at least do not overdo. Better?" Laughter of relief.

"Next Yama; - abstention from greed," Cheng went on. "This includes abstention from attachment, or vairanya. To explain; you don't cling to anything. Or anyone. Every time you attempt to do so the following analogy will help you to stop: think of yourself at those times hanging on to the edge of a cliff. How do you feel? At peace? Free to look around and see clearly? With good feelings about this precipice from which you are hanging by a thread? Of course, 'no' to all those questions. To cling is to be a prisoner every bit as much as a person who hangs from a cliff or is behind bars is a prisoner. So when we abstain from such clinging we receive an extraordinary benefit - knowledge of our past, present and future lives. This in itself gives us experiential proof of reincarnation and of the everlastingness of life itself for us all. As for greed, that is wanting more and more when we already have enough, thus acting immorally to get more. Remember what yoga says about that. 'The path to hell is paved with greed.'"

"And so, ideally these Yamas, abstentions, would be followed without exceptions as to time, place or situation.

Now, let me move on to the Niyamas, or the observances. Again, the Yamas are things to avoid doing while the Niyamas are things to do."

I raised my hand and was acknowledged. I offered, "I would have thought it the other way around. Niyamas sound like things not to do, Yamas like things to do. Isn't this way confusing?" The other way would be easier to remember; 'ni' for 'no.'"

"You have a point," Cheng answered. "So, remember by your memory crutch, but then remember to reverse it. What can I tell you?" he shrugged, at that moment seeming very Jewish.

"So the Niyamas are the observances, not the abstentions. The Yamas are the abstentions, not the observances. Got it?

"The first Niyama is purity. This is cleanliness, external and internal. The body is the temple of our indwelling God, so it deserves to be kept clean. Washing is excellent psychologically, too; it makes us feel that we are cleansing ourselves of mental as well as physical dirt; we feel renewed. We must cleanse our insides by pure water and good food in a sensible diet, and in today's polluted world I will offer that regular herbal cleansings are also advised. A wonderful body purification exercise is to lie in the bathtub in a warm bath of about two cups of sea salt, Epson Salts, or apple cider vinegar. They are all very detoxifying. Just lie there twenty minutes or so to unpeel, to let the thoughts and feelings come up. In fact, it's good to take a bath in the morning, and then to take a shower right afterwards to cleanse you further from the skin which sloughs off in the bath."

Ginger interjected, "And after we're late every morning and get fired from our jobs, does yoga also tell us how to get other work?" We all related (I was lucky to fit in a five minute shower, mornings) and roared.

"You are all laughing but Ginger is right, of course." Cheng offered. "Indeed it is not dharmic to make your boss wait. So the bath might out of necessity be postponed for the evening. Again, viveka, discrimination."

Cheng continued, "A good mental diet is just as important, if not more so, than a good physical one. We want to monitor what we put into our heads by the literature that we read, the films that we watch, the people with whom we socialize, our thoughts and our speech. We do not want to become holier-than-thou, while at the same time we want to understand that this Niyama can be observed only with constant alertness. One newspaper or news broadcast a day is enough and not just before you retire, please, unless you want nightmares. If you have to read a newspaper before going to sleep, read the comics and then only the funny ones.

"Gossip, too much 'light' entertainment and the like become like junk food to the mind. If we indulge in those at first we will feel relaxed, but then we will drift into a dark and impure mind characterized by the three a's; addictions, aversions and anxieties. Rather than acting 'holy,' thus setting us apart from others, set an example with our tone, frankness, sincerity, interests, and interest in others. If we are with those who insist on being consistently negative, in the social sense at least we are advised to decide if we want to continue putting ourselves where they can drink of our energy leaving themselves feeling somewhat better and us drained. Consider limiting our time with such people, and finding more positive company. Negativity will bring us down. We owe it to those who depend upon us, and that includes humanity in general, to not allow our energy to be stolen as above. Discrimination, viveka, once again. To live well we must eliminate judgment but use discernment.

"The next discipline is withdrawing of the mind from sense objects. This mastery of the senses is known as Pratyahara. We need to control the mind. In order to do that we have to get to know it. We can begin by watching our thoughts. Let us now do that. Let us just sit and passively watch our thoughts for five minutes."

After what seemed like an hour, Cheng said, "Alright, five minutes is up."

Somewhat dazed, we looked around at one another. It was clear that time had not flown for any of us.

"I know," Cheng acknowledged, "Ordinarily our predominant fears and desires have become so usual to us that we don't even notice them. Just now you have all seen how negative, flighty and unfocussed your minds actually are most of the time. You do not like what you observed? Be patient. Be kind with yourselves. Watch your minds in this way for a short time period daily, before meditation. When the mind is watched in this manner it starts to feel silly about how it is behaving and begins to calm down. Along with this exercise, in your daily lives I want you to all practice thought-substitution; substitute a positive or effective thought for a negative, useless one. You might place this in the affirmation category. In these ways you will achieve some measure of mental control and begin to create a better reality, so to speak."

Then Cheng looked sternly serious. "It is so easy to make purity unimportant," he warned. "To slip. To think it's fine to eat junk food just this once, to watch that violent movie just one time, to gossip only in this instance. But that junk "food" clings to the inner parts of your body and in turn goes into the meridians, or channels of the subtle body, and it then takes a long time to purify them. Have you seen a friend after no contact for years, who has been diligent in spiritual and health practices, and that person looks so terrific, you think she or he had a face lift? However, what she had was a good thoughts, good spoken words and good actions uplift. On the other hand, haven't you ever seen a friend after a long interlude who appears to have aged so much? What aged her or him? The years? Contrary to popular belief, years of themselves cannot age anybody. How could they? Years cause us to get older, not necessarily to age. However, how we have thought, spoken, acted, conducted our lives, imbibed of food and drink, all that sticks within us and that can age us. Those pull everything down, give us the so-called aging 'long face."

"Beware of arrogance, Dear Ones. Be humble. Remember that whatever others make of you, God doesn't care about your wealth, your beauty or your position in life. Oh, God wants you to have nice things and beauty in your life, all right, but God really only cares about the love in your heart.

Humility is hard to define, but one of its signs is wanting to perform the good deeds neither seeking nor expecting credit for it. A humble person also thinks first of others and indulges in self-scrutiny in order to improve self. A humble person welcomes constructive criticism."

We sat enthralled as Cheng continued. "Dear Ones, respect everyone and everything. When you walk, respect the floor by walking gracefully. Make each of your movements respect for God in their grace. Lose your fears by going to that place inside of you where fear does not exist; spiritual practices diminish fear and eventually eliminate them.

"Do some selfless service, without pay and without looking for reward. If you are not already doing so, I would like each of you to volunteer some service to somebody or to some people who need it. You each have something to offer and some place exists nearby where you can offer it. I will leave it to each of you to discover what and where this is. This is called Seva in Sanskrit, and is work for God, directed at others without thought of personal reward or recognition. Other than that, in your gainful work charge what you feel your services are worth; we are expected to take care of ourselves that way. Being unfairly compensated in either direction creates bad karma for both the receiver and the giver.

"Let the following phrase never leave you and remind you to always have compassion: 'Everyone I meet is going through a hard time.' Release anger as soon as possible or it becomes a cycle; it must stop somewhere; isn't now as good a time as any time ever will be? You need not condone, you need just to be willing to understand and to work on forgiveness."

Cheng paused for a while, then continued, "Our final limb of yoga is Samadhi, or absorption in God. There are several paths to this. The first is loving devotion to God through actual prayer and ritual, and devotion to some special aspect of God or divine incarnation of God. Then there is dedicating the fruits of one's actions to God. The next is through intellectual analysis. And through doing our work well. These categories should not be too strictly defined. Actually, no one limb of yoga can be practiced with absolute exclusion of any of the others. For example, if we love minus discrimination we will invite enormous problems.

"And so, in summary, the eight limbs of yoga are; meditation, or Dyana; the postures, or Asanas; control of prana, or Pranayama; concentration, or Dharana; withdrawal of the mind from sense objects, or Pratyahara; the various abstentions, or Yamas; the observances, or Niyamas; finally, absorption in God, or Samadhi.

"Think of these, Dear Ones. Observe, remember, practice each to the best of your abilities. Resist temptations to do otherwise - temptations that will bring you toward the darkness rather than toward the light. Temptations are everywhere and can be enticing and compelling; everybody is tempted, even the Great Ones like Jesus and Buddha were tempted. When we meet here next time, we will have our next to final Discourse. Blessings."

CHAPTER TWENTY SEVEN: DISCOURSE TEN- The Inner Veils, Or The Enemies

"From attachment, desire is born
From desire, anger arises
From anger, comes delusion, loss of memory
From loss of memory
the destruction of discrimination.
From the destruction of discrimination,
one perishes."

--Bhagavad Gita

"Because we are prepared to give the staff so much, most come in early and work late, although we rarely ask them to. And there is genuine feeling of trust and affection in the office. If you are generous to people, you allow them to give freely; when you are greedy, you take before they can give and often kill their impulse to give."

--Owner of a business firm who follows yogic philosophy.

We, the Cheng Gang, were again assembled and once more Cheng was standing before us. Except this time he had his back to us. It wasn't a chance momentary posture; it was calculated. As I sat trying to figure this out, I felt three staccato taps on my forearm from Nancy, seated to my left.

"Look at him!" she whispered, pointing her chin toward Cheng."Is tonight's lesson on how to be rude, or what?" I whispered back, "I doubt it's that, but whatever it is, it is different."

At that moment Cheng turned 180 degrees to face us. I looked at him, blinked twice, then stared. Clearly, everyone else was reacting similarly. Cheng's face was completely covered with gray material – was it a scarf? – with only his eyes and mouth exposed. Nancy again turned to me and whispered, "Different was an understatement!"

"Dear Ones, good evening," Cheng said in a muffled voice. "Can everybody hear me?"

Serge, seated to my right, leaned toward me and stage-whispered, "I'd hear him better if he'd take that stupid schmata off his mouth. But I don't need one on *my* mouth to know not to tell him that."

"Oh, *you're* good!" I whispered back, rolling my eyes upward.

"This morning," Cheng continued, "you cannot clearly see nor hear the true Cheng because he is obscured by this veil. What is a veil? For this you can just call out answers. Anybody?"

"A veil's for women to cover their faces with in some foreign countries," Mindie ventured. "It's a custom."

"Good. Anyone else?"

Serge raised his hand, prompting Cheng to tell him, "Now we know how to get you to be acknowledged, Serge. Simply tell you it isn't required. Alright then, you can speak now."

"In the Jewish orthodoxy a woman at a funeral covers her face with a black veil," Serge offered.

"Fine. Anyone else?"

Silence.

"I see." Cheng's eyes indicated that beneath his "mask" he was smiling. "So, by this class's definition, veils are for women of *other* cultures unless the women are Jewish. And veils have nothing to do with me."

Again, silence.

Cheng hoisted a large book onto the coffee table, slapped its cover several times, and instructed, "When in doubt, go to Mr. Webster or his colleagues. Val-teen, will you be so kind to look up definition of veil."

As directed, I stood, walked to the front of the room, opened the large book, looked up the word veil, and read the following definition: "Veil: To cover, obscure or conceal."

"Thank you, Val-teen, you can please again sit down. So now we know that a veil covers something. Something covered is obscured." With that statement, Cheng, in one deft motion, untied the gray scarf, yanked it from his face, then waved it in front of us. "Do you like Cheng better with or without the veil?" he asked. "Call out this one further time only."

"Without it," came our unanimous chorus.

"Why so?" Cheng asked.

"Because," Serge answered, "With that mask-thing on you looked like a robber -- an enemy. See," he added. "I remembered not to be acknowledged."

"What else is new?" Andrew remarked dryly, eliciting a smile from Cheng, who then exclaimed with obvious delight, "Yes, Serge!! We all wear such veils, on the *inside*. They *are* the enemy. The do rob us -- of our repose, our contentment, our dignity. They are the enemies to our love, kindness, and generosity. They do mask our higher Selves. I call them the eleven veils. Yoga calls them 'the inner enemies,' and they are as follows: Anger," Cheng said, pulling a black scarf from a basket on the desk and holding it up. Then he proceeded to call out ten further character traits, punctuating each one by pulling out and displaying another scarf of a murky color. "Desire/attachment," Cheng said. "Pride; envy/jealousy; worry; greed; infatuation; sense of unworthiness; sense of separation; dishonesty; lack of self-discipline.

"Can you imagine had I faced you wearing all these veils at once?" Cheng asked pointedly. "Imagine had I tried to communicate with you, stood up to teach you, wearing all those veils! Yet many people, sometimes even teachers of spirituality, do wear them, on the inside. No wonder it's so difficult to see who we all really are.

"Actually, there is only one category of enemy; fear. All the veils- anger, jealousy and the rest, stem from that one. Due to these inner veils we ruin our relationships, cut off our noses to spite our faces, demean ourselves. And unnecessarily. The enemies are just habit patterns, character traits that we've become very attached to. We have carried them with us from many years, many lifetimes.

"They become attached to us by a certain formula; repetition + strong emotion. Anything fed to us with that formula becomes our perceived so-called truth, our ego. The ego tells us the following lies: that we are separate from everyone else, that we are our body-mind, thoughts, emotions.

"The truth is that we have a body, mind, thoughts, and emotions, but they are *not* us. This puts a vastly different perspective on things. The antidote for fear is love. How can we end the patterns, toss off the veils? Yoga tells us how. It is so simple I'm almost embarrassed to tell you. Do the practices. Especially, observe your thoughts as separate from yourself. Knowing that they are no more us than the clouds are the sky, we can watch them come and go and mentally repeat, 'I *have* these thoughts, aren't they interesting? I *am not* my thoughts.' Then we can substitute a positive useful thought, which has more light, a higher frequency, than for the negative thoughts which carry a lower frequency and less light. So when we consciously change a negative thought to a positive one, immediately we change our light. Light is awareness. We have only to look at your English language; "Let's put some light on the subject"; "Lighten up"; "A light switched on"; and the term "enlightened" for the fully conscious person. If the negative thoughts are persistent, compulsive, we can instead choose to first just go deeply into them. A thought is accompanied by a feeling. So, get deeply into the feeling. More on this in a minute. I did mention this previously, if you recall."

"Do Japa, that is, mentally repeat your mantra not only in meditation but in your daily life. You can know that whatever your misdeeds, sins, mistakes committed through this body/mind, your GodSelf always shines very brilliantly within you and within each other person. As you come to know this, the veils evaporate.

"Let me now briefly discuss each of the veils and ways to shed them. This is a vast complex subject which I will outline tonight. Hopefully all of this will be immeasurably useful to each one of you. Those who wish to can pursue the 'For Further Reading' list that I will later give you.

"Now, once again, get deeply into the feeling" Cheng said. "Take fear. When you feel afraid, if possible just sit quietly and feel the feeling. Observe it with interest, as in 'how interesting, now my chest feels tight,' or 'This is intriguing, now my heart is beating fast." Stay with that feeling, really get deep into what's happening in that chest of yours. Keep reminding yourself the feeling is not you and continue to sit quietly and observe it. First it will intensify. Stay with it and observe. As you observe it, it will then diminish, often then vanish. Whereas, if you flee from fear, then you've put fear on top of fear thus now you have double fear. It is not the original fear but the double fear, which consumes you. Know that because God is within you nothing bad can really happen to you. If your fear involves another person, above all avoid acting out of your fear in a manner hurtful to them. Far better in such a situation to admit your fear to the person, or just recognize it within yourself.

Andrew had a question. "Wouldn't a woman think less of me if I said, 'I'm afraid?'"

"If a woman ever does that to you, that would be her problem so don't make it yours." Cheng replied. "The majority of the time that will not happen. You all believe people shun you due to your faults, whereas it is your ugly defenses - uglier than the faults - which offend them. Our stuff is far more attractive, believe it or not, than are our cover-up defenses. So stop working so hard to hide it. Put the energy you used to cover up toward your spiritual growth.

"Let's now discuss attachment/desire. Fix your attention on the energy you're feeling, which at that moment is desire, rather than on the object of desire. Shift focus from the object to the feeling itself. We are now witnessing rather than being consumed by the desire. Miraculous change occurs. Mind gets still. We feel content, balanced. We can ignore the objects of our desire. Next step, pray in your own way. Letting go frees us. Doesn't mean we stop enjoying. We let go of the desire, which causes pain, inner conflict, distress, and consumes us. For the difficult desires, we can pray 'God, I'm out of control; you handle this however you will.'

"Or ask yourself, 'If I took this desire to its logical conclusion, what would the result likely be?' If the answer is fulfillment, you might go for it. If the answer is that the result would be detrimental, simply experience that feeling so that you know that you can have the feeling without necessarily having the object. You see, you can drop the desire for that person or thing and have the feeling." I thought of Brandt.

"Now, infatuation," Cheng continued, "When you find yourself infatuated with another person, feel that feeling inside your heart and picture God sitting there. In this way you don't deny the longing feelings, you transmute them. Before you had put another person where God should be; now you've put God back in His/Her rightful place." Again, I thought of Brandt.

Serge had a question. "I don't understand this enemy, so-called," he offered. "Are you saying spiritual people shouldn't want nice things or to be with a loved one?"

"I am not saying that," Cheng explained. "I am just saying that when we ascribe extraordinary powers or attributes or auric glows to another individual, what we are really seeing in them is our own true nature with which we haven't adequately identified." A third time, Brandt!

"Let's go on to the next veil," Cheng said. "This one is pride. This is like ego. It also goes along with the enemy 'sense of separation.' Pride is the feeling and/or behavior that we are different, somewhat better or worse than others. We must keep reminding ourselves that categorizations of better or worse are all maya, or illusion, because at our essential core we are all the same. It is the insecurity of pride that makes people crave attention and recognition. It is the unlit candle running around shouting, 'Look at me! Look at me!' But nobody looks for long. There's fleeting if any appeal there. But think of the lit candle. It doesn't have to say anything. It just shines its light and like moths to a flame, attracts multitudes. As the Bhagavad Gita says, "I am the strength in the strong but without pride. Pride converts strength into weakness."

"Next veil, 'envy/jealousy,'" Cheng continued. Telling yourself, 'Whatever I perceive about what another person has is only the tip of the iceberg,' can dissipate that. Everyone alive is having a difficult time because just living in this world is difficult. I will envy no one." We never envy an entire picture; we envy the thing or things about another person that we feel we don't have yet want. Concerning anyone whom you envy, ask yourself what they have that you want, and why you want it. Then in your mind, bring having that thing to its conclusion as best you can foresee that probability. Finally, if after that you still want that thing, if you still believe that end result would be beneficial, you can work toward having a semblance of that thing yourself. It's a big universe. There is enough to go around.

"Let us now look at the veil of 'worry.' Worry serves no useful purpose, although you clearly think otherwise judging by the extent to which you indulge in it, is that not so?" Cheng gave his giggle. "Worry not only serves no useful purpose, it in fact makes things worse. For it's a heavy energy, so it intensifies problems. Once you believe that worry is a totally negative habit, when you catch yourself worrying, tell yourself, 'I refuse to worry,' and substitute a positive thought. Then you can go the next step, which is to laugh when a difficulty arises. In this way, the difficulty will dissipate even faster.

"Now greed rears its ugly head," Cheng went on. "The descriptive phrase for greed is 'more, more, more.' Remember, the Bhagavad Gita says, "The path to hell is paved with greed." The antidote is to know, 'I have God within me, I am already enough. I can be content with what I have.'"

Ginger wanted to know, "And not strive for more?"

"Striving is alright, but not out of greed,or out of delusion that things will bring everlasting contentment."

"Dishonesty," Cheng continued, "Is usually due to feelings of unworthiness. The need to impress, the need to lie so as to seem acceptable. One lie leads to another, and then one must remember all the details of the lies. Lying causes tension. In most things we should all strive to be truthful or silent.

"Lack of self-discipline," Cheng continued. "Self-discipline at first feels difficult and unnatural, then as one continues with it, it begins to feel better, after that it feels good, and soon it becomes like breathing; we wonder how we lived without it. Take physical exercise, or meditation as examples. All these steps occur progressively. Lack of self-discipline can lead to sloth or excess. Self-discipline is most necessary for health, maximum effectiveness and general well being. It is certainly necessary for sadhana or spiritual practices.

"As for sense of unworthiness," Cheng went on, "You can see that all the other veils tie into sense of unworthiness. In fact, each one of the veils in some way impacts upon the next; e.g., jealousy/envy and greed often tie-in together.

"Dear Ones," Cheng concluded, "Our primary goal should be to become better functioning people, to live dharmically or rightly, to find our specific soul's purposes in the world and fulfill that. That and faith in our purpose will keep us centered, connected and focussed. It will keep the enemies at bay.

"Your homework," Cheng said, "Is for you to stay alert in order to be aware of when your veils come on, to recognize them honestly. That takes courage. This will be least painful if we identify them but don't identify with them. Veils are not to be ashamed of, merely to be handled and eventually totally eliminated. So when you are in the throes of a veil, remember -- *you have it, you are not it*. In a relationship, if it is between owning up or wrongly blaming the other person, admit to the veils, don't strive to hide them.

Again defenses are uglier by far. Your motivation? The Bhagavad Gita says, 'True bliss is naught but perfect tranquility of the mind, untainted by any fear, anger or greed.'

"Dear Ones, that concludes tonight's Discourse."

With a flourish Cheng gathered up all the veils, dramatically held them up, then one by one threw them into the wastebasket. Finally he walked out of the room.

Again! Surprise the person, still the mind, and throw in the teaching.

I sat quietly after that. Cheng had given me much to think about, including Brandt. I hadn't thought about him for quite some time.

CHAPTER TWENTY-EIGHT: DISCOURSE ELEVEN- The Final One
The Powers, and Knowing God

"A courageous soul who has the strength to stop the wind with his hand and can control an elephant with a lotus stalk, can also protect his chastity and honor."

--Lalleshwari

"It's not what you are that holds you back. It is what you think you are not."

--Denis Waitley

"It's your good fortune, all of you, to be here tonight," Cheng enthused, standing in front of us. "This final Discourse is to give you at least a taste of how magnificent your God Self really is. Tonight you are ready to hear of Siddhis; the Powers of Yoga."

"Sometimes a person is born having some Siddhis, developed from having done sadhana, or, spiritual practices, in past lifetimes," Cheng explained. "Or, they are developed and expanded upon in this lifetime. More likely it's a combination of the two."

"When in meditation you become absorbed in perceiving not the mantra or any externals, rather only the internal sensations, that is called samadhi. That is obtained from concentration on only one thing such as the mantra, or the breath. From this attainment all the powers come under one's control. This is not the highest form of samadhi, but it is samadhi nonetheless. When through long practice that impression is retained by the mind, one can know the past and the future. At that point, if we think of past experiences we will begin to remember all of our past lives. Additionally, when we concentrate on the individuality of another person, we come to know the nature of that person's mind."

Andrew raised his hand, gained recognition and asked, "Do you mean that if I should achieve that state, then I'd know if my girlfriend's criticism is sincere or manipulative?"

"Yes, you would have that acute perception, Andrew," Cheng affirmed. "Additionally, when a yogi has attained such power of concentration that the form and the object have been separated, this yogi can stand in the middle of the room and disappear; which is not to say he necessarily actually disappears, however he just does become invisible to others."

"He *just* becomes invisible to others?" Serge blurted out, while there were audible drawings in of breaths from the rest of us.

"Yes. Although if he wishes he can make himself visible to a select person or persons and invisible to all the others in the same vicinity."

"Oh, well then *that's* different," Serge countered. "At first I had trouble accepting that somebody could make themselves invisible. But once you explained that at the same time he could remain visible to a few, *then* this whole getting invisible thing became a piece of cake. Do you want us to fucking *believe* this?"

"Yes," Cheng said, ignoring Serge's profanity and outburst, "because it's the truth. These powers *can* become available to us all. I shall now continue. I will describe the other siddhis."

Cheng then went on to do just that almost non-stop except for several questions from us students. Mostly, we were too fascinated to interrupt him for any reason.

Specifically, Cheng expounded as follows:

"By concentration on the strength of an elephant and like creatures, the yogi gets the strength of an elephant. Yes, Dear Ones, infinite energy is at the disposal of us all, and the yogi has discovered the science of obtaining it."

"I shall continue in this vein. When we practice concentration on the light in the heart, we can then begin to see things which are very remote, such as happenings in distant places." Again the sound of drawing in of breaths.

"If we are hungry and practice concentration on the hollow of the throat, hunger ceases. Good for dieters, yes? Similar powers come from practicing the limbs of yoga, such as supernatural hearing like hearing sounds uttered many miles away; the yogi can hear anything he wants to. Also the already mentioned supernatural seeing, and super natural tasting, smelling, touching. The yogi can likewise walk on fire, thorns or so forth, know the exact time of his so-called death - which is said to be an advantage because what we think at the time of our death will influence our afterlife and rebirth. The yogi can also be in multiple places at a time."

Jack, after recognition, exclaimed, "Cheng, let me be honest. This seems impossible. I mean, I can accept that it could be possible for certain special great beings. But, for me? Hardly!"

"The special great beings are here to teach us that we are all special great beings. We simply have to grow into that understanding." Cheng paused to make his point, then continued.

"Now having told Serge, Jack, all of you about these Siddhis - and I can attest to the fact that there *are* people much like yourselves who have obtained all of them, and that all of you will obtain some, or all, in time - I must warn you that these Siddhis or powers should be signposts along the way, not goals. The goal is true yoga, true uniting with the pure Self, with God. Do not tempt yourself, nor be tempted by anyone, to make the acquisition of these Siddhis your goal. When they come, they come, that's all. Take note of them, use them quietly to help people if you feel moved to do so, mainly keep moving on toward the final goal, Self-Realization/union with God. In that only is bliss. Only that is the goal of life. Only that will bring you true happiness.

There are so-called gurus who have developed certain Siddhis, which they display publicly to impress and to gain followers. Beware of such teachers. They, not having reached the final goal, enlightenment, cannot lead others to it. If somebody proclaims him or herself a guru, a wise person should investigate how they earned that title. A true guru is not self-proclaimed, rather has been appointed by his own Self-Realized master after many years of sadhana and dedication. Such a one is totally enlightened and qualified for the job. Remember Viveka. The Bhagavad Gita says that one without a sense of distinction between good and evil is headed for ruin. This is so important, thus I repeat it often."

Serge got recognized –and by that simple act inspired us all to keep the faith - and asked, "You mean the bigger the hype the larger the crowds?" Cheng answered, "Not always. It's true that fakes sometimes attract many followers but sometimes so do genuine teachers. Once again, Viveka, discrimination, is necessary.

"And so, tonight already you have been given a complete teaching. What you do with it will, of course, be your responsibility. Now we will proceed to 'Knowing God.'"

But before Cheng could say more, Nancy interrupted with an urgent wave of her hand. Cheng nodded to recognize her.

"Cheng, please wait. I need to understand where personal love fits in here. Or, does it?" she implored.

Cheng smiled benevolently. "I'm assuming you mean romantic love?" Nancy nodded. " Of course it fits in here, Nancy. Love in all its forms is the entire issue to be honored on this planet. Do not be afraid to long for that type love, Dear Ones. Until that comes along, romance *yourself.* Become *your own* lover in a robust wholesome rather than dried up spinster or widower way. That is what we are here to do with ourselves in any case. *Be* with yourself, allow the world to speak to you, and you will never be lonely with or without a mate."

I hardly had the chance to digest that nugget when Cheng paused, took a sip of water and with hardly a breath, no break and nary a note, gave us the next complete teaching."

"A Siddha, or perfected being, sees everyone as the same as his own Self," he said. "You realize, I hope, that whether I use the male or female pronoun I mean he and she. For equality I'll use the female pronoun for a while. A true teacher sees all she teaches as extensions of her own self." At that Cheng grinned, whereby I fell in love with his smile anew.

"Once we can see each person as that, our awkwardness, our defensiveness, our power struggles, should cease," he continued. "In truth, then, blame serves no good purpose. Would we have a dream about somebody harming us, awaken, then rush to his or her door and give that person a punch, saying, 'In my dream you hurt me, so take this!' If we did that the person would rightly think us insane! They'd likely ask, 'Why blame *me*? I didn't do anything. It's *your* dream.' Then why blame another in life? Why hold a grudge? Why not instead think, 'Thank you for showing me where I still get stuck, where I am still affected by others.' But not to get confused here. In a respectful loving way we still must hold others accountable. We must not let them use us as a rug. We can teach others to treat us better. I always think of a former student who told me, 'I wait for anyone for fifteen minutes and no one for sixteen minutes.' This wise lady was teaching people that she and her time deserved to be respected."

"Dear Ones, let us open our hearts and allow our love to flow outward. That love *is* within our hearts. If we feel it, we need not do another thing. Others will feel that love just as the sun's rays emanate effortlessly from the sun and warm everyone in its path."

"We need to learn a new system beyond controlling, Dear Ones. God does what must be done. We can relax and let go. We will then act when we need to and do it correctly. Like riding on a benevolent wave we can go along for the ride. It is so easy. We can have goals, lofty ones, but everything should not depend upon them. Whatever our goals may be, knowing the Self is our primary goal. Without that, the achievement of all other goals will never make us happy. In the new millennium external power will no longer be an effective form of power; the internal power of knowing the Self will be the true power."

Cheng lowered his voice to a whisper. "Dear Ones, let me tell you an important yogic secret. When our mind is focusing on externals, jumping from one desire, one thought, to the next, it's impossible to feel the bliss of the Self. It's always there within us but we can't access it that way.

Each satisfied desire may fake happiness for a while because when we obtain what we set out to obtain, the mind temporarily stops jumping. The mind will do the same when it becomes scared - witness the popularity of horror movies and scary activities. At such times of danger or fright the mind becomes still temporarily, and as I just explained it is when the mind becomes still that it can take us to where the bliss and contentment of the inner Self reside. Practice yoga and you will attain that state permanently. I am not advising that you necessarily give up having and achieving, but I am telling you that if you simply satisfy each desire, each satisfied desire will lead to a further desire, the unfortunate result being a never-ending cycle of dissatisfaction. People who achieve fame or wealth and expect that in itself to bring happiness end up sorely disheartened. "

"Dear Ones, as I believe I have demonstrated through these classes, true closeness with others comes through energy exchange, not mere words. This inner transmission is conveyed through the heart and from out of the eyes." I thought of my earlier teacher's compelling eyes, then looked at Cheng's eyes, even more compelling than their's. It was a fact. All that Cheng taught was true.

"Feel what you feel. Depression is actually a repression of what we truly feel," Cheng continued. "We want to experience our emotions, to become intimate with them. Follow the feeling back to its source. For example, you are about to begin a business but you feel sad rather than elated. Follow that sadness back and you'll learn your unconscious feeling about it. Then you can make a conscious decision about that business. Watch your thoughts and feelings without identifying with them. If you must label them, they are '*an* anger,' not '*my* anger.' Your mind will slow down in that way. I've already told you the wonderful things that happen when your mind becomes still. So, experience your feelings but don't make them yours. Remember, not *my* anger. It is just anger, just feelings, just passing-show. Practice not being the doer, Dear Ones. Watch your mind as it thinks. Watch your body as it walks. Experience that you are not doing it. Eventually it will become perfectly normal for you to be spontaneous. You will hear yourself talking to another even in 'important' situations, without knowing what you are going to say next until you actually hear yourself saying it. Again, when that happens initially you are frightened. Only when you begin to see that in this way everything works out just as well, better than when you controlled each word, do you see it for what it is; a tremendous drop of a burden off your shoulders."

"As we progress on the spiritual path we will increasingly act as the wise ones do. It will be less important to follow the majority or to want their good opinion of us. We will increasingly follow the inner truth rather than other's so-called truths, follow our so called intuition, which is a manifestation of the loving guidance always there for us. Epictetus said, 'Who arc those by whom you wish to be admired? Are these not the men whom you generally describe as mad? What do you aspire to, then? To be admired by madmen?' So, if the majority of ignorant people agree on something, that does not make it right, in fact the reverse is more often true. Or, as George Bernard Shaw put it so well, 'Fifty million Frenchmen can't be *right*.'"

"I will right now tell you the secret of unhappiness: pleasing others. We have to forget that conditioning. If we try to please everybody out there, not only will we never do anything worthwhile, additionally we'll make ourselves crazy. We need to please our true Self within, God, that is all. We can develop the attitude and approach of a warrior by accepting our karma cheerfully and then doing whatever we need to change things. Remember these three things: the nature of life is change, so flow with change, don't resist it. A yogi turns everything to his advantage. And, treat your obligations as a work of art, and one day your obligations will become your treasure."

"I want to address for a moment resolving conflicts in relationships," Cheng continued, "When we feel we have done so, we have really resolved some conflict within ourselves. In this way we can learn to resolve conflicts with anybody in an instant. We never have to change another person – which is impossible anyway. We should never take offense. It is just as bad to take offense as to give offense. It is healthy, it is dharmic, to respond, that is, to choose how to act. It is not so to react. Responding is more conscious, more in tune with the God-Self. Reacting is more from the past samscaras. It is more unconscious."

"Love is the most important thing in life, Dear Ones. Here's the ultimate secret about love. Through yoga we discover the love within ourselves. As we touch that love, we touch the love in all others. We become compassionate without being co-dependent. If we multiply the love of a good mother or father for a child by millions of times, that is the magnitude of the love in our heart. We can be appropriate, and should. Love is not always synonymous with sweetness. Those who think otherwise are in deep mud. We can love and act angry. We can love and correct. Sometimes it's loving not to 'be nice.'"

"Loving is forgiving, silently or verbally affirming, 'I forgive you for whatever you had to do; I love you as you are.' Forgiving is liberation to the one who forgives. Yet, hear this, Dear Ones; at times you may have to hide your forgiveness for a while to allow the other person the space to think and do his/her growth work. When somebody apologizes after repeatedly doing something very hurtful and your immediate response each time is, 'It's alright,' you are teaching them that it's alright to do it the next time. However, suppose the next time that they do it you say, "I hear that you're sorry, however you hurt me so badly that I can't talk with you right now. Maybe another time." And then you turn your back and walk out. *That* is likely to make an impression.

"Remember, the world is maya, illusion, a play. People who seem happy might not be, while those who seem unhappy might be happy. Very wealthy people don't necessarily have greater happiness in their lives than most people, just more activity. Remind yourselves continuously, 'This physical world is just an appearance, not eternal life.' We can still play our appropriate roles."

"The physical world to the average person actually moves very slowly, is rather bulky, heavy and uninteresting, as if we were at the bottom of the ocean weighted down by a suit of steel. It is as we rise spiritually that life goes faster. Now things literally become interesting. It's a progression. When we "die" of course things become even better and more interesting than ever." Cheng giggled in delight, then composed himself and continued.

"Always remember, you are God. We can cover a diamond with dirt; it is still a diamond. We are in the process of uncovering and polishing your diamond. In that process there will be friction. But it is all for good."

"Life is a dream. Awaken from the dream. Know the truth about yourself regardless of what others say about you; they are seeing you from their own perceptions anyway. One of my great teachers once said, 'When something happens in your life, know that you deserve it.' Remember the Zen saying: 'there is nothing in your life for which you did not strike a hard bargain.' The physical world will be full of surprises and shakeups. A spiritually mature person knows this and accepts it. A spiritual moron whines and protests. When we are close to the True Self we experience a humor and lightness in everything. We are aware that what's out there is merely a play."

"When Moses asked God who he was, God answered, 'I am that I am.' In the same way we must each come to know, 'I am THAT, I am!' Try saying it that way. Maya causes this dream to seem very real. Participate without falling for appearances. We can pretend we are two, we are three, we are many; in reality, we are all one. Haven't we experienced some of that here? We must be appropriate. We don't necessarily want to rush up to people and proclaim, 'We're one!' however, we can *feel* it. Practice seeing everyone else as your self. Work on it where you have difficulty. It is powerful. Watch the karmic movie of your life while actively participating. Don't talk negatively about others; it takes one to see one. You might practice being that person, contemplating what it must be like being him or her."

"Let us do a dharana now, an exercise to know Truth. Close your eyes." Cheng began to speak slowly and softly. "Visualize an individual you've had difficulty with. Enter his or her body. See yourself as this person. Feel his/her feelings. Look out at the world from his/her eyes."

Cheng was quiet for five minutes while we did the dharana. I thought of Brandt. I entered his body. I felt two things, fear and insecurity. Brandt?! I was beyond surprised. Then I heard Cheng say, "This is a powerful dharana. It helps us develop compassion. Everyone has their own samscaras, their own karma, to go through. We can't know what that is, so how can we accurately judge or criticize?"

"Eventually most of us will leave this particular body. At that time we will have a true realization that all that is real about us - our mind, ego, feelings, samscaras - is still very much with us. We are eternal. Nobody dies." At those words I thought of my out-of-body experience at Glady's house shortly after I'd been discharged from the hospital, and knew that once again Cheng spoke the truth. "Once we become accustomed to being in our subtle rather than physical body," Cheng went on, "the physical incarnation we just finished will seem like a dream. We will be in a much lighter body instead of the physical heavy body we literally formerly had to drag around with us."

Serge began to speak without first raising his hand, then, realizing his mistake, smacked his forehead with the back of his hand. Immediately following that gesture, he raised that same hand. "Changes may come slowly and we can all slip backward many times," Cheng humorously acknowledged Serge while concurrently slipping in another teaching.

"I'm sorry I forgot again," Serge apologized, then lamented, "God, have I done things wrong! I mean, even more serious things than my behavior here."

"To see our flaws, to admit to ourselves that we've done things unwisely, is a great spiritual practice. It can be wonderful for our sadhana," Cheng responded. "Just, use it to grow, not to feel guilty about."

"We are all in the same earth-boat," Cheng offered. "Eventually each of us will enter the divine light. Not all of us are going to achieve liberation in this lifetime, so many of us will return to the play of this lifetime to repeat the cycle until we make it. Spiritually it is very simple, actually. No need to complicate it. Go within yourself regularly with meditation/contemplation. Remember what the road to hell is paved with – greed. To put yourself or anyone else down is committing spiritual suicide; don't do it; love and respect others as well as yourself. Be cheerful whatever, and see God in everything and everyone. It is easy to know God if we only remember to see Him as the Light within us and in all. I gave you the secret of unhappiness so let me now give you a simple secret of happiness as stated in the Bhagavad-Gita. You wish to be happy? Then spread happiness wherever you go. You wish to feel good? Then see only good in others.

"Each of you *will* achieve Self-Realization. Just before that occurs, you will experience a tremendous chasm. You will feel you simply haven't the strength to go across. At that very moment all your sadhana, all the work that you've done on yourself and all the experiences from which you have grown until then will give you the strength *to* go across."

We were all mesmerized silent. Each of us drew in an audible breath. What specific Truths Cheng had just given us!

"We have achieved the state of family in this classroom," Cheng continued, looking around. "Although this is our last formal class together, hopefully you will all remain a family in whichever ways you select. We have been together in past lifetimes so we met here again in this way. Similarly, if we consider all our many incarnations, we have quite a large family and circle of friends. People we knew in past lifetimes with whom we connected in this lifetime, because we have something to learn from one another for our soul's growth. And that is the true meaning of 'Soul Mates.' We each have many, not just one. Here in the West you confuse 'Soul Mates' with 'Spiritual Intimate Partners.' Even with the latter, there are many possible ones for each of us, not just one. The whole world is our family. Know yourself, and you will know THAT."

"Know you are God and see God in each other as you go do your dharma in the world." Cheng told us. " Mainly, don't slack off. Do the work. Practice all that you have learned here. Most people are advised to benefit by the teachings in these Discourses by this step-by-step process."

It seemed a reach for me to believe that I'd ever be able to do all those things let alone achieve Realization, but I did know yoga brought miracles. Afterall, I was down to two cigarettes a day!

Cheng then passed each of us a handout entitled "Cheng's Summary Of The Discourses and Practices," saying, "I advise most people to follow this outline for a period of one year and then reevaluate themselves. * I promise those who do will be thrilled with their progress and ready to move on to even loftier goals by whatever ways that they decide."

Finally Cheng took a deep victorious breath, then smiled a huge smile while throwing his arms to the ceiling. "And so, Dear Ones, the Discourse classes have come to an end! My heart goes with you. Blessings, blessings and more blessings," he exclaimed.

With that and a wave Cheng disappeared into a back room, leaving us once again with the tea and one another. Only this night there were also many hugs, kisses and tears. Our graduation from the Discourses was bittersweet. For each of us, the real beginning was dawning.

* Chengs Summary Of The Discourses and Practices is reproduced for the reader in the Appendix to this book.

CHAPTER TWENTY-NINE: THE JUNGLE

"Whenever we waiver from our dharma, our duty, our goal becomes hazy and we are unable to see where we want to go."
--Gurumayi Chidvilasanada

"Everyone should carefully observe which way his heart draws him, and then choose that way with all his strength."
--Martin Buber

In choosing and trusting a spiritual teacher one should use discrimination. Here a leap of faith is needed; it is only through personal experience that one gains real proof of any teacher's true value. I was fortunate; progressively I came to experience Cheng's greatest value; all that he had taught us was true.

For example, I *was* experiencing an increase in spontaneity. I would open my mouth and utter things which I'd had no plan to say. Indeed, more often than not these days my utterances were as much a surprise to me as to the listener. Also as Cheng had predicted, at first this made me frightened, but each time that the results were favorable, I increasingly came to trust this spontaneous speech. A perfect example was an instance at the studio several weeks after Cheng had given us the final Discourse.

That morning I'd taken the train with Max as usual. "You're doing your work dharma, aren't you, Max?" I asked, believing I meant it rhctorically.

"You mean, is being a psychiatrist my work dharma? I used to believe so. Lately I worry that I'm not giving enough of the spiritual. But, it will happen."

"Only if you make it."

"Pardon me?"

"I SAID, only if YOU *make* it happen. Spirit suggests to us, it doesn't move us; that's up to us."

After a surprised pause Max answered, "Valentine, you're right, of course. Cheng said most people in the world are mad, so why let madmen dictate our actions? All that's over for me as of now."

"I'm very happy that you've decided that."

"Thank you for the push. And, you, Valentine, what about your work dharma?"

"I'm not doing it. Oh, my work's served its purpose. I'm just... not sure... it's right any more. At the right time I'll know."

"Only if you make yourself know."

"Great comeback, Max. What was that, instant karma?"

* * *

That morning everything at the studio was status quo. Ernie shrieked, models arrived on go-sees and left, people walked on and off the sets, the stereo blared *I Feel For You* by Chakka Khan and other current hits, while Zarela dashed around conveying messages.

I was in the office hurriedly examining some prints when Ernie blew in, his head turned the other way as he shouted to Stu some left over conversation. Recently Zarela had mentioned how Ernie and Stu no longer fought, just conversed loudly sometimes. She labeled it "a miracle."

"WHY THE HELL IS THE PRINT WORK SO SLOW?!," Ernie bellowed at me.

"This month was the busiest month since I came here," I corrected him, adding with some pleasure, "and probably the biggest month you've ever had. Can't you tolerate even one semi-slow day without getting bananas?"

"I like to keep busy. What we got tomorra?"

"Ernie, I'm leaving."

"Ya need a break this early? It ain't even 10:30 yet."

"I didn't mean that. I mean I'm leaving permanently."

Ernie's mouth dropped open, as did mine, I must say. I'd had no conscious idea that I was going to say that.

Apparently Ernie couldn't find his voice, which was just as well with me; I was so shocked and frightened over what I'd just told him that I didn't trust my own voice further. Finally Ernie asked, "Why, V.J?"

"Because it's time." Only after saying it did I realize that it was true.

For several minutes Ernie examined his fingernails, then offered, "Ya want thirty percent instead?"

"You'd do that? Then why didn't I tell you I was leaving two years ago?" I smiled.

Of course Ernie misinterpreted, so jumped in with, "I think...thirty percent...is do-able."

"I very much appreciate the offer, Ernie, but this isn't about money."

"If it ain't about money, what is it about, fer God's sake?!"

"It's about... love."

"What, ya got involved with somebody here at the studio? It din't work out so now ya gotta get away from him? Shit, what did you expect? Ya don't play where ya eat."

"Ernie, no, I'm not involved with somebody at the studio…"

"Oy, I knew it. It's even worse. Ya got involved with one of the clients."

"No, Ernie. I'm not talking about love with a man."

"Not love with a man?" Ernie mulled that over briefly, then smacked his head and shouted out, "Oh, my God…you're a lesbian?"

Ernie looked and sounded so funny that I had to answer between giggles, "Ernie, it isn't that kind of love either."

"What other kind is thea?" he asked, then regarded me with curiosity. "Yer inta somethin kinky?" That started me giggling again. "Ernie, get off it, alright? It isn't romantic love I'm talking about. I can't explain it to you any better than that. What matters is it's just time for me to move on to something else."

"A new career at *your* age? I don't mean ta hurt yer feelins, but..."

"You didn't hurt me, Ernie," I answered. "You just confirmed my decision. You made me realize that any career where I'm thought too old to do something else while I'm still in my thirties is no longer the right career for me!"

Foreigner singing *I Want To Know What Love Is*, boomed from the stereo while Ernie just stared at me, clearly totally perplexed. While I knew I could never make him understand, I still felt I owed him something more of an explanation. "Ernie," I tried, "It isn't about you. I'm leaving the jungle, that's all."

"Leavin' the jungle?" he repeated. "To go where? Where *ain't* it a jungle?"

"To enter the Garden of Eden," I answered.

"Ta enta da Garden of Eden?" Ernie parroted. "Ta say that takes stupidity."

"No, Ernie. It requires wisdom."

Ernie left the room, then returned several minutes later. For awhile he was uncharacteristically silent. Finally I broke the ice.

"I'll be glad to train somebody new. I'll even interview for you if you like."

"When ya plan on goin'?"

"As soon as whatever loose ends need to be tied up are tied. There's no great rush."

Wham's rendition of *Wake Me Up Before You Go-Go* blasted through the stereo.

"Na, I don't need ya to do anythin'. I'll rep myself. What I need another rep fer? I made one hundred fifty thou doin' it on my own."

"I know" I said, smiling, wondering whom I knew who might like to interview for the job.

I stayed on for two more weeks. Not to interview reps, as Ernie wouldn't even admit to me that he needed one much less let me do anything to help him get one. I simply stayed long enough to get it all straight for and with Ernie. Which turned out to work in my favor too, as several sizable checks came in for work that I'd obtained, work that I'd even forgotten about. God Bless Ernie, but had I left earlier, I would not have placed a bet on him turning my percentage over to me. These commissions would tide me over for awhile. "Thank you, God," I prayed in gratitude.

As I've mentioned, it is a small industry. On my last day with Ernie I received a phone call from Cal. "V.J, I've heard you're leaving Ernie. Is it true?" I told Cal that he'd heard correctly. "I'd really like to see you before you go," he said.

I hadn't seen or spoken much with Cal since the nude shoot incident. My initial reaction to hearing from him now was indignation. He had betrayed my trust and now he expected me to jump? But then, Cal had given me my start in New York and been good to me in many ways. So, he made a mistake. Who's perfect?

"I wish I could see you before I leave, but this is my last day so I'm really up to my eyeballs right now," I answered, meaning it.

"You're taking all your things home with you today?"

"I haven't worked all that out in my mind yet. I'll probably come in and get them tomorrow."

"How will you get them home?"

"I don't know yet. Not by car. There's no place to park near the studio. Maybe the train."

"You're planning to lug all that on the TRAIN! Why not a BUS! Look, nutty-one, I can get away tomorrow. Why don't you come in by train in the morning, get your stuff assembled, I'll have my car in front of 296 Park South whatever time you say, then I'll drive you – *and* your stuff - home."

Cal was making it too appealing for me to refuse him. "That's so nice of you, Cal," I told him. "Alright then, I accept. And - I'm not sure if you'll consider this a reward or punishment - afterwards I'll cook us dinner."

It was time for me to leave for the night, my last night. As I gathered my things and headed toward the elevator, I saw Ernie walking toward me.

"I'll carry this ta the elevator for ya," he said. He took my umbrella and raincoat. "What about the rest of ya stuff?"

"I'll come in for it tomorrow if that's allright?"

"Sure, why not? What time ya' comin'? Ernie asked. "Probably late morning," I told him. Ernie said, " I might not be able to be here then… out showin' the book." I had the distinct feeling that Ernie would make it his business to be out when I returned to leave for good.

At the elevator door Ernie pushed his hair out of his eyes, looked away, then back at me, and said, "I'll miss ya, kid."

"Thanks, Ernie." Spontaneously I gave him a hug. "You taught me a lot and it was a very valuable experience. I'm very grateful for both. Good luck to you."

Once more Ernie looked away, then back at me. "You too, kid."

* * *

At ten the next morning I arrived at the studio and immediately began getting my things together. I'd told Cal that I'd be ready to load the car at noon. As I collected my things, the various guys and girls with whom I'd worked –Duke, Dave, Tony, Janine, Dawn, came in and out of the office saying all the, "I'll miss you, good luck" things. As I'd predicted, Ernie was conspicuously absent among them.

I was finally alone in the office, sitting on the carpet surrounded by all my stuff, trying to decide what to keep and what to trash. Remembering the Yama about no-clutter, I was unsuccessfully trying to eliminate things when Jayson quietly walked in, startling me. "Darling!" he raptured, "This is the first time I'm seeing you in jeans. And with your hair in a ponytail…Gorgeous. Gor –GEOUS! If anything could make me straight, it's the way you look right now!"

"Jayson, I want you to promise me that if that should ever happen to you, you'll call me instantly. I'm not so thrilled with the straight men in my life."

"*That's* a no risk commitment that I'll readily make," Jayson chortled, hugging me.

"I'm going to miss you so much, Jayse"

"Where are you going, Siberia? You'll see me, darling. Try to get rid of me."

"Thank you Jayse, that makes me feel so good." Then I sighed. "My ride will be here in a hour, and I can't decide which things to keep and which to get rid of."

"Then let me help you. Decluttering is one of my specialties." Jayson rushed out of the office to reappear two minutes later with a large plastic bag. "To give to charity," he said, pointing to the bag. Then he began to go through my things. "What's this?" he asked, making a face as he lifted one of a pair of fake ponyskin shoes from the pile.

"I thought I'd keep those."

"Why on earth?"

"My aunt on my mother's side bought them for me for my 30th birthday."

"You've had *these* since your thirtieth birthday?! Not a second more." Jayson lifted both shoes and dropped them into the charity bag. "What else have we here?" he asked, holding up my worn red cardigan. Why, pray tell, is *this* still with us?"

"This was a gift from my mother."

"Fight the nostalgia," Jayson said, as he dropped the sweater into the charity bag. "When you're forty you'll thank me for this. Even though that's a miscalculated date, since you'll never pass 27." Next Jason held up my old raincoat. "*Explain* this to me?" he asked. "It would be all right on some street bum. Let's let one have it." The raincoat, too, went into the bag.

So, Jayson, seeming to understand how hard it was for me to let go of things, helped me by being part diplomat, part psychologist, and part pragmatist. When we had finished going through the pile, the large plastic bag was full and I was feeling lighter and freer. It was time to go meet Cal. Jason carried to the elevator my small bag of stuff that was left over after the purge. There we said "goodbye." I pressed the down button, and for the first time ever, the elevator arrived quickly.

***

At the apartment Cal helped me to unload the car. Once everything was in one heap in the foyer, he said, "Excuse me, I almost forgot something," went back to the car and returned with flowers and a bottle of wine which he handed to me ceremoniously. After thanking him profusely for everything, I gestured to the livingroom and said, "Come on in, sit down." I pointed to the couch, which Cal sank into. I took a seat in the armchair across from him. Cal, looked around, then said, "It's surely lovely in here." I answered, "Thanks to you guys. Lucky you didn't see it before that - ugghh!" Cal answered, "Well, it surely is beautiful now. Just like you. I like being here with you among your things." I answered quickly, "I've put a small something together for supper. Are you hungry?" Cal said that he was, then asked, with attempted tact, "Ah..what..is it?" looking so apprehensive that I had to laugh. "Don't worry, no sprouts or anything else exotic. Just egg plant parmagiana. I'll go shove it in the oven now and then it will take only about fifteen minutes. Can I fix you a drink meanwhile? Cal accepted some wine, then asked if he could help me with the meal. "Two people in my size kitchen? Cal, *I* can hardly fit in there" I told him. "There's the television if you like." I handing him the control. "I'll be back here soon."

In the kitchen I leaned against the refrigerator and drew a breath. Had I made a mistake inviting Cal here tonight. "*Of course* you did, dear," I mentally answered myself like a maiden aunt. "But then, you *knew* that." I opened the refrigerator door, removed the egg plant parmigiana which I'd hurriedly put together the night before, put the oven on to 375 and shoved the eggplant casserole in. So I didn't preheat the oven, let the CIO Division of Kitchens, or whatever, come after me. I took out some prepackaged greens, washed the package contents, dried them with a paper towel and put them in a glass bowl. I cut up a red pepper and added that to the mix along with some fresh garlic and diced dried onions. I mixed together some olive oil and fresh lemon juice, tossed that into the salad and placed the bowl back into the refrigerator. Then I rejoined Cal in the livingroom.

Cal broke the ice. "I was sort of afraid to call you before. I thought you were angry at me. I didn't know how you'd respond."

"I was angry, but on the other hand you were great for me in many ways. For one thing, if it hadn't been for you I'd never have gotten to work with someone like Ernie…sorry, bad example."

Cal chuckled. "Ernie's a piece of work alright, but with him what you see is what you get; kind of refreshing in this business."

Then Cal's conversation took another turn. "Valentine," he asked, "Did you think I came on to you in the studio that night because you were just one more woman and I took advantage of a situation?"

I didn't say anything.

"Well, maybe in a way I did take advantage of the situation, but ...I know this sounds egotistical… the truth is, *I* don't have to come on to anybody to get laid."

"I know that. I learned that from Jacy the day I met you. Cal, we don't have to go over this again as far as I'm concerned, but since you brought it up, I must say that what you did that evening with me was a bit beyond 'coming on to 'me!'

"I apologize for that," Cal said, "it's just that I'd wanted you for so long. I still do. Valentine, fucking without love is just friction. I'm in touch with my feelings and I am in love with you. I have been all these years…"

"Please, Cal..."

"Didn't you know?"

"No, I …I don't know what to say..."

"Just say the truth. Say how you feel about me?"

I paused while Cal waited expectantly. Finally I answered, "I like you tremendously. I admire your talent. I respect what you've done with it. I revere your focus, pardon the pun. Beyond that I don't know how I feel about you right now, or about anybody else for that matter."

"I know how I feel." Cal stood up, walked over to me and extended his hand. "I feel that I'd like you to come sit beside me on this couch instead of sitting clear across the room."

"And that's what a man calls getting in touch with his feelings?" I lamented. "I don't understand all you men!" Then I pulled myself up strong. "That's inaccurate," I proclaimed. "I *do* understand. You *talk* love but you *mean* ejaculation. I think all of you should stop using the word 'love' since you haven't the slightest idea what it means!"

"All of us? You are placing me in a category?"

"Yes, Cal, because it all boils down to one thing. Women are from Venus, men are from Penis, and relationships are from hunger. Or, to put it another way, a man is a peculiar animal anatomically. When his penis expands, his brain shrinks."

"The brain in my larger head *has* fallen in love with you," Cal insisted. "Really."

"Then, tell it to fall out of it!" I ordered.

"But why? You've been separated for quite awhile, and you say there's been nobody in your life for a long time…"

"True, and it's going to be still longer. I have a new religion. I'm a Born-Again Virgin."

I was starting to smell the aroma of the eggplant. "I'm just not ready…for any man now… but dinner is. Besides, I have a rule for myself; never go with a man whose waist size is smaller than mine!" I touched Cal's side for emphasis. "Come on, let's have dinner."

As I began to set the table Cal took the silverware from me and put it beside the plates. With his first bite of the casserole, Cal said, "This is delicious." "Especially when one expected sawdust?" I asked, laughing. "It really is great." Cal said. " I'm glad I got to taste this part of you, anyway. Sorry…I'll behave. V.J, I want to give you a farewell party. The crew at Ernie's came up with the idea and I'd like to have it at my studio."

"Cal, that's so… nice of you!" I was genuinely touched.

"Well, I'm a nice guy," Cal said, winking as he added, "Although a bit peculiar anatomically, I've been told. We wanted it to be a surprise, but on second thought we felt it would be better if you'd get us a guest list of those you'd like to have there. So, if you could do that within the next week I'll get out the invitations."

Busy as he was, Cal was going to write invitations?

"You don't have time for that. I can help."

"Don't worry, I pay my secretary. She expects to do something."

After Cal left that night without further incident, I thanked God that it hadn't been still more difficult. Then I sat down and put together the guest list. All the crew from Ernie's, Ernie and Stu, Jayson, Zarela, Dawn, Casse and Albert, Sallee-Mae and Bernie. Cheng and the Gang. Richard. I included Hinda's name and address also, although since she hadn't been in class recently I assumed she was away again.

* * *

I've always loved the magic and mystery of a New York winter night,so I was in delight the evening of the party. Richard and I drove in together.

Cal's studio was packed with people. Comically enough – and I wondered if Cal had done this deliberately – Madonna's *Like A Virgin* played softly in the background as we entered.

Cal was a terrific host, making certain that everyone had filled glasses and glowing introductions. Once Richard had become engaged in conversation with our studio comptroller, I spotted Cheng, Casse, Jayson and Max seated together. They saw me at the same time and called to me to come join them. "An interesting grouping!" I thought as I walked toward them.

"The problem I see with the feminist movement today," Max was saying, "is that many women, seeing that men failed to respect their capabilities and potential, have done the worst thing they could do to themselves – and to men..."

"You are so right, my dear," Jayson interjected. "Women understandably but unfortunately reacted in ways appearing to be imitations of the worst of male qualities."

"Exactly!" Max agreed. " Sadly, when a woman denies her femininity there is great unhappiness to pay...as is true when a man denies his masculinity."

I saw how Max and Jayson were looking at each other and thought, "Maybe...something?" delighted at the possibility.

Casse, obviously bristling with venom, interrupted my musing. "Max," she spat out, "you aren't about to give me that bullshit about men and women being different, are you?"

"I certainly am, call it what you will." Max answered firmly. I watched in fascination and admiration as Max held his own against Casse's aggression. "Social consciousness changes but the nature of men and women doesn't. There is a quintessential difference between men and women, which has always existed, and always will. It might be buried for a time but never annihilated, so again it will emerge. The differences are biological, anatomical, and psychological. Clinical studies have shown early playground behavior of each sex is different. Sexual behavior differs, too; women can't as readily separate sex from love; it's still nine minutes for him, nine months for her."

"Exactly!" Jayson agreed again.

"This makes me angry," Casse told Max.

"I agree with Max and Jayson," I heard myself saying; that was exactly how it was; I *heard* myself.

"THAT makes me furious," Casse said with wrath. She directed her next remark to the others. "Val didn't like PHW since day one."

"That isn't true."

"Don't get angry at Valentine and me," Max stepped in. "We didn't *make* men and women as they are, we're just explaining them. I begin to sense, Cassandra, that your achievements in this world, and they have been laudable, no longer satisfy you and never did fully. That you're about to come to terms with that."

"What do you *mean*?" Casse demanded.

"Allow me to answer, and to explain women, with men…who better qualified?" Jayson interjected with wry amusement in his voice. "Casse, you're actually something like Esther Greenwood, the protagonist in Sylvia Plath's *The Bell Jar*, forcing herself to succeed regardless of how she felt. Yet underneath her Amazon armor was a deep-seated depression due to denial of her femininity."

"Amazon?" I asked, intrigued. The others were obviously equally interested.

"Alright" Jayson said, "I see that I'm being given permission to be the center of attention for a bit longer, which you know I hate but I'll cope." We all laughed. If Max and Jayson were to be a pairing, it would indeed by an interesting one. Jayson was as showy as Max was subdued. Jayson continued, "Yes, the Amazon aspect is what Casse and most of her PHW members are in most of the time. Let us consider the four aspects of woman by naming them as, as Follows: The Amazon, the Courtesan, The Mother, and the Madonna aspects.

"First the Amazon: In the Greek tale the King of Athens, Theseus comes upon the island of the Amazons and seeing these warrior women with their taut bodies and mannish ways, exclaims, 'If these are the women, what are the men like?' Still, he instantly falls in love with Hippolyta, sees the woman in her beneath the man and wants her. She fights him to the death, literally, for she indeed almost kills him. But he nobly defends himself, although he later remarks, "I'm glad I don't have to do this every day!" He tells her, "…meet me, Hippolyta. A queen cannot refuse a king."

The feminine within her feels something which she had lacked, and she allows him to carry her off the field of battle."

"Just like that?" Casse asked, cynically.

"It wasn't easy for Hippolyta," Jayson answered. "In fact, as she feels growing love and closeness and commitment with Theseus, she confesses to him that her surrender to him on the battlefield left her feeling negated. 'Now I am nothing,' she tells him. However, as time passed in this relationship, Hippolyta grew into the full aspects of femininity and came to embrace a rich new identity of her essence as a woman."

"I love this metaphor, Jayson," Cheng exclaimed. "No offense, Casse, but you and your other Amazons have a cynical detachment to the men in your lives. Your feminine feelings need to begin to emerge now, along with the strength and power which you've cultivated and which is, of course, invaluable."

"Exactly," Max added. "Many contemporary women can identify with Hippolyta's conflict. They deeply fear that bonding with men will annihilate their hard-earned power. So they use and discard men, hold them at arms' length, challenge them continuously. Sex with them isn't making love, it's an athletic event or a match with them 'The Umpire' or 'Coach'. As you heard, even Theseus wouldn't have wanted to do battle with such a woman continuously, yet modern day Theseus are continuously being challenged to do just that. Unlike Theseus, most of the men today decide,'Why bother?' and leave such a woman."

Casse, like Hippolyta, wasn't going to easily relinquish the battle. "I'd like to give you some depressing statistics" she stated. "A never-married woman of 30 has a 20 percent chance of marrying. If she's 40 she has a 1 percent chance of same. 14 percent of single men are homosexual. 12 out of 13 American women who marry will eventually become widowed. Women outlive men by an average of 8 to 11 years. The current divorce rate is over 50 percent. 75 percent of these divorced women remarry while 83 percent of men do, leaving 9 million "left over" women in America and currently more than 37 million single women in this country. What do you make of that?"

Max responded, "For one thing, that you've done your statistical homework, Casse. You are saying there are six distinct possibilities: A woman will marry soon, she will marry later-perhaps later than she expected, she won't marry at all, she will marry and live forever with her mate, she will marry and be widowed, or she will marry but ultimately get divorced."

"Right!" Casse said victoriously

"Let me add," Cheng came in, "that even if you will be with a partner for the rest of your life, you must know the importance of owning your own destiny, of cultivating your autonomy. Because in the most basic way we are all responsible for ourselves. So, although in one sense we are all one, in the other sense we are all single, even if married." Cheng looked at each of us pointedly before adding, "If anything about that depresses you, know that is a certain sign that you need to work more on your autonomy."

Profound! So much so that for awhile nobody spoke. However, I had a realization that gladdened me. Whereas what Cheng had just said would once have depressed me, now it did not.

In the silence, Nancy joined our group and quietly I filled her in on what she'd missed.

"I want to hear about the other aspects of woman," she said.

Jayson gladly obliged. "The Mother is the nurturing aspect of woman. Marilyn Monroe had that. She nurtured everyone she knew. This caring aspect works very well with men's natures as long as it's kept in check and doesn't become the smothering mother aspect. Of course no service anywhere is more important than a woman's mothering of her children. The strength through bonding in our families becomes a ripple effect for the family menbers' strength in the world. Here also balance is needed, so the mother gives enough but not too much to her family, thus building, not taking away, their self-worth.

Marilyn also had the Courtesan aspect. This is the very feminine, sexual, playful, childlike, entertaining aspect of woman. Courtesans were not only highly adored throughout history, they were admired and often exhaulted to high positions by the men who had become enthralled with them.

However, Marilyn lacked one necessary aspect of woman, the Madonna, or the Goddess aspect. These are the qualities of spirituality, inspiration, and the part that helps a man restrain his sexual nature until conditions for it are right. It was because Marilyn lacked the Madonna consciousness that she was used and hurt by men. That aspect must be present along with the others for perfect balance."

"You are the Mother, Madonna and Courtesan, Valentine. An ultimate female," he added. "This is why men are so magnetized to you."

By this time Richard and Cal had joined us." I heard the tale end of that," Richard quipped, 'and I agree with most of what you just said about Valentine, except that I haven't experienced the Courtesan aspect lately. Maybe I'm missing something?"

"I agree" Cal offered.

"Didn't you hear what Jason said?" I countered. "Of course you've both experienced the Courtesan in me. Right next to my Madonna, keeping you in check."

Everybody laughed at my semi-prurient remark, and seemed to be enjoying themselves. Cheng chimed in. "Max is correct about you, Val-teen." Then he turned to Casse. "As for you, my dear one, what you need now is to submerge that Amazon that stridently criticizes, confronts and seeks to dominate men automatically. You and your friends need to realize that a woman never gets anywhere in love by challenging her man because he's geared to be combative in challenges. When confronted challengingly, he *must* go to war, so he shouts, gets defensive, doesn't even hear your point. Allow your Mother, Courtesan and Madonna strengths to emerge, and to bring that strength to the area where you are afraid yet seek with inner longing; man-woman love and commitment."

I was watched Casse's face and manner as Cheng spoke. Something remarkable was happening. Every trace of rage and combativeness drained from her. She indeed looked very vulnerable in an attractive way like I'd never seen her before. She looked - pretty. I thought of the Yamas of yoga on how a person who has no anger would render anyone in his or her presence angerless. Clearly, I had seen an example of that here tonight.

"But I think Valentine got some of my Amazon and it did her good," Casse said with a new gentleness about her.

"You are right there," Max answered. "Just as you were like Esther Greenwood, Valentine started like Nora in Henrik Ibsen's *A Doll's House*. Whereas you, Casse, have seen men as weak and inferior while you were independent and powerful, Valentine saw herself as the weak one, dependent on powerful men. While on the one hand that made her feel treasured like a princess, she also felt like Cinderella, relegated to a lesser place, powerless. Valentine had to recognize her veiled rage which formerly she considered threatening, and to allow it to emerge positively."

"She definitely learned to use her Amazon in her work," Cal offered. "You need it in this business or else they'll walk all over you."

"Sure," Cheng once more agreed. "In Hinduism Kali is the Goddess of destruction and creation. She symbolizes the many women who need to develop their power to assert themselves, to say 'no' if that's required, to get angry at times, at their men and even at God. Women have been expected to live for others. It is spiritual to see to one's own needs as well."

Felicia, who had joined us a few seconds before, asked, "How does a woman say 'no' and keep a man in check, as you called it, if she isn't to challenge him?"

"By understanding male psychology," Max said, "and the true power of the woman. A man, from the time he begins to grow up, fears psychological castration, being swallowed by a woman. Being the son of a woman he must psychologically separate from a woman in order to become a free male. This is not pathological nor immature as Amazon women belief, it is normal. A woman in a relationship with a man must not try to change him. She needs to totally accept him from deep in her heart and soul."

"This is true," Richard said. "I never could be told what to do by Valentine, I had to be persuaded. I would not go into her territory, spirituality, until she would enter mine, sports or whatever. I feared loosing control." I looked at Richard in surprise at his degree of self-awareness, honesty and willingness to be open about it.

"And, Richard, you are describing just about all of us men," Max agreed. "If a woman will offer a balanced degree of maternal warmth as a source of refuge and comfort, and express anger and disapproval when he acts badly through silent withdrawal, incredulousness, as in "I find it hard to believe that you said that," direct honest expressions of feeling, such as, "I feel hurt…etc." and/ or feistiness and spunk, e.g., "If you think you can speak to me that way you obviously don't know me very well," said as she quietly leaves the room, she is well on her way to keeping him in check and in love with her. Sometimes even unrefined honest tears can speak louder and more effectively than words. Lightness and laughter, expressions of joy and sexuality, are delightful to the mature man who usually has a disproportionate degree of seriousness to his life. The modern Amazon is afraid to show her man that she needs his help. Women must understand that part of being a man is needing to help the woman in his life. So, for God's sake, let him. You'll be less tired and he'll be happier. This doesn't mean going back to the fifties, giving up your work, your place in the world, your strength."

"Yes, and let us remember one important thing more," Jayson interjected. "The Amazon female has been so out of touch with her feminine, her intuition, that she has been choosing the wrong men and doesn't even know the difference. For a woman to surrender into her femininity with a man, he must be a mature and trustworthy man who loves her. When such women get involved with wrong men, usually they stay in the relationship too long, trying to get that man to want to have a relationship with her. A woman into her Madonna realizes the futility and negative consequences of such a relationship, so moves on in a timely manner." Then with a sly grin Jayson added, "It isn't only women who have had to learn about wrong men. Ask me."

Cheng chuckled. "Sure, love is love" he said. "Val-teen will have an additional challenge. It takes much courage, for a woman particularly, to stand up to the system, to live her own life, to move toward freedom. Any fight for freedom does extract its price. There can be loneliness. Remember, Val-teen, whatever happens, don't sell your soul for a hot dog! Carry the flag. This message applies to many spiritual beings now on earth who prepared for eternities for this, waiting for the right time. That time is now; to spread the power of understanding of God's love for them; to spread the ancient ways of understanding God which might be in conflict with the doctrines of organized religions – that there is in each of us a place where our spirit dwells –that each of us must reconnect with our spirit in order to feel complete. The spiritual beings now on earth are to counteract the satanic forces, let us call them, wanting to dominate the earth, and to do it not just through force but through their nurturing power of love.

At the millennium and for the next 2000 year cycle there will be a great opportunity for many to release more light into the world. Look at our present politics, business, and medicine; do they not need the influence of the spiritual? Look at those in power today and see if they are trying to advance humanity or simply advance their lower selves; you will see that it is primarily the latter. A spiritual person will be able to be spiritual in politics, medicine, academia, business, wherever.

The woman's role will become one of increasing spiritual wisdom while the men will return more to their natural role of protector of the female and of the family. Above all else, we are to love one another, and to never stop growing spiritually, as for most of us there is always yet another spiritual level, each one more beautiful than the one before. So much so that it is well worth reaching, whatever that takes."

I was about to ask Cheng what he'd meant by some of the remarks he'd just directed toward me, but he had once again turned his attention to Casse. "Self esteem for women, as for men, can come in part from the place that she or he has carved for self in society, however, for the most part it must come from within."

"What do you mean from within?" Casse asked.

"You need to make time for inner pursuits now, Casse."

"You mean like meditation, that stuff Valentine does?" Cheng nodded, "yes."

"Oh, come ON. With work, a marriage, a house and social life to maintain, getting my hair done, working out to keep this body from falling apart, how do you expect me to find time for that other stuff?"

Cheng, never one to mince words, responded readily. "Cassandra, keeping physically fit is important but in proportion. If you're choosing to continue making materiality your priority, your spiritual growth will stay stunted and you'll keep looking for contentment in a pair of pants, with you the loser. You don't need to have it all anymore. Your plate of materiality already overflows."

At that moment Sallee-Mae sauntered over, Bernie beside her, *her* femininity overflowing in a low cut flowered dress. She did look pretty.

"Y'all talkin' 'bout men and women?" she asked. "Honey, there can't be no discussion on that subject without this li'l ol' southern expert present. Even Bernie thinks thar's no other woman who can come close to me. A 'cause ah tole him so." Sallee-Mae laughed, looked over at Bernie and winked.

Cheng said, "Sallee-Mae, a job outside the home would be perfect for you now. You should look for something." Before she could answer, Richard added, "In my opinion," he said, "the mistake women made was in leaving us behind."

I saw everybody listening attentively as he continued seriously. "I mean this," he said. "Women are good at revealing their feelings to others; we men are terrible at it. Women explore their feelings with gusto, we avoid ours with terror. It would have been fine for women to forge ahead if only they'd taken us with them, helped us."

"You are absolutely correct," Cheng exclaimed, reaching up to pat Richard on the back. "This state of affairs cannot continue without total destruction. In the nineties the woman you describe will emerge and really become evident at and beyond the Millennium. The strong loving rather than the strong strident woman. The woman who is truly strong stemming from her spirituality rather than from her mock masculinity. That woman will be the Goddess, here to stay, showing men how to join them in the search for self-discovery, for spirituality. Such women will be the conscience of our society in the early 21st century; God and Goddess will come together again; the world will rejoice."

Richard smiled and pointed. "I see food's on the table," he told us. "I don't mean to be macho but, follow me."

On the buffet line Cheng told Richard, "Of course, both men and women *should* live life as Amazon warriors when putting our strengths to the tasks before us. We need to be alert to what life brings us, unafraid because we are in touch with the inner strength and omniscience to do what it takes, along with the wisdom to let go of ourselves at the same time. Like Arjuna in the Bhagavad Gita."

"Isn't that what Castaneda describes in his books?" Richard asked. My head shot up! This was *Richard*, talking about spiritual literature!? Richard continued, "As I remember, don Juan Matus, the Yaqui Indian sorcerer, shows his apprentice Carlos Castaneda how the latter plays victim, complains, fears, worries, clings to guilt, so avoids acting now and dissipates his power. Is that accurate?"

"Sure," Cheng answered. "don Juan tells Castaneda, 'To make oneself strong takes no more effort than to make oneself weak.'"

Richard conversing about spirituality! Miracles didn't cease! I looked at my once-husband with admiration and respect.

Then my eyes circled the room. Sallee-Mae and Ernie were standing in the corner talking, she looking enthralled, he bemused.

Somewhat later Sallee-Mae ran over to me. "Val-tine," she stage-whispered, "What would ya think 'bout ma workin' with Ernie, bein' his rep? I needed to ask you first." More wonders ! "I think it would be great, Sallee-Mae," I told her, truthfully.

Then Sallee-Mae added, looking dejected. "Ah don't think it's gonna happen, Val-tine. At first it was like he asked me, but then he said, 'What do ah need a rep fer? Ah make six figures repping maself.' He did say ah could come see the studio. But why go, since he ain't interested?"

"Go up and see him," I offered, enthusiastically. "That means he wants you."

"THAT means he WANTS me?" she asked. "CRAZY people!"

"You have NO idea! Go."

I was so glad for her. Sallie-Mae's Amazon was there, well hidden, along with her more obvious Courtesan and Mother. She'd handle anything Ernie dished out and then some. Hopefully sometime later she'd find her Madonna as well.

As Sallee-Mae continued talking, her voice faded from my hearing. I gazed around me at all the people that I felt close to, here in one room. Just a few were missing. My children - who of course were not supposed to be here. Hinda, who was away. My parents, who were in Florida, Glady, who hadn't been too well lately. And Brandt. *Did* he belong here? After everything, I still hadn't a clue. How strange life was.

Richard appeared beside me. "Ready to leave?" he asked.

"Just a quick trip to the ladies' room first," I said.

"*Quick* trip to the *ladies*' room is an oxymoron," Richard offered. I looked at him. "Go, go" he said indulgently.

When I walked out of the restroom into the small alcove surrounding it and the men's room, I saw Richard and Cal standing and talking together. They didn't see me. I was getting ready to walk toward them when their voices carried and I realized that they were talking about me. I sensed the most tactful thing to do was to remain standing in the alcove, hidden from their view.

"You're a lucky man, married to Valentine," I distinctly heard Cal say.

"*Was* married to Valentine," Richard corrected.

"Well, then you're a lucky man because you *were* married to Valentine." Cal answered, "She's extraordinary. I'd choose fifteen minutes of extraordinary over a lifetime of nothing- in -particular, *any* time! I'd take a dab of caviar over all the pasta I could eat. Give me two magical days in Paris over two years in Brooklyn..."

Richard gave Cal a certain kind of male bonding knowing look, and said, "I get the idea. You, too, hmm?" then patted him on the shoulder, and added, "Well, welcome to the club." I waited a minute before walking toward them, feeling awkward.

I thanked Cal, told him it had been an incredible party, to say nothing of a needed postgraduate class in female-male psychology! Cal handed me a goody bag of leftovers, for which I again thanked him. Then I told him 'good bye,' kissed him on the cheek, and left with Richard.

As we walked down the corridor Richard said, "Valentine, the way I love you, we should be together."

"What do you call *this?*" I asked.

"I mean really together. Reconcile." Richard emphasized.

"How do you know it's love?" I asked him. "You're probably just used to me."

With surety Richard answered, "I *love* you. I'll *never* get *used* to you!"

"It would really help me if you'd carry this package," I told him.

"So, you paid attention in tonight's class. I give you an A plus." Richard took the package with one hand, put his other arm around me, and together we left the building.

As we entered the New York night, my spirits soared. The hearty laughter and conversation of a party had always been, for me, among the best of times.

CHAPTER THIRTY: VALENTINE'S DHARMA

"Meditate on yourself
Respect yourself
Kneel to yourself
Worship yourself
God dwells within you, as YOU."
--Swami Muktananda

"Unless there is a new millenium inside, the new millenium will not change things much."

---The 14th Dali Lama

And so I became Cheng's successor.

You might want to ask, "Did you feel qualified to step into Cheng's shoes and if so, by what criteria?" My honest answer is "Yes, and No." On the one hand, Cheng had said it was right and because I trusted him I trusted the process. He'd assured me that I'd done much spiritual practice and teaching in past lifetimes; I could believe that because Cheng had said it and because it felt true. On the other hand, I could just imagine asking a surgeon who wanted to operate on me, "Where did you get your training?" and being answered, "You see, I've never gone to medical school. But I was a skilled surgeon in a past life, so..." To use an apt phrase, that wouldn't cut it for me. I believe that before we do anything in this life we first have to pay our dues. As they say in the East, "only one who has obeyed can command."

Had I paid my dues? Well, I guessed I had, at least as much or more so than any other ordinary person I knew. Cheng had seen to that. Did I always feel qualified? Hardly. But Cheng had told me to expect that, and Max had explained that only a saint or a jerk with an over-inflated ego would always feel qualified. And that's in everything. When we have children, regardless of how carefully we've prepared, do we always feel totally qualified to be a parent? Do we always feel totally qualified with every client, patient or customer, as a lover, as a friend? Obviously not. My job as Cheng's successor was very similar. Bottom line, I'd come to know, not just because Cheng had told me so but from within my own being, that becoming his successor was my dharma. So although I had fear, my dedication to my dharma became more important than my fear. Knowing that this was something that I'd come here to do, made it worth going through whatever fears and insecurities came up along the way.

In the beginning Cheng was right there to support me.

The day of the evening that I was to teach the First Discourse from my apartment, which Cheng had advised would work just fine to start with, I told him, "God, I'm nervous!"

"Why?" he asked.

"I don't know why exactly."

"Then, you'll please think about why exactly, now."

I thought for a few minutes. "I guess... I feel... I don't know enough. Not all that you know, Cheng."

"That is the ego ensnaring you once again. Don't fall into its trap. The wise teacher never identifies with the teachings, rather knows it is the Shakti that does everything. The Shakti asks questions, the Shakti gives the answers. It is only the fool who thinks s/he must 'become this great teacher.'"

"But, suppose nobody comes?"

"Obviously you are still too ego-focused to have heard what I just said. We aren't in the numbers game. Whoever should be here will come. You aren't in charge anyway, so give it up and allow the one who IS in charge to do it."

By seven that evening three people had arrived. I whispered to Cheng, "Not exactly breaking down the door, are they!"

"Are you leaving your memory somewhere else lately? Do I have to repeat for you yet a third time?"

"No." I hanged my head.

"Then stand up precisely on time. It wouldn't matter if one person were here. As you know, promptness is crucial," Cheng directed. " Mentally bow to these three and visualize yourself asking them, 'How can I best serve you?' Everyone who stands up before people should do the same. Then begin. It will be fine and then word will spread."

And so, at exactly seven fifteen I stood up, bowed mentally as Cheng had advised, and said, "Welcome, Dear Ones."

When I had finished, a grinning Cheng whispered to me, "I am very very pleased." It was the first time that Cheng had praised my work so effusively. I told him, "I'm thrilled. It means so much to me to hear you tell me that I was very very good." Cheng was silent momentarily, then replied, "You were good. You can leave out the verys. Not very very good for years yet." *My* ego wasn't going to take over, not if my teacher could help it.

Then Cheng threw in a very great warning, one which I was to hear reverberating in my head forever after. "Knowledge is power. For each new level of power comes greater responsibility for how you use it. The greater the number of people you come to influence, the greater your responsibility to influence them with unselfishness and Truth. And the greater your karma if you do not."

* * *

For the next two years I immersed myself in my children, my work dharma teaching the Discourses- Cheng's work - and my spiritual growth.

With great personal reward and I hoped of equal benefit to my students, I taught the Discourses as my teacher had taught them to me, flavoring them with my own developing style and seasoning them with my own personal experiences.

Such as experiences in raising my children. I told my students, "Through my lessons with my own master, Cheng, a really wonderful thing began happening with my children. Whenever they had moods or were naughty, I'd convey to them that they have a beautiful Self inside, that their present behavior was not their real Self. Not only did that change their behavior for the better almost immediately, but it also changed my own perception of my children for the better. It worked miraculously. It made me realize that a parent who knows the Self would naturally begin to teach that to their children, whereas a parent who did not know the Self could teach their children only their own fears and negative projections."

I spoke to them often about the universality of experience, much as Cheng had taught me. "Remind yourself, 'Every person I meet is having a hard time.' I know you don't believe that. You see somebody else laughing while you are crying, or a favorite movie actor or actress partying, and you think, 'What a great life s/he has!' You think you alone are miserable, bored, and lonely. It isn't true. You see people's outsides, not their insides. Some people are just cleverer at covering up. However, everyone experiences feelings of desolation, boredom, loneliness. So, as my teacher taught me, try to remember each time you are with any other person, ' every person I meet is having a hard time,' then try to put something nice into their situation. Or, as my teacher taught, 'If you can't bring something good to others, at least don't be a pest.'"

I recall once, when sharing the above in my class, Miles, one of my students asked, "Then what is the answer? Are we all here to just be miserable, struggle, and finally die?"

"Please raise your hand and be acknowledged first, Miles," I'd told him. Miles was my Serge. I thought of him as left over karma from Cheng's class. After he'd raised his hand, I'd answered, "The answer is to maintain a positive attitude about all that comes up. Refuse to imbibe negative thoughts as you'd refuse to eat garbage. We need only to go deeper into ourselves to experience our own unending happiness. And as we increasingly do that we can increasingly bring happiness to others."

Of course I spoke extensively on the Self. "Inside of you, inside of every human being, is the potential for greatness. Identify your problems, don't identify WITH them. Identify instead with your inner greatness. That core inside of you is powerful. It is smart, knows everything, and figures out the details. Fall into it and free-fall into a new experience of bliss."

I reminded them, "Spiritually we evaluate people differently than the world does. The world at large may see somebody as a magnificent mental giant, whereas spiritually he may be an imbecile. (I thought of Brandt!) Or the reverse may be true." (I thought of Willie).

Just as we had loved it when Cheng had taught us with humor, so did my students love it when I did so. "I used to have incredible give-and-take relationships with men," I told them at one class. "I gave, they took." Everyone laughed. "Then I learned that is *not* what they mean in the East by balance in relationships. I'm getting better."

Increasingly Cheng retired to the background. I knew that he was weaning me away from him as he himself was winding down, so despite my desires to see him, I made such requests of him infrequently. Thereafter, always in my teachings, with fond feelings and bittersweet ones - because I missed him- I interjected anecdotes about my unique, colorful, beloved teacher; Cheng Ho stories which my students came to eagerly anticipate and to love hearing. There was no doubting it; each time I taught, Cheng's Shakti was right there with me.

Word spread as Cheng had predicted it would; each week more people came. Before long I rented a hall for the classes. I found myself approaching the teachings, as well as everything else in my life, with more lightness and humor. I was definitely happier.

I think you'll want to hear about the changes in some of my friends' lives as well.

Casse, with a feminine and this time flattering hairdo, dress and kinder gentler manner, was in therapy with Max. "Discovering my softer side," she told me happily.

Sallee-Mae did go to work with Ernie, and from the things she said I could tell that she was really good at it, fulfilling herself by bringing a bit of the Amazon to all her creativity and cleverness for success with "real work in the world," as she described it to me. I spoke with Ernie a few times when I returned Sallee-Mae's calls from the studio; he sounded well pleased. "Wow!" He told me, "when she walks in they really notice! Not that they didn't with you, but we're talking 42 inches vs. 36, here. Tougher times call for tougher measures." I answered, "Didn't you mean to say 'larger measurements'? By the way, let's keep the statistics straight; I'm 37 inches, not 36." Sallee-Mae had changed her name for the job, to Salma; those days all of us hardly thought of her as anything else.

I intuited that Max and Jayson, without fanfare, were becoming an item. I could not have been more thrilled for any couple. They did seem complete around each other.

Cal had become an internationally known photographer. He took all my publicity photographs for my lectures, classes and writing. Jayson, too, had gone on to bigger better things, traveling between California and New York making up the stars. Whenever he was in town when I was having a photo session he did my make-up. I wouldn't have considered using anyone else but these two.

"You haven't aged," Cal told me during our latest shoot. "How do you manage that?"

"I have you for a photographer," I replied.

"Well, whatever your secret, there are only two words for how you look; Gorg - *eous*!" Cal smiled, then looking serious, added, "Can I ask you something?"

"Shoot."

"Sure, I know- if I'll pardon the pun. What I want to ask is, those nudes we took together, they were for a man, weren't they."

"THAT's a QUESTION?" I reddened.

As Cal turned his crystal green eyes fully upon me, I thought, "Oh, *my*, all those women Cal could have at the crook of his little finger … I can see why!"

"Those photos were years ago," I answered. "It doesn't matter now."

"If it doesn't matter, why not tell me?"

"Alright, then. Yes, they were for a man."

"Anybody I know?"

"Definitely not. I'm not even sure he's anybody *I* know. The only thing I'm sure of right now concerning you is, I have in you not only the best photographer alive but the best friend a woman could have as well."

Brenna entered her teens lovely, despite some of the gangling awkwardness of that stage which she didn't quite escape. Willie grew handsomer than ever, but more importantly grew in other ways as well. I now felt blessed about *both* of my children – for which I owed Cheng hugely.

Richard and I continued to see each other as friends, visiting Willie together, bringing him home every several months at which time we all stayed at the big house together, Richard and I sleeping in separate bedrooms, so that Willie's life could flow normally. I'd consciously practiced Cheng's teaching on how not to worry about money, and had explained it to Richard. It seemed to be working for both of us. Finances improved.

Then a large outer change occurred pivotal to Richard's and my relationship. Glady had a sudden heart attack and passed on. It was a big loss for us, of course especially so for Richard. Not long thereafter Richard again asked me to reconcile with him.

"I love you," he told me, "and now we have this house."

"I hear that, Richard. But there's so much that you don't know about me."

"For instance?"

"My spirituality. I can imagine how you, and others, must have seen me. 'See this selfish woman, thinking of nothing but her meditation,' and the like. It was like I was embarking alone in a small boat while everyone was standing on the dock calling, 'Where are you going? Come back, you can have anything you want if you do.' But I, "selfish woman," went anyway. What none of you realized was that while all of you stayed on the so-called safe dock, I had to venture out on a journey I knew nothing about, over often treacherous waters which I had to navigate with no idea how to do it. Do you think that's been easy?"

"Then why did you do it, and continue to do it?"

"I had no choice. I didn't and don't like the alternative."

"And I was one of those standing on the dock?"

"I perceived you that way."

"Did you also perceive that I deserted Willie?"

"Me and Willie, more accurately."

"Valentine, I didn't think of it that way. I went into a depression over Willie. I felt deprived of the usual father-son relationship. I was angry. I know I directed it at you, too, whereas God knows it was not your fault and you were suffering enough as it is. I was just so... sad. I wasn't able to get beyond it to handle it right, like you did."

I took his face in my hands and answered, "Who knows that I handled it right? You couldn't look, I couldn't look away. We were two extremes; maybe neither was desirable. For my part, I don't feel affairs are the way to go. Telling you about it was even worse. It was my action, so mine to handle, not to dump upon you."

"Maybe it awakened me," Richard admitted.

"If so, too bad it had to take that to do it. How do you feel about Willie now?"

"I've... accepted him. I love him. How do *you* feel about him?"

"I no longer have the goal of wishing him 'normal.' 'Normal' people aren't normal, they are common, which usually means miserable. My goal for Willie is what everyone wants, to be happy. I think Willie is one of the happiest people I know. I believe he's in a high state, a state that very few people are yet able to appreciate. I read a small poem somewhere. 'I asked God to make my handicapped child whole. God said, 'No, his spirit is whole, his body is only temporary.'"

"Well, I'm not sure about his state, but I understand what you mean. I've thought something else lately, too. Something which has made me feel a lot better about Willie."

"What's that?"

"You say we have many lifetimes?"

"It isn't just me, but yes, that's true. We do."

"Then, when Willie... you know... passes on... is it true he won't be autistic any longer?"

"Well, yes, Rick, that is so. There's an organization of scientists who are investigating near-death experiences. They interviewed some people blind since birth. When those individuals had near-death experiences, they saw things like the doctors in the operating room, and later could describe it visually. Isn't that fascinating? In spirit, their disability was gone. That goes for deafness, Alzheimer's, all illnesses. Those are gone upon 'death' as they're of the physical body only. Furthermore, the great masters say this lifetime itself, in terms of our total existence in eternity, is actually about an hour long. So, even if at worst autism were a bad thing, which I don't believe - I believe the only bad thing about it is the lack of understanding by other people - it isn't so bad if we realize it will end in ostensibly an hour. The same is true of all conditions of people. They're temporary."

"That's a great way to think."

"It's the truth."

"Anyway," Richard said, "People can change. I think now you and I could have a very happy life together..."

"Richard, your mother just died. You're lonely..."

"It isn't that. I was going to talk to you about this long before Mom..."

"Richard, I know people CAN change. It's whether they DO. I can't ask you to change for me."

"I think I have changed, though," Richard answered.

"Well, so have I. I've gained some clarity about the place of marriage in my life, if any. Of what I want."

"Can I hear it?" Richard asked eagerly.

I looked at him. This was such a far cry from his former, "Oh, another theory from a women's magazine..."; he was genuinely interested and respectful."Alright," I said, somewhat hesitantly. "I discovered that I can be happy being single if necessary - going where I go, doing the things I like to do. I'd be married again only if he were the right person. There'd be no other reason for me to be married.

"I've learned the qualities I'd require in a marriage partner," I continued.

Now the words flowed from me.

"He'd have to be kind, loving and respectful - to me, to other people and to all living things.

"He wouldn't have to be handsome - although I wouldn't mind - but he'd have to be presentable and to take good care of his body, the temple of the soul.

"He need not have many degrees, or even one, but must be intelligent and use that to live wisely. He need not be famous, but be one who has discovered his individual form of expression in this world, and be dedicated to it with love, discipline and integrity.

"He'd have to be a friend whom I'd also find physically appealing. I'm not looking for a wild infatuation - that stage passes in all relationships in a relatively short time, anyway."

I then told Richard about how I'd learned that there is a natural healthy progression when we relinquish the "in-love" fantasies that we'd projected upon the other person and move into knowing and loving the person that is. That this second stage of discovery and growth is unending and increasingly exciting in a far more profound and fulfilling way than the wild infatuations can ever be.

I told him that I had learned that mature people could move into this next stage and relish its continuous fruits, whereas those people who never grow up refuse to make that transition. "Instead," I said, "they move from partner to partner, seeking repeated infatuation/roller-coaster-rides which in the end are exhausting, unfulfilling and shallow trips to nowhere."

"Finally, Richard," I concluded, "My marriage partner would have to be spiritual, that is, intent on being the best person he can be. He'd have to be my spiritual partner, meaning a partnership between equals for the purpose of mutual spiritual growth."

Richard exclaimed, "That's me!"

When I didn't respond, Richard asked, "Well, do you believe that? If you do, that will give me something."

Without thought my answer came. "Do *you* believe it, Richard?" I asked. "If you do, that will give you everything."

Richard and I looked at each other for a longer time than we had in ages. Then I looked away.

Later that evening in meditation I had a remarkable experience. Glady came to me.

Glady told me that she was in a place far more beautiful than earth, together with Richard's father who had passed on ten years before her and had helped her to cross over. She said that she was watching over us all, especially Willie. I then asked her a question on my mind. "Glady, should Richard and I reconcile? He seems certain it would be right but I'm filled with ambivalence." To my disappointment, Glady said that she could not answer that question for us. "God asks you to please have the patience to wait until you can figure that out for yourself," she told me. "Were I to answer that now, I could stunt your spiritual growth and interfere with you karma." She then added, "But what I can and want to tell you is this: Don't be afraid to pray specifically for what you want, adding 'or something even better, 'if this is God's will for me.' There are God's messenger-angels here catching your prayers and rushing with them to God. Prayers are magic; prayers bring miracles. Believe in miracles as regular occurrences; finally, love is real and the most important thing in the universe. Believe in love. So spread the word to people; tell them that true love, real magic and ordinary miracles are reality. I'm leaving now. Goodbye, my dear."

Cheng had taught those very things about love, magic and miracles; Glady had just confirmed his teachings.

My visit from Glady left me uplifted and hopeful, as is typically the case when individuals are visited by loved ones' spirits. I realized that many people who have passed on try to contact loved ones when the loved ones are receptive, especially during dreams, mediation or prayer. And that this can happen to any of us.

BOOK III

THE BEGINNING

CHAPTER THIRTY ONE: BABA

"Many are the gurus
who are like lamps in homes,
"but great is the Guru who illumines
Like the sun."
--The Kularnava Tantra

Change happens. What's the problem?
-Eshin (Zen Student)

A following developed for my teachings. Simultaneously some of the Siddhis manifested in me, while abilities already present - like the intuitive - became stronger. I had so imbibed Cheng's warning not to make a display of these powers that I veered too far in the other direction. Thus I missed all opportunity to use them to help people. When I became aware how that, too, wasn't right, I strived for some balance here by continuously whispering in my own ear, "You are not the doer." In this way I progressed, and so my spirituality and work became very satisfying to me. Until...

A discontent, a stuckness, grew within me. It progressed relentlessly. Finally I had to talk with somebody about it.

But, to whom? In my early months as a teacher I'd periodically visited Cheng at his home. Each time it was I who initiated our meetings; Cheng no longer contacted me. He always seemed pleased to see me, welcoming me as openly and lovingly as ever, with an additional obvious pride in my, his students' achievements. Even so, he was cutting me loose. This was never said in words; that wouldn't have been Cheng. It was implicit that he trusted me to understand what he was doing, why, and to accept it.

Certainly I understood. Cheng had completed what he was intended to do with me this time around, so now trusted me to go forth without him. It was actually a compliment. I should feel good about this. But accepting it was something else. I did so reluctantly and gradually. As for feeling good about it, I felt as good as a child whose always-doting adoptive parents had just kicked her out into the street. In time, though, as I came to realize how content Cheng was living the solitary life which he now wanted, my happiness for him and desire to honor his choice took precedence over my other feelings. The time had come for Cheng to move on. I would do the same.

So I definitely wasn't going to disturb Cheng now with my wearisome complaints. I'd been blessed as few people are in being protégé of such a gifted teacher. Certainly petty spiritual laments should be behind me by now. "You ought to be ashamed of yourself!" I admonished myself, and assumed the emotion.

Yet if anything the inner gnawing grew worse, until one day I pleaded with God, "Please, define it for me, or just remove it!" After that, feeling only slightly better, I decided to drive to Glady's former house, now Richard's. Richard, knowing that I derived relaxation and pleasure from gardening and aware that the apartment hadn't any back yard to speak of, had invited me to use his whenever I wanted to. When I'd thanked him for his generosity, he'd answered, "Hey, I'm being selfish. A free landscaper and I get to enjoy the results." Typical Richard. God forbid he let anyone know he's nice.

Landscaper was far too lofty a title for my projects in Richard's yard. Today, for example, I stopped at a nursery on the way and bought some begonias to plant in a space I had in mind beside the pond.

Once there I went first to the outdoor faucet where the garden hose was usually attached, planning to pull it over to the pond. It wasn't there - probably stored in the garage for the winter - and the pond was covered over so not a viable source of water this day either. So I decided to use Richard's hidden spare key to find some container in the house, which I'd bring back outside with me, then fill from the outdoor faucet. In the mudroom I located a pail, headed outside with it, on some impulse grabbed the cordless phone off of the counter as well, and then carried both items outside with me.

I went first to the outdoor faucet and filled the pail with water, then proceeded with the planting. I had just finished patting the potting soil around the last begonia when the phone rang. I hesitated to answer. It was Richard's line; I tried to maintain certain boundaries. On the fourth ring I picked up. "Valentine, I'm so glad I've reached you!" After a pause, then a familiar bell-like laugh, the caller announced, "It's Hinda. Had you forgotten me already?"

"Hinda!" I hadn't seen or spoken with her since March. I was both elated and confused. "Of course not. I just wasn't expecting you on Richard's phone. How did you know to call me here?"

"A gut feeling. I called information. Glad Richard's listed. Hope you don't mind the intrusion."

I minded about as much as a drowning person would mind the intrusion of a rescue boat!

"No, I'm glad you called," I answered, striving to sound cool. "Where have you *been*?"

Hinda's voice was, as always, soft and sweet. "Well, as you knew I was in India for awhile. Recently I've been spending most of my time in upstate New York." India! Upstate New York! For a woman with solidly implanted feet, Hinda managed to cover a lot of ground! Before I could question her further, Hinda asked me, "How have YOU been, Valentine?"

My cool crumbled. "I've been better. No, worse than that. I'm that drowning person, going down for the second time. I need the rescue boat, now; I'm afraid you're it."

Hinda urged, "Tell me about it." Then she listened attentively while I told her of my recent inner turmoil. When I'd finished speaking, she asked, "Do you remember the times during Cheng's classes when I went to India?"

"Yes, I do. You called me once from Bombay." Although I managed politeness, I felt impatient with Hinda's irrelevant question. What did any of that have to do with me?

"You're right. I was there to be with Baba Sonn Nath, affectionately called Baba. His name in Sanskrit means winner of all."

"Who...is this person?" I asked, irritated. I had just trusted Hinda with my most intimate thoughts and feelings, told her I was going down for the third time, and her response was to ruminate to me about …some...Indian Guru?

"Baba is the spiritual leader of a long lineage of Self-Realized masters. He's my spiritual master."

Although I still couldn't fathom how this related to my predicament, despite myself I was becoming curious. "This Baba," I asked, "Is he like Cheng?"

"It would be easier to talk in person. May I come to you?"

"When?"

"Now would be good, but if now isn't convenient…

"Please. Come"

Once Hinda and I were seated together under the Wisteria, she reached into her long oblong bag, like Cheng's, and took out a thermos, some pink plastic glasses with green trim and green napkins. It was a pleasing display. Pointing to the thermos, Hinda offered, "Iced mango tea with ginger?" I nodded. She poured and handed me a filled glass. The cold slightly pungent tea was perfect in the day's heat.

"Hinda, how do you manage it? Everything you do is right," I marveled. "Hardly!" Hinda waved my praise away with her hand, then spontaneously lifted one of the napkins, opened it and held it up to the day light. "Look! It matches all the green here in the yard!" she squealed, delighted. Again I was in awe. Hinda was the only person I knew other than Cheng who could genuinely rhapsodize over something as seemingly insignificant as a napkin!

Then she resumed where we had left off over the phone.

"Valentine, you asked if Baba's like Cheng. Cheng's a marvelous teacher and rare person. We both know that. I would have thought him the ultimate until I met Baba. Which is not disloyalty to Cheng. He'd be the first to acknowledge that's true."

"I'm confused. You told Cheng about Baba?"

"The other way around, actually. Cheng knew him first."

"Go on." Now I was not only confused, I was lost.

"Cheng was born and educated here in the United States, a third generation Chinese American," Hinda said. "He went to India looking for a spiritual teacher. There he met Baba, who at that time had only a handful of disciples, or dedicated students. Cheng became one of them. For ten years Cheng studied in India with Baba. Became Baba's star disciple, you might say. Then Baba told Cheng to return to the West to teach that ancient Indian wisdom and philosophy here. In his first class here Cheng had five students. I was one of them. Several years after that Cheng invited me to accompany him to India where, he said, he would introduce me to Baba. I went. Once I met Baba, that was it for me."

"What about the other five students? Did Cheng also take them to India to meet… this… Baba ?"

"No. I was the only one who went."

"Quite an honor, that. Cheng selecting only you!"

"It wasn't so much Cheng selecting me, Valentine. Cheng told all of us in the class about Baba. It was just that I was the only one who felt more than a passing interest. Even before meeting Baba in person I felt magnetized toward him in some magical way."

Suddenly I had a million questions. "So all five of you in the class had equal initial exposure but only you were magically magnetized. How do you explain that?"

"Karma. I see it primarily as my destiny. Baba doesn't withhold himself from anybody like some exclusive club. Just, all people are not intended to follow the same path. Without that destiny factor I would have probably felt as disinterested as my classmates did, or mildly curious at most but minus that pull, that "calling."

My questions tumbled forth. "What's a Siddha guru?"

"A guru is a teacher, a profession, if you will. A Siddha is a self-realized person, a saint, a state of evolvement. A Siddha Guru is a spiritual teacher who is Self-Realized. Baba is a Siddha Guru."

"What happened to the other students who were with you in Cheng's class?"

"I don't know. We went our separate ways, so I guess it was time for our relationships together to end. I expect, at least I hope, that at the right time each of them found their own path."

Although it was a cool day, beads of sweat began to form on my forehead. "Sensory overload. It will pass," I thought, using one of the green napkins to wipe away the wet. Meanwhile Hinda sat quietly, smiling. Just then a cardinal sailed before us, dived into the birdbath near the pond, then perched briefly on the rim appearing to look us over before deciding whether to leave or stay.

"Tame," I muttered.

"Good sign, seeing a red bird. Fortuitous. Something wonderful's in store for you."

"I could use it," I groaned, "I'm sorry, I must sound like the ultimate gloom machine."

"Not a bit. We all go through such mental gymnastics. People like us who get involved with spirituality are the hardest on ourselves. We think we can't ever again have a human feeling. That is, of course, nonsensical."

"Why didn't Cheng tell me about Baba?"

"Because he asked me to tell you, at the right time."

Hinda again opened the flowered bag. This time she extracted a beautifully wrapped package which she handed to me. "I brought you a gift from the ashram."

"Thank you so much."

"Wait for that until you've seen it!"

I unraveled the lavender ribbon and pulled off the pink and peach tissue paper, revealing a blue velvet box the color of midnight. I looked at Hinda, who nodded. I lifted the cover of the box. Facing me was a photograph of an Indian man. "Oh, my God! Hinda... he... I... I mean... Is THIS...?"

"This is Baba," Hinda finished my sentence.

"Hinda," I sputtered, "This is HIM... I mean this man...he once came to me... in my head -- I didn't know who he was. He told me... something important, something I've forgotten. How could he do that...?"

Touching my hand, Hinda said, "Your mystical experience with Baba was a wonderful gift. More people than you can imagine have experienced similar. With variations in details, of course. Which doesn't negate your experience one whit. If anything, it helps to affirm it. A Siddha, you see, is free, unbounded by time and space so able to travel anywhere, any way, any time, to anybody. Just as we all have the potential to do the same. Remember Cheng's last lesson, the Siddhis?"

I could not speak just then, as Baba's eyes were penetrating my very being. I could not tell Hinda then of the impact his picture was having on me. I was actually feeling pulsating waves of bliss throughout my entire body. I was getting high and lightheaded. As if Hinda had given me champagne, not tea. "Siddhis," I repeated mechanically. "The powers." But my eyes remained riveted on Baba's eyes in the photograph.

Then it happened. Waves of electricity surged through me. My entire body began to shake. Lights burst inside of me. It was like a benevolent inner earthquake and thunderstorm combined. The entire experience seemed to last only a minute. When I opened my eyes, all within and outside of me was still. I looked over at Hinda beside me, her eyes closed. I coughed. Hinda opened her eyes.

"You seemed occupied, so I decided I'd meditate for a while," she explained.

"How long since you started meditating?"

Hinda looked at her watch. "Around forty minutes."

Forty minutes! Whatever I had just experienced had lasted forty minutes? I was beyond astonishment. "You can't imagine what just happened to me," I said weakly.

"I think I can," Hinda said, smiling, "but I'd love to hear it anyway."

I described the experience to Hinda as best as I could .

"It sounds like Baba gave you Shaktipat," she said, excitedly.

My eyes became circles. "Shaktipat?" I asked suspiciously, "Is that good... or bad?"

Hinda clearly found my question very amusing; the tiny bells of her laughter really chimed. "It's good, Valentine," she managed between joyful giggles. "It's extraordinary! Through a look, thought or touch, a Siddha Guru gives Shaktipat to one who is ready. It is the transmission of energy, the true awakening of the kundalini inside of you. This begins a purification."

All I could think of at the moment was that magical pull Hinda had said she'd felt toward Baba and whatever he represented. I was feeling it too. Again I had myriad questions. "This Shakitpat, why didn't that happen to me through Cheng?"

"Oh, surely Cheng helped to get you ready for it."

"What else should I know about Shaktipat?"

"For now, just that the fruits of Shaktipat are unsurpassed by anything else. As with all great things, we cannot receive them for nothing. The purification process is ongoing, cumulative, and self-regulating. Ultimately, it is thorough. Although there is nothing to fear about it, at times, when it burns away some of our limitations like a fire, it can seem agonizing. There's a sanskrit word for that burning; tapasya. You experienced that partially through physical symptoms a while back, remember?"

"How could I forget?" I groaned. "By the way, I don't know if I thanked you for being there for me then. So, belated thank you. Your explaining that to me then was a great relief. So is it that everybody who gets Shaktipat gets sick?"

"No, each person gets what he or she needs. It is purification of the mind, body and soul which leads to the state of unbounded ecstasy."

My questions were again coming like a flood. "If I look at Baba's picture again, will I go to the moon again? Can I show this to other people and help them go to the moon too? You mean, Baba can really see me, here, now?"

"Hey, slow down." Hinda laughed. "A Siddha is like the sun. Again, the sun doesn't withhold its light and energy from any receptive person. I believe whether there's receptivity or not very much has to do with one's karma. The fact that Baba came to you years ago in his subtle body and imparted something important was, I believe, due to merits that you earned in the past, this lifetime and/or in prior ones. You were probably with Baba in other lives, as I believe Cheng and I also were. By the way, Shaktipat is experienced in many different ways, not always as dramatically as yours but always with unfailing results."

"I wish I could remember what it was Baba told me," I lamented.

"A Siddha's words influence on two levels," Hinda explained. "There is obviously the outer content, the imparting of knowledge. And, because they speak to us from their state of enlightenment, their words are Chaitanya - alive with their energy - capable of bringing us to a higher state than mere words can ever do. So the meaning of the words are almost secondary. Although at the right time you might also remember Baba's actual words to you."

I needed to be silent. Hinda picked up on that, so for awhile we sat wordlessly beside each other. Finally I turned to her and with a bewildered little laugh, asked, "Well? What now?"

"Valentine, not only did Cheng make me promise to tell you about Baba, he also told me to take you to meet him – at the right time."

"The right time?" I repeated robotically. "And did Cheng tell you when *that* would be?"

"No. He said *you'd* let me know that." Hinda was smiling beatifically. "And clearly you just have. Seems that time is now."

"It's NOW! It's time for me to go to India NOW?" I felt myself pulling back. "I haven't even said… I… want to meet… this…this...guru."

Hinda didn't answer. I shut my eyes, running my index fingers across my eyelids. "A guru. To India, yet." As I let my mind turn away, I felt a diminishment of the expansive feelings I'd been enjoying.

"You're getting contracted." Hinda said. "Expand, float back out. There's nothing to fear. *I'm* not a shadow of my former self, am I?" Again her laughter came, the tiny bells dispensing joy with each peal.

"And not to India," she added, "at least not NOW. How fortunate you are! Only last week Baba arrived at his Western ashram in upstate New York, just a three hour drive from here. He'll be there all summer. That's where I was this past month, doing seva. Selfless service, remember? Many of us devotees were at the ashram helping to prepare for Baba's arrival."

"What kind of... seva... do you do?" I asked, rolling the unfamiliar term around on my tongue.

"I'm a manager of the ashram. For about six months now," Hinda answered simply.

I took a deep breath. I understood how Alice in Wonderland must have felt. "So that's why you weren't in Cheng's class much toward the end?"

"Exactly."

The right time, the right time, the right time. How often I had heard those words from Cheng, and now Hinda!

I tilted my eyes upward toward the sun and watched it squeeze through the clouds. A slight breeze then skimmed my skin, cooling and sobering me. Cheng had been one thing, this was quite another. Seva. Chaitanya. Tapasya. I had trouble with *English*. An ashram, a guru? Me, become one of *those*? I didn't *think* so.

Then I looked at Hinda, serene, strong, centered, her eyes putting to shame the eyes of my Pathways teachers, She was so deeply happy, I felt happy just being *near* her. And Cheng. I thought of his happiness, bliss and wisdom. From day one I'd felt as comfortable with these two people as when I was alone. There was no manipulation, no being too fast with an opinion, no need to keep up a constant chatter; an easiness with both talk and silence. In a word, they were real; in that was their unusualness and appeal. When with them my supposed limitations seemed like mere dust.

Was this the effect those with little ego had on others? Cheng had taught us that the ego is something undesirable, to be annihilated. His work on me had been toward that end. Through it all I'd always somewhat feared that with little or no ego I would be a blob, a robot, a puppet. Yet Cheng and Hinda were the antithesis of blobs. They were each rich, colorful, strong individual personality. With those realizations, my decision seemed sealed. Whatever Cheng and Hinda had, I wanted it; whatever way they had obtained it, I wanted *that*.

I swallowed hard. "Hinda," I said, "I'm ready to go meet Baba."

With those seven words you might say that my life as it had been came to an end.

***

If you analyzed it, physically Baba was not really a large man. But due to his strong aura he seemed mammoth when you were near him. I remembered a similar observation when first meeting Cheng. With Baba it was even more pronounced. He was the freest individual I'd ever conceived of, let alone met. As for happy... strong... loving... he gave new meaning to those adjectives. In fact for him they were nouns.

When Hinda introduced me to Baba, his first words to me, in Hindi (translated into English by the very attractive young Indian woman who stood nearby), stunned me. "Would you like to be a director of one of the meditation centers?" he asked conversationally, as if he had asked, "Is it sunny out?"

"If you would like that," he continued through translation, "Hinda can take you to Swami Sarojeet who will explain it to you further." With that he playfully tapped me three times on the crown of my head, whereupon I felt waves of unbridled joy like those I'd felt with Hinda in the back yard. Baba chuckled happily; the waves subsided.

I sat before Baba transfixed, neither able to speak nor to leave, until Hinda touched my hand and said softly, "Come, we can go now." I allowed her to lead me away from Baba's chair very much like I'd often had to lead a reluctant Brenna away from a store toy counter.

Once we were out of the hall, I exclaimed, "DIRECT ONE OF BABA'S MEDITATION CENTERS! IS HE CRAZY!" thus attracting the attention of several people nearby who had been conversing in very soft voices. Hinda put her index finger to her lips. "Shhh," she said softly. "We'll talk later." I hadn't realized I'd spoken that loudly. My hand flew to cover my mouth.

Once back on Long Island, I met with Richard and told him about Baba and what he had proposed for me to do. "I can't explain, just, it feels right for me. I want to do it." Knowing Richard, I had prepared myself for his typical slowness in acceptance of the new.

"What about Brenna?"

I had thought it out. "You know the sleep-away camp Brenna's friend Betsy went to last year? Betsy's going again this year. Brenna's been pleading with me to send her too. Right along I've thought the experience would be good for her and for all of us. I've only hesitated due to the cost. But maybe we can arrange a time-payment plan with the camp directors. What do you think?"

Richard's instant support stunned me. "You seem very much to want this, so I think you should go. Brenna will love sleep-away camp. It will be quiet around here this summer without her constant chatter. I admit I do not count that as a minus. *I'll* call the director today."

***

That summer was exhilarating, difficult, glorious and painful. It was training with Cheng times 1000! It was Marine boot camp and the land of Oz! It was purgatory mixed with Nirvana!

I lived in quarters the size of a small motel room with ten other women, four of whom I didn't like. One I couldn't stand. I was the only one among them taking the training thus the only one having to be so disciplined, while they were hanging out, going to programs when they wanted to, otherwise not. The room had one tiny bathroom, necessitating three minute showers, maximum; we made every possible arrangement for who would get the bathroom first mornings, including drawing numbers. I lucked out and got the bottom of a bunk bed.

Every morning I arose at 3:30 AM to get to 4:30 meditation followed by chanting, breakfast and classes plus seva. I was five minutes late to the first class that I attended. I was told by the attending monk teacher that if I found myself late the next time, not to bother coming into the classroom in the first place. After that I was always on time if not slightly early.

We ate in a dining hall, cafeteria style, our food placed in compartmentalized plastic trays rather than plates. There were no cloths on the tables. The only flatware we were given was a teaspoon with which we ate everything, including salad. At the first lunch I asked Hinda, "Where are the napkins?" She answered, "No napkins here. We just eat neatly."

I was given numerous sevas that summer –doing dishes, chopping lettuce, washing huge windows, cleaning toilets, vacuuming. I even helped plant and top trees, very physically hard work. We had classes, talks, seva, and exams, written and oral, with no place or time to study beforehand; we were supposed to remember the teachings by sufficiently paying attention to them as we received them .

Tapasya! Burning of the ego! I learned the meaning of the word even before I could correctly pronounce it! Often I felt pushed beyond my supposed limitations to a point which made Cheng's teachings feel like kindergarten. The most difficult thing here was how it was next to impossible to deceive oneself; the Shakti was so powerful that it continuously thrust mirrors in front of our faces. Yet although there were many things very strange and difficult for me about this place, on the other hand I felt contented and comfortable here, as if I'd come home to a place I'd been searching for all of my life. The yearning, the stuckness, were gone.

Mainly, whenever possible I tried to be near Baba. Although I watched him closely all summer I could not detect one selfish action. Even in his everyday behavior he was nothing less than remarkable. He gave a different talk to the assemblage every night of the week, seemingly effortlessly. That would have been an impossible feat for the most accomplished entertainer. Five nights a week he followed his talk with darshan, that is, his blessings to his devotees, and I received every one. We would stand in a line in front of the chair where Baba sat for his talks and programs, called the darshan line, and when it was our turn he'd bless us by touching us with his wand made of peacock feathers. Sometimes he'd not say a word, other times he would say something which Kamla, his translator, would repeat in English. Either way, each darshan was a glorious deepening of my sadhana, a blessing beyond words.

Kamla, Baba's translator, also intrigued me tremendously. A young Indian woman whose inner and outer beauty were so striking that they could have taken her anywhere, brought her anything in life that she desired, seemed to desire nothing beyond being with and serving Baba. She served him so well, thereby easing his way to in turn serve all of us, the multitudes, that she inspired *me* to want to give more than I'd thought *I* was capable of.

I was also so impressed with many of the other people taking the training. They were from around the world. Some had endured inconceivable hardships to get here. For the most part they were a group of extremely disciplined people, very dedicated to their spiritual growth and to Baba's teachings. Many of them had been attending Baba's centers locally for years; some had helped to run those centers with the directors. What was I doing here with them? Half way through the summer I knew that I wasn't going to be selected as a Center Director; I wasn't nearly as qualified or experienced as most of the others. I really didn't care that I wouldn't be chosen. In fact, I was rather relieved that I wouldn't have that responsibility. I just wanted to keep on with this study, with my sadhana, my spiritual practices. I just wanted to remain here with Baba and his teachings.

Finally at summer's end thirty-five people out of almost five hundred training were chosen to be directors of meditation centers. I was one of them. When I learned that, I ran to find Hinda. "This has to be a mistake!" I wailed. "There were people much better qualified than I who weren't selected. Why me and not them?"

"I don't think we can figure that out. The only answer I can give you is that obviously this is something that you were intended to do. Your karma. Remember, Baba himself asked you."

"I can decline the position though, can't I?"

"Of course you have that option. Just first be certain whether you want to do that. Oh, I almost forgot, Baba told me to impart to you your spiritual name. It's Kalyani. It means "Chosen One" Do you like it?"

"Kalyani," I repeated. "As if I didn't have sufficient names already! Seriously, It's beautiful. Much too high for *me*, it seems."

"The spiritual names are often a lot to live up to, but that's good," Hinda answered. "My spiritual name is Sumitra," she offered. "It means, 'the good friend.'"

"You've already lived up to *your* name and then some!" I said, hugging her. "To tell the truth, I thought Hinda was your spiritual name?"

"No, Hinda's my given name," she said, laughing. "My parents were visionary, or maybe just peculiar." Just then something came to me. "Hinda!" I shouted. "I just remembered what I heard Baba say to me when he came to me in my mind. It sounded like cal…cal..cal.."

"So, that was it. He was giving you your spiritual name, Kalyani, before you even met him in body!"

"My God. Even then he knew this was all going to happen?"

"Obviously. Remarkable, isn't it. So, what are you going to do about becoming a center director?"

"Do I have to tell you? You know everything."

* * *

When the summer retreat ended Baba returned to India. I returned home to many inquiries by well-meaning friends and relatives of, "Did you have a nice vacation?" I knew I couldn't possibly explain to them that my summer had been many things, but "vacation" was hardly the adjective I'd have used!

Then I was again in a whirlwind of activity. Brenna had experienced a great time in camp and was full of stories to tell us. I spent a lot of time with her giving her my undivided attention.

I wanted to visit Willie as soon as possible, so Richard and I did so together. Immediately upon arriving home from that visit, I hand wrote a letter to Baba.

"I meant to tell you in person," I wrote, "that I have a son named Willie. He has autism which is considered a developmental disability. I would be so grateful if you would help him to have a happy and meaningful life. Will you help him to talk, please? If it means bringing him to see you in India, please advise and I'll do that. With my love, Valentine ("Kalyani"). I mailed the letter to Baba's ashram near Bombay, India.

Without a break after that, I set about re-establishing my gainful employment. At the same time Hinda and I made plans to open the center.

After we'd invited many people we realized that my apartment might be too small, so I prevailed upon Richard who - again surprisingly - was receptive to our having the opening for this strange activity at his house.

Baba, like Cheng before him and *then* some, had taught us that we should be very clean and neat with ourselves, our houses, our possessions, and of course, in places where spiritual activities would take place. Doing so denoted love and respect for God's world. It helped the Shakti, or energy, to flow unimpeded. So the afternoon of that evening's opening Hinda and I zealously cleaned, polished and organized the den where the presentation would take place.

As we dusted, moved chairs and vacuumed, I felt a joy and bliss unlike anything I'd ever experienced while cleaning house. Finally we arranged the alter, called a puja, the focus for prayer and contemplation, adorning it with a beautiful cloth Hinda had brought, and placing upon it my silver framed shaktipat picture of Baba along with some other small items.

Shortly before everyone was due to arrive I told Hinda, "I'm nervous. How did *I* become a center director!"

"Just remember, you aren't the dooer."

"Perhaps, but *I* can't wait another minute to go to the bathroom and I *am* the one who has to do *that.* I'll be quick."

I was washing my hands when I heard the phone ring a few times, then stop. I realized that Hinda had probably answered it. A potential attendee who had gotten lost on the way, no doubt.

When I returned to the living room Hinda was standing with her back to me and the receiver in her hand. The conversation from her end sounded serious. When she got off the phone and turned around she had tears in her eyes. "Hinda, what is it, what happened?"

"Valentine, it's Swami Sachem from the Ashram with some…sad news. Last night Baba left his physical body. He took Mahasamdhi, that's passing of a saint." Hinda's tears fell; she continued to wipe her eyes.

I could not believe it! How could this have happened? Why, when I'd finally found something that totally fulfilled me, had Baba, my ultimate teacher, been taken from me?

"People will be arriving soon," Hinda reminded me, drying her eyes. "We want to be ready to welcome them."

Panicked, I said, "Hinda, I can't welcome them, not tonight. What do I say to all these people? -'Welcome, the Guru just died'? I can't do it."

Once again Hinda amazed me with her self-discipline. Although obviously she was grief stricken, probably more so than I, having known Baba even longer and better, she now showed herself to be very collected. "Baba would want us to carry on as if he were still here. In fact, he is," she said. "You could tell the group what Swamiji just told me that Baba said shortly before he left his body: 'You'll never know the power of a Siddha until he passes on.'"

And that was exactly what I did tell the almost sixty people who attended that night. I will tell you that the Shakti, the energy, in the house was unbelievable! It was as if Baba were around times ten! Feeling that, I knew without a doubt that Hinda had been right. Baba was indeed present guiding everything I did that night. I could not have done it otherwise; not that night nor in the years to follow.

One by one everyone got up to leave. Each had their say. Casse, still in her work dress, a tailored yet feminine style, told me, "You said that guy in the picture who died last night was in the room with us? I'll tell you the truth, Val, that spooks me. This isn't for me, but I've never seen you look so great. Luck with it, dear." After an air kiss, she departed.

Then Sallee-Mae - sorry, Salma - wearing (for her) a conservatively low-cut-blouse, asked, "Valtin, honah, was that Baba married?" I told her, "No, he was celibate."

Salma replied, "What a waste. Such sexy eyes. Ah loved it, honah. Ah'll come to ya centa some tam." After hugging me some ten times, Salma, too, was gone.

Finally only Hinda, Max, Serge and myself and of course Richard remained.

In a state of elation, Hinda, I, and the men cleaned the room and got everything back in its regular place. Finally Hinda and I dismantled the puja and after Serge helped us pack up our supplies, he left, followed soon by Max.

When I was ready to leave, Richard stepped outside the door with me.

"How did you like it?" I asked.

"Interesting. I must say you're very good at this. Amazing how you keep it going for an hour without notes. After two minutes I'd be saying 'duh…duh…'"

"Thanks, Richard. They taught me to do that up there." Just then I thought of something which made me terribly sad. I felt the need to tell Richard. "Imagine Baba passing on at this of all times."

"Of all times? What do you mean?"

So I told Richard about the letter that I'd written to Baba several weeks earlier asking him to help Willie, offering to bring Willie to India if necessary. I said, "I wasn't going to tell you about the letter because I thought if I did you'd think I was crazy."

Richard answered, "To paraphrase the Jewish Passover Seder service, 'why should this night be different from all other nights?' Alright, explain to me. What does Baba passing on have to do with the letter?"

"Don't you understand, Richard? It could have taken ten days for that letter to reach Baba in India. Considering, Baba probably passed on before he even got to see it."

"Oh, he saw it alright" Richard assured me.

I looked at Richard quizzically. "How could you know that?"

"Simple." Richard replied. "Why *else* do you think Baba passed on except that he got your letter? As soon as he read it, he told himself, 'If she's going to bring *that* kid *here*, *I'm* leaving!'"

Well, I laughed until I cried. When Hinda came outside looking for me, I repeated Richard's statement and we both laughed to that point. When Hinda had finally stopped laughing and crying, she told Richard, "Thank God for you! There's a lot of Shakti in your humor. We need you tonight."

I thanked Richard for that, for the use of the house, and for everything, then told him goodnight. Together Hinda and I walked to the curb in front of the house where our cars were parked.

"Tonight was divine," Hinda said. "You're going to make a really good center director."

Then I asked a question which had been in the back of my mind and now suddenly plagued me. "Hinda, what's going to happen now that Baba is gone?"

"Before he passed on Baba renamed Kamla Guru Shanti Devi. He has pronounced her his spiritual successor."

"You mean *his translator*?!" I was truly stunned.

Hinda nodded. "Evidently he's been training her for this since she was a child."

"But, how could this BE? I'm sorry, but I'm being honest with you, Hinda. Kamla seems very sweet and devotional, but she's retiring, shy. She could be any one of us. Her, the Guru? How could *she* take Baba's place; he was SO... And a woman?"

"She's the first female Siddha Guru in the lineage." Hinda affirmed.

"How will she be accepted, especially by the Indian men? Mainly, how can she take Baba's place?"

Hinda turned her loving gaze upon me. "Baba's judgement has always been impeccable," she offered. "We can trust it. Wait and see."

CHAPTER THIRTY-TWO: SHANTI DEVI

"The company of a Great Being is rare and difficult to attain, but unfailing in its effect."

--Shakti Sutras

"I became aware of a screen of some kind with hundreds of images floating on it, and I realized those were the images of my mind from many lifetimes. Yet at the same time I realized that my mind had nothing to do with my Self. My eyes opened. I was in awe. With my intellect I could not comprehend any of what had just occurred, yet with my heart I understood that it was the most important thing that had ever happened to me."

--True experience of a devotee
after darshan with a Siddha Guru

It was the end of summer and time to go meet Kamla, now Shanti Devi, our new spiritual leader.

Hinda and I slowly moved forward on the darshan line toward Baba's former chair, where Shanti Devi now sat. As we came closer, I watched her bless one person after the next. There were more people at the ashram for her darshan than I'd ever seen there before, yet she greeted each person animatedly, attentively and joyfully, as if he or she were the only one there.

Now we were approaching the front of the line. In a few seconds an assistant gestured with his hand that it was my turn to come forward. I moved toward the chair into the area of sparkling light surrounding Shanti Devi; at that moment it became my light blending into her light. I bowed down in the Indian tradition. While in that position I heard Shanti Devi ask me in a deep mellifluous yet conversational voice, "How's the center coming?" When I looked up into her face, I was too startled to do more than stare. Shanti Devi was looking down at me with penetrating eyes, emanating an enormous degree of love, wisdom and clarity. Gone was Baba's retiring translator. Kamla, the shy attractive woman of the timid voice, was no more. In her place sat this strong, forceful yet gentle woman with lustrous black hair - now cut attractively short from the bun of her Baba days - high cheekbones, almond butter skin, and defined brows above the most incredible eyes I'd ever seen, in a class by themselves except for Baba's before her. She was now of such stunning beauty, energy and authority that I drew in my breath and took two steps backward. Everything about her and coming from her overwhelmed me. Time stood still. This metamorphosis of this girl whom I formerly could have conceived of as a peer to go out with for pizza, into this state of full enlightenment, was the greatest miracle and most encouraging phenomenon that I'd ever witnessed. Kamla had become Shanti Devi. She had become Baba.

I waited on the sideline while Hinda had her darshan after me. Once we were away from the darshan line, I elatedly whispered to Hinda, "Self-Realization *is* a continuum after all, just like Cheng always said! It happened for Kamla; it can happen for me! Her state, in *my* life."

Hinda smiled her angelic smile. "And *that*, Kalyani, *is* the whole *idea!*"

* * *

"Please remove your shoes," Shanti Devi's secretary told me with the kind of polite efficiency that I'd come to expect from those who spent much time around the Great Beings. And so I did, as I looked around. The room, carpeted in red, had white wicker furniture. Everywhere were beautiful flower-filled vases. Then my eyes alighted on Shanti Devi, seated in the corner at her desk wearing her red silk monk's robe, looking at the very least like a young queen.

"You can come right over here," the secretary said, extending her hand toward a chair at the desk, beside Shanti Devi.

I had wanted, no needed, to speak with Shanti Devi privately. So I had contacted the office of her staff; after hearing my request, the secretary had set up a private darshan for me for the following day. However, that morning she had contacted me and said, "Shanti Devi's schedule's become very busy. Can this wait awhile?"

Probably to the secretary's surprise and to mine as well, I'd answered, "No, it cannot. It's very important."

"Then, will you come at three?" she'd asked.

Now, seated beside Shanti Devi I was again overcome by her magnificence. She sat silently for a few minutes. I did the same. Hinda had explained to me that a Siddha's presence influenced us on two levels; their words, and simply their presence. From their words we would gain not only knowledge but also a taste of the enlightened state from which they spoke. Their mere presence gave us that taste too. That certainly seemed to be happening to me now.

Finally Shanti Devi asked me in her deep-voiced accent, "Did you have something that you wanted to talk to me about?"

I could not get over how Baba, and now Shanti, behaved. Although they were the greatest of the great, able to move mountains and beyond, they were most humble, yet not in the least self-effacing. I thought, "some of our arrogant postulating Western doctors should take note of what true greatness looks like."

"Shanti Devi," I told her, "I like your hair much better short." Immediately after that slipped out I was horrified at myself. What could I have been thinking of, taking such familiarity with a Siddha master! But when I dared to look at the guru again, she was smiling, I felt showing me that she liked my ease with her. Weakly I smiled back. She waited for me to go on.

"I have a son, Willie," I finally managed. I couldn't believe how the power of her energy made it difficult for me to speak. "He's autistic - considered disabled in some ways. ...I wondered... I mean, it's been very difficult for him, for us. Should I bring him to meet you? I asked Baba to help him but then he... took mahasamadhi. I don't know if he got to read my letter. Could you... help? Should I bring him here? I'm not sure…I mean, I don't know...if he could handle the energy here…but if you say it's all right…"

Without any hesitation Shanti Devi replied, "Show him the video at home."

"Alright," I said, then thought, "Which video? And at which home?"

"A video of Shanti Devi," she answered immediately, "at your home." I'd become accustomed to Cheng reading my mind, and Baba too. But this seemed even more intense, although I could not have explained how or why. Then I asked the question which I had to ask.

"Shanti Devi, can you tell me any more about Willie? Why is he here in this world?"

Silently, she regarded me for a very long time. I felt an incredible anxiety waiting to hear what she would say. Finally she spoke, slowly, her words carefully chosen. "In India there are Great Beings," she said. "They are called Siddhas. Some act peculiarly by usual standards."

I had read about Siddhas, Cheng of course had spoken about them, also Hinda and I had discussed them. There had been one Siddha who never spoke, another spoke by writing only, and one used to greet people from atop a heap of garbage, at times actually throwing garbage at them. Yet people felt greatness from being in these beings' presence. I thought of a passage from Baba's book: "Never try to understand a Siddha completely. His ways are beyond your comprehension."

Shanti Devi repeated, "Yes, some of them are strange by usual standards. Still, they *are* Great Beings."

I tried to grasp the magnitude of her words. Cheng had said something similar about Willie and the others in his category. I had to take this to the final step. I asked, my tongue stumbling over my words, "Are you telling me, Shanti Devi, that my son and those like him are Great Beings?"

Shanti Devi, saying nothing, just continued to look at me with great love and compassion. I felt she wasn't going to explain further. I'd known Cheng long enough to somewhat understand how these Great Beings, and semi-Great Beings, taught.

"But," I sputtered, "A Great Being comes here to teach others."

"Exactly," she answered simply, maintaining steady eye contact.

With that Shanti Devi had answered my question. I had to look away from her. Tears flooded my eyes. Oh, no, I wasn't going to cry here, now. I must prevent that. It was too late; I broke into sobs. I put my head down on Shanti Devi's desk and let the floodgates open. The years of pain, the months of torment, the days of hope lost. It was all there, and then, sitting before this great master, it was released. I felt slices of my life-pain just blown away.

I wasn't certain how long we sat there that way, with me crying and Shanti quietly watching me cry. Finally I felt her touch on my hand, a small touch transmitting enormous love. "It is fine, GRACE," she said softly. Emphasizing the name 'Grace'. My head came up swiftly. I'd never told her, or anybody here, that my real name was Grace. I hadn't told anybody for that matter. With that use of my given name Shanti Devi showed me that she knew, understood and accepted me better than anyone else ever had. She then added, "Do you know what Grace means? Grace is uncontaminated light. It is divinity." I thought that both my parents and

Baba, in bestowing such names upon me, had given me much to live up to.

However, I was still feeling embarrassed about my tears. "Those were tears of joy," I feebly apologized. Shanti Devi smiled, reached her hand into a dish on her desk, took out a hard candy wrapped in blue cellophane paper and placed it into my hand. I got the feeling that our private darshan was over. A candy! Was it all really so simple? Mentally, I shook my head. FOR HER, probably. When would it become so for me?

I rushed directly from Shanti Devi's quarters to find Hinda. Once I found her I told her everything, then exclaimed, "Hinda, my pain... from Willie, it's gone! Or at least it's far less. I think... Shanti Devi's did something."

"You THINK?" Hinda asked, as only one who knows from experience could.

After many minutes of silence I told Hinda, "I love Cheng, and I loved Baba, yet I must say my love for Shanti Devi is…the greatest love I've ever felt for anyone. Is this normal?"

"Totally" Hinda responded. "I feel the same way about her, in fact, that is the classic way the disciple feels about the master. Since the Guru is without ego, s/he manifest as pure consciousness, so around her it's easier to open our heart tremendously. The love we are feeling is that of our own inner Self. Such a being expands our love-ability in general. Everyone in our life benefits."

* * *

It would probably be an impossibility to totally do justice in the retelling to the numerous and amazing miracles that happened as a result of that private darshan, and of me following my Guru's command. Nor could I prove to doubters that these developments were a direct result of her darshans. But, I just knew, without any doubt that they were. The following are some highlights.

A week after my private darshan I was contacted by a Long Island group home agency telling me that a place for one male resident had unexpectedly just opened up; they would accept Willie if we still wanted that. The reason that this was such a miracle was because when I'd put Willie's name on their list two months earlier, they had told me that they had a five year waiting list, and on top of that, that they gave priority to clients who were not at the time served by any facility. Therefore, Willie's chances of getting in were slim to nil. Now I asked when Willie could move there. I was told as soon as possible.

Richard and I went to visit the group home, which was in Wainscott, on the Eastern end of Long Island, about an hour's ride from Coldport. The staff were lovely people, as was the home itself, on a quiet road within walking distance of a beach. We signed some of the necessary papers of acceptance and prepared ourselves for the extensive red tape for moving Willie there. When you have a child served by state agencies you learn about red tape. But this time it all happened so quickly and smoothly that I had to wonder what went wrong.

A month later Willie was living in the Wainscot group home. When Willie moved, this time we were right by his side, easing his transition. It proved to be a most positive move. For one thing, now we could visit him frequently and bring him home more often. As for following Shanti Devi's command, during each of Willie's home visits I had put a video of Shanti Devi on the VCR, and told Willie, "This is Shanti Devi, a Great Being", then allowed Willie to watch or walk out, as he pleased. I did that at each of his home visits for a year.

One day after that year was up, when we brought Willie to Glady's house for one of his home visits, Willie, who rarely spoke in such full sentences or offered unsolicited information, told me, "Shanti Devi kissed me."

I got chills! "Where, Willie?"

"In my room. Wainscott," Willie answered. "I'll show you."

On home visit weekends usually Richard drove Willie back to Wainscott on Monday mornings, but this one time I wanted to do it. When we arrived there that Monday morning, the manager, Elise told us, "Willie has been telling us that somebody named Shanti someone lives in the air purifier near his bed, and comes out to see him at night. Do you know what any of this means?"

"Well," I said, "It's a long story." I felt ill at ease about telling the house manager the truth, thinking, "Surely they'll write me off as a lunatic, which could reflect upon Willie." But since I was already up on the diving board, about to dive into deep waters, I told myself, "Jump." I then proceeded to explain to Elise about Shanti Devi, and about the video. That for that entire year of showing Willie the video I'd had no idea why I was doing it. I had simply followed Shanti Devi's directive with blind faith. That her purpose had only now become obvious. She had wanted Willie to see the video, so that he would know who she was when she came to visit him in subtle body. To give him Shaktipat, her blessings.

I thought of Cheng's last Discourse about the Siddhis, or powers, especially the Siddhi of being able to be in many places simultaneously. Shanti Devi, a bona fide saint, clearly had all the powers Cheng had described.

But I was in for yet another surprise. When I was through explaining, Elise told me, "I can believe that your teacher did do something here, because since Willie came here our house has changed incredibly for the better. We have the best staff with the least turnover of any house in this agency!"

For a year after this momentous event Willie went through some seemingly very difficult times, which discouraged me enormously until Hinda told me, "Remember what *we* had to go through after Shaktipat and even before that, with Cheng? Willie's got samscaras and a Higher Self just like everyone else does. He's probably throwing off a lot of karma. Be patient. He'll emerge."

"Fine, but how do I explain this to the doctors?" I asked.

"There are some things better left unsaid," Hinda responded, smiling.

What Hinda had predicted came to pass. Soon the manager and assistant manager were telling us, "Willie is doing so wonderfully, it's a miracle!" We could see it ourselves. He was smiling and happy whenever we saw him. Every week his verbal speech seemed to improve. We had tried every kind of medication and natural substance known, and none of them - holistic or allopathic - had helped him. Now a new medication came on the market and I asked them to try it with Willie. Perhaps this new medication was partially attributable as well. Cheng had taught me that God works through all things in the world, and that, "Medication, too, when used wisely, is divine."

At about the same time, new experimental treatments came about. Some of the experts believed that people like Willie had hearing that was too acute. "Too good for this world?" I wondered. They discovered a way to regulate that so that those with such acute hearing could live in our world more comfortably. It was a seventeen day twice a day non-invasive treatment. I made arrangements to bring Willie home for three weeks and to take that time off so that I could bring him for such daily treatments. They seemed to help him.

The next treatment to come down the pike was visual therapy; this doctor prescribed temporary glasses and exercises for what he felt were Willie's visual misperceptions. Again I couldn't definitely say whether or not this helped, but Willie's progress was continuous now. I'd come to realize that even more influential than any proof of efficacy of the treatments was our willingness to do whatever seemed required to make things good for Willie. Although none of this was covered by insurance, somehow we managed it financially.

Remarkably, Willie also began to communicate using letter boards and computers with the help at first of a facilitator supporting his hand or arm, revealing a wealth of inner intelligence and keen perceptions. This technique was known by various names, Facilitated Communication, and Augmentative Communication. He was not the only one; people with autism and the like worldwide began using this successfully. One of the first things Willie wrote was, "I can read." We asked him how he had learned. "I taught myself" he answered. I suspected that was not the whole of it. I thought back to the many tutors we'd hired for Willie, and of the academics that I'd also diligently taught him while he lived at home. Evidently he'd been learning all along and had it stored inside himself. He'd just had no way to express it. As he continued to communicate with letter boards and the like, his verbal speech also improved. The method was controversial. Our fights to get the right for Willie to use it were not always pleasant but well worth it. Now my terror about who would understand Willie when I was no longer here abated quite a bit. It was during all this that I remembered Cheng talking about other ways of communicating, directing those remarks to me especially.

I concluded that each of us here has evolved guides watching out for our needs; for some of us like Willie and me, those guides are on this earth plane, for others, their Great Beings are on other planes. But we all have them. If we don't know who they are we can pray that we be shown and it will happen. Or simply accept that we have them and pray to them without needing to know exactly who they are. I remembered Glady's verification of this, her message to me from spirit about the messenger-angels. Ultimately it is God here for each of us regardless of our religion or spiritual path.

Meanwhile, I continued my training with Shanti Devi and her staff, spending months at a time at the ashram, observing her closely, and absorbing her teachings. Sometimes she spoke of very mundane things, something highly esoteric. Once she told of a woman who'd come to see Baba in India and complained to him that she'd always had an eating problem. Baba had handed her a box of very delectable looking chocolates, saying, "Go out into the courtyard and offer the people each a candy for as long as they last, but don't take one yourself. Then bring the empty box back to me." Baba related that the woman did as commanded. When she returned and handed Baba the empty box, he told her, "In a past lifetime you deprived people of food. That is why you had an eating problem in this lifetime. By giving the people the chocolate while taking none yourself, you just finished burning up that karma. You should no longer have an eating problem." Recalling that, I remembered reading that often people who had certain types of eating problems loved to cook and feed other people but they did not eat much. I wondered if by some unconscious knowing they were using that way of burning up karma.

I also began to consider whether my acts of blind faith for a year in showing Willie that video, had helped burn up some group karma for people involved with autism, as well as for Willie individually. It had been after talking to Shanti Devi about Willie, and after those video showings, that all the new treatment possibilities and interest in autism had flooded the world. I knew if I were to ask Shanti Devi, "Were you/Baba responsible?" I would not get an answer; she never took credit for any miracles that happened around her. But I did ask Hinda.

"What do *you* think?" she asked in return.

"I think yes," I replied.

"I think you're accurate."

The last summer of my training an unpredictable number of people came for Shanti Devi's darshan. I watched her blessing each person. One evening she had been at it for over three hours, and judging by the number of people still waiting, would be there hours more. Yet she was radiant, minus any indication of fatigue or strain in her face and body, as she lovingly, attentively and joyously greeted each one as if they alone were in the room with her.

That summer Shanti Devi chose to show me, as I was sure she did others, more of her Siddhis. She never did this formally in front of any group. Even walking around informally most of the time she would behave in a very ordinary fashion. But the day that she did this for me she appeared in a hallway in the ashram where I was standing. Minutes earlier she's been in a place so far from this spot that I just knew she could not have arrived here so fast by ordinary means. And one time, during a course I was taking, she appeared beside me and stood there. I was puzzled as to why the others taking the course did not crowd around her, as happened wherever she appeared. But here today nobody was even noticing her but me. Finally it dawned on me that they couldn't see her; she had made herself invisible to everyone in the room but me. This was no apparition either. Shanti Devi was as solid and real as ever. As she stood there she told me that I wasn't meditating long enough during the class meditation times. At which point she touched my arm and I went into an hour-long meditation. When I came out of it she had vanished. Even as I tell you these incidents it is difficult for me to believe that they happened. But I assure you that they did.

One of Shanti Devi's talks that summer was on happiness. She said, "Happiness is right inside you. All you have to do is allow it to come forth. Happiness is natural. Unhappiness is not natural, so you have to work so hard to experience it. Somebody does something, says something, you dwell on it, you mull it over, and you won't let it go. *Such* hard work to be unhappy. Then in addition people don't want to be near you because you have a long face. Most people shun darkness and gloom. They like to be near brightness and light. If you know somebody who looks for darkness and gloom instead of brightness and light, think twice about being with that person!" Shanti Devi laughed, and her audience joined in. After a pause, she continued. "Take a moment now," she said, "and feel the happiness in your heart. It is there. Now let it spread throughout you and outside of you." She waited while the thousands assembled did as instructed. Then, with great joy she called out, "And what are you?"

"Happy!" we called back in unison.

Shanti Devi ecstatically raised an arm in the air. "Yes!" she shouted in return. Then she raised her other arm and thrust it toward us. "HAPPY!" she proclaimed, bringing me and I knew the majority of the others as well, to actually taste that happiness. Which was her state.

Shanti Devi's pattern was that always at summer's end she would leave the upstate ashram to travel to other parts of the world and spread her Shakti, or would go back to the Ashram in India. We had heard that she had specific humanitarian projects for the poor underway in India, although they weren't publicized. The following May or June she'd always return to the upstate ashram for the summer. But we all knew that this time would be different. Shanti Devi was going to India not to return here for at least two years; she only explained, "there is much there to be done."

In the final farewell program in Shanti Devi's talk she addressed this issue of her long absence to be.

She said, "I miss you already and I love you very much. But even the baby calf must be weaned to stand on its own, not to keep sucking forever on the mother cow." So - I wondered - was this separation for us as well as for the Indian people? "Know you have God inside you, that it is not just I who can convey blessings," she continued. "You've got the Grace. You can give blessings too, in your world, in your life. Spread those blessings and that love. Make a commitment to it. Then when we meet again, and we *will* meet again, you can know that in doing that you have given me the greatest gift possible. That gift is all I ever want from you."

She then gave another great teaching. "Do the following. When you step out the door to go to work or enter a doorway, or to do anything, always start on the right foot. Then say to yourself, 'Om,' eleven times. At the start of your day, move your eyes to the left, then sweep them to the right. As you sweep them to the right, see yourself bringing God in. Then see God beside you every moment, in whatever you do. My people can see me, other people can see whatever representation of God they wish to. In this way each moment will be as it should be, each experience will be sublime."

It was after this that my most incredible miracle to date - although it was difficult to choose among them- occurred.

That night I silently prayed to Shanti Devi, "Oh, my Guru, my Dear One, you are so completely blissful. Please, let me feel as you feel for even a minute; please, give me a taste of your state." I waited expectantly but nothing happened. I was both disappointed and hungry. I had missed lunch. So I decided to go to one of the ashram restaurants for something to eat.

The restaurant I chose was so crowded that it took an hour before I could be served. After I ate, I returned to the outside meditation hall where the program was still in progress.

As I approached the entrance to the hall, I saw that the primary lights had been lowered. Only the peripheral lights were on. The musicians were playing a beautiful Indian chant. I walked, as if magnetized, toward the hall, then stopped near the doorway. Inside, beyond the hundreds and hundreds of heads of seated devotees, I saw Shanti Devi seated yoga style as always in her chair on the platform at the front of the room. She would chant the words of the chant, then everybody would respond. Again and again that occurred. Then Shanti Devi began to gain momentum with the beat until she was nearly bouncing up and down on her seat. Now she unfolded her legs and stood, starting to sway in place, a free being showing her unmixed bliss to all. One by one the seated attendees, monk teachers and everybody else stood as well, and all began to sway in place to the rhythms.

I stood where I was, watching, transfixed. Then slowly I walked into the hall, starting to sway as I did so. At that moment Shanti Devi pranced down from her chair platform and danced into the crowd, moving clockwise in a circle, motioning for devotees to join her. I looked to my side and realized she was beside me. She looked at me and brought her right hand and arm to her chest and then thrust it out into the air. Telepathically I heard her tell me, "Now YOU do it." I did so. She swayed her body far to the right, then to the left; again, I followed her lead.

Suddenly, everything and everybody in the room became imbued with scintillating blue light. As I tried to absorb the otherworldly beauty of it while continuing to move, suddenly all the people disappeared and it was just Shanti Devi and me, dancing together in the hall. It was the dance of life.

I remembered one of the private lessons with Cheng when he had taught me that our True Selves, our souls, are a shimmering blue, and that a Realized Being sees that shimmering blue light in everyone and everything. With that realization Shanti Devi disappeared too, leaving me dancing alone. At that moment I cried out inwardly, "Oh, Shanti Devi, where are you?" All of a sudden a loud voice, her voice, deep within me, spoke. "My Dear One, I am you." At that any trace of separation left me as I experienced that she is indeed I and I am that. I was dancing totally free, in a way I never had before, similar to at Pathways many years before but freer. Total freedom! Then the other people in the room began to appear, disappear and reappear. As that happened I realized that whether they were there or not didn't make any difference, because when they were there, there was nobody there but me, and when they were not there, they were there because I was part of everyone and everyone was part of me. We are all part of one another!

I *felt* it. I *was* it. Total freedom; bliss beyond measure, complete strength, total love, and total happiness. Nothing could have added to it nor taken from it. There was not a hint of fear, self-consciousness or need in me. Then Shanti Devi appeared beside me again and once more I telepathically heard her say to me, "Grace, this is what you prayed for. My state of being."

At that I closed my eyes in rapture and before I knew it, images of babies rapidly appeared before me, one after the other beginning with Willie as a baby and ending with Brenna. At the same time I heard Shanti Devi's voice inside of me saying, "Willie came to you as autistic to prevent you from having to lose all those other babies, including Brenna, to death, in this lifetime and in future ones."

I did not remain in that state that Shanti Devi had so bountifully visited upon me, however nor did I quite return to where I'd been before the experience. Shanti Devi, in giving me my desire to experience her state had also shown me what my sadhana was for and had given me the motivation to continue it. For I had learned that whatever it took and however long it might take, that state of Self-Realization is the birthright of every one of us, and worth striving for. There is no way anyone could have even a minute of it and not want it permanently.

By showing me the babies, Shanti Devi had also given me total acceptance of Willie. More than acceptance. Reverence was more the word. Willie! What a great being he indeed *was*!

I only wished that Richard could experience a semblance of that reverence. I told that to Hinda, adding, "But, it can't happen."

"Why NOT?"

"Well...because I can't give him that."

"You can't, but God can."

"You mean, bring Richard to the Guru?"

"No, don't *bring* him. Richard's too big for you to carry. *Invite* him."

Richard accepted my invitation. I was able to arrange a private darshan for him and me, directly after her evening's talk.

As we entered the ashram we faced a huge photograph of Baba on the wall. "That's my man," Richard exclaimed. I looked at him, thinking he was joking, but he was totally serious.

When Richard stood in front of Shanti Devi and she greeted him, I realized with a mixture of awe and regret that she had given him more love in that one second than I had given him in our entire married life. As we walked away from that darshan, Richard remarked, "She's quite a change from that old man Baba." He then pursed his lips into a wolf whistle. I could see that he was totally taken with her.

I smiled. "People are bewitched by her outer beauty," I said, "But her inner beauty is really what captivates."

"Like with you, babe," Richard said. "It's what people, and certainly men, get from you."

With a downward thrust of my hand I scoffed, "I have a long way to go before I'm in *her* league - BABE."

"Didn't you LISTEN to her talk tonight!" Richard argued, "when she said we all have that greatness within us."

"Richard, you amaze me with what you know."

"It isn't just knowing," Richard answered. "It's experiencing."

"Meaning what?"

"She came into my room and spoke to me."

I gulped. "When? What did she say?"

"I couldn't hear it. I just know she gave me the feeling that I can do anything I need to do."

As I looked at Richard, my eyes brimmed over. Miracles were becoming an ordinary occurrence.

* * *

Through Shanti Devi's leadership the ashram grew in size and into a place of extraordinary splendor and beauty. Due to her travels throughout the world uplifting humanity, more and more people awakened to the joy inside of themselves. As Shanti Devi and Cheng before her had said, "Happiness is inside us. It is our birthright. All we need do is allow it to be."

However, I was experiencing one unexpected downside to my new found happiness - other people's reactions to me. I suppose I'd expected they'd all be delighted for me. After all, my caring for them remained the same, in fact, had increased. But they did not all react positively. Richard's first reactions when I was back on Long Island had been, "What did they DO to you up there?"

I heard similar from Casse. It happened one day when we were having lunch together. She'd begun to badmouth somebody we both knew. I didn't say anything; I simply didn't feel like joining in. This caused Casse to snarl, "Oh, forgive me. I'd forgotten I'm with Saint Valentine." I got other negative reactions from other friends and relatives. It was difficult and confusing. Had sadhana condemned me to loneliness or confined me only to that minority who understood me through their own experience?

Max helped. "This is understandable, Valentine," he explained. "When one person in a relationship changes, the entire relationship must go through re-adjustments. This is not what these people were accustomed to from you. They are implicitly being asked to shift their concepts of you. This unsettles them, at least initially."

"Do they adjust, Max?"

"Some do. Some never do. The friendships of the first category usually develop into deeper finer relationships."

"And those in the other group?"

"They often end."

Hinda helped, too. "I know," she said. "I've been there."

"Well, your use of the past tense is encouraging, anyway. You mean your friends and family finally accepted it?"

"Some did. Others, like my then-husband, didn't."

"I hadn't known you were married."

"Oh, yes, to a clinical psychiatrist. Very prominent person here on L.I. He thought my kundalini experiences, which were very pronounced at the time, meant I was crazy. I tried for five years after that to make the marriage work. Unfortunately my husband was so conditioned by his academic training that he never allowed himself to consider what was really occurring in me. I had to leave so as not to lose myself. It was difficult because I had loved him, especially so because he blamed me entirely for our break-up." Hinda's tone was bittersweet.

"Would you... marry again?" I asked. "Is there... anyone now?"

Hinda smiled. "To the first question, 'Yes,' if we were on the same wavelength; to the second question, 'no, unfortunately.' But that's all right for now. Anyway, my advice to you about others is, don't expect them to act adversely to you - that breeds paranoia - but expect that they might, and - strange to hear – don't take it personally. Understand they're feeling off-balance and frightened.

So, the formula is: understand, be loving, be patient. Those who will accept will in time, those who won't will fly out the window eventually and new people will fly in. That's how it is. One more thing. Resist proselytizing. We're happy, we can't wait to help those we love be as happy, so we drown them in our preaching. That isn't to say that we should not share this. We just need to read when. Know when to start, when to stop, and when to remain quiet. Stay astute; take their pulse first. If they want to hear about it they'll find a way to ask you. Even then stay alert as to how much they can handle at any given time. Baba used to tell us, 'if someone asks for a glass of water, don't hose them down.'"

I related. At that moment I was feeling rather hosed-down myself.

CHAPTER THIRTY-THREE: BELIEVE IN LOVE

"What can crooked people do to me now?
Because I have always sought God,
I became worthy of His love.
Now who has the strength
to bring about my downfall?
O friends!
Hear me and trust what I say.
Seek the Inner Shiva (God)
See Him and be free."

--Lalleshwari

"I'm finally ready to own my own power, to say, 'All right, this is who I am. If you like it, you like it. And if you don't, you don't. So watch out! I'm gonna fly!' "

--from Oprah Winfrey:
The Real Story by George Mair

Spring, 1985

Among the many things that I had to be happy for lately, Richard's spiritual awakening ranked high. I felt delighted for him, also interested in where this would take him. Soon after that realization of mine, he invited me out for dinner, "To celebrate your new profession, spiritual teacher. It's belated. Do you mind?"

"No, I'm touched."

"Touched? It should only happen!"

"*Tell* me about it!"

"Hmm. Well, seeing that we agree on one thing..." Richard moved closer.

I blocked his pass, so to speak. I'd learned that I had a rather normal female condition. Despite what the feminists of the seventies had touted, most of us weren't very good about separating sex from emotional bonding. I told Richard, "I think it's sweet of you to invite me out for dinner."

"I'm nothing if not sweet. You choose the place. I don't suppose the Golden Dove would be an option?"

"Please, don't. If I even think of that evening I'll laugh till I cry and smear my mascara."

"Same with me, without the mascara problem. When I think about you that night, inventing excuses for why we had to leave early, kicking me under the table each time… Why am I laughing? By the end of the evening I needed orthopedic surgery!"

Now I *was* laughing. "I'm sorry for that. I couldn't stand Sallie…I mean, Salma, one minute more. If anyone had told me then that I'd come to love her as I have…unfathomable. Of course Cheng was right about that too; my judging of her certainly did limit my perceptions of her total being." Suddenly I had an idea. "Rick" I asked," instead of dinner how about taking me to a Knicks' game?"

Richard jaw fell open. "You are of course kidding!" Looking at me more closely he concluded, "You *aren't* kidding! I can't believe *that's* where you'd like to go!"

" I'd like to try it once."

"Really? You aren't pulling my leg this time instead of kicking it?"

"Really."

"You were right. Miracles do happen! I'll see what I can do about getting tickets."

I was surprised at how much I actually enjoyed the game. Watching the players' interactions, the spectators' reactions, experiencing the flavor of just being there, was kind of exciting. Richard was elated about my presence there, a pal sharing his passion and his thrill when the Knicks won. I felt good about all that too.

Afterwards, over dessert at a neighborhood diner, Richard asked me, "What made you decide to come to a game with me?"

"I just figured since you and millions of other people love it, there had to be *something* to it."

"And?"

"I found out there is."

"Wow! So from now on you're an avid fan, huh! "

"Let's not get carried away. Just, I liked it enough to go again sometime."

"I guess it's the same for me about your ashram."

"Speaking of the ashram," I told Richard," I've decided to use my real name Grace, from now on."

"Really!?"

"Yes. Can you remember to call me that?"

"If that's what you want, I'll surely try."

My work dharma was now a real source of fulfillment and satisfaction. As I joyfully and abundantly gave everything I felt that I could and more to those students and clients who came to me on their journey to knowing the Self, the universe in turn gave to me. My money situation improved along with the rest of my life.

As the many pieces of my life came together, like an onion unpeels, those places where I was still stuck, and the loose ends in my life, became more noticeable to me. Like a sore thumb.

Brandt was a loose end. There had been no real coming to terms with anything between us. Only that abysmal scene several years ago. We hadn't seen nor spoken with each other since. I'd long ago given up all mind-wrenching analyses of, "What is Brandt really? A special knight with an aura fifty feet outward, or a skirt-chasing womanizer in sheep's clothing? A narcissist, or a real honey? A sociopath, or a man with such special powers that he'd made walled-in Valentine Jordan feel again? Had it been, as Brandt had intimated, mere fantasy based on the distance and paltry number of times we'd actually been together? Or, as I'd believed, a love affair more real than reality itself, since true love is mainly of the heart in any case.

When I thought of Brandt these days I was certain of only one thing, and it was all that concerned me. Some very harsh words had been spoken, imploding the relationship to ruins in minutes. No amends, no closure. Spiritually that wasn't dharmic, it wasn't right. Up until this point, when I'd thought about Brandt's and my relationship, I'd felt that I had been the wronged person; it had been Brandt who had hurt *me*. Of course he had done that, however now it also became clear to me that I'd said some very harsh things to him. Since I was the one doing sadhana, my words had more power than his did – to hurt as well as to help the recipient.

As much as I wished it were otherwise, these thoughts would not let go of me. Every time I tried to divert my mind, thoughts of Brandt kept yanking me back as if tied to a five hundred-pound mule. So I brooded about all of that, wanting to rectify it but having no idea where or how to begin. A letter or phone call seemed inadvisable. Brandt could too easily misinterpret my motivation. I didn't want to add insult to injury by conveying a false idea of how I felt about him or of what I wanted between us; after this much time had elapsed, how could I even know how I felt or what I wanted? I was so frustrated about my hands being tied with this, that finally I belatedly surrendered the whole dilemma to God. (Hell-ooo-oo! I'm a spiritual teacher. I couldn't have thought of this sooner?)

About a week after doing that, I was sitting in the dentist's reception room, waiting to have my teeth cleaned. Taking good care of my physical body had become a pleasing priority; having enough money to have my teeth professionally cleaned was nice. I was idly skimming through a Long Island newspaper which I rarely read, when the dental hygienist came out to tell me that it was my turn. I was about to put the paper down when a press release jumped out at me. Brandt was coming to Long Island the following week to give a speech at a school for special children! I could hardly believe it. God was obviously far more effective with this so-called relationship than either Brandt or I were. I wanted to shout out, "Thank you!"

The night of the meeting, after I'd dressed in a simple white blouse and skirt and applied light make-up, it occurred to me that Brandt had probably never seen me looking this way, this undolled-up.

I deliberately arrived fifteen minutes early and took a seat in the third row. Having surrendered the entire evening to God, I can not say I was nervous. It was something more like being on automatic pilot.

I carefully scrutinized the faces and demeanor of all the people who walked into the lecture hall. When finally Brandt sauntered through the doorway I spotted him instantly. He was thinner than before with more gray in his sideburns and a new style glasses. But it was his slow lion walk that I saw first; I would have known it anywhere.

Brandt ambled to the front of the room accompanied by a small entourage, like the Pope, an amusing analogy. One of the men who had walked with him moved a lectern and lowered the microphone. The room grew quiet as a short, dark man stepped to the mike and introduced himself as Dr. Irwin Fresoff, Director of the Institute. He then proceeded to give Brandt a lengthy introduction *at least* worthy of the Pope, if not of a eulogy, during which Brandt by turns fidgeted in embarrassment and basked in the praises.

Finally Dr. Fresoff concluded his introduction, stepped down from the lectern, whereupon the first man walked over to the microphone and raised it higher. Then Brandt stepped up. He casually removed index cards from his jacket pocket, scanned the content of each, stuck the stack back in his pocket, looked up, saw me, and froze! I mouthed the words "It's all right," wanting to tell him at the least that I wasn't there to make trouble or to embarrass him. I thought that helped him relax somewhat about me, because directly after that he began his speech and was rather fluent. On second thought, what choice did he have? He knew he wasn't booked to stammer through speeches.

As always the audience responded enthusiastically to Brandt's lecture. His charisma had most assuredly not vanished. After the talk it took at least a half-hour for the crowds of young mostly female admirers around him to thin out. I thought, "They are so thirsty for answers, the new ones, welcoming it from this attractive charmer rather than from some crusty old scientist. I once was like them."

When finally only a handful of the entranced remained, I made my way up to the group and stood behind them. Within a few seconds Brandt saw me. At first he just looked at me. I had no idea what he would do next. Then he excused himself to the group, stepped forward past them to where I stood, and kissed me near but not on the mouth. He said, "I'm glad you came heeaaa..."

"So am I. I thought your speech was very fine."

I became aware of the small group straining to hear our words, so I stepped a few feet away from them; Brandt followed. In a lowered voice I asked him, "How long before you go back?"

"I'll be heaa 'til tomorrow night." So, the charisma and the accent were the same. I wondered if everything else was. "What will you do tomorrow, then?"

"Well, I have a post-confaance lunch meeting at noon..."

"So, you're busy…it's understandable…that's fine.." My heart sank, the realization of which bothered me.

"Why did you aask?"

"Really, it's not important…"

"But it is. Tell me."

"Oh…I just thought … if you weren't doing anything we'd spend a few hours…but, no problem."

Brandt appeared to be thinking. Then he said, "When they told me about this meeting I didn't get the puupose of it; I still don't, so theaa likely isn't one. They can do this one without me. I'd rather be with you." That disarming grin appeared; my heart sailed upward again.

I looked over at the faces of the young group of followers, then nodded toward their direction. "They've been patient. Shouldn't you go back to them?"

"You aaa right, I'd betta. Please wait heaa. I'll be back"

Within three minutes Brandt returned to me, as one by one the small group filed out of the lecture hall.

"So, for tomaaoo, what did you have in mind?"

"We could go to Jones Beach? The ocean's great this time of year. I mean to look at. It's still too cold to go in. The board-walk's nice, and there are a few decent places for lunch. Would you like that, or…"

"It sounds relaxing. These days I could use some relaxation."

"I would imagine. You always did work hard.'

"It's work, and eveathing else."

"Well, we'll talk. So, I can call for you tomorrow morning?"

"Fine."

"What time?"

"You tell me."

"Eleven, then. Where are you staying?"

"At a motel."

"I'll need to know more," I said lightly.

"Brandt fumbled around in his wallet and came up with a slip of paper from which he then read aloud. "Atlantic Royal Motel." As he said the name I drew in my breath as my heart fluttered. *I* certainly remembered. Brandt and I had stayed together and made beautiful love at the Atlantic Royal the last time he'd lectured on Long Island over eight years ago. I looked at him for some sign of recollection. He gave me none. I didn't say anything. Finally Brandt broke the silence by asking me, "Do you know wheaa that is?" I answered "I know exactly where that is," and continued to look at him. If he did remember he gave no indication. Regardless of how much I felt like it…and that was very much…I was not about to ask him.

I'd come to see Brandt tonight clear in my head about where I *didn't* want this to go more than where I did. For years I'd worked hard on myself. I never again wanted to lose myself in a man. I'd been certain that could never happen to me again. But now as I looked at Brandt I felt my skin grow hot. I was feeling sexual excitement like I'd forgotten existed. At that moment I wanted only to be in Brandt's arms again if only for an hour. Feeling what I had felt, before. Why call for Brandt in the morning when I could be in his bed tonight? I was just about ready to put my hand on Brandt's, to look at him, to convey my desire through my eyes and body language, when suddenly an inner voice shouted at me, "Valentine, don't do it!" It had to be a powerful force, because almost instantly after that my skin and all the rest of me cooled down as if a door had been opened and a cold wind had blown in upon me.

I looked at Brandt, hoping he hadn't detected my state of heat a few seconds ago. I cleared my throat. "Is noon a better time to call for you, so you can sleep in longer?" I asked.

"ANY time is good" There was arousal evident in Brandt's seductive smile and gleaming eyes. Brandt *had* picked up on my state. Men didn't usually miss such things. Damn! Now he'd perceive me as conveying mixed messages.

I managed a steady tone. "I'll meet you outside at 12, then. At the rear left parking lot. There's a small coffee shop attached to the motel on that side. You can't see it from the street but it is there. At least, it was. Anyway, I'll be in that area of the parking lot at noon in my silver Toyota."

Brandt's smile faded. After a pause he said, "Alright. If that's what you want, I'll meet you then."

On my ride home I wondered what Brandt's reaction had been to my familiarity with the motel layout, and decided "that's his problem." I felt a momentary satisfaction from that, but then almost immediately an inner voice sounding like Cheng's told me, "And contemplating your motivation is *your* problem." Contritely, I did just that. Had I been practical, or simply bitchy? My Self told me, "Don't rule bitchy out completely." Damn again! I was falling into the same pattern with Brandt that I'd come here to rectify. How could I? That was terrible of me, and beside that, simply stupid! But in the next breath it was like Cheng whispering in my ear, "Mentally tell Brandt, 'Thank you for showing me where I'm still stuck.'"

* * *

We sat at an outdoor table. The sun was warm, although not excessively so, while the relentless waves kept rising, cresting and crashing in front of us. "There is a heaven," I thought. Closing my eyes, I lifted my face to the sun.

"Do you come here often?" Brandt asked.

I faked indignation. "Of course not. Do I look like that kind of girl? This is my first time. I'm just here out of curiosity."

Brandt first looked puzzled, then chuckled. "You're still the same funny nut at times."

"I can't fathom what makes you say that. However, if your next question's, 'What's your sign?' I'm out of here." Then I said, "To give you a straight answer to your question, no, not often enough. I should remember to come here more. What time's your flight back to L.A? You still live in L.A., don't you?"

" I'm still theeaa. Flight's at 6:20 PM."

"How were you going to get to the airport?"

"Limousine, probably."

"I could drive you. Of course if you'd rather…"

"You're aasking me if I'd rathaa look at you than the back of the bald head of a limo drivaa? What do you think? I accept youaa offaaa. Thank you."

I caught Brandt scrutinizing me. "Something? I asked.

"You making-up differently?"

"Not to speak of. I wear a little less than when I was modeling, that's all."

"Your eyes look diffaant."

"My students have been saying that too. I'm not doing anything to them though."

"You're more beautiful than evaaa"

A waitress approached our table. "Give us a few more minutes, please," Brandt told her. After she'd walked away we looked over our menus. Brandt asked me, "How's the seafood? I guess heeaa it should be good. " I answered, "I haven't had it but somebody mentioned it's very tasty." Brandt said, "Then I'll ordaa the scrod. Look good to you?"

"No, I don't eat fish. I'm a vegetarian."

"Then, would you have chicken?"

I laughed a little. "I keep wondering why people think a chicken is a carrot. I don't eat meat, chicken or fish."

"How long's *that* been going on?"

"A while now."

"Would you rathaa, then...I mean, should I ordaa something else...?"

"Not at all. Most of my friends eat flesh food. Enjoy what you like. I'll have the Greek salad. The small one. I have a feeling here it's huge." That had been considerate of Brandt to ask wheather I'd rather he not eat flesh in front of me.

When our food arrived Brandt enthusiastically cut into his scrod. Suddenly he began to laugh. "Oh, reminds me of a joke" he said. "A man comes to Long Island and hails a cab. He tells the drivaa, 'Take me where I can get scrod. The driver says, 'Alright, mistaa, I'll be glad to. But I never heaad it asked foa in the past plupaafect befoaa.' "Brandt roared.

He'd told me the joke before, but it struck me funny again so I had no difficulty laughing along with him. After a while Brandt said, "You're not eating. I *thought* you were a little too thin."

"I'm too thin *now*? When you first met me I was probably ten pounds less - the camera puts on at least that much. You didn't seem to object then." I hadn't meant it that way. The minute it was out I wished I'd bitten my tongue.

Brandt's reaction was to reach over, put some salad onto my fork and put it to my mouth, saying, "Here, you have to eat." I ate it. He continued to feed me. I thought, "This is ridiculous!" but made no attempt to stop him, because to tell you the truth I was liking it. Then all at once Brand put my fork down on my plate and then his hand was on my neck and his lips to mine. "daa...ling," he murmured. "It's still theaa, isn't it!"

At that moment I felt so unsettled and vulnerable that I only hoped Brandt didn't sense the extent of it. I strived for some control. "Please, Brandt. I don't want to get confused about what I'm doing." "*I'm* not confused" Brandt answered, nibbling my neck." Gently I pushed him away. "Brandt, please, let's talk this time. I think it was a mistake...*I* made a mistake...that it became sexual between us almost from the beginning."

"It never BECAME sexual," Brandt corrected me. "From the beginning it WAS. Innately sexual. But it wasn't just sex for me. You were nevaa -- just another gill."

"I believe...our meeting was destined. I also believe we have some free will within destiny. I'm not going to use karma as an excuse. Technically I was married. End of story."

Brandt, wiping his forehead with his napkin, replied, "I was legally sepaa-ated." I could have done him bodily harm for that remark, even if it hadn't been my clear recollection – which it in fact was - that his and Mary's separation had never been formalized. Deciding that strangling was not an option, I answered, "Separated is another word for married, honey-lamb." I knew that if Brandt hadn't deserved that, I'd pay for it immediately with the remorse and guilt which would soon fill me. I waited. Not a trace came.

Over his coffee and my herbal tea, Brandt offered me a cigarette. I shook my head "no."

"Come to think of it you haven't lit up all day. Did you quit?"

"Yes, a few years ago."

Brandt lit one for himself and took a drag. "No more meat, coffee, cigarettes? What's it all about?"

"I think it's from meditation. It's made me boring."

"Haadly!" Brandt stubbed out his cigarette in the ashtray. "You're right about this at least. It's bad stuff."

Just then I said,"Oh, there's something that you don't know about me. Valentine isn't my real name, it's Grace."

"What's wrong with Valentine?"

I answered, "It's what my father called me when I was a child. It's a little girl's name. Do you think you could learn to call me Grace?"

"I don't think I could switch to Grace, I'm used to Valentine."

I wanted very much to tell Brandt about my life since we'd last been in touch. I didn't know where to start so I just began talking, giving him a synopsis of my spirituality and the work I'd been doing. "I'm helping people, Brandt," I said excitedly. "To heal their bodies and their minds. Helping them use their psychic abilities, their intuition. Psychic like I did with you. Do you remember?"

"Yes, I remembaa. Look, I'm sorry, but I put this mumbo-jumbo in the same class with hypnosis and fortune tellaas."

Before I would have let it go but it seemed now I was being told, "Answer."

So I did my best in this unfamiliar terrain. "Brandt, just because something is not traditional doesn't necessarily mean it is not to be respected. The Great Beings throughout history always talk about Beginner's Mind. A scientist Robert Bernstein said the same thing. That it's often the novice scientists who had recently changed into that field that made the best discoveries, because *they* approach things without preconceptions. I'd be more comfortable about your work if you would…"

"You'd be more comfaatable about my work if I would *what,* Valentine?"

I flinched at Brandt's stare and aggressive response. "If you'd open your mind a bit more."

"To this new-age stuff? I caan't, Valentine. I'm too conseaavative."

"Start where you are then, with autism. You could be positive with the parents who come to you. It doesn't have to be presented as a tragedy. To be honest, from the beginning every time I've heard you refer to them as 'these poor unfortunate children,' I've flinched."

Brandt's face was coloring. "What aa they? Foaatunate? It would be wrong of me to offaa these already distressed parents false hopes."

"I don't get how hope can ever be false. Why not throw some their way, give them some positive answers."

"I have none," was his sad admission. "Nobody does."

"Then open yourself. You'll get some."

"You want me to do scientific study…on… mysticism?"

"I'm not suggesting that. It probably couldn't even be done, not yet. Brandt, did you ever read Nietzsche?"

"Nah. Did you?"

"A little."

"I was probably reading my medical books when you read that stuff."

"Maybe. Anyway, his Zarathustra said, 'Nothing is outside us. But we forget this at every sound.' Nietzsche said Superman lies within the depth of each soul, that the human mind can rise to levels almost inconceivable to most of us, Brandt. There's evidence of that in the Gospels, in the Upanishads, and in other Eastern scriptures, in the works of art such as the Great Sphinx at Gizeh. This isn't new age, Brandt, it's ancient."

Brandt remained silent. I went on. "Brandt, from what I've been taught, but mainly from my own experience, I've come to know that the external world isn't a reliable source of truth. The recognition of truth has to happen within us. Something lights up telling us, 'Yes, this is true!' I'll give you an example. Quite awhile ago something lit up in me about people with autism. That they are not disabled. They are differently-abled. What makes us think that *we're* right?" Had I gone too far with him?

"I understand why it makes you feel bettaa to think that way," Brandt answered, his voice patronizing "but it's magical-thinking, just a fancy word for denial. I'm a scientist, I caant allow myself to go there."

"The truth isn't about what field a person is in," I responded immediately. "Meditation accelerates recognition of truth within. I see similarities between meditation and psychoanalysis, actually."

"How?"

"Both are processes of acknowledging all feelings including not particularly pleasant ones. Meditation takes it one step further. In fact, Brandt, scientists have said the same thing."

"What do you mean?" Brandt asked, appearing intrigued. I then remembered that Brandt liked to hear anything as long as it was interesting.

I felt encouraged. "The point of both is to make the unconscious conscious, that is, to increase self-awareness. However, Freud's aim was to bring people to 'ordinary misery' and stop there, whereas Eastern meditation takes it one giant step further. Traditional therapy can expose the pain, meditation can remove it. The end result isn't ordinary misery, rather permanent happiness. Psychology actually means healing of the soul, which can't happen unless there is knowledge of one's soul. That's the work I'm doing, Brandt. Helping people become aware of the existance of their soul natures so that real healing is possible."

"It's irresponsible to make people believe theaa can be peaa-fect happiness. Theaa aae a lot of crazy people in L.A. doing theaapy who talk that way. I nevaa thought I'd heaaa it from you."

With those words from Brandt I began to feel that crushed sinking feeling, that almost apologetic feeling for believing and thinking in ways which set me apart from most. Contracted, Hinda would call it. I also realized that I was on thin personal ice here with Brandt. I had never before challenged him in the area of his work; he'd become defensive. Thirteen years ago he had gotten himself hooked up with an adoring model and young mother hungry for help with her autistic child, and now this? If I'd forgotten about Brandt's appeal to woman, the fan club of women after last's night's lecture would have been ample reminder. He'd not have a problem finding a companion who would make his every opinion her's, just to be near him.

But then, from the recesses of my being, strength surged. Why, I asked, should I feel guilt or any fear of loss for not subscribing to harmful, distorted and superficial ideas which, although popular, were in my opinion harmful to people? I would no longer feel that way! I was more than that! Stronger in Truth than were they in their ignorance! As for Brandt, I had to let him see all that I'd become and then figure out if I was what he wanted. I had to see him as he was and then do the same about him. As Cheng had taught us in Discourse One, if we feared loosing anything, we didn't have it in the first place.

I expanded again. I was back. From that place my words came smoothly and easily. "Brandt, you'd agree that a normally constructed 'truth' of a scientific discovery lives, as a rule, no longer than fifteen or twenty years? I didn't want to put my faith in anything so transient. But the truths of the ancient sages have stood the test of thousands of years. That's why I like them so much. In fact, more than a few scientists have come to similar realizations. Barbara McClintock said about her success in science, 'I identify so completely with the material that I become a part of it.' The person who discovered the carbon atom said, ' I first asked myself how I would combine with the carbon atom.' The ancient Indian scriptures tell us that the essential nature of everything is worth being known. Be one with that and the answer will come."

"And that's where my work comes in. What I teach and use in my work, Brandt, is a modern synthesis of many thousands of years of accumulated wisdom in how to help people become more conscious, joyous, secure and healthy. Open to all possibilities."

Brandt looked away, coughed a few times nervously before answering. "I can only tell you I do my reseaach slowly and carefully."

"But open to all possibilities?" The inner Shakti told me, "Let it lay there. No more now. Change the subject and your location." I responded immediately. "Want to walk on the boardwalk?" I invited.

As we walked we spoke of Brandt's work, his children. Heather, one of his daughters, was the same age as Brenna. I recalled how I used to wonder if they'd ever become stepsisters, and if so, how Brenna would like having "normal" siblings. As it was our children didn't know of each other's existence, even though when Brandt and I had met they were playing with blocks and now were beginning to baby sit and to think about boys.

Brandt and I walked a while more, and then I indicated a wood bench. We sat down upon it, facing the ocean. After removing my sandals I found a small stone and worked it through the boardwalk slats with my foot. I shook my hair in the breeze. I was feeling centered again… and loving the feeling.

At that very moment, out of the blue, Brandt asked me, "Valentine, do you… love me?"

His question took me so totally by surprise that for a few minutes I couldn't speak. I couldn't even find my center. Even when I again could, I didn't want to answer until I knew what I felt. I wanted to give Brandt the truth to the extent that I knew it. To allow nothing he or I had done in the past to color that. Finally I took a few deep breaths and answered from my heart

"I first need to tell you that I know I said some hurtful things that last night, and I regret that very much. I'm sorry."

"It's alright, I forgive you." He said just that. No, "Well, I'm sure I gave you reason," or, "I'm sorry for how I hurt you too." I attributed this to Brandt's Leo moon. I had read, "Leos can be wonderful people if you don't mind being with somebody who is never wrong."

I continued from my heart. "About you and me, Brandt, I can best talk about how it *was*. A lot of time's passed since we were last together. I know that for *me* it *was* love. What I don't know is, what was it for you? Were you involved or was I in this alone?"

I looked into Brandt's eyes and waited for his answer. Brandt looked at my watch - I remembered he rarely wore one - then asked, "How faa are we from the aaaipot?"

"One half hour, give or take." There he went, changing the subject again! And I'd wondered if anything about him was the same? But I too glanced at my watch. I couldn't believe how fast the time had flown. Thank goodness Brandt had called the time to my attention. "Heavens, we have to leave now," I said.

As we walked to the car the weather suddenly changed. The sun went down, there was a slight steady wind and I felt a hint of drizzle. I shivered, maybe not so much from the wind as from the complexity of Brandt's last question. I was cognizant of my many disconnected thoughts, my inability at that moment to see the ocean for the waves. I felt cold, and shivered. Seeing that, Brandt removed his jacket and placed it over my shoulders. I was surprised at how warm and comforting it was.

Once inside the car I handed Brandt's jacket back to him. "Rain slows things down a bit," I muttered. As I drove toward Kennedy, I thought, "If we should miss Brandt's plane he'd have to sleep over." Did I really have to drive that slowly?

"How do you like driving the... Toyota?" Brandt asked

"I like it. It's very reliable."

"You used to drive a... Porsche, wasn't it?"

"That was long ago." He remembered!

"Do you miss it?"

"No. It was hard to let it go at the time, but it was also a relief. A Porsche on Long Island with 55 mile an hour speed limit was absurd. So was the expense."

"Mary and I aaa still sepaated," Brandt said.

Well, what had I expected, consistency? I had my spiritual master in India, and Brandt, my Master of Changing the Subject, in the next seat.

"Same with Richard and me."

"What's going to happen theeaa?"

"Richard wants us to get back together?"

"Is that what you want?"

"No. I mean I don't know, yet. I believe when the time is right, I will know. I don't force decisions anymore. It's best that way."

"Somebody has to make decisions. They don't just happen."

"That is true, but there's a right time. First we have to get clear within ourselves about things. Then the right decisions can be made."

"I'm sorry to say it again, but that also sounds like one of those left-oveaa kooks from the sixties. I don't get it."

"You could."

"How?"

"Meditate. I could teach you."

"Maybe anotheaa time. Right now I have otheaa things on my mind. I need to know what's going to be with us. I need to know that soon, Valentine."

I'd had some unbelievable experiences and persons in my life but this man was *really* unbelievable! I didn't know where to begin answering that. I told Brandt, "I didn't hear a word from you for years. Not a phone call, not a letter, not a postcard. If I hadn't read in the newspaper about your lecture and attended, we wouldn't even be here now. Yet suddenly you want to know if I love you and what our future together will be like?"

"Have you faagotten *why* we haven't had any contact for so long? Because yeaas ago *you* told *me* it was all ova, Valentine you sent me away, not the otheaa way around." I wanted to respond, "And you did nothing to provoke that, except to throw your affair with your colleague in my face?" But give me credit, I didn't say it. It would have accomplished nothing.

"Mary and I have been in limbo for yeaas," Brandt continued. "She's pressuring me to move back in with heaa and the children, or give her a divoss. If I should move back I caan't move out again, it would put the kids onto the flooa.. But if you and I..."

His words so startled me that I barely saw a car pass us on the right.

"I'm sorry, that car noise must have drowned you out. Or, I need my hearing checked. I actually thought you said that if you and I aren't going to get together you'll go back with Mary and your family. Please tell me what you *actually* said."

"That *is* what I said."

The adjective "exasperating" leaped to mind.

"Brandt," I answered, suprisingly patiently, "You first need to decide what you want with Mary *irrespectiv*e of anyone else, me included. Beyond that, we haven't been in contact for so long, how could either of us really know just now what we want or don't want with each other?"

Brandt said, "It could be between us like it was befoaa."

"No, Brandt, it could never be that again."

Surprisingly, we pulled into Kennedy with time to spare. I offered to teach Brandt meditation in the car. Brandt accepted, so I instructed him, then meditated beside him. At one point during the process Brandt anxiously called my name several times.

"Brandt?"

"I felt... like... I was sinking..." he said, obviously frightened.

I realized he'd felt he had lost control which had terrified him "Think of it as floating. That's was great, Brandt." I told him. "Will you do this at home now that you know how?"

"I don't know. I'll see. What time is it?"

"Time to go in."

As I turned quickly to look at Brandt, my heart melted with the warm feelings I felt for this man with whom I'd clearly had a strong tie, whom I'd wanted so much to touch with my love, whom I'd wanted to help touch the world that I had touched, so that he could experience some of its joy and then spread it. From the start we'd been so close in some ways, so far apart in others.

At that moment something happened which was the most unexpected from Brandt that I'd ever experienced (which, all considered, was really saying something!) I heard him tell me, loudly and clearly, that despite the strong attraction and bond we'd felt from the first, he had serious doubts about our ever having a successful life-long pairing. For one thing, he went on, he was not at all sure that he'd be able to remain faithful to me, which would hurt me immeasurably. Whether I believed it or not, that was the last thing that he wanted to do to me. He knew, and always had known, that I deserved better, he said. Being with him, then, would be a gamble. It would depend on whether or not I wanted to take the risk. He then told me that whatever the outcome between us, our relationship had helped us both. It had helped him to understand what love could be like. It had let me realize that real love gives unconditionally. He said that while Willie had first taught me that and my Eastern teachers next, he, Brandt, had accelerated the lesson. The relationship had helped us both to move beyond our perceived limitations.

Stunned, I looked at Brandt again and was doubly surprised to find him silently gazing out of his side of the window, lost in thought. It was then that I realized that not a word of what I'd just heard from him had passed his lips, that I had not heard the words audibly at all. Yet they *had* been Brandt's words, clearly transmitted to me telepathically. It had been the most authentic communication with which he had ever gifted me.

Cheng had always said that life is a mirror. My striving to be honest with Brandt must have touched a place within him. At least, at last, this once, his spirit had responded to mine.

I looked at Brandt; he appeared the most peaceful I'd ever seen him.

The din and roar of planes taking off and landing captured my full attention. It was then that I realized that something had drastically changed in me. I could have comfortably and easily boarded any one of those planes at that moment. My fear had gone. I was free - to fly!

Exhilarated by that knowing I walked with Brandt through the drizzle to the terminal. The thunder of the aircraft drowned out any possibility of conversation, so I just walked beside him looking at him, tall, the hint of muscle rippling through his shirt. I accompanied him to the ticket counter, then walked with him to the boarding gate. We stood awkwardly for a while. Finally Brandt cleared his throat and said, "I suppose... we can... talk... moaa about this... ovaa the phone?"

"I suppose."

An announcement came over the loudspeaker, "Passengers for Flight 348 Trans World Airlines now boarding, gate 318."

"That's me," Brandt said. "You'll call me soon, then?"

I was overcome, right then, with a deja vu experience of the first time Brandt and I became lovers, right here at Kennedy Airport at the Inn at Kennedy. So many years ago to the month. I remembered how just prior to that when he and I had been making arrangements by phone, he'd asked that I meet him upstairs in the room. When I'd hesitated, he had asked, "You want me to meet you down in the lobby? Would that be bettaa?" Then without waiting for my answer, he had said, "Yes, we'll do that, that will be bettaa."

Here, now, I was emotionally overcome by my nostalgia. Brandt, noting my hesitation this time too, said, "You want ME to call YOU? Would that be bettaa? We'll do that then, that will be bettaa."

I shivered, partly from the chill of the terminal, mostly from the memories. Brandt, noticing me shaking, removed his jacket again and held it toward me, offering its warmth to me. I smiled at him but shook my head, "No." Brandt shrugged, put the jacket down with his suitcase and then walked toward me.

I nodded, managing a slight smile. There had been so many promises of closeness with Brandt, followed by so many disappointments and partings.

Brandt drew me close and kissed me hard. I let him, then I let him go. He lifted his carry-on, hung his jacket over his sleeve, turned and walked down the corridor to his plane. I watched him carefully, looking to see if the shiny silvery aura was still surrounding him. It wasn't. But his lion walk was evident still; watching it carry him away, I trembled.

I had come to Brandt this time to do the dharmic thing, be myself, as kind yet honest as I knew how. And I had done that. Perhaps he would like the woman that he had seen and would call me. If so, then we'd see. If I didn't hear from him I'd not call him ever; I knew that way it could never be good. Realizing that, a new chill spread through me. Giving up control is never easy.

Outside it had grown dark and the wind had strengthened. With no man's jacket around my shoulders now, I shivered slightly, my aloneness descending upon me as the darkness did. Just then I remembered the first class of Cheng's that I'd attended, where he had told us, "You don't want somebody to love you, you want the experience of love. That comes from knowing the Self, God." But he had also said that love in all its forms, romantic love included, is to be honored. As an observer, I watched my legs walk toward my car.

Suddenly it was stunningly present, the shimmering light within me rendering invisible the atmospheric mist surrounding me. That shimmer inside of me whispering truths about love.

Bringing me instant - after *how many* years of living and seeking – wisdom.

Part of it - a large part - was self-forgiveness for my misunderstandings about love. Forgiveness for my belief that it had been better to walk a complex path than to come into the simplicity of the wound and to go beyond it. For my delusion that I had to fear and shun the intensity of my childlike longing for love, to hide it under a cloak of sophistication rather than to recognize that a child's love, so pure, so enthusiastic, so honest, is a perfect model for adult love.

And, recognition that there was nothing to forgive myself *for*. Not for all those crevices where I'd stuck those feelings. Not for all the hidden places, for the many secret corners, for the boxes I'd built to stuff love into, for all the keys and locks, all the webs and tangles my ego had invented. Not even for those I'd hurt due to my ego's ploys or for those who had hurt me due to theirs. They aren't there.

Yes, I saw it! Our Western psychologies, born also of egos, had created categories and rules having nothing to do with love. "We must rid ourselves of wanting somebody!" "A strong person doesn't feel need!" "Work it out! Get cured about love!" Our constructs point fingers, create guilt, diminish us. "Co-Dependent!" An abused and misused monster-term sprung ugly from the useful entity that it was born to be and was originally. "Women Who Love Too Much!" Love can be indiscriminately directed and misused, but *where love is concerned, too much is not even enough!* I would put aside the diagnoses, the rules, and the notion that there is anything about my need that is a problem.

"I want to be yours." I don't want you to ever leave me." "I'm afraid if I don't have you I'll have nothing" Oh Lord, what was this!

"Never fear" the shimmering light whispered. "Is there something wrong with admitting, 'I don't want to live in loneliness?' Is this not the basis upon which are built all spiritual paths and practices? Is this not a prayer to God? Isn't this realization of a way of opening to eternity and to unbounded strength?" I knew it was so! "I want you, I need you, and I love you" while not the same, are not so far apart as they may seem. " Help me not to feel empty anymore," the heart implores. Is this not part of an ancient prayer which yearns for that something which does not change? Is it undignified to yearn for eternity? In no way! It is an intrinsic longing for completion.

For the first time I was staring my need for love in the face and seeing it with respect, and seeing myself with respect for having it. For the first time I was looking at it with ease and seeing it for what it is; a gift. And seeing my need for that gift as one gift more. My God, this was it! Love between people is a window and a gate. Love provides the window; we can look through to what lies beyond. Then we can walk through the gate toward that final destination, the Ultimate. So, we long for love with a person because we know God is the love that we want.

But should I again create stories making this a wrong thing, to be dealt with in some categorical or diverse manner, I would again turn from the gate and walk away.

Do I want to turn from that gate again? Or learn to walk through it? But of course to walk though. It is safe to use love with a man as a gate. My willingness now to enter into the fear can become one more experience, one of the most precious of experiences, in which I meet and touch the warm hand which will lead me to the only Presence which I *can* fully trust; to always be with me, doing the best for me every second, through eternity.

Now I knew! There is no shame or guilt in *any* love experience I have ever had.

It is okay to admit to myself, and then to the special man, "I need you." "I want you!" "My heart calls out for your presence!"

There is something in me that needs that person and I can love them with my need and through my need, and that is more than all right. I want this person so much to be with me! I want to rush to him. This is not the story of weakness; it is a way of going about discovering strength. In that experience I will be able to hear the whisper of immortality, the winds of eternity. The song of the soul.

This is me! I feel safe with this fundamental human experience. I'm a spiritual student and a spiritual teacher and I will walk though that gate. I will respect and honor it.

I will never again call it "neurotic" or "unenlightened."

Because now I know! I am like everybody and everybody is like me. We are all identical about love. Whatever the boxes or keys we select to lock it away, part of our human experience is needing somebody else. To come to this is an act of courage, not of cowardice. It is Godlike, not a sin. It is the inverse side of something holy.

Then the whisper and the light within took my understanding all the way: When I could sit with something and not expect it to be just as I wanted it to be, that's the way God had always come to me. Now I could let go of the hiding places and whisper, speak or shout out to that right man, whomever or wherever he is, "I want to touch you." "I want to hold you." I want you to hold me." "I want your help" "Out of my longing for you, I'll weep like the rain." And he would come to me at the right time as an echo of the holy thirst and an example of how it is quenched. As one instance of faith's prayers answered by God.

So, this is what all my study and practice and my teaching of others had come to. It had dissolved the categories, taken me through and beyond the ideologies, philosophies, principals and yes even the formal spiritual teachings. And here I now stood in dignity, with myself and my overflowing heart, knowing that to be with God doesn't mean having to first overcome all forms of specialness.

I had become ready to invite a man into the temple of my being. A great temple. With my limiting attitudes and behaviors I had trivialized this temple space, perceiving what was within as so much sawdust. It wasn't that the men in my life had done this to me –trivialized love. They had merely been my reflection. I had done it to myself. But this evening I had returned to the temple and seen within not sawdust but particles of gold. Now I could go to the sanctified temple within the gates with a worthy man, a fellow traveler, and our life together would be a prayer of eternal love. What a blessing, this person! Allowing me to gently divert the prayer from him into the sanctity of the Infinite One, without shame or any diminishment of the flame between us. Is this not what friends and lovers are really for?

Yes! I prepare a plate to feed him. Everything we share will be a feast together. To work out misguided prayers and indiscriminate behaviors, and when the prayers are wise and the behaviors from God, not ego, to soar higher and higher together and to share the unadulterated love that results. Then, finally, to connect with eternity.

Listen to this! Everything I feel is a gift. There is nothing in us that speaks of shame. Thank you God for who I am! For letting me feel! For my want! For my need! Thank you God for the one whom you will bring. How can I run from this? I no longer can, when I know there is no place to run, no place to hide, no escape. The experience must be had. I can only honor it and go through it, to the light. Oh my God! He and I together can walk, with you, to the gate as equals. And finally together enter the kingdom. Anything he feels for love, anything everyone feels for love, is exactly the same. Equals looking for the gift. We are the same; we all enter the gate as one. The Universal dance to the soul's song.

The whispering stopped and I realized that it had started to rain. As I continued to stand where I was I felt the raindrops on my hair, some seeping through onto my scalp, others dripping onto my forehead. "Auspicious!" I could hear my Eastern teachers' words. "Rain with any event brings good."

I raised my face upward and let the rain pour down upon me, as I allowed myself to feel and embrace it all: the wet, the chill, the pain, and the loneliness, the longing.

Then I lowered my head and I did cry like the rain. And as the wet from both sources became one and dripped down my face, I felt the heavenly cleanse. Mostly I felt the love. Love as I had never felt love before. And gratitude for the gift.

Suddenly I looked upward at the mist through the moon, and the feeling that came over me was so powerful that it stopped me where I was standing. Then, as I continued to stare up into the atmosphere, all at once, through the golden-gray blur, I saw them. He was running toward her and she toward him, her arms outstretched and her hair flying. Now she was throwing her arms around his neck, while his arms encircled her waist without restraint. They belonged together.

The woman was clearly me; that this was so was quite appropriate. I'd never again put any man where God should be. I'd never again think I needed a man to be happy. But, not needing didn't mean not wanting.

I stood in fascination and awe. I had done my spiritual practices long and well and one of my rewards was this glimpse of my future. Cheng had taught the truth. My heart overflowed.

I strained now to see who the man was; Brandt? Richard? Cal? Somebody I hadn't yet met? It was no use. I couldn't tell who the man was or even what he was wearing. Suprisingly that didn't matter. It only mattered that because I had continued to believe in love, it would be mine, all of it; true love, real magic and ordinary miracles.

Epilogue

Dear Reader,

If you'd like to get in touch with me about this book, for a free brochure of my services, a schedule of workshops and events, (including "The Saving Grace Discourses And Other Spiritual Mysteries" course) or just in general, you are welcome to e-mail me at PTTherapy@aol.com, telephone me at my office at 631-269-5330, or write to me: Phyllis-Terri Gold c/o Infinity Publishing, 519 West Lancaster Avenue Haverford, PA 19041. I will receive and respond to your communications.

To quote from Saving Grace: A Spiritual Love Story, *Chapter Thirty-Two...*

You have God inside of you.
You can give blessings too.
In your world, in your life,
spread those blessings
and that love.

With love and blessings,

Phyllis-Terri Gold, Ph.D., NCC.

Cheng's Summary Of The Discourses And Practices

Discourse One (Chapter Nine): The One You Are Looking At Is The One Who Is Looking. Discernment and Judgement, and The Eight Magic Words

- Yoga, unlike Western psychology, is a finished product with predictable, guaranteed results if one practices it consistently and correctly. It is to lead you to knowledge of your Self.
- Really listen to another person. It will make you feel very connected to the moment and make that person feel cared about.
- Stay tuned in to the Shakti, the life force. It will tell you when to speak, when to remain silent, when to stay and when to go.
- In any relationship, we have Connecting Spirit (C.S.) or we get B.S.
- Love: User Friendly (for our selfish needs) and Other Centered (Unselfish). Love must be appropriately expressed or pain ensues.
- Nobody knows enough to judge, but we must evaluate. Judgement says, "I know this for what it/she/he is and proclaim it inferior." Evaluation says, "I see this person or thing as it is and do not choose to align myself with it/her/him at this time." The most dangerous bad is that which counterfeits as good. We evaluate better if we keep emotion out of it. Emotion distorts reality.
- If you fear losing your happiness, you didn't have it in the first place.
- Those whom we attract to us will be our reflections.
- From the year 2000 and beyond, the majority of people are going to be feeling dissatisfaction. Everybody thinks they want somebody to love them, but what they really want is the experience of love. That comes from within. To the degree that we need love we are unhappy. To the degree that we give love, we are happy.
- Love yourself. Make a 'YES' list of all the things that would make you feel fulfilled, and if they're constructive give them to yourself. Similarly make a 'NO' list, of all the things which you are doing now which make you feel unhappy and unloved. Stop doing each of them. Expect some flack from others when you begin to say, "No, I am sorry I cannot do that", or "Yes, I am going to do this for myself."
- Practice being your higher Self. Ask yourself, "Is this how I really feel, what I really want?" Then drop your disguises one by

one. Decent people will usually like what you are once they figure out what that is. Put yourself out there regardless of how it is received.

- As much as possible, live by the traits of your higher Self. Then there is less need to work through the lower tendencies; they will drop away.
- Name a person's game.
- Attempts to control are simply insecurities masquerading as necessities.
- Anger is darkness, love is light. We will experience the opposite of the lessons that we need to learn, e.g., if we need to learn non-anger, we will live in a world of angry people.
- Be the change that you want to happen. If you want to see less hatred in the world, put more love into the world.
- A Dharana, or exercise, to let go of control and to feel safe. Feel yourself rising above yourself to connect with a stream of light. Now follow that light to its source, God. Feel it also flowing to the one whom you are trying to control at that time. Now let go of any connection with that person through control and relate to that person from your knowing of your higher connection with him or her via the light.
- Make a list of everything that you're doing for others that you don't want to do. Eliminate those things.
- We are always in one of three states. 1) We know what to do. 2) We don't know what to do and we know we don't know. 3) We don't know what to do but we don't know we don't know. Only the third makes the problem worse.

Discourse Two (Chapter Eleven): The Mind And Meditation

- One of many good ways to meditate:

✧ Sit comfortably, feet on floor if on a chair, or crossed in front of you if on the floor.

✧ Elongate your back and neck slightly, but keep body relaxed.

✧ Gently put together the thumbs and adjoining fingers of both hands and place each hand on the corresponding knee in a palms-down position.

✧ Visualize a sparkling blue light in the form of a line moving toward your nose and entering your nostrils. Do not strain. As you do so, breathe in and think "Om." As you exhale, see the blue line going outward and again think "Om."

✧ When thoughts come, just return to the above process.

✧ Establish a regular time to meditate.
✧ Begin with five minutes if that's all the time you have. (You can use a non-ticking timer.)
✧ Then open your eyes slowly.

In addition to meditating on your own, find a support group to meditate with regularly. For further details on meditation, please refer back to this entire chapter again, particularly the last six pages where meditation and its results are summarized.

Discourse Three (Chapter Fourteen): S.E.s: Coincidences Which Don't Exist, and Stepping Into Your Life

- The only thing that makes us really happy is going within and discovering how strong and powerful we really are. When we grow through our so-called problems, we become happier.
- Avoid The Agony of the Haves and Have Nots with its resulting discontent by reminding yourself that everything that you have as well as everything that you lack brings within it its unique advantages as well as disadvantages.
- Pretend that you are your own Angel Rescue Squad, stepping into your Virtual Reality Life with no past or background in it, just chosen to step in as the best person to solve this person's particular life-challenges. Make your best moves -- after all, YOU were chosen -- and look forward to the results, whatever.
- Synchronistic Events (S.E.s). Nothing is a coincidence.

Discourse Four (Chapter Sixteen): The Most Concise Simple Rule for Assuring That Nothing Will Go Wrong In Your Life

- Think only thoughts which feel good and refuse to think thoughts that make you feel bad. e.g., "This is not a difficult time, it is an exciting challenge." The pains of life come from the negative thoughts which we entertain. Begin a Three Week Pleasant Thought Diet. If a negative thought arises, change it to a positive one.
- Discern whether a challenge is a barrier to move away from or a stepping stone to step over and continue in the same direction.

Discourse Five (Chapter Seventeen): Karma

- Three Step Process For Knowing The Truth:

1. *External Contemplation.* Drawing of the circle labeled "(your problem)" and writing every thought about it in circles, pro to the

right, con to the left. Connect the circles with lines (as in a flow chart). Study it.
2. *Internal Contemplation.* Relax. Breath slowly in and out, think a phrase that calms you (e.g., "God Responds") with each inhalation and exhalation. When very calm, internally ask your question, listen for answers, tell yourself, "I will remember this." If no answers come, say, "I know I will receive an answer."
3. Ask for a sign, a Synchronistic Event. (S.E.)

- *Karma, the four kinds.*

1. White karma (produces happiness)
2. Black karma (produces pain)
3. White and black karma (produces happiness and misery)
4. Neither black nor white karma (produces neither pain nor sorrow. This kind is most desirable.)

- *Three Main Types*

Type One: *Prarabdha Karma.* Things which happen which we didn't *make* happen. e.g., family we're born into, our gender, things we generally can't change. We are free from the karma attached to these things when we undergo them cheerfully and with detachment.
Type Two: *Sanchita Karma.* Stored up from our past actions in this and prior lifetimes; seeds waiting to sprout. Spiritual practices, and our present right actions, can nullify and burn these seeds so these events, destined to otherwise happen, won't, or will occur but in a greatly watered-down way.
Type Three: *Kriyama Karma.* Our present thoughts, actions and words which become Sanchita Karma, eventually Prarabdha Karma. In other words, this is the type of kharma that we are creating now with our thoughts and actions, to fructify in our future. Check out your every thought, word and action, because they will return in kind.

- Laughing at your troubles and bearing them cheerfully makes them go more quickly.
- Whatever is happening, in the entire span of existence, relatively speaking, lasts about one minute. There is little we cannot tolerate for one minute. Train your mind to desire what the situation demands.

Discourse Six (Chapter Twenty): Living our Dharma. Doing What Is Right Vs Doing What Is Wrong Or Merely Pleasurable.

Dharma is your unique and appropriate form of expression in the world, including but not limited to your work. What is right for one is not necessarily right for another, so, ' It is better to do our own dharma imperfectly than to do someone else's dharma well.' It is up to each of us to discover our own dharma. To discover if you are in your correct work dharma, ask yourself, "If I were a multi-millionaire, would I be doing my present work?" If the answer is yes, you are probably doing your work dharma.

Discourse Seven (Chapter Twenty-Three): Non-Doership And Dharma

-Act in a non-attached way ("I am not the doer.") We just act in the appropriate way and do not take the credit or blame. Four Ways:
One: Defer all actions to God. Ask what we should do.
Two: Follow God's instructions.
Three: Be non-attached to the results.
Four: Act without fever, but give yourself totally to what you do.
-The highest dharma: Ask yourself, "Does this further my path to the truth? Is it good for everybody?" This turns karma into dharma.

-As a result, we become spontaneous, "in the flow." We can just talk, walk and act while observing it all.

-Every effort you expend in self-discipline will return to reward you many times that.

Discourse Eight (Chapter Twenty-Five): Yoga; The Eight Disciplines By Which Permanent Happiness Is Achieved, Part One

Yoga means union with our True Self, with God. It is the breaking of contact with pain. It consists of eight limbs, or categories of practices. Discourse Eight covers four of the eight limbs of yoga; Discourse Nine covers the remaining four.

1. The physical postures, or hatha yoga.
2. Meditation, or dhyana.
3. Breathe or Pranayama,.
4. Concentration, or dharana.

A simple secret to happiness: You wish to be happy? Then spread happiness wherever you go.

Keeping your emotions clear, you will become increasingly lighter. Hear what the intuition is saying and honor it.

A simple Pranayama exercise: Alternate Nostril Breathing
(A natural tranquilizer to the central nervous system)
Breathe in through your nose.
Close your right nostril with your thumb.
Breathe out through your left nostril.
Breathe in through your left nostril.
Close off your left nostril with your pinky and ring finger.
Breathe out through your right nostril.
Breathe in through your right nostril.
Close your right nostril with your thumb.
Exhale through your left nostril.

That is one round. You can do five to ten rounds in a sitting.

Discourse Nine (Chapter Twenty-Six): The Eight Disciplines By Which Permanent Happiness Is Achieved, Part Two

5. Abstentions (yamas) and their benefits.

-. Live so as not to cause harm or pain to others. (May have to be tempered somewhat; please read details again in chapter twenty-eight.)
Benefit: When we renounce violence others become non-violent and harmless in our presence.

-. Abstain from falsehood. Let our words, thoughts and actions coincide and be truthful. However, if to tell the truth would hurt and do no good, remain silent.
Benefit: When we renounce falsehood, whatever we say comes true.

-. Abstain from theft. (Wasting, taking others' work and calling it our own, etc. is stealing.)
Benefit: When we renounce theft, wealth comes to us.

-. Abstention from incontinence (sexual excess). Conserve our sexual energy.
Benefit: We achieve purification of our heart, cheerfulness of mind, the power of concentration, control of the passions, all leading to the ultimate goal: connection with God.

-. Abstention from greed. (Don't cling to anyone or anything.)
Benefit: We receive knowledge of our past, present and future lives which is experiential proof of reincarnation and the everlastingness of life itself.

6. Observances (Niyamas)
- Purity. Cleanliness, internal and external. Monitor what we put into our bodies and into our heads and the kind of company we keep.
- A good mental diet.
- Good company in what we read, with whom we associate, with our entertainment and the like.
- Withdrawal of the mind from sense objects. Watch our thoughts for five minutes without censoring. Our mind will slow down. Do this for a short while each time before meditation. The mind will feel silly and begin to calm down.
- Final limb of yoga. Samadhi, or absorption in God.

Methods can include:

A. Prayer and ritual.
B. Devotion to some divine incarnation of God or special aspect of God.
C. Dedicating the fruits of your actions to God.
D. Intellectual analysis.

Chapter Thirty: Glady's message: Pray specifically for what you want, adding, "this or something better, if this is God's will for me." God's Messenger-Angels are here rushing with your prayers to God; prayers are magic. They bring miracles. Believe in miracles as regular occurrences; love is real and the most important thing in the universe. Believe in love.

Discourse Ten (Chapter Twenty-Seven): The Eleven Inner Veils, or The Enemies

The Inner Enemies are anger, desire/attachment, envy/jealousy, worry, greed, infatuation, sense of unworthiness, sense of separation, dishonesty, lack of self-discipline. They rob of us of our love, kindness and generosity. They all stem from one emotion; fear. There are really only two emotions, love or fear. The enemies are just habit patterns. To learn how to deal with each inner enemy, please again review chapter 27.

<u>Discourse Eleven</u> (Chapter Twenty-Eight): The final one; The Powers, and Knowing God

The Siddhis (powers which often come to one as a result of the spiritual practices of yoga):
1. Knowing the past and future.
2. Obtaining the strength of an elephant.
3. Supernatural hearing, seeing, sensing and control of senses such as the appetite.
4. Ability to walk on fire, thorns or so forth.
5. Knowing the exact time of our death.
6. Ability to be in more than one place at a time.
7. Ability to be invisible at will.

What to do when observing siddhis in others? (A true Siddha Guru does not make a display of his powers. There are so-called gurus who have developed certain siddhis, but because they have not reached the final goal, cannot bring others there.) Be astute.

What to do about siddhis in ourselves? Take note of them, use them, but don't make a display of them, and keep moving on to the final goal of oneness with God.

"So now you have received a complete life teaching. What you do with it is up to you. I advise you to practice it all to your best ability for a period of one year from today. Your entire life will change for the better. It is, after all, very simple.

1. To put yourself or anyone else down is committing spiritual suicide. Don't do it.
2. Love and respect others and yourself.
3. Be cheerful, whatever.
4. See God in everyone and everything.

It is easy to know God if we see Him as the light within us and within everyone."

And so, Dear Ones, my heart goes with you. Blessings, blessings, and more blessings."

From Cheng

(With love and blessings, too, from Valentine)

For Further Reading

There are many excellent books on pertinent subjects, so these are just a sampling from Valentine's and Phyllis-Terri's personal favorites. With simple desire to know, the reader will find other wonderful books on her/his own.

MEDITATION

Journey of Awakening. Ram Dass. Bantam, 1990 (includes a list of groups that teach meditation, or you might find a local group on your own).
Meditate. Swami Muktananda. State University of New York Press, 1980
My Lord Loves A Pure Heart. Swami Chidvilasananda. SYDA Foundation, 1994

YOUR DHARMA

Do What You Love, The Money Will Follow. Dr. Marsha Sinetar. Bantam Doubleday Dell Publishing, 1987

YOGA

How To Know God. Swami Prabhavananda/Christopher Isherwood. Vedanta press, 1953
The Sacred Power. Swami Kripananda. SYDA Foundation, 1995

MIRACLES

The Women's Wheel of Life. Elizabeth Davis and Carol Leonard. Viking, 1996
Expect a Miracle. Dan Wakefield. Harper Collins, 1995

PROSPERITY

The Trick to Money is Having Some. Stuart Wiled. Hay House, 1989
The Dynamic Laws of Prosperity. Catherine Binder. Prentice Hall, 1962
The Richest Man in Babylon. George S. Clason. Clason Signet, 1955
The Ultimate Secret to Getting Absolutely Everything You Want. Mike Hernacki. Berkeley Books, 1988

AUTISM
Nobody Nowhere. Donna Williams. Times Books, 1992
Somebody Somewhere. Donna Williams. Times Books, 1994
There's a Boy In Here. Judy and Scott Barron. Simon and Schuster, 1992
Please Don't Say Hello. Phyllis-Terri Gold. Human Sciences Press, 1975, 1983 (About to be revised and republished. Please contact author.)

VEGETARIANISM
Vegetarian Times Complete Cookbook. The editors of Vegetarian Times and Lucy Moll. Simon and Schuster, 1995
Elegant Dinner Parties For The Vegetarian Host In A Hurry. Cecilia Norman. Thorsons Publishing Group, 1988
Transition to Vegetarianism. Rudolph Ballentine, M.D. Himalayan Publishers, R.R.1, Box 405, Honesdale, PA 18341; 1-800-822-8547
The New Vegetarian Epicure. Anna Thomas. Knoph, 1996
Repacking Your Bags: Lighten Your Load For The Rest Of Your Life. Berret-Koehler, 1996
Timeless Healing: The Power And Biology Of Belief. Herbert Benson, M.D.
Scribner, 1996

HEALTHY EATING
Eat More, Weigh Less. Dean Ornish, M.D. Harper Perennial, 1993
Fit For Life. Harvey and Marilyn Diamond. Warner Books, 1985
Intuitive Eating. Humbert Santillo, N.D. Holm Press, 1993
Healing With Whole Foods. Paul Pitchford. North Atlantic Books, 1993

REINCARNATION AND AFTERLIFE
We Don't Die. George Anderson. Berkeley Books, 1988
We Are Not Forgotten. George Anderson. Berkeley Books, 1990
Many Lives, Many Masters. Brian Weiss, M.D. Simon and Schuster, 1988
Only Love Is Real. Brian Weiss, M.D. Warner Books, 1996
One Last Time. John Edward, Berkly Books, 1998
Talking To Heaven. James Van Praagh, Dutton, 1997

SPIRITUALITY (GENERAL)

The Dragon Doesn't Live Here Anymore. Alan Cohen. Fawcett, 1987

Divine Revelation. Susan G. Shumsky. Simon and Schuster, 1996

Journey To The Heart. Melody Beattie. Harper, 1996

Second Sight. Judith Orloff, M.D. Warner Books, 1996

In Heaven As On Earth: A Vision Of The Afterlife. M. Scott Peck, M.D. Hyperion, 1996

WOMEN'S INTERESTS

(Look for the book, How To Be A Woman by Phyllis-Terri Gold, now in progress.)

What Women Want. Patricia Ireland. Dutton, 1996

Women's Bodies, Women's Dreams. Patricia Garfield, Ballantine, 1988

When Bodies Lose Their Beat. Deon Black, Ph.D. Tapestry Press, 1990

The Herbal Menopausal Book. Amanda McQuaide Crawford. The Crossings Press, 1996

The Pause: A Positive Approach to Menopause. Lonnie Barbach, Ph.D. Signet, 1994 (and her other books)

A Woman's Worth. Marianne Williamson. Ballantine, 1993

Women's Bodies, Women's Wisdom. Christiane Northrop, M.D. Bantam Books, 1996

INDIAN WISDOM

Mahabharata. Narayan, R.F. Heinemann, 1978

The Bhagavad Gita. Winthrop Sargeant (or any version)

SPIRITUAL HEALING/ALTERNATIVE MEDICINE

The Therapeutic Touch. Domores Krieger, Ph.D., R.N. Prentice Hall, Inc., 1979

Accepting Your Power To Heal. Domores Krieger, Ph.D., R.N. Bear And Co., 1993

Quantum Healing. Deepak Choprah. Bantam, 1980

Reiki, Universal Life Energy. Boganski and Shalila Sharamon. Life Rhythm, 1988

Hands of Light. Barbara Brennan. Bantam, 1988

Light Energy. Barbara Brennan. Bantam, 1994

Prayer Is Good Medicine. Larry Dossey, M.D. Harper Collins, 1996

SPIRITUAL HEALING/ALTERNATIVE MEDICINE
Healing Words. Larry Dossey, M.D. Harper Collins, 1993
Healing And The Mind. Bill Moyers. Doubleday, 1993
Compassionate Laughter: Just For Your Health. Commune-A-Key Publishing, 1996
The Complete Family Guide to Alternative Medicine. C. Norman Shealy, M.D., Ph.D., Editor. Element Books, 1996
Dr. Whitaker's Guide to Natural Healing. Julian Whitaker, M.D. Prima Publishing, 1996
Alternative Medicine. Compiled by the Burton Goldberg Group. Future Medicine Publishers, 1993

MEN AND WOMEN
John Grey's books
Barbara De Angelis' books

MEN'S CONCERNS
The Angry Man: Why Does He Act That Way?. David Stoop. Dallas World Publishing, 1991
Men's Friendships. Peter Mardi, Editor. Sage Publications, 1992
Against The Wall: Men's Reality in a Co-Dependent Culture. John Hough. Hazeldine Foundation, 1991
The Intimate Male. Lonnie Barbach. Anchor Press, 1983